SELECTED STORIES

from the

SOUTHERN REVIEW

1965–1985

SELECTED STORIES

_(t._

from the

SOUTHERN

REVIEW

1965–1985

Edited by
LEWIS P. SIMPSON · DONALD E. STANFORD
JAMES OLNEY · JO GULLEDGE

LOUISIANA STATE UNIVERSITY PRESS
BATON ROUGE and LONDON

TO ALL CONTRIBUTORS
TO
THE *SOUTHERN REVIEW*

Designer: Sylvia Loftin
Typeface: Goudy Old Style
Typesetter: The Composing Room of Michigan, Inc.
Printer: Thomson-Shore, Inc.
Binder: John Dekker & Sons

"Memories of Uncle Neddy" from *The Collected Prose* by Elizabeth Bishop.
Reprinted by permission of Farrar, Straus and Giroux, Inc.
"Opening the Door on Sixty-second Street" from *The Designated Heir* by
Maxine Kumin. Copyright © 1973 by Maxine Kumin. Reprinted by permission
of Viking Penguin Inc.

10 9 8 7 6 5 4 3 2 1

Library of Congress Cataloging-in-Publication Data

Selected stories from the Southern review, 1965–1985.

1. Short stories, American.   2. Short stories,
English.   3. American fiction—20th century.
I. Simpson, Lewis P.   II. Southern review (Baton Rouge, La.)
PS648.S5S45   1988   813'.01'08   87-21383

ISBN 0-8071-1443-X (cloth)
ISBN 0-8071-1490-1 (paper)

CONTENTS

PREFACE

For *An Anthology of Stories from the* Southern Review (1953) Cleanth Brooks and Robert Penn Warren selected twenty-four short stories from among the seventy-nine published during the seven-year life of the original series of the *Review.* For the collection that follows we have chosen twenty-five out of the nearly three hundred stories published during the first twenty years of the second series. In deciding on the stories to include in the present volume we have had a relatively more difficult task than Brooks and Warren had, especially because we faced the necessity of accommodating our choices to a volume of strictly limited length. Convinced—in view of our regard for the high quality of all our fictional offerings—that we could not approach the problem of selection merely on the basis of picking out the "best" stories, we have attempted to put together a group of stories that represents excellence in the craft of fiction and the diversity of authorship and subject matter that we have always sought to present in our pages of fiction each quarter. Our editorial policy in this respect follows the cosmopolitan inclination of the original series, which, contrary to superficial historical accounts stressing its regional bent, was devoted to modern Western literature and culture. Meanwhile, we remain aware that we could easily compile another volume or two of fiction published in the *Southern Review* during the sixties, seventies, and eighties with no diminution of quality. We are grateful to all the storytellers we have been privileged to publish. A number of them have found early publication with us. Others have come into our pages in the maturity of their careers. We have always kept in mind the provision of a place in which new and established writers come together.

The national literary conference held at Louisiana State University in October, 1985, to mark the fiftieth year of the establishment of the original series of the *Southern Review* and the completion of twenty years of the second series pursued the theme of southern letters and modern literature. Possibly a conference twenty years hence might adopt as its theme southern letters and postmodern literature. But we expect the *Southern Review* to continue to hold to the idea that storytelling fundamentally transcends time and place, being the basic mode of our perception of ourselves and the world.

The Editors

SELECTED STORIES

from the

SOUTHERN

REVIEW

1965–1985

MEMORIES OF UNCLE NEDDY

Elizabeth Bishop

IT'S raining in Rio De Janeiro, rain-
ing, raining, raining. This morning the papers said it is the rainiest rainy
season in seventy-six years. It is also hot and sticky. The sea—I'm writing
in a penthouse apartment, eleven floors up, facing southeast over the
sea—the sea is blurred with rain, almost hidden by the mixture of rain
and fog, that rarity here. Just close enough inshore to be visible, an
empty-looking freighter lunges heavily south. The mosaic sidewalks are
streaming; the beach is dark, wet, beaten smooth; the tide line is marked
by strands of dark seaweed, another rarity. And how it rains! It is seeping
in under the French doors and around the window frames. Every so often
a weak breeze seeps in, too, and with it a whiff of decay: something or
other spoiled, fruit or meat. Or perhaps it's a whiff of mildew from my
own old books and old papers, even from the shirt I have on, since in this
weather even clothes mildew quickly. If the rain keeps up much longer
the radio will stop working again and the hi-fi will rust beyond repair. At
flood tide the sea may cross the avenue and start rising slowly up the base
of the apartment building, as it's been known to do.

And Uncle Neddy, that is, my Uncle Edward, is *here*. Into this wildly
foreign and, to him, exotic setting, Uncle Neddy has just come back,
from the framer's. He leans slightly, silently backwards against the damp-
stained pale-yellow wall, looking quite cheerfully into the eyes of whoever happens to look at him—including the cat's, who investigated him
just now. Only of course it isn't really Uncle Neddy, not as he was, or not
as I knew him. This is "little Edward," before he became an uncle, before
he became a lover, husband, father or grandfather, a tinsmith, a drunkard, or a famous fly-fisherman—any of the various things he turned out
to be.

Except for the fact that they give me asthma, I am very fond of molds and mildews. I love the dry-looking, gray-green dust, like bloom on fruit, to begin with, that suddenly appears here on the soles of shoes in the closet, on the backs of all the black books, or the darkest ones, in the bookcase. And I love the black shadow, like the finest soot, that suddenly shows up, slyly, on white bread, or white walls. The molds on food go wild in just a day or two, and in a hot, wet spell like this, a tiny jungle, green, chartreuse, and magenta, may start up in a corner of the bathroom. That gray-green bloom, or that shadow of fine soot, are just enough to serve as a hint of morbidity, attractive morbidity—although perhaps mortality is a better word. The gray-green suggests life, the sooty shadow—although living, too—death and dying. And now that Uncle Neddy has turned up again, the latter, the black, has suddenly become associated with him. Because, after all these years, I realize only now that he represented "the devil" for me, not a violent, active Devil, but a gentle black one, a devil of weakness, acquiescence, tentatively black, like the sooty mildew. He died, or his final incarnation died, aged seventy-six, some years ago, and two or three years before that I saw him for the last time. I don't know how he held out so long. He looked already quite dead then, dead and covered with shadow, like the mold, as if his years of life had finally determined to obscure him. (He had looked, too, then, like a dried-out wick, in the smoke-blackened chimney of an oil lamp.)

But here he is again now, young and clean, about twelve years old, with nothing between us but a glaze of old-fashioned varnishing. His widow, Aunt Hat, sent him to me, shipped him thousands of miles from Nova Scotia, along with one of his younger sisters, my mother, in one big crate. Why on earth did Aunt Hat send me the portrait of her late husband? My mother's might have been expected, but Uncle Neddy's came as a complete surprise; and now I can't stop thinking about him. His married life was long drawn-out and awful; that was common knowledge. Can his presence here be Aunt Hat's revenge? Her last word in their fifty-odd year battle? And an incredible last straw for him? Or is he here now because he was one of a pair and Aunt Hat was a fiend for order? Because she couldn't bear to break up a set of anything? He looks perfectly calm, polite—quite a pleasant child, in fact—almost as if he were glad to be here, away from it all.

(The frames these ancestor-children arrived in were a foot wide, painted and repainted with glittery, gritty gilt paint. They were meant to hang against dark wallpaper in a hair-cloth-and-mahogany northern parlor and brighten it up. I have taken the liberty of changing them to narrow, carefully-dulled, gold ones, "modern." Now the portraits are reduced to the scale suitable for hanging in apartments.)

Uncle Neddy stands on an imaginary dark red carpet, against a dun-colored wall. His right arm rests on the back of a small chair. This chair is a holy wonder; it must have been the painter's "property" chair—at least I never saw anything like it in my grandmother's house. It consists of two hard-looking maroon-colored pads, both hung with thick, foot long, maroon fringes; the lower one makes the seat, the upper one, floating in the airless air, and on which Uncle Neddy's arm rests, the back. Uncle Neddy wears a black suit, velveteen, I think; the jacket has pockets and is gathered to a yoke. He has a narrow white collar and white cuffs and a double black bow of what appears to be grosgrain ribbon is tied under the jacket collar. Perhaps his face is more oblivious than calm. Its not actually belonging to the suit or the chair gives it an extraneous look. It could almost have drifted in from another place, or another year, and settled into the painting. Plump (he was never in the slightest plump, that I can remember), his hair parted neatly on the left, his cheeks as pink as a girl's, or a doll's. He looks rather more like his sisters than like Uncle Neddy—the later versions of him, certainly. His tight trousers come to just below the knee and I can make out three ornamental buttons on each side. His weight rests on the left leg; his right leg is crossed in front of it and the toe of his right boot barely touches the other boot and the red carpet. The boots are very small, buttoned. In spite of his peaceful expression, they probably hurt him. I remember his telling me about the copper-toed boots he wore as a child, but these have no copper toes and must be his "good" boots. His body looks neatly stuffed. His eyes are a bright hazel and in the left one—right, to me—the painter has carefully placed a highlight of dry white paint, like a crumb. He never looked so clean and glossy, so peaceful and godly, so presentable, again—or certainly not as I remember him.

But of course he did have a streak of godliness somewhere, or else of a hypocrisy so common then, so unrecognized, that it fooled everyone including himself. How often did my grandmother tell me that as a small boy my Uncle Neddy had read the Bible, Old and New Testaments, straight through three times? Even as a child, I never quite believed this, but she was so utterly convinced that perhaps it really was true. It was the thing for children to do. Little Edward had also been a great text-memorizer and hymn-singer, and this much I did believe because when I knew him he often quoted texts, and not the well-known ones that everybody quoted, either; and he sang in the church choir. He also said grace before meals. Rather, he read grace. His memory for texts apparently didn't go that far. He had a little black book, printed in black on yellowish paper, with "artistic" red initial letters at the top and middle of each page, that gave two graces for every day in the year. This he held just under the edge of the table, and with his head down read the grace for that day and meal to his family, in a small, muffled voice. The little book was so worn with use that the pages were loose. Occasionally a few would fall out onto the floor and have to be retrieved when grace was over, while my little cousin Billy (Uncle Neddy's youngest child, a year or two younger than I was) and I, if I happened to be present, rolled our eyes at each other and giggled. My grandparents rather disapproved of their son for using a book. After all, my grandfather thriftily said the same grace every time, year in, year out, at all our regular meals. "Oh Lord," it began, "we have reasons to thank Thee"—but this sounded like "raisins," to me. (But then, at this time I also confused "as we forgive our debtors" with "taters," a word I'd heard used humorously for "potatoes.") However, if we had company to dinner or "tea," my grandfather was perfectly capable of producing a longer, more grateful one, or even making up one of his own to suit the occasion.

Until age or drink had spoiled it, Uncle Neddy had a very nice baritone voice, and Sundays when he was well enough to go to church he appeared in the back row of the choir. On those days he wore a navy blue suit and a hard collar, a dark blue satin tie with a red stripe, and a stickpin with a small, dead diamond in it, much like the white highlight in his left eye that I am contemplating right now.

But I want to try to be chronological about this little boy who doesn't look much like a little boy. His semidisembodied head seems too big for his body; and his body seems older, far less alive, than the round, healthy, painted face which is so very much in the present it seems to be taking an interest in it, even here, so very far away from where it saw such a very different world for so long.

The first dramatic episode of his life that I know about was when his foot got scalded. He told me the story more than once, usually as a warning to keep away from something hot. It concerned his boots, not these in the painting but his first pair of copper-toed boots, real little boots, no buttons or laces. Out of curiosity, he stood too near someone who was dipping boiling water out of the big boiler on the back of the kitchen stove and somehow a dipperful fell straight into a boot top. The boot was pulled off immediately, and then his sock. "And the skin came with it," Uncle Neddy always said, proud and morbid, while an icicle suddenly probed the bottom of my stomach. The family doctor came, and for a long time poor Uncle Neddy couldn't walk. His mother and sisters—he was the only son, the second child—all said he had been a very stoical boy; on that occasion he had only given one scream. Later on he had performed prodigies of stoicism in respect to the Nova Scotian winter cold. He couldn't endure being bundled up and would run out of the house and all the way to school, with the thermometer at ten, or twenty, below, without his overcoat. He would condescend to wear mittens and a muffler, but no more, and his ears had been frostbitten over and over again, and once one was frozen.

After these feats of endurance, his life, except for the Bible reading, is unknown to me for a long time. No—it was Uncle Neddy who dug all the wax off the face of my mother's big wax doll from France, with his fingernails and chewed it like chewing gum. The delicacy of the doll's complexion depended on this wax; without it she was red-faced and common. Uncle Neddy and my mother were playing upstairs; when my mother protested, he pushed her downstairs. Then when she pretended to faint and lay there at the foot of the stairs with her eyes shut, in great remorse he ran and got a quart dipper full of icy well water and threw it over her, crying out that he had killed his little sister.

And although she has been dead for over forty years, his little sister is here now, too, beside him. *Her* imaginary carpet is laid out geometrically in dark red, green and blue, or is it supposed to be tiles? and her wall is darker than his. She leans on a fairly normal round table, draped in a long red tablecloth, and her left leg is crossed over her right one. She must be about nine. She wears a small bustle and a gold brooch, but her black hair is cut short all over, with a fringe over her eyes, and she looks almost more like a boy than he does.

The paintings are unsigned and undated, probably the work of an itinerant portrait painter. Perhaps he worked from tintypes, because in the family album the little girl's dress appears again. Or did she have only the one dress, for dress-up? In the painting it is dark blue, white-sprigged, with the bustle and other additions purple, and two white frills making a sort of "bertha." (In the tintype the French wax doll appears, too, seated on her lap, big and stiff, her feet sticking out in small white boots beneath her petticoats, showing fat legs in striped stockings. She stares composedly at the camera under a raffish blond wig, in need of combing. The tintype man has tinted the cheeks of both the doll and my mother a clear pink. Of course, this must have been before the doll had lost her waxen complexion under Uncle Neddy's fingernails.)

Or perhaps the painter did the faces—clearer and brighter than the rest of the pictures, and in Uncle Neddy's case slightly out of proportion, surely—from "life," the clothes from tintypes, and the rest from his imagination. He may have arrived in the village with his canvases already filled in, the unrecognizable carpets, the round table and improbable chair, ready and waiting to be stood on and leaned on. Did Uncle Neddy insist, "I want to be painted with the chair"? Did the two children fight, more than seventy years ago, over which one would have which background?

Well, Uncle Neddy grew up; he skated a great deal, winters (without bundling up), went through all the grades of the village school, and very early (I heard much later) began to fall in love and to—alas for Neddy— "chase women." I even heard, overheard, rather, that there had been prolonged family worry about a "widow." He must have begun drinking about this time, too, although that was never mentioned until years later when he became, on occasion, a public disgrace. It was hard to know what to do with him; he showed all the classical symptoms of being "wild." In vain family prayers morning and night, the childhood Bible-reading, choir practice, Sunday school ("Sabbath School" my grandfather called it), church itself, Friday prayer meetings, and the annual revivals at which Uncle Neddy went forward and repented of all. At one of these, Uncle Neddy even took the "pledge," the temperance pledge that he could still recite to me years later, although he had broken it heaven only knew how many times by then:

> Trusting in help from heaven above
> We pledge ourselves to works of love,
> Resolving that we will not make
> Or sell or buy or give or take
> Rum, Brandy, Whisky, Cordials fine,
> Gin, Cider, Porter, Ale or Wine.

Tobacco, too, we will not use
And trust that we may always choose
A place among the wise and good
And speak and act as Christians should.

This was called the "Pledge of the Iron Age Band of Hope." The "Band of Hope" was an inspirational society for younger members of the church, but why "Iron Age"? Uncle Neddy didn't know and I never found out. It became vaguely associated in my mind with his profession. Because, after all these moral incentives, Uncle Neddy inevitably, immediately, began to show signs of being "wild" all over again and finally he was apprenticed to a tinsmith, to learn a trade—tinsmithing and installing and repairing wood-burning furnaces. And then, still very young, he married Aunt Hat. I got the impression later (I was a little pitcher with big ears) that perhaps he "had" to marry her, but I may be doing him an injustice.

Redheaded, rawboned, green-eyed, handsome, Aunt Hat came from "Galway Mines," a sort of ghost town twenty miles off, where iron mining and smelting were still carried on in a reduced and primitive way. It had once been more flourishing, but I remember boarded-up houses, boarded-up stores with rotting wooden sidewalks in front of them, and the many deep black or dark red holes that disfigured the hills. Also a mountainous slag heap, dead, gray, and glistening. Long before I was born, one of these slag heaps, built up for years, I don't know why, right beside or on the river that further downstream ran through our village, had given way and there had been a flood. I heard this story many times because my grandparents' house was on the lower side of the village, near the river, and it had been flooded. A warning had been given, but in the excitement of rescuing the older children, the clock, the cow and horse, my grandmother forgot the latest baby (later my aunt), and my grandfather had dashed back into the house to find her floating peacefully in her wooden cradle, bobbing over the kitchen floor. (But after this the poor baby had erysipelas.)

If Uncle Neddy was a "devil," a feeble, smokey-black one, Aunt Hat was a red, real one—redheaded, freckled, red-knuckled, strong, all fierce fire and flame. There *was* something of the Old Nick about her. They complemented each other; they were devils together. Rumor had it that the only other redhead for miles around was the parish priest at Galway Mines—the only Catholic community in the county. True or not, the village gossips drew their strictly Protestant and cruel conclusions.

My own recollections begin now, things I saw or heard: Uncle Neddy is a tinsmith, a married man, the father of three living and one or two dead children. He has a big shop across the green from my grandparents' house, in the only part of my grandfather's former tannery not torn down. (The local tanning trade had come to an end before I was born, when chemicals replaced tanbark.) From the entrance, with double doors, the shop starts out fairly bright; a large section is devoted to "store" galvanized pails and enameled pots and pans, two or three or more black kitchen ranges with nickle trimmings, farming implements and fishing rods—the last because fishing was Uncle Neddy's passion. But the farther in one goes the darker and more gloomy it becomes; the floor is covered with acrid-smelling, glinting, black dust and the workbench stretching across the far end is black, with glints of silver. Night descends as one walks back, then daylight grows as one reaches the dirty windows above the workbench. This night sky of Uncle Neddy's is hung with the things he makes himself: milk pails, their bottoms shining like moons, flashing tin mugs in different sizes, watering pots like comets, in among big dull lengths of stove pipe with wrinkled blue joints like elephants' legs dangling overhead.

When he was at work, Uncle Neddy always wore a black leather cap, or perhaps it was so shiny with wear it looked like leather, and black, black overalls. He chewed tobacco. The plugs of chewing tobacco had a little red tin apple pressed into one corner; these he took off and gave to me. He loved children and was very good with them. When he kissed me, he smelled violently of "Apple" chewing tobacco and his sooty chin was very scratchy—perhaps he shaved only on Sundays. Frequently he smelled of something else violent, too, and I remember a black or dark brown bottle, unlabeled, kept in the murk under the workbench, being lifted out for a hasty swig.

The shop was full of fascinating things to look at, but surely most of their charm lay in the fact that, besides being brand-new, they were all out of place. Who would expect to see comfortable-looking kitchen stoves, with names like "Magee Ideal" and "Magic Home" on their oven doors, standing leaning sidewise, in a shop? Stone cold, too, with empty, brand-new teakettles hanging from the rafters over them and the stove-lid lifters hanging up in a bunch, like dried herbs? Or pots and pans, enameled brown or a marbelized blue-and-white, sitting on the floor? Or dozens of tin mugs, the kind we used every day of our lives and that Uncle

Neddy actually made, hanging overhead, brilliantly new and clean, not dull and brown, the way they got at home? And kitchen pumps, sticky red or green, and the taller, thinner variety of pump for the barnyard, lying on the floor? Besides all these things there were fascinating black machines attached to the workbench and worked by hand. One was for rolling the blue-black sheet iron into stovepipes; one made turned-over edges on strips of tin so that they wouldn't cut the fingers, and there were others of more mysterious functions, all black and sinister. There were blowtorches and a sort of miniature forge, little anvils, heavy shears in all sizes, wooden mallets, boxes of stubby, gray-blue, flat-headed rivets and, best of all, solder. It came in thick silver rods, with a trade name stamped along them. What I liked best was to watch Uncle Neddy heat the end of a rod to the melting point and dribble it quickly to join a wide ribbon of tin and make a mug, sometimes a child-size mug, then solder on a strip already folded under on both sides in the folding machine for the handle. When they were cold, drops of solder that fell to the dirty floor could be picked up, pure silver, cool and heavy, and saved. Under the bench were piles of bright scraps of tin with sharp edges, curved shapes, triangles, pieces with holes in them, as if they'd been cut from paper, and prettiest of all, thin tin shavings, curled up tight, like springs. Occasionally Uncle Neddy would let me help him hold a stick of solder and dribble it around the bottom of a pail. This was thrilling, but oh, to be able to write one's name with it, in silver letters! As he worked, bent over, clipping, hammering, soldering, he chewed tobacco and spat long black spits under the bench. He was like a black snail, a rather quick but cautious snail, leaving a silvery, shiny trail of solder.

Probably the paying part of his business was installing furnaces, but that didn't interest Billy and me, although Billy was sometimes allowed to go along. They went off, with a helper, down the shore, to places like Lower Economy, the red wagon loaded with furnace parts and stovepipes, pulled by Nimble, our horse.

While Uncle Neddy worked away, chewing and spitting and drinking, with an occasional customer to talk to (there were two kitchen chairs in the front of the shop where men sometimes sat and talked, about fishing, mostly), or with a child or two to keep him company, his wife was cleaning house. Scrub, scrub and polish, polish, she went, all day long, in the house, next door but up higher, on a grass-covered slope. The house was shingled, painted bright red, the only red house in the village, and although it seemed big enough for Uncle Neddy's family, it was never quite finished; another veranda, a spare room, were always in the process of being added on, or shingled, but never quite completed, or painted. A narrow veranda led from the street to a side door, the only one used, and chickweed grew profusely underneath it, down the slope. My grandmother would send me across the street to pick some for her canaries and Aunt Hat would come out, lean over, and ask me crossly what I was doing, or just bang a dust mop on the railing, over my head. Her sharp-jawed, freckled face and green eyes behind gold-rimmed glasses peered over at me, upside down. She had her good days and her bad days, as my grandmother said, but mostly they seemed to be bad and on those she did everything more vigorously and violently. Sometimes she would order me home, where I meant to go, anyway, and with my innocent handful of chickweed, I ran.

Her three living children—there were two girls, older than Billy and I—all had beautiful curly hair. The girls were old enough to comb their own hair, but when Billy's curls were being made, really made, for Sunday school, his shrieks could be heard all the way across the green to our house. Then Billy would arrive to go to Sunday school with me, his face smeared with tears, the beautiful red-brown curls in perfect tubes, with drops of water (Aunt Hat wet the curls and turned them over her finger with a hard brush) falling from the end of each onto the white, ruffled collar of his Sunday blouse. Mondays, Aunt Hat energetically scrubbed the family's clothes, summers, down below, out back. On good days she occasionally burst quite loudly into song as she scrubbed and rinsed:

> Oh, the moon shines tonight on pretty Red Wing,
>   The breeze is sighing,
>   The night bird's crying.
> Oh, far beneath the sky her warrior's sleeping
>   While Red Wing's weeping
>   Her heart awa-a-y . . .

This song is still associated in my mind not with a disconsolate Indian maiden and red wings but with a red house, red hair, strong yellow laundry soap, and galvanized scrubbing boards (also sold in Uncle Neddy's shop; I forgot them). On other weekdays, Aunt Hat, as I have said, cleaned house: it was probably the cleanest house in the county. The kitchen linoleum dazzled; the straw matting in the upstairs bedrooms looked like new and so did the hooked rugs; the "cosy corner" in the parlor, with a red upholstered seat and frilled red pillows standing on their corners, was never disarranged; every china ornament on the mantelpiece over the airtight stove was in the same place and dustless, and Aunt Hat always seemed to have a broom or a long-handled brush in her hand, ready to take a swipe either at her household effects or any child, dog, or cat that came her way. Her temper, like her features, seemed constantly at a high temperature, but on bad days it rose many degrees and she "took it out," as the village said behind her back, in cleaning house. They also said she was "a great hand at housework" or "a demon for housework," sometimes, "She's a Tartar, that one!" It was also remarked on that in a village where every sunny window was filled with houseplants and the ladies constantly exchanged "slips" of this and that desirable one, Aunt Hat had "no luck" with plants; in fact nothing would grow for her at all.

Yes, she was a Tartar; it came out in her very freckles. She sunburned easily. When we went on a picnic, one hour in the northern sun and the vee of her neck was flaming. Uncle Neddy would say, almost as if he were proud of it, "Hat's neck looks as if I'd taken a flat-iron to it!" Wearing a straw hat and a gray cardigan instead of his black work clothes, even in the sunlight he still looked dark. But instead of being like a dark snail, he was a thin, dark salamander, enjoying, for a moment, his wife's fieriness.

His married life was miserable, we all knew that. My girl cousins whispered to me about the horrible, endless fights that went on, nights, under the low, slanting ceiling of their parents' bedroom, papered all over with small, pained-looking rosebuds, like pursed mouths. When things got too bad he would come to see "Mother" and they would shut themselves in the front parlor, or even in the pantry, standing up, for a talk. At our house, my grandmother was the one who did all the complaining; my grandfather never complained. When she said things about her daughter-in-law that he felt were too harsh, he merely murmured, "Yes, temper . . . temper . . . too bad," or maybe it was "too sad." (To Billy and me, when we quarreled, he said, "Birds in their little nests agree," a quotation I have never been able to place and even then didn't altogether agree with, from my observation of birds in their little nests.) There were days and weeks when these visits from a bedeviled-looking Uncle Neddy occurred often; dramas of which I knew nothing were going on; once in a while I made out that they concerned money, "deeds," or "papers." When Uncle Neddy had finally gone back to his shop, my grandmother would collapse into her kitchen rocking chair and announce: "*She* makes the balls and he fires them . . ." Then she would start rocking, groaning and rocking, wiping her eyes with the edge of her apron, uttering from time to time the mysterious remark that was a sort of chorus in our lives: "Nobody knows . . . *nobody knows* . . ." I often wondered what my grandmother knew that none of the rest of us knew and if she alone knew it, or if it was a total mystery that really nobody knew except perhaps God. I even asked her, "*What* do you know, Gammie, that we don't know? Why don't you tell us? Tell me!" She only laughed, dabbing at her tears. She laughed as easily as she cried, and one very often turned into the other (a trait her children and grandchildren inherited). Then, "Go on with you!" she said, "Scat!"

From the rocking chair by the window, she had a good view of all the green, the people on their way to the general store just around the corner, or on Sundays, to the tall white Presbyterian church opposite, and, diagonally to the right, of Uncle Neddy's shop and the red house. She disapproved of the way Aunt Hat fed her family. Often, around time for "tea," Billy or one of the girls could be seen running across to the store, and a few minutes later running back with a loaf of bread or something in a paper bag. My grandmother was furious: "Store bread! Store bread! Nothing but store bread!" Or, "More canned things, I'll bet! More *soda crackers* . . ." I knew from direct observation, that when he was far too big for the family high chair, Billy was squeezed into it and given what was called "pap" for *his* "tea." This was a soup plate full of the soda crackers, swimming in milk, limp and adhesive, with a lot of sugar to make them go down. The "pap" would be topped off by two pieces of marble cake, or parkins, for dessert. Aunt Hat did bake those, if not bread, and her parkins were good, but, as if out of spite, hard enough to break the teeth.

Sometimes I inadvertently brought on my grandmother's tears myself, by repeating things Billy told me. Perhaps he, too, was firing the balls made on the other side of the green, or pebbles, suited to the verbal slingshot of his tender years. "Is it true that Nimble (the one horse— later there were two horses, the second unfortunately named Maud, the name, straight from Tennyson, of one of my aunts)—is it true that Nimble belongs to Uncle Neddy? Billy says he does. And that Nelly and Martha Washington do, too?" (The cow and her calf; I had named the calf myself.)

My grandmother grew indignant. "I *gave* your Uncle Edward that horse on his tenth wedding anniversary! Not only that, but he sold him back to me two years afterwards and he still keeps saying I haven't finished paying him yet! When I have! And he uses that horse all the time, much more than we do!"

"Oh pshaw, mother," said my grandfather. "That's an old story now."

"Oh yes," said my grandmother. "Nimble, and the buffalo robe, and the dinner service, and *pew rent*—they're all old stories now. *You'd* never remember anything. But *I* won't forget. *I* won't forget." And she set the rocking chair rocking as if it were, as it probably was, a memory machine.

I have a few more memories of Uncle Neddy at this period in his life when the tinsmith business was still going on, and the furnace business, flourishing or not, I don't know, but before the obvious decline had set in and before I went away to Boston and saw him at less and less frequent intervals. One memory, brief but poignant, like a childhood nightmare that haunts one for years, or all one's life, the details are so clear and so awful, is of a certain Christmas. Or maybe it was a Christmas eve, because it takes place after the lamps were lit—but of course it grew dark very early in the winter. There was a large Christmas tree, smelling overpoweringly of fir, in the parlor. It was rather sparsely decorated with colored paper chains, strings of tinsel and popcorn, and a very few glass balls or other shiny ornaments: a countryfied, home-made tree, chopped down and brought fresh from the snow-covered "commons." But there were a few little silver and gold baskets, full of candies, woven from strips of metal by "the blind children," and clips holding twisted wax candles that after many warnings were finally lit. One of my aunts played "Holy Night" on the piano and the candles flickered in time to our singing.

This was all very nice, but still I remember it as "the Black Christmas." My other grandparents, in the States, had sent a large box of presents. It contained woolen caps and mufflers for Billy and me, and I didn't like them at all. His set was dark blue but mine was *gray* and I hated it at sight. There were also mittens and socks, and some of these were red or blue, and the high black rubber boots I'd wanted, but my pair was much too big. Laid out under the tree, even by flickering candlelight, everything looked shapeless and sad, and I wanted to cry. And then Santa Claus came in, an ordinary brown potato sack over his shoulder, with the other presents sagging in it. He was terrifying. He couldn't have been dressed in black, but that was my impression, and I did start to cry. He had artificial snow sprinkled on his shoulders, and a pointed red cap, but the beard! It wasn't white and wooly at all, it was made of rope, a mass of frayed-out rope. This dreadful figure cavorted around the room, making jokes in a loud, deep, false voice. The face that showed above the rope beard looked, to me, like a Negro's. I shrieked. Then this Santa from the depths of a coal mine put down his sack that could have been filled with coal, and hugged and kissed me. Through my sobs, I recognized, by touch and smell and his suddenly everyday voice, that it was only Uncle Neddy.

This Christmas, so like a nightmare, affected me so that shortly afterward I had a real nightmare about Uncle Neddy, or at least about his shop. In it, I crossed the road and was about to go into the shop when the door was blocked by a huge horse, coming out. The horse filled the doorway, towering high over me and showing all her big yellow teeth in a grin. She whinnied, shrill and deafening; I felt the hot wind coming out of her big nostrils; it almost blew me backward. I had the presence of mind to say to the horse, "You are a nightmare!" and of course she was, and so I woke up. But awake, I still felt uncomfortable for a long time about Uncle Neddy's possibly having been inside, his escape cut off by that fearful animal.

I said that Uncle Neddy was a great fisherman; it was the thing he did best of all, perhaps the only thing he did perfectly. (For all I know, his tinware, beautiful and shiny as it was, may have been badly made.) He could catch trout where no one else could and sometimes he would go off before daybreak and arrive at our house at seven o'clock with a string of rose-speckled trout for his mother's breakfast. He could cast into the narrowest brooks and impossibly difficult spots and bring out trout after trout. He tied beautiful flies, for himself and friends, and later for customers by mail.

> Our uncle, innocent of books,
> Was rich in lore of fields and brooks . . .

Whittier wrote of his, and it was true of mine.

But he was not altogether innocent of books. There had been all that childhood Bible reading that had left the supply of texts from which he still quoted. And also, in his parlor, on a shelf above the "cosy corner" and in a small bookcase, there was an oddly assorted collection of books. I wasn't familiar with them the way I was, with the outsides, at least, of every single book on the shelves in the upstairs hall at my grandmother's

(*Inglesby's Legends; Home Medicine; Emerson's Essays*, and so on), but this was only because of Aunt Hat. Every time I managed to be alone in the parlor with Uncle Neddy's books, she soon found me and shooed me off home. But I did get to look at them, or some of them, usually the same ones over and over. It was obvious that Uncle Neddy had been strongly affected by the sinking of the *Titanic;* in his modest library there were three different books about this catastrophe, and in the dining room, facing his place at the table, hung a chromograph of the ship going down: the iceberg, the rising steam, people struggling in the water, everything, in full color. When I was left alone in the parlor, an ear cocked for Aunt Hat, I could scarcely wait to take out the *Titanic* books—one very big and heavy, red, with gilt trimmings—and look at the terrifying pictures one more time. There were also *The Tower of London;* a book about Queen Victoria's Diamond Jubilee; *Advice to Young Men* ("Avoid lonely walks . . ."); and several of a religious nature. Also some little fat books about a character named "Dolly Dimples" that looked nice, and were pleasant to hold, but proved boring to read. But the *Titanic* books with their pictures, some of them actual photographs, were the best.

The other chief attraction in Uncle Neddy's parlor was an Edison phonograph, very old, that still worked. It had a flaring, brown-and-gold horn and played thick black cylinders. My girl cousins were allowed to play it. I remember only two out of the box of cylinders: a brief Sousa march that could have marched people about fifty yards, and "Cohen on the Telephone," which I loved. I knew that it was supposed to be funny, and laughed, although I hadn't any idea who or what a Cohen was or what I was laughing at, and I doubt that Uncle Neddy entirely understood it, either.

I suppose that Uncle Neddy's situation in life, his fortune and prospects, could never have been considered happy, even in his small world, but I was very young, and except for an occasional overheard, or eavesdropped-on remark and those private conversations in the parlor or pantry that always upset my grandmother, nothing untoward came to my knowledge, consciously that is, for years. Then even I began to hear more about Uncle Neddy's drinking, and the shop began its long deterioration. There was no place to buy liquor in the village; the nearest government liquor store was in a town fifteen miles away. At first this meant a daylong drive behind Nimble or Maud; sometimes an overnight stay at the house of a relative, niece or cousin, of my grandfather's. Probably when Uncle

Neddy went to town he brought back a supply of rum, the usual drink, heavy, dark and strong. All I knew of alcohol at that time was the homemade wines the ladies sometimes served each other, or the hot toddy my grandfather sometimes made himself on freezing winter nights. But finally phrases like "not himself," "taken too much," "three seas over," sank into my consciousness and I looked at my poor uncle with new eyes, expectantly. There was one occasion when he had to be taken away from the home funeral of Mrs. Captain McDonald, an old woman everyone was very fond of. What at first passed for Uncle Neddy's natural, if demonstrative grief, had got "out of hand." My grandmother moaned about this, in fact she moaned so loudly in her bedroom across the hall from mine that I could hear almost every word. "He'll disgrace us all; you'll see. I've *never* . . . There's *never* been a drunkard in *my* family . . . *None* of my brothers . . ." This time my grandfather remained quite silent.

Then Uncle Neddy bought a Model T Ford. There were very few cars in the village then; the family who had driven the coach to the railroad station, four miles off, for years and years, had been the first to acquire one, and there were only two or three more. Uncle Neddy got his Ford somehow, and the younger daughter, fifteen or so, with long curls just like Mary Pickford's, drove it hell-for-leather, expertly. Perhaps she drove her father the fifteen miles to town, in no time, to buy rum—anyway, he got it, and when he didn't have it, there was another unbelievable overheard remark, that he drank *vanilla*.

Meanwhile, the shop was changing. First, there were many more things for sale and less and less work seemed to be done at the old black-and-silver glinting workbench. There were many household effects that came ready-made: can openers, meat grinders, mixing spoons, gray-mottled enamel "sets" of saucepans. There were more fishing rods and then gorgeous barbed fish lures, displayed on cardboard stands. The stoves were now all, or almost all, white enamel, and there were white enamel kitchen sinks, and faucets, and electric water pumps. The chewing tobacco with the little tin apple in the corner was still on sale, but next to it one day there were chocolate bars: Moir's and Cadbury's, with nuts, without nuts, or in little sections with a different cream in each. These were magnetic, of course, but they cost five cents, or ten cents, and Billy and I had rarely had more than a penny to buy anything in our lives. Uncle Neddy was as kind to us, to any children, as always. He would take a whole ten-cent bar, divide it into its little squares, and share it out. A punchboard appeared, two or three of them. For ten cents one could punch out a little rolled-up paper with a number on it and, with luck, the number would win a whole big box of chocolates or a tin of biscuits. It was still a fascinating place to go, but not nearly as fascinating as when Uncle Neddy had been making tin mugs and soldering.

Then I went away to live in the States and came back just for the summers. Perhaps two or three years went by, I'm not sure, but one summer a gasoline pump appeared in front of the shop. Cars stopped to be filled up; not very often, but there were more of them although the road was still dirt and gravel, "crowned" in the middle. Billy and I competed with each other as to which one had seen the most and the biggest trucks. If a truck stopped for gasoline, we rushed to examine it: red or blue paint, decorated with white lines or gold lines, with arrowheads, what load it was carrying, and where it was going. Sometimes Uncle Neddy poured water into its radiator from one of his own watering cans while it stood steaming and trembling. Another summer, and the road had been covered with tar. The red house still had an unpainted wing, its "new" shingles already gray. Another summer the governor general drove through and stopped to make a speech in front of Uncle Neddy's shop. Another little girl, not me, curtsied and presented a large bouquet of flowers to his wife, Lady Bing.

Although there are more, these are all the memories I want to keep on remembering—I couldn't forget them if I tried, probably—and remembering clearly, as if they had just happened or were still happening. My grandfather dies. My grandmother goes to live with a daughter in Quebec. I go away to school, then to college. I come back at longer and longer intervals to Uncle Neddy's village. Once I go fishing with him and he deplores my casting, but, as always, very gently. He grows older—older, thinner, bent, and more unshaven, the sooty bristles mixed with silver. His voice grows weaker, too, and higher pitched. He has stomach ulcers. He is operated on, but won't stop, can't stop drinking—or so I am told. It has taken the form of periodic bouts and an aunt tells me (I'm old enough to be confided in) that "Everyone knows" and that "It will kill him." However, when he dies it is of something quite different.

The last time I saw him he was very weak and very bent. The eyes of the man who used to lean down to hug and kiss me were now on a level with mine. When I kissed him, the smell was only half the same: rum—

he no longer chewed tobacco. I knew, and he said it, that he was "not long for this world." Aunt Hat had aged, too. The red hair had faded to pink, but her jaw, her freckles, and her disposition were exactly the same. She no longer shooed me out of the house. Now she expressed her feelings by pretending not to see the presents from the States, clamping her jaw tight, and swatting at flies. Some days she refused to speak, others, she spoke—disparagingly, of whatever subject came up. The filling station was owned and manned by others.

I don't believe that Uncle Neddy ever went anywhere in his life except possibly two or three times as far as Boston after his daughters had moved there and married, and I'm not sure of that. And now he is here, on the other side of the Equator, with his little sister, looking like the good boy in a Horatio Alger story: poor, neat, healthy, polite, and by some lucky accident—preventing a banker from having his pocket picked, or catching a runaway horse—about to start out being a "success" in life, and perhaps taking his little sister along with him. He is overdressed for this climate and his cheeks are so pink he must be sweating in his velveteen suit.

I am going to hang them here side by side, above the antique (Brazilian antique) chest of drawers. In spite of the heat and dampness, they look calmly on and on, at the invisible Tropic of Capricorn, at the extravagant rain still blotting out the southern ocean. I must watch out for the mildew that inevitably forms on old canvases in the rainy season, and wipe them off often. It will be the gray or pale-green variety that appears overnight on dark surfaces, like breath on a mirror. Uncle Neddy will continue to exchange his direct, bright-hazel, child's looks, now, with those of strangers—dark-eyed Latins he never knew, who never would have understood him, whom he would have thought of, if he had ever thought of them at all, as "foreigners." How late, Uncle Neddy, how late to have started on your travels!

THE PARTY

Pat Esslinger Carr

I STEADIED the present on my lap and took a deep breath that stopped at my tight damp skirt band. The streetcar wheels clicked, clicked against the rails. I resisted the impulse to push back wet strands of hair at my temples and mash what little curl was left.

I didn't want to be on the hot trolley and I didn't want to go.

I pushed my glasses back up my greasy nose and wiped under the rims, carefully, not touching the glass with my knuckles. I had wanted so much more to stay in the porch swing with my book. John had just started telling his story; he was still with Beau and Digby, and we had all been together beneath sun spots of heat and sand, hearing the curses of the Legionnaires, smelling hot leather and camel fuzz. And then I had had to splash tepid water over my face, change from my shorts and wrap the hasty present my mother had bought at the dime store that morning. Matching fingernail polish and lipstick whose perfume made me slightly nauseated, but that Jan would probably like all right. I guessed she would, anyway, but I didn't much care. I begrudged the time I was having to lose. Over forty minutes each way on the trolley, and I would have to stay at least until 4:30 before I could break away politely. They usually played some kind of games until about 3:30 or so before they let you eat and escape.

I looked at the fat bland face of the watch hanging in its leather sheath beside the conductor: 2:20. I'd be a little late as it was and that would mean even more minutes lost at the end of the party; my mother said you should always stay at least two hours for politeness' sake. And I had the other two Beau books waiting in their faded blue covers when I finished this one. My whole Saturday afternoon wasted.

The click of the metal wheels chipped away at my world of sand and dry hot fortresses until the desert sun fell into pieces and then dissolved. I scooted the damp package higher up on my lap. I could feel drops of sweat collecting under my bare knees.

We were passing the cemetery. The gawky stone angels dotted the tombs and oozed green slime. They all had the same faces, the same stone cataracts for eyes. Guardian angels, stiffened and blind.

I settled back against the wooden seat, feeling the wet patch of blouse on my skin as we swayed along. It would be another ten minutes on the trolley and then an eight-block walk. My whole Saturday wasted.

When I climbed down from the awkward trolley steps, I realized the afternoon was even hotter than when I had started from home. The drops behind my knees gathered into rivulets that crawled with itching slowness down to the tops of my anklets. Hot branches hung like lank hair over the street, lifting and drooping with a faint hot breeze almost as if they were panting.

Half a block away I saw the house with its tight cluster of balloons tacked to the front door and its pink ribbon trailing from the brass knocker. Up close, I wasn't quite sure how to knock around the pink satin ribbon, so I finally used my knuckles and left damp imprints on the white door.

The door popped open immediately and a lady I guessed must be Jan's mother stood there beaming greedily at me.

"Here's your first guest," she half turned back and called happily without taking her eyes off me. "Do come in," she added to me and tried to open the door wider except that it was already open about as far as it could go. She reached out to take my arm, but when she saw me looking at her a little dumbfounded she didn't touch me and just motioned me in with her hand. I saw Jan behind her.

"Hi," I said, blinking a little with the shadow of the room as the door closed out the bright streak of balloons. I held out the little package with its moist wrapping paper.

"Hi," she said and took the package.

"Aren't you going to introduce your little friend to me, Jan?" her mother said brightly, birdlike, from beside me.

I winced and glanced at her as Jan mumbled my name and held the present in her hands, not seeming to know what to do with it. Although not as fat as Jan, her mother had the same tight curly hair and the same plump cheeks. She said something else bright and pecking while I was looking at her that I didn't hear and then she put a hand on each of our shoulders and pushed us slightly ahead of her into the next room.

"We decided to stack all the presents on the buffet, and yours can be the first." I could hear her beam behind us.

The room was a dining room, but it was so covered with pink crepe paper I couldn't tell at first. Pink twisted streamers bulged low from the overhead light and swung to the molding of every wall. The tablecloth was scalloped with pink crepe paper held on by Scotch tape, and the buffet where Jan's mother put my present was skirted with more taped pink paper. A massive pink frosted cake with a circle of twelve pink candles in flower holders sat in the center of the table, and the whole rest of the table top was jammed with pink paper plates holding a pink snapper each and a pink nut cup stuffed with cashew nuts. Enough for the whole class I guessed.

"We thought we'd just stand up for the cake and ice cream," her mother's voice smiled around me. I knew we would have pink ice cream with the cake. "We just don't have thirty-three chairs in the house," she almost giggled.

I didn't know what to say and Jan didn't say anything, so her voice added, "Why don't you show your little friend your new room, Jan? I'll be down here to catch the door as the rest of your guests arrive."

Jan made a kind of shrugging nod and led the way out the other side of the room, up some stairs that smelled of newly rubbed polish to a converted attic room.

Everything in the room was yellow. Bedspread, curtains, walls, lampshade on the desk. It was a bit like having been swallowed by a butterfly, but it wasn't as bad as the pink downstairs.

"It's new," Jan said offhandedly. "Daddy finished the walls and my mother made the bedspread and curtains." She glanced around casually, but I caught the glint of pride before she covered it up.

"It's nice," I said. "I like yellow."

"It's so sunny." I could almost hear her mother saying it.

I nodded and grappled for something else to talk about. "What's that?" I pointed to a cloth-covered scrap book. The cover was a tiny red and white check, and I somehow knew Jan had chosen that herself.

"Just some sketches." But she couldn't cover up the pride this time.

"Can I see them?" I said too heartily, but she didn't notice as she put the book tenderly on the bed.

I started turning the pages, commenting on each one. Some of them were bad, the heart-lipped beauties in profile we all tried once in a while in math class, a few tired magnolias, some lopsided buildings; but then I got to the animals. Round, furred kittens that you knew were going to grow into cats. Zoo monkeys, hanging on the bars, pretending to be people. Fat pigeons strutting among cigarette wrappers on their way to drop white splatters on Robert E. Lee.

I glanced up at her. She was watching me with the hungry expression I had seen on her mother at the door. "These are good." I couldn't keep the surprise out of my voice.

"Do you think so?" She waited to lap up my praise, her mouth parted and her plump cheeks blushing a little.

I nodded, turning to the animals again, telling her what I thought about each one. I don't know how long we were there when she said, "I guess we'd better go down." I hadn't heard anything, but she carefully closed the book and placed it on her desk.

Her mother was at the foot of the stairs waiting for us. There was a tight pulled look at the corners of her mouth. "What time is it, dear?" she said with that glittering, bird-sharp voice.

I saw the hall clock behind her in a brass star. The shiny brass hands had just slipped off each other and were pointing to 3:20.

"I can't imagine what has happened." Her voice slivered a little.

"You live pretty far out," I said, the excuse sounding pretty bad even to me.

She nodded abstractedly. "I suppose so." Then she added, "I'd better see about the ice cream."

She bustled off and Jan and I stood aimlessly at the foot of the stairs. I could see the pink crepe paper through the door of the dining room.

The silence lengthened uncomfortably and the hall clock pinged 3:30.

"You want to go in the back yard?" Jan said at last.

"Okay."

We trudged through the kitchen. Her mother was standing beside the refrigerator where I guessed she had just checked the cartons of ice cream. "You two go on outside. I'll be here to catch the door." Her voice was brittle, like overdone candy cracking on a plate.

I thought as we filed past that it would be better if she went up to take a nap and could have the excuse later of maybe having missed the knocker. It was getting awfully late.

We went out and took turns sitting on the swing in the oak tree they had out back and I told her about the book I was reading. I didn't much want to share it, but I had to talk about something. I told her she could have it after I finished even though I had intended to let my best friend Aileen read it next so we could make up joint Foreign Legion daydreams. We rocked back and forth a while, not really swinging, just sort of waiting and trying to limp along in a kind of conversation. I knew we were both listening, straining to hear a knock, a footstep on the sidewalk out front.

Her mother appeared at the back screen. "I thought you girls would like a preview lemonade. It's so hot this afternoon."

"It really is," I agreed hastily. She somehow made me feel awful. I guess it was the word "preview" that did it. As if there were really going to be something to follow, the birthday party when the other thirty-one guests arrived. "Pink lemonade sounds great." I hadn't meant to say "pink," and as soon as I said it I could have stuffed my sweaty fist in my mouth.

She gave a little stilted laugh and I couldn't tell if she noticed. "It's all made."

We waited and took turns in the swing until she brought the two glasses out on a little tray. I saw her coming from the corner of my eye and said, "I bet you can't guess what I got you for your birthday."

Jan shook her head, looking at me and sort of grinning.

"It's something to wear," I said prolonging it. Then as her mother got there with the lemonade, I looked up, startled, as if I hadn't seen her. "That looks good," I said a little too loudly at the pink liquid. There wasn't any ice in it; the freezer part of their box was probably full of ice cream.

She strained out a smile. I thought I saw her lower lip quiver a little.

"I got so hot coming out here. I didn't know you lived so near the end of the trolley line." I tried to put over the idea of distance and maybe a confusion about their address. "This is great." I took a quick sip.

"Really great," Jan chorused.

But her mother was already on her way back to the kitchen, into the house where she'd be able to hear the door.

We stayed there in the hot shade, alternately leaning against the rough tree trunk and sitting in the swing until I guessed it must have been about 4:00 or so. We were still listening too hard to talk much.

"Want something to eat?"

I couldn't face that pink dining room with the crepe paper streamers and the thirty-three nut cups. I hesitated.

She must have understood. "We have some cupcakes, in case we ran out of. . . ." Her voice trailed off.

"Fine. I love cupcakes," I said hurriedly.

As we came in her mother came from the front of the house.

"We thought we'd have a cupcake," Jan said.

"Oh, yes. That's a fine idea," she began. "And have a dip of the ice. . . ." Then her face crumpled like a sheet of wadded paper. Her lips wavered over the word and a great sob hiccuped through her throat. She put her hand over her mouth as she turned and ran toward the hall, and I saw her back heaving as she disappeared beside the stairs.

We pretended we hadn't seen anything. Jan got the little pink cakes from a bin and dished out two great heaps of strawberry ice cream, and we stood beside the sink and ate them.

I had separate sensations of dry warmish crumbs and iced smoothness passing across my tongue, but I couldn't taste anything. But I ate the little cake and the bowl of ice cream and when she offered me another cupcake and more ice cream, I took them and ate them too.

I repeated some of my compliments about her sketches and added more as I thought of them and spooned up the chopped bits of strawberry in the bottom of the dish. We dragged out the ritual until shadows began to ease into the kitchen and I saw by the kitchen clock that it was after 5:30. I told her I had better leave to be able to get home before dark with such a long trolley ride back uptown. "Tell your mother," I began, but I couldn't think what she should tell her mother for me and I stopped.

As we went toward the front door I saw the pink paper of the dining room glowing in the afternoon sun.

"See you Monday. I'll bring the book," I said loudly at the front door.

She waved her hand and shut the door. The knot of balloons jogged, settled lightly against one another beneath the pink satin ribbon on the door knocker as I went down the sidewalk.

PLEADINGS

John William Corrington

DINNER was on the table when the phone rang, and Joan just stared at me.

—Go ahead, answer it. Maybe they need you in Washington.

—I don't want to get disbarred, I said. —More likely they need me at the Parish Prison.

I was closer than she was. It was Bertram Bijou, a deputy out in Jefferson Parish. He had a friend. With troubles. Being a lawyer, you find out that nobody has trouble, really. It's always a friend.

—Naw, on the level, Bert said. —You know Howard Bedlow?

No, I didn't know Howard Bedlow, but I would pretty soon.

They came to the house after supper. As a rule, I put people off when they want to come to the house. They've got eight hours a day to find out how to incorporate, write a will, pull their taxes down, or whatever. In the evening I like to sit quiet with Joan. We read and listen to Haydn or Boccherini and watch the light fade over uptown New Orleans. Sometimes, though I do not tell her, I like to imagine we are a late Roman couple sitting in our atrium in the countryside of England, not far from Londinium. It is always summer, and Septimus Severus has not yet begun to tax Britain out of existence. Still, it is twilight now, and there is nothing before us. We are young, but the world is old, and that is all right because the drive and the hysteria of destiny is past now, and we can sit and enjoy our garden, the twisted ivy, the huge caladiums, and if it is April, the daffodils that plunder our weak sun and sparkle across the land. It is always cool in my fantasy, and Joan crochets something for the center of our table, and I refuse to think of the burdens of administration that I will have to lift again tomorrow. They will wait, and Rome will never even know. It is always a hushed single moment, ageless and serene, and I am with her, and only the hopeless are still ambitious.

Everything we will do has been done, and for the moment there is peace.

It is a silly fantasy, dreamed here in the heart of booming America, but it makes me happy, and so I was likely showing my mild irritation when Bert and his friend Howard Bedlow turned up. I tried to be kind. For several reasons. Bert is a nice man. An honest deputy, a politician in a small way, and perhaps what the Civil Law likes to call *une bon pere du famille*—though I think at Common Law Bert would be "an officious intermeddler." He seems prone to get involved with people. Partly because he would like very much to be on the Kenner City Council one day, but, I like to imagine, as much because there lingers in the Bijou blood some tincture of piety brought here and nurtured by his French sires and his Sicilian and Spanish maternal ascendants. New Orleans has people like that. A certain kindness, a certain sympathy left over from the days when one person's anguish or that of a family was the business of all their neighbors. Perhaps that fine and profound Catholic certainty of death and judgment which makes us all one.

And beyond approving Bert as a type, I have found that most people who come for law are in one way or another distressed: the distress of loss or fear, of humiliation or sudden realization. Or the more terrible distress of greed, appetite gone wild, the very biggest of deals in the offing, and O, my God, don't let me muff it.

Howard Bedlow was in his late forties. He might have been the Celtic gardener in my imaginary Roman garden. Taller than average, hair a peculiar reddish gold more suited to a surfing king than to an unsuccessful car salesman, he had that appearance of a man scarce half made up that I had always associated with European workmen and small tradesmen. His cuffs were frayed and too short. His collar seemed wrong; it fit neither his neck nor the thin stringy tie he wore knotted more or less under it. Once, some years ago, I found, he had tried to make a go of his own Rambler franchise, only to see it go down like a gutshot animal, month by month, week by week, until at last no one, not even the manager of the taco place next door, would cash his checks or give him a nickel for a local phone call.

Now he worked, mostly on commission, for one used car lot or another, as Bert told it. He had not gone bankrupt in the collapse of the Rambler business, but had sold his small house on the west bank and had paid off his debts, almost all of them dollar for dollar, fifty here, ten there. When I heard that, I decided against offering them coffee. I got out whiskey. You serve a man what he's worth, even if he invades your fantasies.

As Bert talked on, only pausing to sip his bourbon, Bedlow sat staring into his glass, his large hands cupping it, his fingers moving restlessly around its rim, listening to Bert as if he himself had no stake in all that was passing. I had once known a musician who had sat that way when people caught him in a situation where talk was inevitable. Like Bedlow, he was not resentful, only elsewhere, and his hands, trained to a mystical perfection, worked over and over certain passages in some silent score.

Bedlow looked up as Bert told about the house trailer he, Bedlow, lived in now—or had lived in until a week or so before. Bedlow frowned almost sympathetically, as if he could find some measure of compassion for a poor man who had come down so far.

—Now I got to be honest, Bert said at last, drawing a deep breath. —Howard, he didn't want to come. Bad times with lawyers.

—I can see that, I said.

—He can't put all that car franchise mess out of mind. Bitter, you know. Gone down hard. Lawyers like vultures, all over the place.

Bedlow nodded, frowning. Not in agreement with Bert on his own behalf, but as if he, indifferent to all this, could appreciate a man being bitter, untrusting after so much. I almost wondered if the trouble wasn't Bert's, so distant from it Bedlow seemed.

—I got to be honest, Bert said again. Then he paused, looking down at his whiskey. Howard studied his drink, too.

—I told Howard he could come along with me to see you, or I had to take him up to Judge Talley. DWI, property damage, foul and abusive, resisting, public obscenity. You could pave the river with charges. I mean it.

All right. You could. And sometimes did. Some wise-ass tries to take apart Millie's Bar, the only place for four blocks where a working man can sit back and sip one without a lot of hassle. You take and let him consider the adamantine justice of Jefferson Parish for thirty days or six months before you turn him loose at the causeway and let him drag back to St. Tammany Parish with what's left of his tail tucked between his legs. Discretion of the Officer. That's the way it is, the way it's always been, the way it'll be till the whole human race learns how to handle itself in Millie's Bar.

But you don't do that with a friend. Makes no sense. You don't cart him off to Judge Elmer Talley who is the scourge of the working class if the working class indulges in what others call the curse of the working class. No, Bert was clubbing his buddy. To get him to an Officer of the Court. All right.

—He says he wants a divorce, Bert said. —Drinks like a three-legged hog and goes to low rating his wife in public and so on. Ain't that fine?

No, Bedlow acknowledged, frowning, shaking his head. It was *not* fine. He agreed with Bert, you could tell. It was sorry, too damned bad.

—I'm not going to tell you what he called his wife over to Sammie's Lounge last night. Sammie almost hit him. You know what I mean?

Yes I did. Maybe, here and there, the fire is not entirely out. I have known a man to beat another very nearly to death because the first spoke slightingly of his own mother. One does not talk that way about women folk, not even one's own. The lowly, the ignored, and the abused remember what the high-born and the wealthy have forgotten.

—Are you separated, I asked Bedlow.

—I ain't livin with the woman, he said laconically. It was the first time he had spoken since he came into my house.

—What's the trouble?

He told me. Told me in detail while Bert listened and made faces of astonishment and disbelief at me. Bert could still be astonished after seventeen years on the Jefferson Parish Sheriff's squad. You wonder that I like him?

It seemed that there had been adultery. A clear and flagrant act of faithlessness resulting in a child. A child that was not his, not a Bedlow. He had been away, in the wash of his financial troubles, watching the Rambler franchise expire, trying hard to do right. And she did it, swore to Christ and the Virgin she never did it, and went to confinement carrying another man's child.

—When, I asked. —How old is . . . ?

—Nine, Bedlow said firmly. —He's . . . it's nine . . .

I stared at Bert. He shrugged. It seemed to be no surprise to him. Oh, hell, I thought. Maybe what this draggle-assed country needs is an emperor. Even if he taxes us to death and declares war on Guatemala. This is absurd.

—Mr. Bedlow, I said. —You can't get a divorce for adultery with a situation like that.

—How come?

—You've been living with her all that . . . nine years?

—Yeah.

—They . . . call it reconciliation. No way. If you stay on, you are presumed . . . what the hell. How long have you lived apart?

—Two weeks and two days, he answered. I suspected he could have told me the hours and minutes.

—I couldn't take it any more. Knowing what I know . . .

Bedlow began to cry. Bert looked away, and I suppose I did. I have not seen many grown men cry cold sober. I have seen them mangled past any hope of life, twisting, screaming, cursing. I have seen them standing by a wrecked car while police and firemen tried to saw loose the bodies of their wives and children. I have seen men, told of the death of their one son, stand hard-jawed with tears running down their slabby sunburned cheeks, but that was not crying. Bedlow was crying, and he did not seem the kind of man who cries.

I motioned Bert back into the kitchen. —What the hell . . .

—This man, Bert said, spreading his hands, —is in trouble.

—All right, I said, hearing Bedlow out in the parlor, still sobbing as if something more than his life might be lost. —All right. But I don't think it's a lawyer he needs.

Bert frowned, outraged. —Well, he sure don't need one of . . . them.

I could not be sure whether he was referring to priests or psychiatrists. Or both. Bert trusted the law. Even working with it, knowing better than I its open sores and ugly fissures, he believed in it, and for some reason saw me as one of its dependable functionaries. I guess I was pleased by that.

—Fill me in on this whole business, will you?

Yes, he would, and would have earlier over the phone, but he had been busy mollifying Sammie and some of his customers who wanted to lay charges that Bert could not have sidestepped.

It was short and ugly, and I was hooked. Bedlow's wife was a good woman. The child was a hopeless defective. It was kept up at Pineville, at the Louisiana hospital for the feebleminded, or whatever the social scientists are calling imbeciles this year. A vegetating thing that its mother had named Albert Sidney Bedlow before they had taken it away, hooked it up for a lifetime of intravenous feeding, and added it to the schedule for cleaning up filth and washing, and all the things they do for human beings who can do nothing whatever for themselves. But Irma Bedlow couldn't let it go at that. The state is equipped, albeit poorly, for this kind of thing. It happens. You let the thing go, and they see to it, and one day, usually not long hence, it dies of pneumonia or a virus, or one of the myriad diseases that float and sift through the air of a place like that. This is the way these things are done, and all of us at the law have drawn up papers for things called "Baby So-and-so," sometimes, mercifully, without their parents' having laid eyes on them.

Irma Bedlow saw it otherwise. During that first year, while the Rambler franchise was bleeding to death, while Bedlow was going half crazy, she had spent most of her time up in Alexandria, a few miles from the hospital, at her cousin's. So that she could visit Albert Sidney every day.

She would go there, Bert told me—as Bedlow had told him—and sit in the drafty ward on a hard chair next to Albert Sidney's chipped institutional crib, with her rosary, praying to Jesus Christ that He would send down His grace on her baby, make him whole, and let her suffer in his place. She would kneel in the twilight beside the bed stiff with urine, and stinking of such excrement as a child might produce who has never tasted food, amidst the bedlam of chattering and choking and animal sounds from bedridden idiots, cretins, declining mongoloids, microcephalics, and assorted other exiles from the great altarpiece of Hieronymus Bosch. Somehow, the chief psychologist had told Howard, her praying upset the other inmates of the ward, and at last he had to forbid Irma coming more than once a month. He told her that the praying was out altogether.

After trying to change the chief psychologist's mind, and failing, Irma had come home. The franchise was gone by then, and they had a secondhand trailer parked in a run-down court where they got water, electricity, and gas from pipes in the ground and a sullen old man in a prewar De Soto station wagon picked up garbage once a week. She said the rosary there, and talked about Albert Sidney to her husband who, cursed now with freedom by the ruin of his affairs, doggedly looking for some kind of a job, had nothing much to do or think about but his wife's abstracted words and the son he had almost had. Indeed, did have, but had in such a way that the having was more terrible than the lack.

It had taken no time to get into liquor, which his wife never touched, she fasting and praying, determined that no small imperfection in herself should stay His hand who could set things right with Albert Sidney in the flash of a moment's passing.

—And in that line, Bert said, —she ain't . . . they . . . never been man and wife since then. You know what I mean?

—Ummm.

—And she runs off on him. Couple or three times a year. They always find her at the cousin's. At least till last year. Her cousin won't have her around any more. Seems Irma wanted her to fast for Albert Sidney, too. Wanted the cousin's whole family to do it, and there was words, and now she just takes a room at a tourist court by the hospital and tries to get in as often as that chief psychologist will let her. But no praying, he holds to that.

—What does Bedlow believe?

—Claims he believes she got Albert Sidney with some other man.

—No, I mean . . . does he believe in praying?

—Naw. Too honest, I guess. Says he don't hold with beads and saying the same thing over and over. Says God stands on His own feet, and expects the same of us. Says we ain't here to shit around. What's done is done.

—Do you think he wants a divorce?

—Could he get one . . . ?

—Yes.

—Well, how do I know?

—You brought him here. He's not shopping for religious relics, is he?

Bert looked hurt. As if I were blaming him unfairly for some situation beyond his control or prevention.

—You want him in jail?

—No, I said. —I just don't know what to do about him. Where's he living?

—Got a cabin at the Bo-Peep Motel. Over off Veterans Highway. He puts in his time at the car lot and then goes to drinking and telling people his wife has done bastardized him.

—Why did he wait so long to come up with that line?

—It just come on him, what she must of done, he told me.

—That's right, Bedlow said, his voice raspy, aggressive. —I ain't educated or anything. I studied on it and after so long it come to me. I saw it wasn't *mine*, that . . . thing of hers. Look, how come she can't just get done mourning and say, well, that's how it falls out sometimes and I'm sorry as all hell, but you got to keep going. That's what your ordinary woman would say, ain't it?

He had come into the kitchen where Bert and I were standing, his face still wet with tears. He came in talking, and the flow went on as if he were as compulsive with his tongue as he was with a bottle. The words tumbled out so fast that you felt he must have practiced, this country man, to speak so rapidly, to say so much.

—But no. I tell you what: she's mourning for what she done to that . . . thing's real father, that's what she's been doing. He likely lives in Alex, and she can't get over what she done him when she got that . . . thing. And I tell you this, I said, look, honey, don't give it no name, 'cause if you give it a name, you're gonna think that name over and over and make like it was the name of a person and it ain't, and it'll ruin us just as sure as creaking hell. And she went and named it my father's name, who got it after Albert Sidney Johnston at Shiloh . . . look, I ain't laid a hand on that woman in God knows how many years, I tell you that. So you see, that's what these trips is about. She goes up and begs his pardon for not giving him a fine boy like he wanted, and she goes to see . . . the thing, and mourns . . . and goddamnit to hell, I got to get shut of this . . . whole *thing*.

It came in a rush, as if, even talking, saying more words in the space of a moment than he had ever said before, Bedlow was enlarging, perfecting his suspicions—no, his certainty of what had been done to him.

We were silent for a moment.

—Well, it's hard, Bert said at last.

—Hard, Bedlow glared at him as if Bert had insulted him. —You don't even know hard . . .

—All right, I said, —We'll go down to the office in the morning and draw up and file.

—Huh?

—We'll file for legal separation. Will your wife contest it?

—Huh?

—I'm going to get you what you want. Will your wife go along?

—Well, I don't know. She don't . . . think about . . . things. If you was to tell her, I don't know.

Bert looked at him, his large dark face settled and serious. —That woman's a . . . Catholic, he said at last, and Bedlow stared back at him as if he had named a new name, and things needed thinking again.

A little while later they left, with Bedlow promising me and promising Bertram Bijou that he'd be in my office the next morning. For a long time after I closed the door behind them, I sat looking at the empty whiskey glasses and considered the course of living in the material world. Then I went and fixed me a shaker of martinis, and became quickly wiser. I considered that it was time to take Zeno seriously, give over the illusion of motion, of sequence. There are only a few moments in any life and when they arrive, they are fixed forever and we play through them, pretending to go on, but coming back to them over and over, again and again. If it is true that we can only approach a place but never reach it as the Philosopher claims, it must be corollary that we may almost leave a moment, but never quite. And so, as Dr. Freud so clearly saw, one moment, one vision, one thing come upon us, becomes the whole time and single theme of all we will ever do or know. We are invaded by our own one thing, and going on is a dream we have while lying still.

I thought, too, mixing one last shaker, that of the little wisdom in this failing age, Alcoholics Anonymous must possess more than its share. I am an alcoholic, they say. I have not had a drink in nine years, but I am an alcoholic, and the shadow, the motif of my living is liquor bubbling into a glass over and over, again and again. That is all I really want, and I will never have it again because I will not take it, and I know that I will never really know why not.

—It's bedtime, Joan said, taking my drink and sipping it.

—What did they want?

—A man wants a divorce because nine years ago his wife had a feebleminded baby. He says it's not his. Wants me to claim adultery and unclaim the child.

—Nice man.

—Actually, I began. Then no. Bedlow did not seem a nice man or not a nice man. He seemed a driven man, outside whatever might be his element. So I said that.

—Who isn't, Joan sniffed. She is not the soul of charity at two-thirty in the morning.

—What? Isn't what?

—Driven. Out of her . . . his . . . element?

I looked at her. Is it the commonest of things for men in their forties to consider whether their women are satisfied? Is it a sign of the spirit's collapse when you wonder how and with whom she spends her days? What is the term for less than suspicion: a tiny circlet of thought that touches your mind at lunch with clients or on the way to the office, almost enough to make you turn back home, and then disappears like smoke when you try to fix it, search for a word or an act that might have stirred it to life?

—Are you . . . driven, I asked much too casually.

—Me? No, she sighed, kissing me. —I'm different, she said. Was she too casual, too?

—Bedlow isn't different. I think he wants it all never to have happened. He had a little car franchise and a pregnant wife ten years ago. Clover. He had it made. Then it all went away.

Joan lit a cigarette, crossed her legs and sat down on the floor with my drink. Her wrapper fell open, and I saw the shadow of her breasts. —It always goes away. If you know anything, you know that. Hang on as long as you can. 'Cause it's going away. If you know anything . . .

I looked at her as she talked. She was as beautiful as the first time I had seen her. It was an article of faith: nothing had changed. Her body was still as soft and warm in my arms, and I wait for summer to see her in a bathing suit, and to see her take it off, water running out of her blond hair, between her breasts that I love better than whatever it is that I love next best.

—Sometimes it doesn't go away, I said. Ponderously, I'm sure.

She cocked her head, almost said something, and sipped the drink instead.

What made me think then of the pictures there in the parlor? I went over them in the silence, the flush of gin, remembering where and when we had bought each one. That one in San Francisco, in a Japanese gallery, I thinking that I would not like it long, but thinking too that it didn't matter, since we were at the end of a long difficult case with a fee to match. So if I didn't like it later, well . . .

And the Danish ship, painted on wood in the seventeenth century. I still liked it very much. But why did I think of these things? Was it that they stood on the walls, amidst our lives, adding some measure of substance and solidity to them, making it seem that the convention of living together, holding lovely things in common, added reality to the lives themselves. Then, or was it later, I saw us sitting not in a Roman garden in Britain, but in a battered house trailer in imperial America, the walls overspread with invisible pictures of the image of a baby's twisted unfinished face. And how would that be? How would we do then?

Joan smiled, lightly sardonic. —Ignore it, and it'll go away.

—Was there . . . something I was supposed to do, I asked.

The smile deepened, then faded. —Not a thing, she said.

II

The next morning, a will was made, two houses changed hands, a corpo-ration, closely held, was born, seven suits were filed and a deposition was taken from a whore who claimed that her right of privacy was invaded when the vice squad caught her performing an act against nature on one of their members in a French Quarter alley. Howard Bedlow did not turn up. Joan called just after lunch.

—I think I'll go over to the beach house for a day or two, she said, her voice flat and uncommunicative as only a woman's can be.

I guess there was a long pause. It crossed my mind that once I had wanted to be a musician, perhaps even learn to compose. —I can't get off till the day after tomorrow, I said, knowing that my words were inapposite to anything she might have in mind. —I could come Friday.

—That would be nice.

—Are you . . . taking the children?

—Louise will take care of them.

—You'll be . . . by yourself?

A pause on her side this time.

—Yes. Sometimes . . . things get out of hand.

—Anything you want to talk about?

She laughed. —You're the talker in the family.

—And you're what? The actor. Or the thinker?

—That's it. I don't know.

My voice went cold then. I couldn't help it. —Let me know if you figure it out. Then I hung up. And thought at once that I shouldn't have and yet glad of the miniscule gesture because however puny, it was an act, and acts in law are almost always merely words. I live in a storm of words: words substituting for actions, words to evade actions, words hinting of actions, words pretending actions. I looked down at the deposition on my desk and wondered if they had caught the whore *talking* to the vice squad man in the alley. Give her ten years: the utterance of words is an act against nature, an authentic act against nature. I had read somewhere that in Chicago they have opened establishments wherein neither mas-sage nor sex is offered: only a woman who, for a sum certain in money, will talk to you. She will say anything you want her to say: filth, word-pictures of every possible abomination, fantasies of domination and degradation, sadistic orgies strewn out in detail, oaths, descriptions of rape and castration. For a few dollars you can be told how you molested a small child, how you have murdered your parents and covered the carcasses with excrement, assisted in the gang rape of your second grade teacher. All words.

The authentic crime against nature has finally arrived. It is available somewhere in Chicago. There is no penalty, for after all, it is protected by the first amendment. Scoff on, Voltaire, Rousseau, scoff on.

My secretary, who would like to speak filth to me, buzzed.

—Mr. Bijou.

—Good. Send him in.

—On the phone.

Bert sounded far away. —You ain't seen Howard, have you?

—No, I said. —Have you?

—Drunk somewhere. Called coughing and moaning something about a plot to shame him. Talking like last night. I think you ought to see Irma. You're supposed to seek reconciliation, ain't you?

—I think you're ripe for law school, Bert. Yes, that's what they say do.

—Well, he said. —Lemme see what I can do.

I was afraid of that. When I got home there was a note from Louise, the childrens' nurse. She had taken them to her place up in Livingston Parish for a day or two. They would like that. The house was deserted, and I liked that. Not really. I wondered what a fast trip to the Gulf coast would turn up, or a call to a friend of mine in Biloxi who specializes in that kind of thing. But worse, I wasn't sure I cared. Was it that I didn't love Joan anymore, that somewhere along the way I had become insulated against her acts? Could it be that the practice of law had slowly made me responsive only to words? Did I need to go to Chicago to feel real again?

I was restless and drank too many martinis and was involved so much in my own musings that time passed quickly. I played some Beethoven, God knows why. I am almost never so distraught that I enjoy spiritual posturing. Usually, his music makes me grin.

I tried very hard to reckon where I was and what I should do. I was in the twentieth century after Christ, and it felt all of that long since anything on earth had mattered. I was in a democratic empire called America, an officer of its courts, and surely a day in those courts is as a thousand years. I was an artisan in words, shaping destinies, allocating money and blame by my work. I was past the midpoint of my life and could not make out what it had meant so far.

Now amidst this time and place, I could do almost as I chose. Should it be the islands of the Pacific with a box of paints? To the Colorado mountains with a pack, beans, a guitar, pencils, and much paper? Or, like an anchorite, declare the longest of nonterminal hunger strikes, this one against God Almighty, hoping that public opinion forces Him to reveal that for which I was made and put in this place and time.

Or why not throw over these ambiguities, this wife doing whatever she might be doing on the coast of the Gulf, these anonymous children content with Louise up the country, contemplating chickens, ducks, and guinea-fowl. Begin again. Say every word you have ever said, to new people: hello, new woman, I love you. I have good teeth and most of my mind. I can do well on a good night in a happy bed. Hello, new colleagues, what do we do this time? Is this a trucking firm or a telephone exchange? What is the desiderata? Profit or prophecy?

Bert shook my arm. —Are you okay? You didn't answer the door.

I studied him for a moment, my head soft and uncentered. I was nicely drunk, but coming back. —Yeah, I said. —I'm fine. What have you got tonight?

—Huh? Listen, can I turn down that music?

—Sure.

He doused the Second Symphony, and I found I was relieved, could breathe more deeply. —I brought her, he said. —She's kinda spaced out, like the kids say.

He frowned, watched me. —You sure you're all right?

I smiled. —All I needed was some company, Bert.

He smiled back. —All right, fine. You're probably in the best kind of shape for Irma.

—Huh?

He looked at the empty martini pitcher. —Nothing. She's just . . .

His voice trailed off and I watched him drift out of my line of sight. In the foyer, I could hear his voice, soft and distant, as if he were talking to a child.

I sobered up. Yes, I have that power. I discovered it in law school. However drunk, I can gather back in the purposely loosed strands of personality or whatever of us liquor casts apart. It is as if one were never truly sober, and hence one could claim back from liquor what it had never truly loosed. Either drunkenness or sobriety is an illusion.

Irma Bedlow was a surprise. I had reckoned on a woman well gone from womanhood. One of those shapeless bun-haired middle-aged creatures wearing bifocals, smiling out from behind the secrecy of knowing that they are at last safe from any but the most psychotic menaces from unbalanced males. But it was not that way. If I had been dead drunk on the one hand, or shuffling up to the communion rail on the other, she would have turned me around.

She was vivid. Dark hair and eyes, a complexion almost pale, a lovely body made more so by the thoughtless pride with which she inhabited it. She sat down opposite me, and our eyes held for a long moment.

I am used to a certain deference from people who come to me in legal situations. God knows we have worked long and hard enough to establish the mandarin tradition of the law, that circle of mysteries that swallows up laymen and all they possess like a vast desert or a hidden sea. People come to the law on tiptoe, watching, wishing they could know which words, what expressions and turns of phrase are *the ones* which bear their fate. I have smiled remembering that those who claim or avoid the law with such awe have themselves in their collectivity created it. But they are so far apart from one another in the sleep of their present lives that they cannot remember what they did together when they were awake.

But Irma Bedlow looked at me as if she were the counselor, her dark eyes fixed on mine to hold me to whatever I might say. Would I lie, and put both our cases in jeopardy? Would I say the best I knew, or had I wandered so long amidst the stunted shrubs of language, making unnatural acts in the name of my law, that words had turned from stones with which to build into ropy clinging undergrowth in which to become enmeshed?

I asked her if she would have a drink. I was surprised when she said yes. Fasts for the sake of an idiot child, trying to get others to do it, praying on her knees to Jesus beside the bed of Albert Sidney who did not know about the prayers, and who could know about Jesus only through infused knowledge there within the mansions of his imbecility. But yes, she said, and I went to fix it.

Of course Bert followed me over to the bar. —I don't know. I think maybe I ought to take care of Howard and let *her* be your client.

—Don't do that, I said, and wondered why I'd said it.

—She's fine, Bert was saying, and I knew he meant nothing to do with her looks. He was not a carnal man, Bert. He was a social man. Once he had told me he wanted either to be mayor of Kenner or a comedian. He did not mean it humorously and I did not take it so. He was the least funny of men. Rather he understood with his nerves the pathos of living and would have liked to divert us from it with comedy. But it would not be so, and Bert would end up mayor trying to come to grips with our common anguish instead of belittling it.

—I never talked to anyone like her. You'll see.

I think then I envisioned the most beautiful and desirable Jehovah's Witness in the world. Would we try conclusions over Isaiah? I warn you, Irma, I know the Book and other books beyond number. I am a prince in the kingdom of words, and I have seen raw respect flushed up unwillingly in the eyes of other lawmongers, and have had my work mentioned favorably in appellate decisions which, in their small way, rule all this land.

—Here you are, I said.

She smiled at me as if I were a child who had brought his mother a cool drink unasked.

—Howard came to see you, she said, sipping the martini as if gin bruised with vermouth were her common fare. —Can you help me . . . help him?

—He wants a divorce, I said, confused, trying to get things in focus.

—No, she said. Not aggressively, only firmly. Her information was better than mine. I have used the same tone of voice with other attorneys many times. When you know, you know.

—He only wants it over with, done with. That's what he wants.

Bert nodded. He had heard this before. There goes Bert's value as a checkpoint with reality. He believes her. Lordy.

—You mean . . . the marriage?

—No, not that. He knows what I know. If it *was* a marriage, you can't make it be over. You can only desert it. He wouldn't do that.

I shrugged, noticing that she had made no use of her beauty at all so far. She did not disguise it or deny it. She allowed it to exist and simply ignored it. Her femininity washed over me, and yet I knew that it was not directed toward me. It had some other focus, and she saw me as a moment, a crossing in her life, an occasion to stop and turn back for an instant before going on. I wondered what I would be doing for her.

—He *says* he wants a divorce.

She looked down at her drink. Her lashes were incredibly long, though it was obvious she used no makeup at all. Her lips were deep red, a color not used in lipsticks since the forties. I understood why Bedlow drank. Nine years with a beautiful woman you love and cannot touch. Is that your best idea?

—He told you . . . I'd been unfaithful.

Bert was shaking his head, blushing. Not negating what Howard had said, or deprecating it.

—He said that, I told her.

—And that our baby . . . that Albert Sidney wasn't . . . his?

—Yes, I said. Bert looked as if he would cry from shame.

She had not looked up while we talked. Her eyes stayed down, and while I waited, I heard the Beethoven tape, turned down but not off, running out at the end of the "Appassionata." It was a good moment to get up and change to something decent. I found a Vivaldi Chamber Mass, and the singers were very happy. The music was for God in the first instance, not for the spirit of fraternity or Napoleon or some other rubbish.

—What else, she asked across the room. I flipped the tape on, and eighteenth-century Venice came at us from four sides. I cut back the volume.

—He said you . . . hadn't been man and wife for nine years.

—All right.

I walked back and sat down again. I felt peculiar, neither drunk nor sober, so I poured another one. The first I'd had since they came.

—Howard didn't seem to think so. He said . . . you wouldn't let him touch you.

She raised her eyes then. Not angrily, only that same firmness again.

—That's not true, she said, no, whispered, and Bert nodded as though he had been an abiding presence in the marriage chamber for all those nine long years. He could contain himself no more. He fumbled in his coat pocket and handed me a crumpled and folded sheet of paper. It was a notice from American Motors canceling Howard Bedlow's franchise. Much boilerplate saying he hadn't delivered and so on. Enclosed find copy of agency contract with relevant revocation clauses underlined. Arrangements will be made for stock on hand, etc.

It was dated 9 May 1966. Bert was watching me. I nodded. —Eight years ago, I said.

—Not ten, Bert was going on. —You see . . .

—He lost the business . . . six months after . . . the . . . Albert Sidney.

We sat looking at the paper.

—I never denied him, Irma was saying. —After the baby . . . he couldn't. At first, we didn't think of it, of anything. I . . . we were lost inside ourselves. We didn't talk about it. What had we done? What had gone wrong? What were we . . . supposed to do? Was there something we were supposed to do?

—Genes went wrong . . . hormones, who knows, I said.

Irma smiled at me. Her eyes were black, not brown. —Do you believe that?

—Sure, I said, startled as one must be when he has uttered what passes for a common truth and it is questioned. —What else?

—Nothing, she said. —It's only . . .

She and Bert were both staring at me as if I had missed something. Then Irma leaned forward. —Will you go somewhere with me?

I was thinking of the Gulf coast, staring down at the face of my watch. It was almost one-thirty. There was a moon and the tide was in, and the moon would be rolling through soft beds of cloud.

—Yes, I said. —Yes I will. Yes.

III

It was early in the morning when we reached Alexandria. The bus trip had been long and strange. We had talked about east Texas where Irma had grown up. Her mother had been from Evangeline Parish, her father a tool-pusher in the Kilgore fields until he lost both hands to a wild length of chain. She had been keeping things together working as a waitress when she met Howard.

On the bus, as if planted there, had been a huge black woman with a little boy whose head was tiny and pointed. It was so distorted that his eyes were pulled almost vertical. He made inarticulate noises and rooted about on the floor of the bus. The other passengers tried to ignore him, but the stench was very bad, and his mother took him to an empty seat in back and changed him several times. Irma helped her once. The woman had been loud, aggressive, unfriendly when Irma approached her, but Irma whispered something, and the woman began to cry, her sobs loud and terrible. When they had gotten the child cleaned up, the black woman put her arms around Irma and kissed her.

—I tried hard as I could, miss, but I can't manage . . . oh, sweet Jesus knows I wisht I was dead first. But I can't manage the other four . . . I got to . . .

The two of them sat together on the rear seat for a long time, holding hands, talking so softly that I couldn't hear. Once, the boy crawled up and stopped at my seat. He looked up at me like some invertebrate given the power to be quizzical. I wondered which of us was in hell. He must have been about twelve years old.

In the station, Irma made a phone call while I had coffee. People moved through the twilight terminal, meeting, parting. One elderly woman in a thin print dress thirty years out of date even among country people kissed a young man in an army uniform good-bye. Her lips trembled as he shouldered his dufflebag and moved away. —Stop, she cried out, and then realized that he could not stop, because the dispatcher was calling the Houston bus. —Have you . . . forgotten anything? The soldier paused, smiled, and shook his head. Then he vanished behind some people trying to gather up clothes which had fallen from a cardboard suitcase with a broken clasp. Somewhere a small child cried as if it had awakened to find itself suddenly, utterly lost.

Irma came back and drank her coffee, and when we walked outside it was daylight in Alexandria, even as on the Gulf coast. An old station wagon with a broken muffler pulled up, and a thin man wearing glasses got out and kissed Irma as if it were a ritual and shook hands with me in that peculiar limp and diffident way of country people meeting someone from the city who might represent threat or advantage.

We drove for twenty minutes or so, and slowed down in front of a small white frame place on a blacktop road not quite in or out of town. The yard was large and littered with wrecked and cannibalized autos. The metal bones of an old Hudson canted into the rubble of a '42 Ford convertible. Super deluxe. There was a shed which must have been an enlarged garage. Inside I could see tools, a lathe, work benches. A young man in overalls without a shirt looked out at us and waved casually. He had a piece of drive shaft in his hand. Chickens ambled stupidly in the grassless yard, pecking at oil patches and clumps of rust.

We had eggs and sausage and biscuits and talked quietly. They were not curious about me. They had seen a great deal during the years and there was nothing to be had from curiosity. You come to learn that things have to be taken as they come and it is no use to probe the gestations of tomorrows before they come. There is very little you can do to prepare.

It turned out there had been no quarrel between Irma and her sister's family. Her sister, plain as Irma was beautiful, who wore thick glasses and walked slowly because of her varicose veins, talked almost without expression, but with some lingering touch of her mother's French accent. She talked on as if she had saved everything she had seen and come to know, saved it all in exhaustive detail, knowing that someone would one day come for her report.

—It wasn't never any quarrel, and Howard had got to know better. Oh, we fussed, sure. My daddy always favored Irma and so I used to take after her over anything, you know. Jesus spare me, I guess I hated my own little sister. Till the baby come, and the Lord lifted the scales from my eyes. I dreamed He come down just for me. He looked like Mr. Denver, the station agent down to the L & N depot, and He said "Elenor, I had enough stuff out of you, you hear? You see Albert Sidney? You satisfied now? Huh? Is that enough for you? You tell me that, 'cause I got to be getting on. I don't make nobody more beautiful or more smart or anything in this world, but I do sometimes take away their looks or ruin their minds or put blindness on 'em, or send 'em a trouble to break their hearts. Don't ask why 'cause it's not for you to know, but that's what I do. Now what else you want for Irma, huh?"

Tears were flowing down Elenor's face now, but her expression didn't change. —So I saw it was my doing, and I begged Him to set it right, told Him to strike me dead and set it right with that helpless baby. But He just shook His head and pushed up his sleeves like he could hear a through-freight coming. "It's not how it's done. It ain't like changing your mind about a hat or a new dress. You see that?"

—Well, I didn't, but what could I say? I said yes, and he started off and the place where we was began getting kind of fuzzy, then He turned and looked back at me and smiled. "How you know it *ain't* all right with Albert Sidney," he asked. And I saw then that He loved me after all.

Then, when I could hardly see Him, I heard Him say, "Anything you forgot, Elly," but I never said nothing at all, only crossed myself the way Momma used to do.

Elenor touched her sister's shoulder shyly. Irma was watching me, something close to a smile on her lips. —Well, Elenor said, —we've prayed together since then, ain't we, hon? Irma took her sister's hand and pressed it against her cheek.

—We been close since then, Charlie, Elenor's husband said. —Done us all good. Except for poor Howard.

It seemed Howard had hardened his heart from the first. Charlie had worked for him in the Rambler franchise, manager of the service department. One day they had had words and Charlie quit, left New Orleans which was a plague to him anyway, and set up this little backyard place in Alex.

Why the fight, I asked Charlie. He was getting up to go out to work. — Never mind that, he said. —It . . . didn't have nothing to do with . . . this.

Elenor watched him go. —Yes it did, she began.

—Elenor, Irma stopped her. —Maybe you ought not . . . Charlie's . . .

Elenor was wiping her cheeks with her apron. —This man's a lawyer, ain't he? He knows what's right and wrong.

I winced and felt tired all at once, but you cannot ask for a pitcher of martinis at seven-thirty in the morning in a Louisiana country house. That was the extent of my knowledge of right and wrong.

—A couple of months after Albert Sidney was born, I was at their place, Elenor went on. —Trying to help out. I was making the beds when Howard come in. It was early, but Howard was drunk and he talked funny, and before I knew, he pulled me down on the bed, and . . . I couldn't scream, I couldn't. Irma had the baby in the kitchen . . . and he couldn't. He tried to . . . make me . . . help him, but he couldn't anyhow. And I told Charlie, because a man ought to know. And they had words, and after that Charlie whipped him, and we moved up here . . .

Elenor sat looking out of the window where the sun was beginning to show over the trees. —And we come on up here.

Irma looked at her sister tenderly. —Elly we got to go on over to the hospital now.

As we reached the door, Elenor called out. —Irma . . .

—Yes . . . ?

—Honey, you know how much I love you, don't you?

—I always did know, silly. You were the one didn't know.

We took the old station wagon and huffed slowly out of the yard. Charlie waved at us and his eyes followed us out of sight down the blacktop.

IV

Irma was smiling at me as we coughed along the road. —I feel kind of good, she said.

—I'm glad. Why?

—Like some kind of washday. It's long and hard, but comes the end, and you've got everything hanging out in the fresh air. Clean.

—It'll be dirty again, I said, and wished I could swallow the words almost before they were out.

Her hand touched my arm, and I almost lost control of the car. I kept my eyes on the road to Pineville. I was here to help her, not the other way around. There was too much contact between us already, too much emptiness in me, and what the hell I was doing halfway up the state with the wife of a man who could make out a showing that he was my client was more than I could figure out. Something to do with the Gulf.

—There's another washday coming, she whispered, her lips close to my ear.

Will I be ready for washday, I wondered. Lord, how is it that we get ready for washday?

The Louisiana State Hospital is divided into several parts. There is one section for the criminally insane, and another for the feebleminded. This second section is, in turn, divided into what are called "tidy" and "untidy" wards. The difference is vast in terms of logistics and care. The difference in the moral realm is simply that between the seventh and the first circles. Hell is where we are.

Dr. Tumulty met us outside his office. He was a small man with a large nose and glasses which looked rather like those you can buy in a novelty shop—outsized nose attached. Behind the glasses, his eyes were weak and watery. His mouth was very small, and his hair thin, the color of corn shucks. I remember wondering then, at the start of our visit, whether one of the inmates had been promoted. It was a very bad idea, but only one of many.

—Hello, Irma, he said. He did not seem unhappy to see her.

—Hello, Monte, she said.

—He had a little respiratory trouble last week. It seems cleared up now.

Irma introduced us and Dr. Tumulty studied me quizzically. —A lawyer . . . ?

—Counselor, she said. —A good listener. Do you have time to show him around?

He looked at me, Charon sizing up a strange passenger, one who it seemed would be making a round trip. —Sure, all right. You coming?

—No, Irma said softly. —You can bring him to me afterward.

So Dr. Tumulty took me through the wards alone. I will not say everything I saw. There were mysteries in that initiation that will not go down into words. It is all the soul is worth and more to say less than all when you have come back from that place where, if only they knew, what men live and do asleep is done waking and in truth each endless day.

Yes, there were extreme cases of mongolism, cretins and imbeciles, dwarfs and things with enormous heads and bulging eyes, ears like tubes, mouths placed on the sides of their heads. There was an albino without nose or eyes or lips, and it sat in a chair, teeth exposed in a grin that could not be erased, its hands making a series of extremely complicated gestures over and over again, each lengthy sequence a perfect reproduction of the preceding one. The gestures were perfectly symmetrical and the repetition exact and made without pause, a formalism of mindlessness worthy of a Balinese dancer or a penance—performance of a secret prayer—played out before the catatonic admiration of three small blacks who sat on the floor before the albino watching its art with a concentration unknown among those who imagine themselves without defect.

This was the tidy ward, and all these inventions of a Bosch whose medium is flesh wore coveralls of dark gray cloth with a name patch on the left breast. This is Paul whose tongue, abnormally long and almost black and dry, hangs down his chin, and that, the hairless one with the enormous head and tiny face, who coughs and pets a filthy toy elephant, that is Larry. The dead-white one, the maker of rituals, is Anthony. Watching him are Edward and Joseph and Michael, microcephalics all, looking almost identical in their shared malady.

—Does . . . Anthony, I began.

—All day. Every day, Dr. Tumulty said. —And the others watch. We give him tranquilizers at night. It used to be . . . all night, too.

In another ward they kept the females. It was much the same there, except that wandering from one chair to another, watching the others, was a young girl, perhaps sixteen. She would have been pretty—no, she was pretty, despite the gray coverall and the pallor of her skin. —Hello, doctor, she said. Her voice sounded as if it had been recorded—cracked and scratchy. But her body seemed sound, her face normal except for small patches of what looked like eczema on her face. That, and her eyes were a little out of focus. She was carrying a small book covered in imitation red leather. My Diary, it said on the cover.

—Does she belong here, I asked Tumulty.

He nodded. —She's been here over a year.

The girl cuddled against him, and I could see that she was trying to press her breasts against him. Her hand wandered down toward his leg. He took her hand gently and stroked her hair. —Hello, doctor, she croaked again. —Hi, Nancy, he answered. —Are you keeping up your diary?

She smiled. —For home. Hello, doctor.

—For home, sure, he said, and sat her down in a chair opposite an ancient television locked in a wire cage and tuned, I remember, to "Underdog." She seemed to lose interest in us, to find her way quickly into the role of Sweet Polly, awaiting the inevitable rescue. Around her on the floor were scattered others of the less desperate cases. They watched the animated comedy on the snow-flecked, badly focused screen with absolute concentration. As we moved on, I heard Nancy whisper, —There's no need to fear . . .

—Congenital syphilis, Tumulty said. —It incubates for years, sometimes. She was in high school. Now she's here. It's easier for her now than at first. Most of her mind is gone. In a year she'll be dead.

He paused by a barred window, and looked out on the rolling Louisiana countryside beyond the distant fence. —About graduation time.

—There's no treatment . . . ?

—The cure is dying.

What I can remember of the untidy wards is fragmentary. The stench was very bad, the sounds were nonhuman, and the inmates, divided by sex, were naked in large concrete rooms, sitting on the damp floors, unable to control their bodily functions, obese mostly, and utterly asexual with tiny misshapen heads. There were benches along the sides of the concrete rooms, and the floors sloped down to a central caged drain in the center. One of the things—I mean inmates—was down trying slowly, in a fashion almost reptilian, to lick up filthy moisture from the drain. Another was chewing on a plastic bracelet by which it was identified. Most of the rest, young and older, sat on the benches or the floor staring at nothing, blubbering once in a while, scratching occasionally.

—Once, Dr. Tumulty said thoughtfully, —a legislator came. A budgetary inspection. We didn't get any more money. But he complained that we identified the untidy patients by number. He came and saw everything, and that's . . . what bothered him.

By then we were outside again, walking in the cool Louisiana summer morning. We had been inside less than an hour. I had thought it longer.

—It's the same everywhere. Massachusetts, Wyoming, Texas. Don't think badly of us. There's no money, no personnel, and even if there were . . .

—Then you could only . . . cover it.

—Cosmetics, yes. I've been in this work for eighteen years. I've never forgotten anything I saw. Not anything. You know what I think? What I really *know?*

—. . . ?

Tumulty paused and rubbed his hands together. He shivered a little, that sudden inexplicable thrill of cold inside that has no relationship to the temperature in the world, that represents, according to the old story, someone walking across the ground where your grave will one day be. A mockingbird flashed past us, a dark blur of gray, touched with the white of its wings. Tumulty started to say something, then shrugged and pointed at a small building a little way off.

—They're over there. One of the attendants will show you.

He looked from one building to another, shaking his head. —There's so much to do. So many of them . . .

—Yes, I said. —Thank you. Then I began walking toward the building he had indicated.

—Do . . . whatever you can . . . for her, Dr. Tumulty called after me. —I wish . . .

I turned back toward him. We stood perhaps thirty yards apart then.

—Was there . . . something else you wanted to say, I asked.

He looked at me for a long moment, then away. —No, he said. —
Nothing.

I stood there as he walked back into the clutter of central buildings,
and finally vanished into one of them. Then, before I walked back to join
Irma, I found a bench under an old magnolia and sat down for a few
minutes. It was on the way to becoming warm now, and the sun's softness
and the morning breeze were both going rapidly. The sky was absolutely
clear, and by noon it would be very hot indeed. A few people were
moving across the grounds. A nurse carrying something on a tray, two
attendants talking animatedly to each other, one gesturing madly. Another attendant was herding a patient toward the medical building. It was
a black inmate, male or female I could not say, since all the patients'
heads were close-cropped for hygienic purposes, and the coverall obscured any other sign of sex. It staggered from one side of the cinder path
to the other, swaying as if it were negotiating the deck of a ship in heavy
weather out on the Gulf. Its arms flailed, seeking a balance it could never
attain, and its eyes seemed to be seeking some point of reference in a
world awash. But there was no point, the trees whirling and the buildings
losing their way, and so the thing looked skyward, squinted terribly at the
sun, pointed upward toward that brazen glory, almost fell down, its
contorted black face now fixed undeviatingly toward that burning place
in the sky which did not shift and whirl. But the attendant took its
shoulder and urged it along, since it could not make its way on earth
staring into the sun.

As it passed by my bench, it saw me, gestured at me, leaned in my
direction amidst its stumblings, its dark face twinkling with sweat.

—No, Hollis, I heard the attendant say as the thing and I exchanged a
long glance amidst the swirling trees, the spinning buildings, out there
on the stormy Gulf. Then it grinned, its white teeth sparkling, its eyes
almost pulled shut from the effort of grimace, its twisted fingers spieling a
language both of us could grasp.

—Come on, Hollis, the attendant said impatiently, and the thing
reared its head and turned away. No more time for me. It took a step or
two, fell, and rolled in the grass, grunting, making sounds like I had
never heard. —Hollis, I swear to God, the attendant said mildly, and
helped the messenger to its feet once more.

The nurse in the building Tumulty had pointed out looked at me
questioningly. —I'm looking for . . . Mrs. Bedlow.

—You'll have to wait . . . she began, and then her expression changed. —Oh, you must be the one. I knew I'd forgotten something. All right, straight back and to the left. Ward Three.

I walked down a long corridor with lights on the ceiling, each behind its wire cover. I wondered if Hollis might have been the reason for the precaution. Had he or she or it once leaped upward at the light, clawing, grasping, attempting to touch the sun? The walls were covered with an ugly pale yellow enamel which had begun peeling long ago, and the smell of cheap pine-scented deodorizer did not cover the deep ingrained stench of urine, much older than the blistered paint. Ward Three was a narrow dormitory filled with small beds. My eyes scanned the beds and I almost turned back, ready for the untidy wards again. Because here were the small children—what had been intended as children.

Down almost at the end of the ward, I saw Irma. She was seated in a visitor's chair, and in her arms was a child with a head larger than hers. It was gesticulating frantically, and I could hear its sounds the length of the ward. She held it close and whispered to it, kissed it, held it close, and as she drew it to her, the sounds became almost frantic. They were not human sounds. They were Hollis' sounds, and as I walked the length of the ward, I thought I knew what Tumulty had been about to say before he had thought better of it.

—Hello, Irma said. The child in her arms paused in its snufflings and looked up at me from huge unfocused eyes. Its tongue stood out, and it appeared that its lower jaw was congenitally dislocated. Saliva ran down the flap of flesh where you and I have lips, and Irma paid no mind as it dripped on her dress. It would have been pointless to wipe the child's mouth because the flow did not stop, nor did the discharge from its bulging, unblinking eyes. I looked at Irma. Her smile was genuine.

—This is . . . I began.

—Albert Sidney, she finished. —Oh, no. I wish it were. This is Barry. Say hello.

The child grunted and buried its head in her lap, sliding down to the floor and crawling behind her chair.

—You . . . wish . . . ?

—This is Albert Sidney, she said, turning to the bed next to her chair.

He lay there motionless, the sheet drawn up to what might have been the region of his chin. His head was very large, and bulged out to one side in a way that I would never have supposed could support life. Where his eyes should have been, two blank white surfaces of solid cataract seemed to float lidless and intent. He had no nose, only a small hole surgically created, I think, and ringed with discharge. His mouth was a slash in the right side of his cheek, at least two inches over and up from where mouths belong. Irma stepped over beside him, and as she reached down and kissed him, rearranged the sheets, I saw one of his hands. It was a fingerless club of flesh dotted almost randomly with bits of fingernail.

I closed my eyes and then looked once more. I saw again what I must have seen at first and ignored, the thing I had come to see. On Albert Sidney's deformed and earless head, almost covering the awful disarray of his humanity, he had a wealth of reddish golden hair, rich and curly, proper aureole of a Celtic deity. Or a surfing king.

V

We had dinner at some anonymous restaurant in Alexandria, and then found a room at a motel not far from Pineville. I had bought a bottle of whiskey. Inside, I filled a glass after peeling away its sticky plastic cover that pretended to guard it from the world for my better health.

—Should I have brought you, Irma asked, sitting down on the bed.

—Yes, I said. —Sure. Nobody should . . . nobody ought to be shielded from this.

—But it . . . hasn't got anything to do with . . . us. What Howard wants to do, does it?

—No, I said. —I don't think so.

—Howard was all right. If things had gone . . . the way they do mostly. He wasn't . . . isn't . . . a weak man. He's brave, and he used to work . . . sometimes sixteen hours a day. He was very . . . steady. Do you know, I loved him . . .

I poured her a drink. —Sometimes, I said, and heard that my voice was unsteady. —None of us know . . . what we can . . . stand.

—If Howard had had just any kind of belief . . . but . . .

—. . . He just had himself . . . ?

—Just that. He . . . his two hands and a strong back, and he was quick with figures. He always . . . came out . . .

—. . . ahead.

She breathed deeply, and sipped the whiskey. —Every time. He . . . liked hard times. To work his way through. You couldn't stop him. And very honest. An honest man..

I finished the glass and poured another one. I couldn't get rid of the smells and the images. The whiskey was doing no good. It would only dull my senses prospectively. The smells and the images were inside for keeps.

—He's not honest about . . .

—Albert Sidney? No, but I . . . it doesn't matter. I release him of that. Which is why . . .

—You want me to go ahead with the divorce?

—I think. We can't help each other, don't you see?

—I see that. But . . . what will you do?

Irma laughed and slipped off her shoes, curled her feet under her. Somewhere back in the mechanical reaches of my mind, where I was listening to Vivaldi and watching a thin British rain fall into my garden, neither happy nor sad, preserved by my indifference from the Gulf, I saw that she was very beautiful and that she cared for me, had brought me to Alexandria as much for myself as for her sake, though she did not know it.

—. . . do what needs to be done for the baby, she was saying. —I've asked for strength to do the best . . . thing.

—What do you want me to do?

—About the divorce? I don't know about . . . the legal stuff. I want to . . . how do you say it . . . ? Not to contest it?

—There's a way. When the other person makes life insupportable . . .
Irma looked at me strangely, as if I were not understanding.

—No, no. The other . . . what he says.

—Adultery?

—And the rest. About Albert Sidney . . .

—No. You can't . . .

—Why can't I? I told you, Howard is all right. I mean, he could be all right. I want to let him go. Can't I say some way or other what he claims is true?

I set my glass down. —In the pleadings. You can always accept what he says in your . . . answer.

—Pleadings?

—That's what they call . . . what we file in a suit. But I can't state an outright . . . lie . . .

—But you're his counsel. You have to say what he wants you to say.

—No, only in good faith. The Code of Civil Practice . . . if I pleaded a lie . . . anyhow, Jesus, after all this . . . I couldn't . . . . Plead adultery . . . ? No way.

—Yes, Irma said firmly, lovingly. She rose from the bed and came to me.

—Yes, she whispered. —You'll be able to.

VI

The next evening the plane was late getting into New Orleans. There was a storm line along the Gulf, a series of separate systems, thin monotonous driving rain that fell all over the city and the southern part of the state. The house was cool and humid when I got home, and my head hurt. The house was empty, and that was all right. I had a bowl of soup and turned on something very beautiful. *La Stravaganza.* As I listened, I thought of that strange medieval custom of putting the mad and the demented on a boat, and keeping it moving from one port to another. A ship full of lunacy and witlessness and rage and subhumanity with no destination in view. *Furiosi,* the mad were called. What did they call those who came into this world like Irma's baby, scarce half made up? Those driven beyond the human by the world were given names and a status. But what of those who came damaged from the first? Did even the wisdom of the Church have no name for those who did not scream or curse or style themselves Emperor Frederic II or Gregory come again? What of those with bulbous heads and protruding tongues and those who stared all day at the blazing sun, all night at the cool distant moon? I listened and drank, and opened the door onto the patio so that the music was leavened with the sound of the falling rain.

It was early the next morning when Bert called me at home. He did not bother apologizing. I think he knew that we were both too much in it now. The amenities are for before. Or afterward.

—Listen, you're back.

—Yes.

—I got Howard straightened up. You want to talk to him?

—What's he saying?

—Well, he's cleared up, you see? I got him to shower and drink a pot of coffee. It ain't what he says is different, but he *is* himself and he wants to get them papers started. You know? You want to drop by Bo-Peep for a minute?

—No, I said, but I will. I want to talk to that stupid bastard.

—Ah, Bert said slowly. —Un-huh. Well, fine, counselor. It's cabin 10. On the street to the right as you come in. Can't miss it.

I thought somebody ought to take a baseball bat and use it on Howard Bedlow until he came to understand. I was very tight about this thing now, no distance at all. I had thought about other things only once since I had been back. When a little phrase of Vivaldi's had shimmered like a waterfall, and, still drunk, I had followed that billow down to the Gulf in my mind.

There were fantasies, of course. In one, I took Irma away. We left New Orleans and headed across America toward California, and she was quickly pregnant. The child was whole and healthy and strong, and what had befallen each of us back in Louisiana faded and receded faster and faster, became of smaller and smaller concern until we found ourselves in a place near the Russian River, above the glut and spew of people down below.

Acres apart and miles away, we had a tiny place carved from the natural wood of the hills. We labored under the sun and scarcely talked, and what there was, was ours. She would stand near a forest pool, nude, our child in her arms, and the rest was all forgotten as I watched them there, glistening, with beads of fresh water standing on their skin, the way things ought to be, under the sun.

Then I was driving toward Metairie amidst the dust and squalor of Airline Highway. Filling stations, hamburger joints, cut-rate liquor, tacos, wholesale carpeting, rent-a-car, people driving a little above the speed limit, sealed in air-conditioned cars, others standing at bus stops staring vacantly, some gesticulating in repetitive patterns, trying to be understood. No sign of life anywhere.

The sign above the Bo-Peep Motel pictured a girl in a bonnet with a shepherd's crook and a vast crinoline skirt. In her lap she held what looked from a distance like a child. Closer, you could see that it was intended to be a lamb curled in her arms, eyes closed, hoofs tucked into its fleece, peacefully asleep. Bo-Peep's face, outlined in neon tubing, had been painted once, but most of the paint had chipped away, and now, during the day, she wore a faded leer of unparalleled perversity, red lips and china blue eyes flawed by missing chips of color.

Bert sat in a chair outside the door. He was in uniform. His car was parked in front of cabin 10. The door was open, and just inside Howard Bedlow sat in an identical chair, staring out like a prisoner who knows there must be bars even though he cannot see them. He leaned forward, hands hanging down before him, and even from a distance he looked much older than I had remembered him.

Bert walked out as I parked. —How was the trip?

We stared at each other. —A revelation, I said. —He's sober?

—Oh, yeah. He had a little trouble last night down at the Kit-Kat Klub. Bert pointed down the road to a huddled cinderblock building beside a trailer court.

—They sent for somebody to see to him, and luck had it be me.

Howard looked like an old man up close. His eyes were crusted, squinting up at the weak morning sun, still misted at that hour. His hands hung down between his legs, almost touching the foor, and his forefingers moved involuntarily as if they were tracing a precise and repetitious pattern on the dust of the floor. He looked up at me, licking his lips. He had not shaved in a couple of days, and the light beard had the same tawny reddish color as his hair. He did not seem to recognize me for a moment. Then his expression came together. He looked almost frightened.

—You seen her, huh?

—That's right.

—What'd she say?

—It's all right with her.

—What's all right?

—The divorce. Just the way you want it.

—You mean . . . like everything I said . . . all that . . . ?

—She says maybe she owes you that much. For what she did.

—What she did?

—You know . . .

—What I said, told you?

—Wonder what the hell that is, Bert put in. He walked out into the driveway and stared down the street.

Bedlow shook his head slowly. —She owned up, told you everything?

—There was . . . a confirmation. Look, I said. —Bert will line you up a lawyer. I'm going to represent Ir . . . your wife.

—Oh? I was the one come to you . . .

I took a piece of motel stationery out of my pocket. There was a five-dollar bill held to it with a dark bobby pin. I remembered her hair cascading down, flowing about her face. —You never gave me a retainer. I did not act on your behalf.

I held out the paper and the bill. —This is my retainer. From her. It doesn't matter. She won't contest. I'll talk to your lawyer. It'll be easy.

—I never asked for nothing to be easy, Bedlow murmured.

—If you want to back off the adultery thing, which is silly, which even if it is true you cannot prove, you can go for rendering life insupportable . . .

—Life insupportable . . . ? I never asked things be easy . . .

—Yes you did, I said brutally. —You just didn't know you did.

I wanted to tell him there was something rotten and weak and collapsed in him. His heart, his guts, his genes. That he had taken a woman better than he had any right to, and that Albert Sidney . . . but how could I? Who was I to . . . and then Bert stepped back toward us, his face grim.

—Shit, he was saying, —I think they've got a fire down to the trailer court. You all reckon we ought to . . .

—If it's mine, let it burn. Ain't nothing there I care about. I need a drink.

But Bert was looking at me, his face twisted with some pointless apprehension that made so little sense that both of us piled into his car, revved the siren and fishtailed out into Airline Highway almost smashing into traffic coming from both directions as he humped across the neutral ground and laid thirty yards of rubber getting to the trailer court.

The trailer was in flames from one end to the other. Of course it was Bedlow's. Bert's face was working, and he tried to edge the car close to the end of it where there were the least flames.

—She's back in Alex, I yelled at him. —She's staying in a motel back in Alex. There's nothing in there.

But my eyes snapped from the burning trailer to a stunted and dusty cottonwood tree behind it. Which was where the old station wagon was parked. I could see the tail pipe hanging down behind as I vaulted out of the car and pulled the flimsy screen door off the searing skin of the trailer with my bare hands. I was working on the inside door, kicking it, screaming at the pliant aluminum to give way, to let me pass, when Bert pulled me back. —You goddamned fool, you can't . . .

But I had smashed the door open by then and would have been into the gulf of flame and smoke inside if Bert had not clipped me alongside the head with the barrel of his .38.

Which was just the moment when Bedlow passed him. Bert had hold of me, my eyes watching the trees, the nearby trailers whirling, spinning furiously. Bert yelled at Bedlow to stop, that there was no one inside, an inspired and desperate lie—or was it a final testing.

—She is, I know she is, Bedlow screamed back at Bert.

I was down on the ground now, dazed, passing in and out of consciousness not simply from Bert's blow, but from exhaustion, too long on the line beyond the boundaries of good sense. But I looked up as Bedlow shouted, and I saw him standing for a split second where I had been, his hair the color of the flames behind. He looked very young and strong, and I remember musing in my semiconsciousness, maybe he can do it. Maybe he can.

—. . . And she's got my boy in there, we heard him yell as he vanished into the smoke. Bert let me fall all the way then, and I passed out for good.

VII

It was late afternoon when I got home. It dawned on me that I hadn't slept in over twenty-four hours. Huge white thunderheads stood over the city, white and pure as cotton. The sun was diminished, and the heat had fallen away. It seemed that everything was very quiet, that a waiting had set in. The evening news said there was a probability of rain, even small-craft warnings on the Gulf. Then, as if there were an electronic connection between the station and the clouds, rain began to fall just as I pulled into the drive. It fell softly at first, as if it feared to come too quickly on the scorched town below. Around me, as I cut off the engine, there rose that indescribable odor that comes from the coincidence of fresh rain with parched earth and concrete. I sat in the car for a long time, pressing Bert's handkerchief full of crushed ice against the lump on the side of my head. The ice kept trying to fall out because I was clumsy. I had not gotten used to the thick bandages on my hands, and each time I tried to adjust the handkerchief, the pain in my hands made me lose fine control. My head did not hurt so badly, but I felt weak, and so I stayed there through all the news, not wanting to pass out for the second time in one day, or to lay unconscious in an empty house.

—Are you just going to sit out here, Joan asked me softly.

I opened my eyes and looked up at her. She looked very different. As if I had not seen her in years, as if we had lived separate lives, heights and depths in each that we could never tell the other. —No, I said. —I was just tired.

She frowned when I got out of the car. —What's the lump? And the hands? Can't I go away for a few days?

—Sure you can, I said a little too loudly, forcefully. —Anytime at all. I ran into a hot door.

She was looking at my suit. One knee was torn, and an elbow was out. She sniffed. —Been to a fire-sale, she asked as we reached the door.

—That's not funny, I said.

—Sorry, she answered.

The children were there, and I tried very hard for the grace to see them anew, but it was just old Bart and tiny Nan trying to tell me about their holiday. Bart was still sifting sand on everything he touched, and Nan's fair skin was lightly burned. Beyond their prattle, I was trying to focus on something just beyond my reach.

Their mother came in with a pitcher of martinis and ran the kids back to the television room. She was a very beautiful woman, deep, in her thirties, who seemed to have hold of something—besides the martinis. I thought that if I were not married and she happened by, I would likely start a conversation with her.

—I ended up taking the kids with me, she said, sighing and dropping into her chair.

—Huh?

—They cried and said they'd rather come with me than stay with Louise. Even considering the ducks and chickens and things.

Hence the sand and sunburn. I poured two drinks as the phone rang. —That's quite a compliment, I said, getting up for it.

—You bet. We waited for you. We thought you'd be coming.

No, I thought as I picked up the phone. I had a gulf of my own. It was Bert. His voice was low, subdued.

—You know what, he was saying, —he made it. So help me Christ, he made it all the way to the back where . . . they were. Can you believe that?

—Did they find . . .

Bert's voice broke a little. —Yeah, He was right. You know how bad the fire was . . . but they called down from the state hospital and said she's taken the baby, child . . . out. Said must have had somebody help . . .

—No, I said. —I didn't, and as I said it I could see Dr. Tumulty rubbing his hands over nineteen years of a certain hell.

—Never mind, listen . . . when the fire boys got back there, it was . . . everything fused. They all formed this one thing. Said she was in a metal chair, and he was like kneeling in front, his arms . . . and they . . . you couldn't tell, but it had got to be . . .

I waited while he got himself back together. —It had got to be the baby she was holding, with Howard reaching out, his arms around . . . both . . .

—Bert, I started to say, tears running down my face. —Bert . . .

—It's all right, he said at last, clearing his throat. There was an empty silence on the line for a long moment, and I could hear the resonance of the line itself, that tiny lilting bleep of distant signals that you sometimes hear. It sounded like waves along the coast. —It really is. All right, he said. —It was like . . . they had, they was . . .

—Reconciled, I said.

Another silence. —Oh, shit, he said. —I'll be talking to you sometimes.

Then the line was empty, and after a moment I hung up.

Joan stared at me, at the moisture on my face, glanced at my hands, the lump on my head, the ruined suit. —What happened while I was gone? Did I miss anything?

—No, I smiled at her. —Not a thing.

I walked out onto the patio with my drink. There was still a small rain falling, but even as I stood there, it faded and the clouds began to break. Up there, the moon rode serenely from one cloud to the next, and far down the sky in the direction of the coast, I could see pulses of heat lightning above the rigolets where the lake flows into the Gulf.

TWO GIRLS WEARING PERFUME IN THE SUMMER

Robb Forman Dew

THOSE Natchez girls were still young enough so that they could drink coffee all day long. They had coffee at breakfast and again at lunch. They often had coffee as they worked in the early afternoon, and they always made some fresh when Lucy got home and then even had one more cup each after dinner. At night they slept easily despite a gentle trembling of their nerves, not because they were especially untroubled but because they were unencumbered. And when they had drunk so much coffee that they became giddy, they merely regarded this thin energy as one more barrier against the lethargy that threatened to engulf them in the heat. And now as Lucy leaned back against the cooling bricks and sipped her mug of sweetened coffee, she felt lightheaded and altogether less substantial than she knew she was by rights as the humid weight of the air lifted in the New Orleans twilight. Sarah was tapping the ash of her cigarette into her saucer with an agitated rustle of her long fingers against the paper. She sat with her head tilted to one side and her chin tucked in, as she often did when she was repressing irritation; she was so good-natured. But at last she leaned back in her chair and abruptly flicked her cigarette over the railing. "I don't know why you want to go," she said to Lucy, but with her eyes on the street. "There's something wrong about him. Is it that he's . . . coarse? Oh, there's a pretense I don't like somehow. You know, Lucy, *you* don't have a coarse bone in your body!"

Lucy's blouse lay across her back in damp streaks, and she had been thinking that it would be hard to go anywhere this evening because of the effort it would entail, but she didn't say so. "It's what I've thought I've always needed," she said to Sarah, "just one coarse bone in my body." The dark interior of their rooms lay in serene disarray beyond the French windows, and she was in no hurry to leave. In the living room the morning newspapers still lay in sections across the couch, and the sandals she had just stepped out of stood together right inside the door. She yearned half-heartedly to do nothing more right now than lie on her cool sheets and rest, simply allowing herself to settle into the disordered sensuality of the bedroom. Sarah's helmeted hair dryer always stood open on the desk; it sat perched there like a sated pelican. And on the floor in the vicinity of the mirror were strewn shoe boxes of hair rollers, a hand-held blow dryer, powder, makeup, nail polish, shoes, and various pieces of clothing, so that the way in which the room was furnished without these things could no longer be determined. Lucy always left that room with a feeling of regret, lingering over one last cigarette while her dates waited in the long living room. But she went on anyway with what she had meant to say, "Besides, *coarse* isn't the word you want. You might say Dan is *brash.* No, not that either, exactly. Well, I know what you have in mind. Just because he doesn't seem like someone who would write, though . . . his *wife* said for us to come, you know! I'm not interested in him, Sarah, but I do like working with him at the *Review.* And you must think he's attractive, at least?"

Sarah was beginning to feel the solace of the evening, and her expression remained so placid that it gave no hint of an opinion as she sat gazing out into the street, hardly following Lucy's voice. She knew, though, that *brash* was not what she thought about Dan—*arrogant* came closer. "Oh well, it's been so hot today . . . I'm really tired. And, you know, I've been thinking all day that we could probably have gotten by on a cocktail party education. Do you know what I mean? A few interesting facts to fill the spaces, good manners. It seems to me we worked too hard to have ended up doing what we're doing."

Lucy turned her head to consider Sarah. "You could have gotten by, I think. You have just the right kind of looks. Well, but then it depends on the kind of cocktail party, too, doesn't it?" They smiled at each other and out at the street, which was beginning to appear shadowed. On their balcony they were caught in the last shaft of light before the sun disappeared behind the building across the street. "I'm going to get dressed," Lucy said. "Do you want to bathe first?"

"Oh, he's your poet! I'm not even going to look in the mirror before we go!" Sarah was so at ease that when Lucy went in she made no attempt to pull herself away. She remained on the balcony seated close up against the wall on the pretext of watching Lucy's cat, but the cat, who had not yet reconciled himself to Sarah, had turned his back and was carefully washing his paws. In order to keep his company Sarah chose not to mind his air of condescension, and she was coming, in any case, to respect the sort of animal he was. Lucy said he was an unusual sort of cat in that he would live within a fence. Only, of course, if the fence were built around the yard to which he was already accustomed. Sarah was prepared to believe this, although the cat did not live within the wrought-iron railings that enclosed their courtyard. She gathered from this that the move to New Orleans had emboldened him, but she thought that it had not served his appearance well. He had been a Natchez cat with a glistening coat, and he had been so much a part of his household that he was missed now in that vicinity. He had become lean and hollow-sided from his new street adventures.

Lucy and Sarah were missed as well, even though there are always so many young girls in Natchez just waiting in the wings. No one said— perhaps no one really thought—"Ah, now, those two girls . . . too bad they've gone!" In Natchez, events continued as they always had, celebration after celebration and births and deaths. But for all their lives Lucy and Sarah had been the focus of a great deal of attention as their stars ascended in the dense familial atmosphere of Natchez. One can't presume anything about such girls. They weren't beauties by any means, not really, but all of Natchez could see in Sarah's face, for instance, as it narrowed toward the chin, the line of her father's jaw and her mother's gentle, down-turned mouth. And Lucy, well, her head at a certain angle was so like both her uncle's and her father's that it was uncanny. This strong resemblance was often taken for beauty, and Lucy and Sarah themselves took it so as they looked in the mirror at faces so keenly stamped with their own lineage. But over the years they had come to understand that something was expected in return for so much sympathetic scrutiny, and each of them had developed a ferocious charm, even guile, that was, at least, tempered a little by compassion. But they always came out ahead, it seemed to Sarah, who even this moment was relaxing in the same self-congratulation exhibited by the cat now that he was well-groomed and sitting neatly in the last spot of sun. The cat, in fact, was a case in point. No pets were allowed in this apartment, and yet these two girls were blessed with such good fortune that they possessed a cat with charm and cunning of his own, a cat who fled the rooms to the farthest corners of the closet when the landlord visited. What luck they had!

And yet, Sarah's mind tick-ticked with restlessness, as though she had ambitions, or as though she ought, at least, to have some plans. And charm or no, here she was in this city on her own balcony, and yet she stayed well out of the air, against the wall, because to lean out against the balustrade was to indicate solidarity with the street community just below. Sometimes, to her surprise, she was mistaken for someone else, or greeted, at any rate, as though she were known to some person on the street, and that assumption by a stranger made her feel peculiarly vulnerable. And it made her lonely as well, watching all those people going in and out of each other's doorways and nodding and speaking to one another as they passed. She often saw a tall woman enter the storefront Italian restaurant directly across the street and settle at a table by the window, where she would draw out a book from her straw bag and read. She always had one glass of wine before dinner and a second with her meal. It was not the woman who so beguiled Sarah; it was the woman's self-sustenance—she seemed to feel no need to beguile anyone. Thinking of this Sarah leaned out from the wall and lightly stroked the cat, who slunk down and away from her hand, affronted by such a liberty.

And to have found this apartment, that had been such good luck too. It was a series of huge rooms strung out railway fashion, and it had bookshelves and a fireplace. But today the bedroom at the rear of the apartment had received the sun all day, and now it was hot and still, and humid too, so that although Lucy had said she was going to dress she was still just sitting in her slip on the edge of the bed, waiting for the window air conditioner to make some impression on the temperature. She was thinking that she must change her clothes, and that she needed to refresh herself somehow after the wilting day. And she was wondering what Dan's wife could be like. One afternoon in the *Review* office he and Lucy had been sitting at their desks with sandwiches and coffee for a quick lunch. Dan had been self-contained all morning, much like her own cat, Lucy had thought, when he's not hungry.

"Such a strange thing happened last night," he said all of a sudden, and Lucy had turned full around with attention, looking at him more intently than she would have meant. It wasn't often in her experience that she had come across a man so absolutely handsome, and she meant not to notice this; it must be an embarrassment to him sometimes.

"Lilah and I went out for a beer. Just to a little neighborhood place. We were sitting in the front room and people were coming in and going through to the back." He was eating all the while between sentences, so

Lucy had nodded her continued attention as he chewed. "Well, it's not a fancy place, or anything—no waiters—and I went back to get us another beer. I heard this guy talking about some beautiful woman sitting out front, so when I took our drinks back I looked all around; I didn't see *anybody!*" He looked at Lucy expectantly, and she could see that he was ready to laugh with her, so she began a smile. "It was *Lilah,* you see!" he said. "He was talking about Lilah!" He was so plainly delighted that Lucy had smiled at him.

"Oh, I see," she said. "But, you know, I haven't met her yet." At that moment all that she had recognized was that depression was overtaking her at the thought of Dan's having such a beautiful wife. In fact, all that afternoon she had felt dragged out, though not forlorn. She had her own life, after all; this was just her job! But as she had walked from her bus stop down Royal Street, it had suddenly struck Lucy that *he* hadn't known; he hadn't thought it could be Lilah who was sitting in the front room of that bar being so beautiful. Well, perhaps Dan had only been trying to tell her something about the nature of his marriage, how little he and his wife really saw each other anymore, that sort of thing. So now, thinking back on it with deliberation, she forced herself to take heart, and she roused herself long enough to call through the vast rooms to Sarah to, for God's sake, remember to call the landlord about this air conditioner! Then she bathed in tepid water, and when she stepped out of the tub she carefully dried herself and dusted her whole body with cool, dry powder, so that now in the general fog of the bathroom she almost felt a chill along her wrists and ankles. She had read somewhere that if immediately upon stepping from a bath one rubs one's hands over a steamy mirror the glass will clear, and she tried this, but the effect was that the mirror remained streaked with stubborn condensation. It was getting late, though, so standing still damp and nude she brushed her teeth and strapped on her slender watch, but after a moment she took it right off again to step on the scales. She stepped on and off again several times just to make sure, and then she felt even better. So with very little consideration she chose her clothes and dressed with pleasure, and finally sprayed her throat and wrists and the backs of her knees with Blue Grass perfume.

Lucy always wore Blue Grass in the summer, but Sarah wore Chanel No. 5 the year round. Oh, these girls walked in an effusion of scent, the two of them. And as they left their apartment and walked down Dumaine Street to catch their bus, Lucy idly reached out her hand to brush a mimosa branch that flowered along the brick wall they passed. Her hand jumped away all of itself when the bloom disintegrated even at that light touch. Just—poof—it became a drift of silken wisps and powder in the heavy New Orleans air. It had so surprised her expectations that it made her smile, and a lady sitting in a city bus parked along the curb smiled as well. The perfumes of these two girls had drifted through her open window just as the mimosa fell into so many parts, and the lady thought, "Oh, my, what girls! What pretty girls! Imagine, wearing perfume on such a hot day in summer!"

When Sarah and Lucy transferred on Canal Street and boarded the trolley, they could not speak to each other any longer because of the tremendous roar of the metal wheels on the track. Quaint as it was, and picturesque too, neither of them liked to ride it at all. The trolley set up a terrible swaying once it gathered speed, and so they sat gripping their seats grimly and pondering their separate thoughts. Lucy was growing more and more apprehensive, hating herself for sweating where the hair curled onto the back of her neck, and so sweating more.

But it was adventure they were setting off to. Everything was adventure these days in this city. "Look, Sarah," Lucy had said when they had first moved into the Quarter. "They put their garbage in these sorts of holes! They aren't manhole covers at all! I wondered why there were so many of them." They had stood struck with admiration, gazing along a sidewalk dotted with numerous metal discs which enclosed sunken cans. They were enchanted! Such ingenuity! But then at two o'clock in the morning they had been awakened by the clanking all down the street of the heavy lids being thrown roughly off as the trash was taken away. Nonetheless, they were pleased every morning when they awoke and found themselves where they were. "I don't think there could be any other city quite like New Orleans," they said to each other now and then. These girls, though, had never been to any of the other cities to which people go on purpose. Or, at least, the cities to which they had gone had been visited with some specific purpose in mind: shopping, or a doctor's appointment. Even so, they had not made their way through a childhood in Natchez and emerged naïve. No—in fact the intensity of relationships in such close quarters had left them at once languid and on edge. There was nothing left to surprise them except, perhaps, their own feelings, so they were left on the brink of what might happen to them in all their lives. They had come to New Orleans, and they were pleased with it, because new possibilities still seemed to open before them like morning glories.

In the mornings they ate beignets and drank café au lait alongside the truckers who made early deliveries to the French Market. They would never tire of this; how could they? And being the girls they were, they, too, left an impression wherever they went in the city. Waiters remembered them; the truck drivers took note of those two girls, so easy-limbed somehow, all at home with their own bodies though neither of them possessed extraordinary grace. But they were so clearly not awkward. A social life had blossomed around them immediately; they had only to be there. And as the trolley reeled down St. Charles, Sarah was wondering if perhaps they had plunged in without enough discretion. She knew she would have to approach Robert Leland about the broken air conditioner sooner or later, because it turned out that it was she who dealt best with businessmen—privately she was wary of them, but only because they made no pretense of altruism in their various dealings. This seemed to Sarah a social gaffe, and she had no method of dealing with it. These men were mysterious, she thought: they had wealth disproportionate to their vaguely suspicious origins. Well, she didn't know what to make of them. And it was through one of these men that she had met Mr. Leland and finally rented their apartment.

At first he had shown them a number of small efficiencies, scarcely taking any notice of them and seeming to them almost handsome, but sleek, too, like a beetle in his black suit. Finally Sarah had said again, but with more apparent despair, "But, you see, I need a whole separate room just for my sewing!" He had looked around at her sharply while he fitted the key of another small apartment and led the way inside. He sat down wearily on the fold-down couch and stretched his arms along its back. "Why don't you girls look for another apartment out around Metairie? There are lots of bigger places out there. Do you know how hard it is to find a decent apartment in the Quarter?"

Sarah had felt so dejected; Metairie was no different than a suburb of Natchez. She turned from the window to see his face. "But we haven't got a car," she said. "And neither of us likes to be out so far." Mr. Leland appeared to be staring off into space, so Sarah sat down on the far end of the couch and watched his face for some hint. In the small, musty room he seemed large and heavily fleshed, though not fat. He frowned, finally, to himself, and nodded at them absently.

"All right, girls, come with me, but there are no pets allowed in this one."

Sarah and Lucy had both begun to feel relief as they had followed him through the one-way streets; they felt this might be it, and they had been looking for so long that they had been about to give up the search. "Are all these yours?" Sarah had asked as they walked. "Do you own all these? I mean the entire buildings of each of the apartments we've seen? How does this sort of thing work?"

He had given her a quick look of interest. "Oh well, it's pretty complicated." When he had shown them the huge apartment on Dumaine Street with the courtyard and the goldfish pond downstairs, they had been overwhelmed and had walked all around it looking into closets while he sat in the kitchen noting down something on one of his pads. Eventually he had followed them into the living room. "I'm glad you like it," he said, looking around vaguely. "So you sew," he said to Sarah, looking at her bluntly. "I wouldn't have guessed it. You look like you own the place."

Fleetingly she had pictured herself among her fabrics, and she had thought of explaining that what she did was not exactly "sewing"; it was almost like architecture; it was design—her job! But she had no idea what good luck had gotten them this apartment, so she just nodded while Mr. Leland explained all the details of renting.

One evening a month or so after they had moved in, Sarah had happened to meet him on the street, and they had gone to have a drink together, so now she must call him Bob, at least in person. And one weekend when Lucy had gone home to Natchez, Sarah had locked herself out, and she and her date had had to locate Mr. Leland and get a second key. First she had had to telephone a central office and explain the situation to the night operator. "Well, isn't there anywhere else you could spend the night?" the operator had asked irritably and to Sarah's astonishment. But out of force of habit Sarah always tried to oblige, and she duly cast her eye over the man waiting for her at the table in the little bar from which she was phoning.

"No, I'm afraid not," she had said at last.

It had been nearly one o'clock in the morning, but Mr. Leland's apartment was very near her own as it turned out, and he had met them in the lobby wearing a dark green silk robe and pajamas. She saw that he was amused; perhaps he had only been watching television and had not really had to disturb himself on her account. At least that was what she had found herself hoping. All the way from his building to her own, however, as she went along the sidewalk, she had had a slight queasy feeling; it might have left her far less unsettled if he had shown some sign of irritation.

He had dropped by in the middle of that next week to retrieve his key, and Sarah had felt that she must offer him a drink. He had sat contentedly in the living room still seeming amused, and he had relaxed into an attitude so peculiarly sedentary it was as though he might never move from his chair. And he did stay some time, so that eventually the cat crouching in the bedroom on the upper shelf of the closet let out a low guttural yowl of impatience, but it went unnoticed, or at least unremarked upon.

Thinking back on it, Sarah thought that it was only that she had been a victim of that particular day which had been so mild. The lighter, unoppressive air had seemed to demand an expansion of the spirit, and Sarah had felt herself to be beautifully displayed, like a butterfly on a page, by the flat, dry rectangle of sun that lay across the brown rug and all over the couch where they sat. The rest of the room lay in shadow and surrounded them like a curtain. She had felt . . . well, gaiety she called it now, but it had stemmed from a sudden realization of her own perfect balance and control. Just as if she *had* looked down and discovered corresponding spots on her translucent wings. It had filled her with sensuality, this momentary assurance, and there she had finally been, only kissing Robert Leland on that pale afternoon, but finding it pleasant to have his heavy torso leaning over her. Eventually he had stood up and gone to hang his coat carefully in the closet and then to make a drink, rolling back his sleeves fastidiously to run the water and shake the ice from the trays. He came to sit beside her again, clasping his hands around his drink, which he held between his knees. She was feeling an affection for all that was excessive about him—the weight of him and even the abundance of dark, wiry hair that grew thickly along his arms and across the backs of his hands. And then she noticed on the inside of his arm, a little above his wrist, a delicately traced tattoo of a flowering vine which spiraled its way up at least to the bend of his elbow, and perhaps beneath his rolled sleeve it continued beyond that. Her stomach felt leaden with distaste. She almost sighed with relief just sitting there, because at least she had not gotten herself into even deeper water. When he once again laid his arm along the back of the couch and brushed her cheek, she arose and withdrew. "I've got to go out in a few minutes, I hadn't noticed the time," she had said. "Why don't I walk down with you?"

But now that she must get in touch with him, how could she ask a favor without some sort of consequence? And if Robert Leland himself came to look at the air conditioner, what would she do this time about the cat? She gave it up, finally, tired of mulling it over, and just sat in the swaying trolley staring out at the houses as they lurched by.

Lucy and Sarah could walk from the trolley's terminus to Dan's house, and they had little to say to each other in the early dark. Sarah was hoping that they would have a good meal, and Lucy, wishing for a chance to comb her hair before they got there, was distressed by her own agitation. She felt even less at ease when they arrived and were seated amidst strangers in a cream-colored room filled with massive furniture decorated only by its own wood grains. She had an impression of large, floating planes of soft color. She had never been in a room like this in the whole of her social life, and the statement these surroundings made to her was that they possessed no history; the atmosphere was brittle with an air of immediacy. Her perspective was thrown off kilter, and she felt her neck beneath her hair grow damp with sweat once again.

But Sarah sat bemused, since she had nothing to lose and had already decided that these people wouldn't interest her. She, too, was perplexed by this environment, but it had occurred to her right away that it was for the people who would live in these rooms that she designed the dresses she sold to the little boutiques in the Quarter. Not for herself, with her full body which was better suited to gentle prints and such. No, she made neat, quick slips of dresses like flexible arrows of color. Brilliant and clean. She had never seen anyone wearing one; she made them for sizes 6, 8, and 10, when she herself wore a 12, but she was delighted to have found, at least, the proper place for them, and she simply sat still trying to absorb it all. She didn't think to come to Lucy's aid; she didn't even notice whether aid was required.

Lucy was sitting next to a small, slender man with glasses and such a pale, dusty look that she might not have seen him at all if she hadn't been sitting right there. No one had told her who he was, and he gave no sign of being interested in conversation, but she was beginning to feel uncomfortable just sitting silent. "I feel I've used up a whole evening's energy already, just getting here," she said, though he remained seated as he was, with his head lolled back against the wall and his eyes closed. Then all at once he turned just his head and looked at her sharply, like a sparrow. "We came on the trolley," she explained, "and it's exhausting."

She thought he was regarding her impassively, but suddenly he spoke with a surprising passion. "The trolley is *filthy*; it's just filthy! If they're going to go in for that sort of nostalgia, for God's sake, they ought to do a decent job of it. Like the cable cars!"

Lucy was amazed at how drunk this man was beneath his gray facade. "Are you from California?" she asked softly, hoping to persuade him by her example to lower his voice.

"Yes," he said, and once more leaned back in his chair and closed his eyes.

"I've never been to California," Lucy said. "I don't think I even know anyone in California, but I've heard that parts of it are lovely."

He began to giggle in a strange, choked manner as though, with his head tilted back as it was, he were strangling on his own laughter. Lucy looked at him with dismay. "Don't *know* anybody in California," he repeated with the same rasping giggle. "My God!" he announced loudly. "Here is a girl—right here—who knows *no one* in California!"

A general silence fell over the room as everyone looked their way and paused for a moment to take his drunkenness into account. When conversation in the room resumed, he roused himself and moved away to leave Lucy to herself. He crossed the room and hung over Lilah's chair as she earnestly listened to a pretty woman in a caftan. Lucy was relieved that no one was noticing her for the moment, because she needed the time to get her bearings. She especially wanted a moment to study Lilah, whom she had scarcely even seen. She was trying to interpret Lilah's attraction, because it was plainly apparent, but her looks were not of Lucy's experience. Lilah had greeted them at the door wearing red velour shorts and a man's shirt tied at the waist. "We swam earlier," she had said, gesturing at herself with a hint of apology, but still Lucy had been very nearly insulted by the lack of formality. Lilah's hair was long and very curly, a light brown, and she had simply clasped it at the back of her neck with a wide, tortoise-shell barrette. But she was devastating anyway; Lucy could see that in spite of herself. Thinking of her own soft face with its blunt features, she envied Lilah above all else the precise and elegant lines of her face, almost sharp. When she spoke, her small, even teeth put one in mind of some quick animal. She certainly gave one pause, Lucy thought, but still, she hardly seemed the type to be noticed in a New Orleans bar.

Dinner was nowhere apparent. There was no hint of it in the air or anywhere in the dining room, but Lilah was making frequent trips to the kitchen to see about something, and both girls hoped it was food. Lucy was now sipping her third glass of pale yellow wine, which was too sweet, she thought, but was all that had been offered to her, and Sarah was just hungry. Lilah approached from across the room, but not with a smile as hostesses do; instead she looked grave, so that Lucy was expecting their first exchange to be of some import. But Lilah simply hesitated in front of them for a moment uncertainly and then sat down right there with a sigh. "Maybe you girls would help me with the lettuce," she said with a very delicate reluctance and a slight frown. "I hate to do lettuce, you know. Would you mind?"

Neither Lucy nor Sarah had ever thought about whether they liked to do lettuce or not—they had salads sometimes, but who usually fixed them? They couldn't think, and as they followed Lilah to the kitchen they were both uncertain about their ability to do lettuce at all.

"I hear you're a huge help at the *Review*," Lilah said as she handed them the colander. "You're Lucy, aren't you? Dan's described you, of course—soft and southern and pretty—but both of you are that." Lucy was watching as Lilah bent to retrieve a pan from beneath the sink, and it seemed to Lucy that Lilah's face at that angle was the most delicate of triangles, a fragile wedge, with so little of laxity about it that, whatever her expression, there was always an inherent tension implied. Lilah smiled up at them, and it became clear that a smile from Lilah was a statement; she smiled apart from her speaking. "Oh—charming—I should say that about both of you," she said as she considered them with a quiet pleasure. "So charming!"

The girls were surprised and smiled back at her. "Well," said Lucy, "the *Review* fascinates me. I'm getting a chance to read a lot of things I never would have come across on my own. And it still leaves me time to work on my own writing in the evenings."

"Do you write?" Lilah appeared to be even more interested. "Dan didn't say so. Oh, I wrote too once, when I was younger." She looked down into the colander, into which Sarah had begun to tear pieces of lettuce. "Be sure not to put the stems in! I'm going to get one more glass of wine and see how everyone's doing, then I'll slice the mushrooms." And she headed out toward the makeshift bar on the buffet.

"Well," Sarah said finally, "busy hands, you know." Lucy put down the lettuce and took another sip of wine.

At last the party was seated wherever there was room. Everyone settled their plates on their laps to eat however they could manage and drink more wine. Dan sat down next to Lucy on the rug, and they braced themselves one against the other companionably. Lilah sat above them on the couch between Sarah and the same persistent pale moth of a man who despised the trolley. He had pursued Lilah all evening, so this was the first time he had sat down in several hours, as far as Lucy could remember.

"You'd better eat, Jimmy," Lilah said to him with concern.

"Eat! Oh God, Lilah!" And for a moment he looked alarmingly distressed as he passed a hand briefly across his eyes. But then he looked down and studied his food with surprise. "There are too many distractions. Where did you get these girls?" And he bent forward, almost folding himself onto his own plate as he leaned around Lilah to indicate Sarah and Lucy. "These pretty, pretty girls?"

Dan grinned just in general, which he did sometimes, and which, Lucy thought, erased from his face its look of ponderous responsibility, which could occasionally be so dampening to the spirit. "Now, Jimmy," he said, "these are my girls, you know. I discovered them. And how do you think you'll make Lilah feel, letting your eye rove like that?"

Lilah smiled her detached smile and looked vaguely around the room, not seeming to pay anyone much heed. But all of a sudden she turned back to them. "No, that's right, Jimmy," she said. "Don't ever fall in love with anyone else! I think I would be . . . well, distraught. Unless she were just the right person. You're too innocent, you know, to look after your own interests."

Lucy had a twinge of severe uneasiness, just as though she were sitting with grownups whose conversation had risen above her head. Dan was grinning now with even greater pleasure, which seemed an odd thing to her.

"Lilah couldn't do without you, Jimmy!" he said between bites. "I think that's the truth. She needs to have people in love with her, not just loving her."

Lilah smiled directly down at him, and it was a peculiar look they exchanged, their faces were so barren of pretense. Dan went back to finishing his meal, and Lilah reached out and massaged his shoulder with a light pressure. "You know," she said lazily, "I think you're right, Love. I suppose you and I know each other so well we've become like one sex. Do you see what I mean? We've been married almost seventeen years." She sat with her hand just resting now on Dan's shoulder, apparently considering this thought for the first time, but Dan only laughed.

"Well, which sex is it, Lilah?" he said.

Lilah settled back on the couch and smiled a very slow, almost disappointed smile, as though her point had been missed. "Oh, a little of each, I guess. But, Jimmy, don't take up with girls like these! In case you were thinking of it." She linked her arm through Sarah's and pressed it to her side fondly. "As charming as these two are . . . they still could be eaten alive. Or else they'll become pretty fierce." She smiled around at Lucy and Sarah to show that she was teasing them. "You're too vulnerable, Jimmy. I don't know what might happen to you. And," she added, "it might not be so good for them either. Bad all the way around."

Sarah and Lucy exchanged a glance, each thinking how drunk everyone had become in such short order.

It was late when the girls boarded the trolley once more for the return trip, and there were only one or two people aboard, none of whom seemed interested in them or in the least threatening. Besides, those two girls had no idea of real fear. They walked around the streets of the Quarter any time of day or night to do their laundry or go to the drugstore. They couldn't have been called brave; it was just that they had assimilated such a powerful sense of identity through all their lives in Natchez that in their minds it would simply be too much of a coincidence to be *who* they were and still have something terrible happen to them. So it never occurred to them to dread the long ride home other than for the discomfort of it. They sat together on a bench along the side and gave themselves up to the swaying of the trolley.

"Do you remember that song we sang at summer camp the last year we went?" Sarah asked over the roar of the wheels, and then she began to sing it:

> We are the Natchez girls
> We wear our hair in curls
> We wear our dungarees

> Way up above our knees
> We wear our daddy's shirts
> And boy are we big flirts
> We saw the boys today
> That's why we feel this way
> Ta rah rah boom te ay
> We saw the boys today
> Ta rah rah boom te ay
> That's why we feel this way.

Lucy looked around at the other passengers with embarrassment, but these people riding the trolley so late at night had taken no notice of them. They barely saw two pretty girls who were only two more people, slightly drunk, having to get from one place to another.

The next few days were lost to the girls for so many reasons. It took all of Saturday to recover from the night before, and they stayed out of each other's way in the big apartment. Sunday, Monday, and Tuesday were consumed by the terrible heat. Tuesday morning, as she walked from her bus stop to the *Review* office, Lucy reflected bitterly that there was no breathing in this heavy air. At least in Natchez, as hot as it often got, there had always been the possibility that the season would change. But here, this was endless; she was sure it would continue this way forever. She had not been able to think, so absorbed had she been by the heat, and even the Quarter had been less rowdy throughout the last few oppressive nights. She envisioned all the inhabitants sitting by their windows, soporific with the warm weight of the atmosphere. What could there be to talk about or to celebrate when one's skin was lightly slick and damp with a film of sweat? Before she began to sort the mail she tried to phone Sarah to remind her to get in touch with Mr. Leland about the air conditioner, even though in the huge bedroom it would probably have no more effect than the pleated paper fans the girls fashioned for themselves from magazine covers.

Sarah had already called Robert Leland that morning, but she had been made so uneasy by a slight pause in his voice, a slight change in tone, that immediately after hanging up she had left the apartment. She was sitting in Walgreens with a glass of iced tea while she waited for the cool air to stop her from sweating. She looked around her with a little interest and decided that no one can be hot and look good at the same time, so she felt a little better about her own dishevelment.

She had arranged for Mr. Leland to come in the evening so Lucy would be there, but she hoped he wouldn't come at all, that he would send some repairman. "It's not working at all?" he had asked. "Hard to keep a curl in your hair, I bet." She sipped her tea and put him out of her mind for the moment, but on the way out she bought a small toy for the cat as reparation for the time he would spend in seclusion that evening. When she got home she wandered around the rooms, unable to settle to serious sewing, and finally she opened the cat's gift and proffered it. But the cat inspected it with disdain—it was only a small plastic ball containing a bell—and almost as an afterthought he gave it a casual bat as he was walking by. When the bell tinkled he flicked his back in irritation. Well, she thought desultorily, he is not to be placated.

By the time Lucy had come home, Sarah was depressed and had eaten too many chocolate cookies, but she had taken the time to change her clothes. The cat was asleep on Lucy's bed, and they weren't sure what to do with him. The closet was no refuge this time, because it was in the same room as the air conditioner. Finally they closed him outside on the balcony and decided that if he were noticed they could claim he belonged to somebody else.

Mr. Leland arrived just as they finished dinner, and Lucy had begun washing up. He was brisk and in a hurry tonight and showed no inclination to linger. But checking the air conditioner took some time. After flipping various switches in the apartment, he had to make several trips back and forth down the stairs to the basement, and on the third trip he arrived back at their door red-faced and sweating so that his shirt clung wetly to his chest and back. Sarah gave him some iced tea, which he drank in one long swallow while standing in the doorway. Sweat had dampened the hair above his ears, and he made her think of a seal.

"Thanks," he said when he handed her back the glass. "I'm not sure what's wrong with that thing. We may have to get you a new one. I imagine we can turn one up somewhere." They were all three standing in the doorway of the kitchen, which was the only entrance to the apartment, and he was leaning against the doorframe looking worn out, but suddenly he began to smile, and then he laughed. "I've got to get going," he said, not looking directly at either of them. "I'll see if we can't get this fixed or replaced at least by the first of the week." He turned to go and shook his head ruefully. "I'll tell you," he said with a quick glance at them, "with apartments as hard to find as they are these days, you've really got to be something special to get away with drinking your milk off the floor!" And he smiled with unnerving satisfaction as he headed toward the stairs, still shaking his head. Sarah closed the door behind him and turned to look at Lucy, and they both looked down to see the cat's bowl full of milk in plain sight under the kitchen table. They simply stood there for a moment, and then Sarah looked at Lucy apologetically. "I took his food out to the balcony," she said, "but I forgot about his milk."

Lucy left the room, though Sarah couldn't tell if she were angry or tired, or perhaps both. After all, she reminded herself, it is Lucy's cat! Sarah slowly went about the business of straightening up where Lucy had left off, and then she mixed two very tall gin and tonics, though she supposed in the long run the drinks would make them even warmer. "I've fixed you a drink," she called through the rooms to Lucy. And when Lucy came in they both sat exactly in their places at the table, sipping their drinks through straws Sarah had found in the cupboard.

"At the very least," Lucy said, "really, the least we can do . . . we've got to get rid of that cat!" She sat tracing rings around her glass with her index finger, thinking that she could take him home this weekend if she made a special trip, or perhaps when she went up on the 24th. Of course, she supposed, there was no real hurry.

SECOND-HAND MAN

Rita Dove

VIRGINIA couldn't stand it when someone tried to shorten her name—like Ginny, for example. But James didn't. He set his twelve-string guitar down real slow.

"Miss Virginia," he said, "you're a fine piece of woman."

Seemed he'd been asking around. Knew everything about her. Knew she was bold and proud and didn't cotton to no silly niggers. Vir-gin-ee-a he said, nice and slow. Almost Russian, the way he said it. Right then and there she knew this man was for her.

He courted her just inside a year, came by nearly every day. First she wouldn't see him for more than half an hour at a time. She'd send him away; he knew better than to try to force her. Another fellow did that once—kept coming by when she said she had other things to do. She told him he do it once more, she'd be waiting at the door with a pot of scalding water to teach him some manners. Did, too. Fool didn't believe her—she had the pot waiting on the stove and when he came up those stairs, she was standing in the door. He took one look at her face and turned and ran. He was lucky those steps were so steep. She only got a little piece of his pant leg.

No, James knew his stuff. He'd come on time and stay till she told him he needed to go.

She'd met him out at Summit Beach one day. In 1921, that was the place to go on hot summer days! Clean yellow sand all around the lake and an amusement park that ran from morning to midnight. She went there with a couple of girl friends. They were younger than her and a little silly. But they were sweet. Virginia was nineteen then. "High time," everyone used to say to her, but she'd just lift her head and go on about her business. She weren't going to marry just any old Negro. He had to be perfect.

There was a man who was chasing her around about that time, too. Tall, dark Negro—Sterling Williams was his name. Pretty as a panther. Married, he was. Least that's what everyone said. Left a wife in Washington, D.C. A little crazy, the wife—poor Sterling was trying to get a divorce.

Well, Sterling was at Summit Beach that day, too. He followed Virginia around, trying to buy her root beer. Everybody loved root beer that summer. Root beer and vanilla ice cream—the Boston Cooler. But she wouldn't pay him no mind. People said she was crazy—Sterling was the best catch in Akron, they said.

"Not for me," Virginia said. "I don't want no second-hand man."

But Sterling wouldn't give up. He kept buying root beers and having to drink them himself.

Then she saw James. He'd just come up from Tennessee, working his way up on the riverboats. Folks said his best friend had been lynched down there, and he turned his back on the town and said he was never coming back. Well, when she saw this cute little man in a straw hat and a twelve-string guitar under his arm, she got a little flustered. Her girl friends whispered around to find out who he was, but she acted like she didn't even see him.

He was the hit of Summit Beach. Played that twelve-string guitar like a devil. They'd take off their shoes and sit on the beach toward evening. All the girls loved James. "Oh, Jimmy," they'd squeal, "play us a *loooove* song!" He'd laugh and pick out a tune:

> I'll give you a dollar if you'll come out tonight,
> If you'll come out tonight,
> If you'll come out tonight.
> I'll give you a dollar if you'll come out tonight
> And dance by the light of the moon.

Then the girls would giggle. "Jimmy," they screamed, "you oughta be 'shamed of yourself!" He'd sing the second verse then:

> I danced with a girl with a hole in her stockin',
> And her heel kep' a-rockin',
> And her heel kep' a-rockin';
> I danced with a girl with a hole in her stockin',
> And we danced by the light of the moon.

Then they'd all priss and preen their feathers and wonder which would be best—to be in fancy clothes and go on being courted by these dull factory fellows, or to have a hole in their stockings and dance with James.

Virginia never danced. She sat a bit off to one side and watched them make fools of themselves.

Then one night near season's end, they were all sitting down by the water, and everyone had on sweaters and was in a foul mood because the cold weather was coming and there wouldn't be no more parties. Someone said something about hating having the good times end, and James struck up a nice and easy tune, looking across the fire straight at Virginia:

> As I was lumb'ring down de street,
> Down de street, down de street,
> A han'some gal I chanced to meet,
> Oh, she was fair to view!
>
> I'd like to make dat gal my wife,
> Gal my wife, gal my wife.
> I'd be happy all my life
> If I had her by me.

She knew he was the man. She'd known it a long while, but she was just biding her time. He called on her the next day. She said she was busy canning peaches. He came back the next day. They sat on the porch and watched the people go by. He didn't say much, except to say her name like that.

"Vir-gin-ee-a," he said, "you're a mighty fine woman."

She sent him home a little after that. He came back a week later. She was angry at him and told him she didn't have time for playing around. But he'd brought his twelve-string guitar, and he said he'd been practicing all week just to play a couple of songs for her. She let him in then and made him sit on the stool while she sat on the porch swing. He sang the first song. It was a floor thumper.

> There is a gal in our town,
> She wears a yellow striped gown,
> And when she walks the streets aroun',
> The hollow of her foot makes a hole in the ground.
>
> Ol' folks, young folks, cl'ar the kitchen,
> Ol' folks, young folks, cl'ar the kitchen,
> O' Virginny never tire.

She got a little mad then, but she knew he was baiting her. Seeing how much she would take. She knew he wasn't singing about her, and she'd already heard how he said her name. It was time to let the dog in out of the rain, even if he shook his wet all over the floor. So she leaned back and put her hands on her hips, real slow.

"I just *know* you ain't singing about me."

"Virginia," he replied, with a grin would've put Rudolph Valentino to shame, "I'd *never* sing about you that way."

Then he pulled a yellow scarf out of his trouser pocket. Like melted butter it was, with fringes.

"I saw it yesterday and thought how nice it would look against your skin," James said.

That was the first present she ever accepted from a man. Then he sang his other song:

> I'm coming, I'm coming!
> Virginia, I'm coming to stay.
> Don't hold it agin' me
> For running away.
>
> And if I can win ya,
> I'll never more roam,
> I'm coming Virginia,
> My dixie land home.

She was gone for him. Not like those girls on the beach: she had enough sense left to crack a joke or two. "You saying I look like the state of Virginia?" she asked, and he laughed. But she was gone.

She didn't let him know it, though, not for a long while. Even when he asked her to marry him, eight months later, he was trembling and thought she just might refuse out of some woman's whim. No, he courted her proper. Every day for a little while. They'd sit on the porch until it got too cold, and then they'd sit in the parlor with two or three bright lamps on. Her mother and father were glad Virginia'd found a beau, but they weren't taking any chances. Everything had to be proper.

He got down, all trembly, on one knee and asked her to be his wife. She said yes. There's a point when all this dignity and stuff get in the way of Destiny. He kept on trembling; he didn't believe her.

"What?" James said.

"I said yes," Virginia answered. She was starting to get angry. Then he saw that she meant it, and he went into the other room to ask her father for her hand in marriage.

But people are too curious for their own good, and there's some things they never need to know, but they're going to find them out one way or the other. James had come all the way up from Tennessee and that should have been far enough, but he couldn't hide that snake anymore. It just crawled out from under the rock when it was good and ready.

The snake was Jeremiah Morgan. Some fellows from Akron had gone off for work on the riverboats, and some of these fellows had heard about James. That twelve-string guitar and straw hat of his had made him pretty popular. So, story got to town that James had a baby somewhere. And joined up to this baby—but long dead and buried—was a wife.

Virginia had been married six months when she found out from sweet-talking, side-stepping Jeremiah Morgan who never liked her nohow after she'd laid his soul to rest one night when he'd taken her home from a dance. (She always carried a brick in her purse—no man could get the best of her!)

Jeremiah must have been the happiest man in Akron the day he found out. He found it out later than most people—things like that have a way of circulating first among those who know how to keep it from spreading to the wrong folks—then when the gossip's gotten to everyone else, it's handed over to the one who knows what to do with it.

"Ask that husband of your'n what else he left in Tennessee besides his best friend," was all Jeremiah said at first.

No no-good Negro like Jeremiah Morgan could make Virginia beg for information. She wouldn't bite.

"I ain't got no need for asking my husband nothing," she said, and walked away. She was going to choir practice.

He stood where he was, yelled after her like any old common person. "Mrs. Evans always talking about being Number One! It looks like she's Number Two after all."

Her ears burned from the shame of it. She went on to choir practice and sang her prettiest; and straight when she was back home she asked:

"What's all this Number Two business?"

He broke down and told her the whole story—how he'd been married before, when he was seventeen, and his wife dying in childbirth and the child not quite right because of being blue when it was born. And how when his friend was strung up he saw no reason for staying. And how when he met Virginia, he found out pretty quick what she's done to Sterling Williams and that she'd never have no second-hand man, and he *had* to have her, so he never said a word about his past.

She took off her coat and hung it in the front closet. She unpinned her hat and set it in its box on the shelf. She reached in the back of the closet and brought out his hunting rifle and the box of bullets. She didn't see no way out but to shoot him.

"Put that down!" he shouted. "I love you!"

"You were right not to tell me," she said to him, "because I sure as sin wouldn't have married you. I don't want you *now.*"

"Virginia!" he said. He was real scared. "How can you shoot me down like this?"

No, she couldn't shoot him when he stood there looking at her with those sweet brown eyes, telling her how much he loved her.

"You have to sleep sometime," she said, and sat down to wait.

He didn't sleep for three nights. He knew she meant business. She sat in their best chair with the rifle across her lap, but he wouldn't sleep. He sat at the table and told her over and over that he loved her and he hadn't known what else to do at the time.

"When I get through killing you," she told him, "I'm going to write to Tennessee and have them send that baby up here. It won't do, farming a child out to any relative with an extra plate."

She held onto that rifle. Not that he would have taken it from her— not that that would've saved him. No, the only thing would've saved him was running away. But he wouldn't run either.

Sitting there, Virginia had lots of time to think. He was afraid of what she might do, but he wouldn't leave her, either. Some of what he was saying began to sink in. He had lied, but that was the only way to get her—she could see the reasoning behind that. And except for that, he was perfect. It was hardly like having a wife before at all. And the baby— anyone could see the marriage wasn't meant to be anyway.

On the third day about midnight, she laid down the rifle.

"You will join the choir and settle down instead of plucking on that guitar anytime anyone drop a hat," she said. "And we will write to your aunt in Tennessee and have that child sent up here." Then she put the rifle back in the closet.

The child never made it up to Ohio—it had died a month before Jeremiah ever opened his mouth. That hit James hard. He thought it was his fault and all, but Virginia made him see the child was sick and was probably better off with its Maker than it would be living out half a life.

James made a good tenor in the choir. The next spring, Virginia had her first baby and they decided to name her Belle. That's French for beautiful. And she was, too.

THE LAST PERSON
Charles East

Today I found a marble. I was raking leaves near those trees where we hung the hammock that summer, and the rake uncovered it. It was blue and chipped, larger than the average marble. I seem to remember bringing Steve a bag of marbles once—large ones just such as this. Perhaps I bought them in some airline terminal. Newark? Atlanta? I've tried to remember, which is of course absurd: why should it matter? Why should it matter what we wrote on the wall of a house? It was the first house we owned—a house with two bedrooms and a bath and an attic fan and floor furnaces. I still pass it occasionally. They've enclosed the porch and added a carport. It always gives me a funny feeling. There was a wall in Steve's bedroom where, when he was small, we kept a record of his height: a horizontal line in pencil and a date. Lines climbing a wall, until at some point we no longer went to that wall and the lines and dates remained only marks to be painted over by the people who would one day buy the house from us.

Kathy was a baby then. By the time she came along we needed a larger house. A year or so later we bought this one. There are no marks in the room where she grew up, only the snapshots we took there in the yard or at the beach those long-ago summers. And the note of course. I saw it just the other day, or rather the envelope in which Ann placed it, there in the box marked IMPORTANT PAPERS. Car titles, house insurance, life insurance, tax receipts, warranties: the assorted pieces of paper that tell us we are safe, we are secure, we have six months or 1,000 miles or a lifetime to go, and that tell us nothing really. And the envelope in which Ann placed Kathy's note. I did not open it. I have not opened it for a long time now, but I can recite it from memory. There is no date, but I know that too. And there is no signature, just Kathy's familiar handwriting. The letters almost seem drawn: *Dear Mom and Dad, If I've hurt you I'm sorry.*

No unsteadiness, no slip of a *t* or slide of an *s*, nothing to tell us what she might have been thinking. *If I've hurt you I'm sorry.* Was it really so simple? At first Ann tried to make herself believe it was an overdose, an accident, putting the note out of her mind: it was merely a letter Kathy had started. We no longer talk about it, but I'm sure she has at some point come to accept it, the irrefutable truth of it. These things, after all, happen. We hear stories every day. But why Kathy? What could we have done that might have made things turn out differently?

I wish we had saved some of her letters. There must have been clues there: in the letters she wrote that last year, for instance. She and Jack had broken up. She was beginning to have doubts about what she wanted to do, about whether she should go ahead with her master's. She thought she might like to go into teaching. *But that's like throwing away four years,* she wrote. *Not counting what it's cost to send me to college. I know I'm a problem.*

It's true we worried about her. When we didn't hear from her, we called her. I remember how surprised we were when she told us about Jack. Yes, she said, it really was over. She didn't want us worrying. "I'm fine. I'm OK. I'm OK, Dad. You don't believe me?"

From that time on, I think, her letters were different. We had never met Jack. The winter we flew up he was spending the holidays with his family. But Kathy sent us a color transparency. She had asked someone to take her camera and snap their picture, which is slightly out of focus. A boy and a girl in the New England summer. Kathy looks happy. The boy with his arm around her is blond and bearded and wears cutoffs, and he's looking into the camera. We never met him but we got a letter he wrote a few weeks after it happened. He was working at a ski lodge in New Hampshire. A friend of his had written him. *Kathy,* he wrote, the litany of the young, *was a beautiful person.*

Ann cried of course. She said, "He sounds like a nice boy." Later she wrote him.

I wonder whether he knew her—Kathy, I mean; whether there was something about her he knew or saw that we didn't. Do the young see the young? I don't think her friends I talked to knew her. Did I know Ann once? Did Ann know me? I thought she did. I am no longer so certain. Whatever happened, if it did, happened long before Kathy. Perhaps somewhere along the way we simply lost touch with each other.

"Kathy," Ann said, "was always different, even as a child. Oh, it was nothing you could put your finger on, but . . . well, different."

Different from Steve, certainly. Kathy was the loner. She was more apt to be up in her room with her nose in a book than down the street playing. She never had the friends Steve had. Yet there was something that drew you to her. Once Ann accused me of showing partiality and I suppose she was right, though I was reluctant to admit it. The truth is, I never felt I was getting through to Steve. I was always onto him about something. It wasn't that I didn't love him. I did. But Kathy was special—not, I think, in the way Ann means. More . . . what is the word? *Sensitive?* No, but that too. I always thought that her feelings ran deeper. Is the word I am looking for the thing Ann was unable to put her finger on? *Private?*

Yet sometimes surprisingly open. I remember a conversation we had, I think her senior year, the spring before she went away to college. She had come in from a date and Ann and I were still up, watching Johnny Carson, and we got to talking. She hadn't had the greatest evening in the world—in fact, she said, forcing a smile, "A real bummer." The boy had brought her home early. "But it wasn't his fault," she said. "I guess it's just me. I'm not exactly a fun kind of person." Ann and I were full of platitudes and excuses: what the kids called fun nowadays was sleeping together and smoking marijuana. No, she said, that wasn't what she meant, it didn't have anything to do with sex or smoking pot or drinking. She meant enjoying herself. Enjoying being with people. Already she was beginning to dread the trip her class had planned the week before graduation. She didn't want to go, but she knew if she didn't go they'd ask her why and she wouldn't know what to tell them. In the end, she went—I think because we insisted.

That night after we had gone to bed I remember Ann and I were talking. "When we were Kathy's age," she said, "did we have fun?" Yes, I said, we had fun. "You know," she said, "the sad thing is, it's true. Kathy's never known how. Don't ask me why. I don't understand it."

I don't think Kathy ever lied to us. I think if we had asked her whether she had smoked marijuana she would have told us yes if she had, which of course was why we never asked her. Our children know us better than we know ourselves. We expect lies, deception. We never got it from Kathy. I remember the winter Ann and I flew up to spend the holidays with her.

She was living in an apartment near the campus and we stayed in a Holiday Inn which was within walking distance. "Did you notice," Ann asked one evening when we had gone back to our room, "his things in the other closet?" She meant Jack's things. Kathy had told us he was home for the holidays. Ann was upset: I had known, even before she asked the question, that something was bothering her. "Do you think they're living together?"

I was certain that they were, but I was not certain how to answer her. "Do you?"

"Isn't that what they're all doing," I said, "living together?"

"Well," she said, "it does look like she would have tried to keep it from us," and I thought: because that's what *we* would have done. Everything out of sight, nothing showing. But, then, it never would have happened. In the first place, Ann wouldn't have had an apartment, and if she had, I wouldn't have had my things there—not, at least, on a weekend when her parents were coming. Ann sat there on the side of the bed with her gown in her hands. I had already gotten into my pajamas. Finally she asked if I thought she ought to say something.

"What would you say?"

"God," she said, "I don't know. I just hope she's on the pill. Maybe that's what I should say." She looked at me and laughed, I suppose surprised that she had actually said what she was thinking. Then, as suddenly, I saw that she was crying. "What happened, Joe? What turned everything upside down? I know I've failed but I don't know how I've failed. I don't know how to cope with it."

I told her she hadn't failed: if she had failed, I had failed. "It's just that they changed all the rules on us."

Later Kathy would write us, one of those letters I wish we had saved, *Jack wants me to marry him. But,* she said, *I don't know . . . I have this fear . . . I'm not sure I'm ready for that. I'm not sure either of us is.* I wondered what her fear was. Perhaps the same fear I had when I married Ann, not so much I think a fear of commitment as a fear of loss: of privacy, of identity—God, just when you're beginning to think you know who you are, the fear of becoming another person. But those were different times. I started to say nicer times, but I'm not really so very certain. All that went on in the name of love in the back seats of those cars moved into the motels and then into the apartments and perhaps, in a funny way, there is more love involved in it—at least, the possibility. That, after all, is all that we can hope for, isn't it?

"I think she knew we loved her," Ann said. "I don't think she ever doubted that we loved her . . ."

My mother had said that, or something close to that: "You never know what's right. You make mistakes. But if a child knows you really love him . . ." Meaning: everything will end happily. But it doesn't happen that way. It didn't for Kathy. It hasn't for Steve. It didn't for me either. It would be so simple, so easy, if I could believe that love had anything to do with it. I have often asked myself what it was that was missing, what was the source of my own sense of loneliness and insecurity. Should I blame my mother? Was she in effect saying to me long ago what Ann would say later: "I know I've failed but I don't know how I've failed. I don't know how to cope with it"?

"Looking back," Ann said, "that winter we were there for the holidays, I can see that Kathy was a very mixed-up person."

Looking back, I can see now that I was a very mixed-up person. Looking back, I can see that Ann was a very mixed-up person. Was there ever, I wonder, anyone twenty . . . twenty-one who was not a mixed-up person?

"I think we *know*," Ann said, "I think it's right there in front of us, I think we're skirting it."

I don't think we are. I don't think we've ever been close to knowing why Kathy did it. I remember talking to her friends and I remember what one of them said, not an explanation, because they had none, or if they did it was not something that they could share with her father: "You never felt you really knew what Kathy was thinking." I remember going back to her apartment to get her things together: her clothes, her books, the stereo and the records, the wine bottles she had made into candle holders, our letters. I read one, a letter from Ann written three months or more earlier. *Kathy baby, is everything all right? It's been weeks since we heard from you. When we don't hear from you we . . .* And the note the police handed me. I read it again. They had found it there beside her. To satisfy the requirements of the law they had had to do an autopsy. It would be another three hours before they released the body. I sat there on the bed for a long time, wondering what in God's name had made her do it, and then I placed a long distance call to Ann and told her that I had done everything that had to be done, that I would be flying home in the morning.

Strange the things that you remember: trivial things, the sound of a voice, the smell of a room, the thought you had at a particular moment. I remember leaving the plane that morning and seeing Ann and Steve waiting in the terminal and I remember thinking: At least we have Steve. I had left Ann a day and a half earlier; it had been a year or more since I saw Steve—the summer after the wedding. Ann was wearing dark glasses. Steve had grown a mustache and his hair was cut shorter. They looked like strangers to me waiting there.

We had only a few days together. Steve had to get back. No, to his job, not to Toni—that hadn't worked out. "In another six months," he said, "our divorce will be final." So Ann was right, her instincts were better than mine: she said it wouldn't last and it didn't. I doubt that Steve really had to get back as soon as he said. He was restless. He stayed in the car a good bit of the time. It may have been us. It may have been Kathy. I don't think it hit him until he saw her.

When I drove him to the airport, neither of us did very much talking. Ann had planned to go with us but she changed her mind at the last moment. I knew that telling him goodbye would be hard for her. "You think Mom is going to be all right?" he asked me. Yes, I said, I thought she'd be all right, but it would take time and of course she would never really get over it, neither of us would. No, he said, it wasn't the kind of thing you got over. He wondered if I had ever thought of taking early retirement. "You and Mom could sell the house and come out to California." I laughed and told him that I was still a long way from early retirement, and as for living in California . . . well, he could have California. Mostly he talked about his friends from the old days, how few of them there were still around. I suppose he'd been looking for someone to go out with him. After a while I turned the radio on to save us the necessity of making conversation. I'm sure we were both thinking of Kathy. Why had she done it? I had asked him that that first morning. I thought he might be able to tell us something, but he couldn't. "I just never would have thought . . ." he said. "Kathy was the last person . . ."

I wonder who the last person is. I suspect it depends less on the person than the circumstances, no one thing, a combination of things coming together. There must be a point. I've always said I could never do it, which may be another way of saying I've never reached the point, probably never come close to it. But it's there all the same, and perhaps we're never certain until we reach it. When I said goodbye to Steve before he boarded the flight to Los Angeles, we shook hands and he put his hand on my shoulder and I thought: I don't really know you either. Oh, I was there when you were born, I was out there in that hospital corridor, I was your father, you were my son, we lived in the same house until you went off to college. I know your shirt size, the after shave you use, how many beers you can drink—all the statistics. But I don't really know you any better than I knew Kathy.

I remember a house, lines on a wall, Ann lying beside me those hot summer nights when the attic fan was going: she was pregnant with Steve and I remember her saying, "I think it's going to be a boy, Joe," because she knew that was what I wanted. What else was it that I wanted? There's so much I've forgotten. For Steve to do well in school? He of course didn't. At one time I had hoped he would go into law, but he never could have made it. Perhaps I wanted too much, not only from Steve but from Kathy. What impossible dream of perfection had I constructed . . . had we constructed for Kathy? But Ann was wiser. I remember her saying once, "You can't make Steve into someone he isn't." He was in many ways, I suspect, typical. Into pot when he was sixteen, probably earlier. God, how well I remember that night: the call from the police, Ann's face when I told her, the ride home from the station with Steve, neither of us talking. "Goddam it," I said finally, "say something." Dropped out of school when he was twenty. Married at twenty-one, divorced at twenty-three: the statistics are mounting.

Ann said, "I just thank God there weren't any children." I didn't say so but I was wishing there were, even one child, something left to show for it. Oh, I know the story. I was, as they say, the child of a broken home myself. But I don't think I was ever sorry about what happened. It was wrong from the start, or at least for as long as I can remember. I saw what it did to my mother.

Ann blames Toni: too much like her mother, she says. We met her parents when we flew out for the wedding. Her father was an Air Force colonel. Toni was spoiled, she says. "So self-centered. I never had the feeling she loved him." On the other hand, I had the same feeling about Steve. Perhaps we have somehow lost the capacity for loving.

Those few days he was here, Ann tried to get him to open up to us.

"You and Toni . . ." she said. "We had no idea. What on earth happened?"

"Let's just say it was a mistake," he said, "from the beginning."

"Then there's no chance you'll go back together?"

"No chance," he said.

"Steve, you and Toni . . ." I knew what Ann was thinking: whether to tell him what she had felt about Toni. I wanted to say "Ann, don't, you've gone far enough," but Steve beat me to it.

"Look, Mom," he said, "would you mind? I'd rather not talk about it."

In the meantime he's found another job and he's going with a girl with two children he says he plans to marry as soon as her divorce is final. Ann says she wishes he'd find someone else. She's never met Vivian, neither of us has, but she doesn't like the idea of his taking on the responsibility of another man's children. She also wishes he'd come home: there are earthquakes in California. What she means is, she wants to see him. It's been almost two years now—not since Kathy's funeral. We seldom hear from him anymore. A call now and then. An occasional letter. He's fine. He and Vivian are planning to drive up the coast for a few days. He wishes (*ha, ha*—he underlines the words) we were there to stay with Vivian's children. *Vivian says she guesses if we can't find a sitter, we'll have to take them with us.*

Don't make the same mistake twice, Ann writes. Spoken like a mother.

I showed Ann the marble I found. "Probably one of Steve's," I said. "I was raking leaves out by the trees and the rake hit it."

"The children used to play back there," she said. There was a smile on her face that I had not seen for such a long time, before Kathy's death, perhaps a long time before that. "I had this dream the other night," she said. "It was so real. We were living in the little house we used to live in. I had forgotten what it was like. The children were small, and I woke up thinking nothing had happened."

"That two-bedroom house," I said.

She nodded. "I couldn't go back to sleep. I must have lain there an hour, and I kept thinking . . . you know what crazy things you think in the middle of the night? . . . I kept thinking maybe that was where we made our mistake, we never should have moved, we should have stayed in that two-bedroom house forever."

"We couldn't," I said, "we outgrew it."

"Yes," she said, "we outgrew it." The smile suddenly vanished. "What did we do wrong, Joe? What happened?"

"Nothing," I said. "Nothing I did or you did. Nothing either of us did."

"The terrible thing is," she said, "I woke up from that dream thinking we had it all to do over. I don't think I'd want it to do over. Joe . . ." She looked at me so strangely. "There's something I never told you. After Kathy . . . after what happened I did a lot of thinking and I . . . I guess I blamed you for it. God knows, don't ask me why. I blamed myself too. Anyway," she said, "I was going to leave you, but I couldn't go through with it." Her voice was strained. I saw that her hands were trembling. "Does that surprise you?"

I nodded. I wanted to say something, I was not certain what, perhaps what it had taken me half of my life, more than half, to discover: that there are things which should never be said, that most of all that runs through our heads between the moment we are born and the moment we die must forever remain private.

"The truth is," she said, "I can't be sure anymore how I feel about you . . . or how you feel about me. I guess what scares me is the thought that we've stayed together all these years just out of habit."

"Ann . . ."

"No," she said, "it's true. I mean, I just don't know anymore. It's as if we were strangers."

I remembered the thought I had that morning when I flew back on the plane with Kathy's body and saw Ann and Steve there in the terminal waiting. *At least we have Steve.* But we didn't, did we? I have lost them all, I thought. Everyone I ever loved. Kathy, Steve, Ann even.

"Joe, are you listening?"

"Yes," I said, "I'm listening."

I remember now where I bought the bag of marbles. It was in the Atlanta terminal. I had flown to Chicago and on the way home I had a stopover in Atlanta and I wandered into a gift shop and picked up those marbles for Steve and a doll kit for Kathy and a bracelet for Ann. We were young then and there were years and years ahead of us. At thirty thousand feet, in the air over Montgomery, I was thinking that: there are years and years ahead of us. Steve will grow up and Kathy will grow up and they will marry and Ann and I will grow old and love each other and we will enjoy our grandchildren. Nothing can stop that.

But something has. Ann is standing there before me with a stricken look on her face and Steve is up the coast with a girl whose children are with a babysitter back in Los Angeles and I am standing here holding a chipped blue marble that I bought such a little while ago in the airport in Atlanta. Something has.

ABROAD

Nadine Gordimer

MANIE Swemmer talked for years about going up to Northern Rhodesia for a look around. His two boys, Thys and Willie, were there, and besides, he'd worked up there himself in the old days, the early Thirties.

He knew the world a bit although he was born in Bontebokspruit. His grandmother had been a Scots woman, Agnes Swan, and there was a pack of relatives in Scotland; he hadn't got that far, but in a sergeants' mess in Alex just before Sidi Rezegh, when he was with the South African First Division, he had met a Douglas Swan who must have been a cousin—there was quite a resemblance about the eyes.

Yes, he thought of going up, when he could get away. He had been working for the Barends brothers, the last five years, he had put up the Volkskas Bank and the extensions to the mill as well as the new waiting rooms for Europeans and non-Europeans at the station. The town was going ahead. Before that, he worked for the Provincial Public Works Department, and had even had a spell in Pretoria, at the steel works. This was after the motor business went bust; when he came back from the war he had sold his share of the land to his uncle, and gone into the motor business with the money. Fortunately, as Manie Swemmer said to the people he had known all his life, in the bar of Buks Jacobs' hotel on Saturdays after work, although he'd had no real training there wasn't much in the practical field he couldn't do. If he'd had certificates, he wouldn't have been working for a salary from Abel and Johnnie Barends, to-day, that was for sure; but there you are. People still depended on him; if he wanted to take his car and drive up North, he needed three weeks, and who could Abel find to take his place and manage his gang of boys on the site?

He often said he'd like to drive up. It was a long way but he didn't mind the open road and he'd done it years ago when it was strip roads if you were lucky, and plain murder the rest of the way. His old '57 Studebaker would make it; he looked after her himself, and there were many people in the town—including Buks Jacobs from the hotel with his new Volkswagen combi—who wouldn't have anybody else touch their cars. Manie spent most of his Saturday afternoons under somebody's; he had no-one at home (the boys' mother, born Helena Thys, had died of a diseased kidney leaving him to bring up the two little chaps, all alone) and he did it more out of friendship than for anything else.

On Sundays, when he was always expected at the Gysbert Swemmer's, he had remarked that he'd like to go up and have a look around. And there were his boys, of course. His cousin Gysbert said, "Let them come down and visit you." But they were busy making their way; Thys was on the mines, but didn't like it, Willie had left the brewery and was looking for an opening down in the capital. After the British Government gave the natives the country and the name was changed to Zambia, Gysbert said, "Man, you don't want to go there now. What for? After you waited so long."

But he had moved around the world a bit: Gysbert might run three hundred head of cattle, and was making a good thing out of tobacco and chillies as well as mealies on the old Swemmer farm where they had all grown up, but Gysbert had never been further than a holiday in Cape Town. Gysbert had not joined up during the war. Gysbert sat in their grandfather's chair at Sunday dinner and served roast mutton and sweet potatoes and rice to his wife and family, including Manie, and Gysbert's mother, Tante Adela. Tante Adela had her little plot on the farm where she grew cotton, and after lunch she sat in the dark *voorkamer*, beside the big radio and record player combination, and stuffed her cotton into the cushion-covers she cut from sheets of plastic foam. There was coffee on the stoep, handed round by pregnant daughters and daughters-in-law, and there were grandchildren whose mouths exploded huge bubbles of gum before Oom Manie and made him laugh. Gysbert even still drank *mampoer*, home-made peach brandy sent from the Cape, but Manie couldn't stand the stuff and never drank any spirits but Senator Brandy— Buks Jacobs, at the hotel, would set it up without asking.

At the end of the Sunday Manie Swemmer would drive home from the old family farm that was all Gysbert knew, past the fields shuffling and spreading a hand of mealies, then tobacco, and then chilli bushes

blended by distance, like roof-tiles, into red-rose-yellows. Past the trac-
tor and the thresher with its beard of torn husks, and down into the dip
over the dried-up river bed, where they used to try and catch leguaans, as
youngsters. Past the cattle nibbling among the thorn bushes and wild
willow. Through the gates opened by picannins running with the kaffir
dogs, from the kraal. Past the boys and their women squatting around
paraffin tins of beer and pap, and the Indian store, old Y. S. Mia's,
boarded up for Sunday, and all the hundred-and-one relations those
people have, collected on the stoep of the bright pink house next to the
store. At that time in the late afternoon the shadow of the hilly range had
taken up the dam; Manie looked, always, for the glittering circles
belched by fish. He fished there, in summer, still; the thorn trees they
used to play under were dead, but stood around the water.

The town did not really leave the lands behind. His house in Pretorius
Street was the same as the farm houses, a tin roof, a polished stoep on
stumpy cement pillars darkening the rooms round two sides, paint the
colour of the muddy river half-way up the outside walls and on the
woodwork. Inside there was flowered linoleum and a swordfern in a
painted kaffir pot that rocked a little on its uneven base as he walked in.
The dining table and six chairs he and Helena had bought when they got
married, and Tante Adela's plastic foam cushions, covering the places on
the sofa-back where the kids had bounced the springs almost through. He
had a good old boy, Jeremiah, looking after him. The plot was quite big
and was laid out in rows of beetroot, onions and cabbage behind a quince
hedge. Jeremiah had his mealie patch down at his *khaya.* There were half-
a-dozen Rhode Island Reds in the *hok,* and as for the tomatoes, half the
town ate presents of Manie Swemmer's tomatoes.

He'd never really cleared out his sons' room, though once there'd been
a young chappie from the railways looking for somewhere to rent. But
Willie was only sixteen when he went up North to have a look round—
that's how kids are, his brother Thys had gone up and it was natural—he
might want to come back home again sometime. The beds were there,
and Willie's collection of bottle-tops. On the netted-in stoep round the
back there was his motorbike, minus wheels. Manie Swemmer often
thought of writing to ask Willie what he ought to do with the bike; but
the boys didn't answer letters often. In fact, Willie was better than Thys;
Thys hadn't written for about eighteen months, by the time the place had
gone and changed its name from Northern Rhodesia to Zambia. Not that

the change would frighten Manie Swemmer if he decided to make the trip. After all, it wasn't as if he were going to drag a woman up there. And it might be different for people with young daughters. But for someone like him, well, what did he have to worry about except himself?

One September, when the new abbatoir was just about off his hands, he told the Barends brothers that he was taking leave. "No, not down to Durban—I'm pushing off up there for a couple of weeks—" His rising eyebrows and backward jerk of the head indicated the back of the hotel bar, the mountain range, the border.

"Gambia, Zambia! These fancy names. With the new kaffir govern-ment. Dr. or Professor or whatever-he-calls-himself Kaunda," said Carel Janse van Vuuren, the local solicitor, who had been articled in Johan-nesburg, making it clear by his amusement that he, too, knew something of the world.

"Tell your sons to come home here, man. *Hulle is onse mense.*" Dawie Mulder was hoping to be nominated as a candidate for the next provin-cial elections and liked to put a patriotic edge on his remarks.

"Oh they know their home, all right, don't you worry," Manie Swem-mer said, in English, because some of the regulars on the commercial travellers' run, old Joe Zeff and Edgar Bloch, two nice Jewish chappies, had set up the beers for the group. "They'll settle down when they've had their fling, I'm not worried."

"Up in this, uh, Northern Rhodesia—I hear the natives don't bother the white people on the mines, eh?" said Zeff. "I mean you don't have to worry, they won't walk into your house or anything—after all, it's not a joke, you have a big kaffir coming and sitting down next to us here? It's all you're short of."

Sampie Jacobs, the proprietor's wife and a business woman who could buy and sell any man in Bontebokspruit, if it came to money matters, said, "Willie was a bea-utiful child. When he was a little toddler! Eyes like saucers, and blue!" She hung the fly-swatter on its hook, and men-tally catching somebody out, scratched at some fragment of food dried fast to a glass. "If Helena could have seen him"—she reminded Manie Swemmer of the pimple-eroded youth who had bought an electric guitar on credit and gone away leaving his father to meet the installments.

"They'll settle down! Thys is earning good money up there now, though, man. You couldn't earn money like that here! Not a youngster."

"Twenty-six—no, twenty-seven by now," said Sampie Jacobs.

"But Willie. Willie's not twenty-one."

Buks Jacobs said, "Well, you can have it for me, Oom Manie."

"Man, I nearly died of malaria up there in thirty-two," Manie Swemmer said, putting a fist on the counter. "Good lord, I knew the place when it was nothing but a railhead and a couple of mine shafts in the bush. There was an Irish doctor, that time, Fitzgerald was his name, he got my boss-boy to sponge me down every hour . . ."

On the third day of the journey, in the evening, the train drew into the capital, Lusaka. Manie Swemmer had taken the train, after all; it would have been different if there had been someone to drive up with him. But the train was more restful, and, with this trip in the back of his mind all the time, it was some years since he'd taken a holiday. He was alone in the second-class compartment until the Bechuanaland border, wondering if Abel Barends wouldn't make a mess, now, of that gang of boys it had taken years to get into shape, a decent gang of boys but they had to know where they were with you, the native doesn't like to be messed around, either. He mouthed aloud to himself what he had meant to say to Abel, "Don't let me come back and find you've taken on a lot of black scum from the location." But then the train stopped at a small station and he got up to lean on the let-down window; and slowly the last villages of the Transvaal were paused at and passed, and as he looked out at them with his pipe in his mouth and the steam letting fly from beneath the carriage, Barends and the building gang sank to the bottom of his mind. Once or twice, when the train moved on again, he checked his post office savings book (he had transferred money to Lusaka) and the indigestion pills he had put in with his shaving things. He had his bedding ticket (Everything under control, he had joked, smiling to show how easy it was if you knew how, to Gysbert and his wife and Sampie Jacobs, who had seen him onto the train) and a respectful coloured boy made up a nice bunk for him and was grateful for his five cent tip. By the time the train reached Mafeking after dinner, he felt something from the past that he had forgotten entirely, although he talked about it often; the jubilant lightness of moving on, not a stranger among strangers, but a new person discovered among new faces. He felt as if he had been travelling forever and could go on forever. The hills, the bush, the smell of a certain shrub came back to him across thirty years. It was like the veld at home, only different. The balancing rocks, the white-barked figs that split them and held them in tightspread roots, the flat-topped trees turning red with spring—yes, he remembered that—the bush becoming tangled forest down over the rivers, the old baobabs and the kaffir-orange trees with their green billiard-balls sticking out all over, the huge vleis with, far off, a couple of palms craning up looking at you. Two more days slid past the windows. He bought a set of table mats from a picannin at a siding; nicely made, the reeds dyed pink and black—he saw Sampie Jacobs putting them under her flower arrangements in the hotel lounge, far, far away, far, far ahead. When the train reached the Rhodesian-Zambian border there was a slight nervous bracing of his manner: he laid out his open passport— HERMANUS STEFANUS SWEMMER, national of the Republic of South Africa. The young Englishman and the black man dressed exactly like him, white socks, gold shoulder tabs, smart cap, the lot, said, "Thank you sir"; the black one scribbled and stamped.

Well, he was in.

As the train neared Lusaka he began to get anxious. About Willie. About what he would say to Willie. After all, five years. Willie's twenty-first was coming up in December. He forgot that he was drawing into Lusaka through the dark, he forgot that he was travelling, he thought: Willie, Willie. There were no outskirts to Lusaka, even now. A few lights at a level crossing or two, bicycles, native women with bundles—and they were in the station. The huge black sky let down a trail of rough bright stars as close as the lights of a city. Bells rang and the train, standing behind Manie Swemmer, stamped backwards. People sauntered and yelled past him: white people, Indians, natives in moulded plastic shoes.

Willie said, "Hell, where were you?"

Tall. Sideburns. A black leather jacket zipped up to where the button was missing at the neck of the shirt. The same; and Manie Swemmer had forgotten. Never sent a snap of himself, and naturally you'd expect him to have changed in five years.

They spoke in English. "I was just beginning to wonder did the letter get lost. I was just going to take a taxi. Well, how's it! Quite a trip, eh? Since Wednesday, man!" Manie knew how to behave; he had his hands on the kid's biceps, he was pushing him and shaking him. Willie was grinning down the side of his mouth. He stood there while his father talked about the train, and why he hadn't driven up, and what Gysbert said, that backvelder tied to Tante Adela's apron, and the good dinner the dining car had put up. "Give us your things," Willie said. "What's this?" The mats were tied up in a bit of newspaper. "Presents, man. I can't go back empty-handed." "Just hang on here a minute, ay, Dad, I'mna get some smokes." Held his shoulders too high when he ran; that was always his fault, when he did athletics at Bontebokspruit High. Willie. Couldn't believe it. Suddenly, Manie Swemmer landed in Lusaka, knew he was there, and exhilaration spread through his breast like some pleasurable form of heartburn.

Willie opened the pack and shook out a cigarette, tenting his hands round the match. "Where were you gunna take the taxi?"

"Straight to your place, man. I've got the letter on me."

"I've pushed off from there."

"But what happened, son, I thought it was so near for work and everything?"

Willie took a deep draw at his cigarette, put his head back as if swallowing an injury and then blew smoke at it, with narrowed eyes; there was a line between them already, his father noticed. "Didn't work out at Twyford's Electric. So I had to find a cheaper room until I get fixed up."

"But I thought they told you there was prospects, son?"

"I'm going to see someone at the cement works Monday. Friend of mine says he'll fix me up. And there's a job going at a motor spares firm, too. I don't want to jump at anything."

"For Pete's sake, no. You must think of your future. Fancy about Twyford's, eh, they started up in the thirties, one of the first. But I suppose the old boy's dead now. Watch out for the motor spares outfit—I don't trust that game."

They were still standing on the platform; Willie was leaning against one of the struts that held up the roof, smoking and feeling a place near his left sideburn where he had nicked himself. That poor kid would never be able to get a clean shave—his skin had never come right. He seemed to have forgotten about the luggage.

"So where you staying now, Willie?" Everyone from the train had left.

"I'm at another chap's place. There's a bed on the stoep. There's five people in the house, only three rooms. They can't put you up."

"What's wrong with a hotel?" Manie Swemmer consoled, chivvying, cheerful. "Come let's take this lot and get into town. I'll get a room at the

Lusaka Hotel, good Lord, do I remember that place. I know all about the posh new one out on the Ridgeway, too. But I don't have to splash it. The Lusaka'll do me fine."

Willie was shaking his head, hang-dog.

"You'll never get *in*, man, Dad. You don't know—you won't get a room in this place. It's the independence anniversary next week—"

"When? The anniversary, eh—" He was pleased to have arrived for a festival.

"I dunno. Monday. I think. You haven't a hope."

"Wait a minute, wait a minute." They were gathering the luggage. Manie Swemmer had put on his hat to emerge into the town, although he had suddenly realized that the night was very hot. He looked at his son.

"I thought maybe it's the best thing if you go straight on to the Copper Belt," said Willie. "To Thys."

"To Thys?" He lifted the hat to let the air in upon his head.

"I dunno about a train, but it's easy to thumb a lift on the road."

"The Regent!" Manie Swemmer said. "Is there still a Regent Hotel? Did you try there?"

"What you mean try, Dad, I told you, it's no use to *try*, you'll never get *in*—"

"Well, never mind, son, let's go and have a beer there, anyway. Okay?" Manie Swemmer felt confused, as if the station itself were throwing back and forth all sorts of echoes. He wanted to get out of it, never mind where. There was only one clear thought; silly. He must put new buttons on the kid's shirt. A man who has brought up two youngsters and lived alone a long time secretly knows how to do these things.

Lusaka was a row of Indian stores and the railway station, facing each other. In the old days.

Manie Swemmer was a heavy man but he sat delicately balanced, forward, in the taxi, looking out under the roof at the new public buildings and shopping centers lit up round paved courts in Cairo Road, the lights of cars travelling over super markets and milk bars. "The post-office? Ne-ver!" And he could not stop marvelling at it, all steel and glass, and a wide parking lot paved beside it. Here and there was a dim landmark—one of the Indian stores whose cracked verandah had been a quay above the dust of the road—with a new shopfront but the old tin roof. No more sewing machines going under the hands of the old natives on the verandahs; even just in passing, you could see the stuff in the smart window displays was factory-made. Fishing tackle and golf clubs; shiny sets of drums and electric guitars; a grubby-looking little bar with kaffir music coming out. "Looks as if it should be down in the location, eh?" He laughed, pointing it out to Willie. There were quite a few nicely dressed natives about, behaving themselves, with white shirts and ties. The women in bright cotton dresses, the latest styles, and high-heeled shoes. And everywhere, Europeans in cars. "Ah, but the old trees are still going strong!" he said to Willie. Along the middle of the Cairo Road there was the same broad island with red-flowering trees, he recognized the shape of the blooms although he couldn't see their color. Willie was sitting back, smoking. He said "They don't leave you alone, with their potatoes and I don' know what." He wasn't looking, but was speaking of the natives who hung around even after dark under the trees—vendors, young out-of-works.

The way to the Regent was too short for Manie Swemmer's liking. He could have done with driving around a bit; this kind of confusion was different—exciting, like being blind-folded, whirled around, and then left to feel your way about a room you knew well. But in no time they were at the hotel, and that had changed and hadn't changed, too. The old rows of rooms in the garden had been connected with a new main building, but the "garden" was still swept earth with a few hibiscus and snake plants.

They found themselves in what had been the verandah and was closed in with glass louvres and called the terrace lounge. Willie made no suggestions, and his father, chatting and commenting in the husky undertone he used among other people, was misled by the layout of the hotel as he remembered it. "Never mind, never mind! What's the odds. We'll have a drink before we start any talking, man, why not? This'll do all right," and with his big behind in its neat gray flannels rising apologetically toward the room, he supervised the stowing of his two suitcases and newspaper parcel beside the small table where he urged Willie to sit. He ordered a couple of beers, and looked around. The place was filling up with the sort of crowd you get on hot evenings; one or two families with kids climbing about the chairs, young men buying their girls a drink, married couples who hadn't gone home after the office—men alone would be in the pub itself. There was only one coloured couple—not blacks, more like Cape Coloureds. You'd hardly notice them. Willie didn't know anyone. They went, once again, over the questions and answers they had exchanged over Willie's prospects of a new job. But it had always been hard to know what Willie was thinking, even when he was quite a little kid; and Manie Swemmer's attention kept getting out of range, around the room, to the bursts of noise that kept coming, perhaps when some inner door connected with the bar was opened—to the strange familiar town outside, and the million and one bugs going full blast for the night with the sound of sizzling, of clocks being wound, and ratchets jerking. "What a machine shop, eh?" he said; but of course, living there five years, Willie wouldn't even be hearing it anymore.

"Who's running the place these days?" he suggested to Willie confidentially, when the beer was drunk. "You know the chap at all?"

"Well, I mean I know who he is. Mr. Davidson. We come here sometimes. There's a dance, first Saturday of the month."

"Do you think he'd know you?"

"I don't know if he knows me," said Willie.

"Well, come on, let's see what we can do." Manie Swemmer asked the Indian waiter to keep an eye on the luggage for a moment, and was directed to the reception desk. Willie came along behind him. A redhead with a skin that would dent blue if you touched it said, "Full up, sir, I'm sorry, sir—" almost before Manie Swemmer began speaking. He put his big, half-open fist on the counter, and smiled at her with his head cocked: "Now listen here, young miss, I come all the way from a place you never heard of, Bontebokspruit, and I'm sure you can find me just a bed. Anywhere. I've travelled a lot and I'm not fussy." She smiled sympathetically, but there it was—nothing to offer. She even ran her ballpoint down the list of bookings once again, eyebrows lifted and the pretty beginnings of a double chin showing.

"Look, I lived in this town while you were still a twinkle in your father's eye—I'd like to say hello to Mr. Davidson, anyway. D'you mind, eh?" She called somewhere behind a stand of artificial roses and tulips, "Friend of Mr. Davidson's here. Can he come a minute?"

He was a little fellow with a recognizable way of hitching his arms forward at the elbow to ease his shirt cuffs up his wrists as he approached: ex-barman. He had a neat, patient face, used to dealing with trouble.

"Youngster like you wouldn't remember, but I lived in this hotel thirty years ago—I helped build this town, put up the first reservoir. Now they tell me I'll have to sleep in the street to-night."

"That's about it," the manager said.

"I can hear you're a Jock, like me, too!" Manie Swemmer seized delightedly upon the hint of a Scots accent. "Yes, you may not believe it but my grandmother was a Miss Swan. From the Clyde. Agnes Swan. I used to wear the kilt when I was a kiddie. Yes, I did! An old Boer like me."

The little man and the receptionist conferred over the list of bookings; she knew she was right, there was nothing. But the man said, "Tell you what I'll do. There's this fellow from Delhi. He h's a biggish single I could m'be put another bed in. I promised him he'd have it to himself, but still an' all. He can't object to someone like yourself, I mean."

"There you are! The good old Regent! Didn't I say to you, Willie?" Willie was leaning on the reception desk smoking and looking dazedly at the high heel of his Chelsea boot; he smiled down the side of his mouth again.

"I'll apologize for barging in on this chap, don't you worry, I'll make it all right. You say from Delhi—India?" Manie Swemmer added suddenly. "You mean an Indian chappie?"

"But he's not one of your locals," said the manager. "Not one of these fellows down here. A businessman, flown in this morning on the V.C. 10."

"Oh, he's well-dressed, a real gentleman," the receptionist reassured in the wide-eyed recommendation of something she wouldn't care to try for herself.

"That's the way it is," the manager said, in confidence.

"O.K., O.K., I'll buy. I'm not saying a word!" said Manie Swemmer. "Ay, Willie? Somewhere to lay my head, that's all I ask."

The redhead took a key out of the nesting boxes numbered on the wall. "Fifty-four, Mr. Davidson? The boy'll bring your luggage, sir."

"Good Lord, you've got to have a bit of a nerve or you don't get anywhere, eh?" Manie walked gaily close beside his son along the corridors with their path of flowered runner and buckets of sand filled with cigarette stubs, stepping round beer bottles and tea-trays that people had put outside their doors. In the room that the servant opened for him, he at once assumed smug possession. "I hope the oriental gentleman's only going to stay one night. This'll do me fine." A divan, ready made-up with bedding and folded in the middle like a wallet was wheeled in. He squeaked cupboards open, forced up the screeching steel flyscreens and pushed the windows wide—"Air, air, that's what we need." Willie sat on

the other bed, whose cover had already been neatly turned back to allow
a head to rest on the pillow; the dent was still there. The chap's things
were on the dressing table. Willie fingered a pair of cufflinks with red
stones in them. There was a tissue-paper airmail edition of some London
newspaper, an open tin of cough lozenges, and a gold-tooled leather
notebook. Rows of exquisitely neat figures, and then writing like something off a fancy carpet: "Hell, look at this, eh?" said Willie.

"Willie, I always taught you to respect other people's belongings no
matter who they are."

Willie dropped the notebook finickily. "Okay, okay."

Manie Swemmer washed, combed his moustache and the back of his
head, where there was still some hair, put back on again the tropical-
weight jacket he had bought especially for the trip. "I never used to look
sloppy, not even when the heat was at its height," he remarked to Willie.
Willie nodded whether he had been listening to what you said or not.

When they had returned the key to the reception desk Willie said,
"We gunna eat now, Dad," but there wasn't a soul in the dining room but
a young woman finishing supper with her kiddies, and if there was one
thing that depressed Manie Swemmer it was an empty hotel dining room.

In fact, he was attracted to the bar with a mixture of curiosity and
shyness, as if Manie Swemmer, twenty-three years old, in bush jacket and
well-pressed shorts, might be found drinking there. He strolled through
the garden, Willie behind him, listening to the tree frogs chinking away
at the night. In spite of the town, you could still smell woodsmoke from
the native's fires. But youngsters don't notice these things. The street
entrance to the bar was through a beer garden now, screened by lattice.
Coloured bulbs poked red and blue light through the pattern of slats and
dark blotches of creeper. There were loud voices in the local native lingo
and the coughs of small children. "It's for them, let's go this way," Willie
said, and he and his father went back into the hotel and entered the bar
from the inside door.

It was full, all right. Manie Swemmer had never been what you would
call a drinker, but for a man who lives alone there is no place where he
feels at home the way he does among men in a bar. And yet there were
blacks. Oh yes, that was something. Blacks sitting at the tables, and some
of them not too clean or well-dressed, either. Looked like boys from the
roads, labourers. Up at the bar were the white men, the wide backs and
red necks almost solidly together; a black face or two above white shirts at

the far end. The backs parted for father and son: they might have been expected. "Well, what's the latest from Thys, man?" Manie Swemmer was at ease at last, wedged between the shoulder of a man telling a story with large gestures, and the bar counter ringed shinily, like the dark water at Gysbert's dam.

"Nothing. Oh this girl. He's got himself engaged to this doll Lynda Thompson."

"Good grief, so he must have written! The letter's missed me. Getting engaged! Well, I've picked the right time, eh, independence anniversary and my son's engagement! We've got something to drink to, all right. When's the engagement going to be?"

"Oh it was about ten days ago. A party at her people's place in Kitwe. I couldn't get a lift up to the Copper Belt that weekend."

"But if I'd known! Why'n't Thys send me a telegram, man! I'd have taken my leave sooner!"

Willie said nothing, only looked sideways at the men beside him.

Manie Swemmer took a deep drink of his beer. "If he'd sent a telegram, man! Why'n't he let me know? I told him I was coming up the middle of the month. Why not just send a telegram at least?"

Willie had no answer. Manie Swemmer drank off his beer and ordered another round. Now he said softly, in Afrikaans, "Just go to the post office and write out a telegram, eh?"

Willie shrugged. They drank. The swell of other people's spirits, the talk and laughter around them lifted Manie Swemmer from the private place where he was beached. "Well, I'll go up and look at Miss Lynda Thompson for myself in a few days. Kitwe's a beautiful town, eh? What's the matter with the girl, is he ashamed of her or what? Is she bowlegged and squint?" He laughed. "Trust old Thys for that!"

At some point the shoulder pressing against his had gone without his noticing. A native's voice said in good English, "Excuse me, did you lose this?" The black hand with one of those expensive calendar watches at the wrist held out a South African two rand note.

Manie Swemmer began struggling to get at his pockets. "Hang on a tick, just let me . . . yes, must be mine, I pulled it out by mistake to pay with . . . thanks very much."

"A pleasure."

One of the educated kind, some of them have studied at universities in America, even. And England was just pouring money into the hands of these people, they could go over and get the best education going, better than whites could afford. Manie Swemmer said to Willie, but in a voice to be overheard, because after all, you didn't expect such honesty of a native, it was really something to be encouraged: "I thought I'd put away all my money from home when I took out my Zambian currency in the train. Two rand! Well, that would have been the price of a few beers down the drain!"

The black said, "The price of a good bottle of brandy down there." He wore a spotless bush jacket and longs; spotless.

"You've been to South Africa?" said Manie Swemmer.

"You ever heard of Fort Hare College? I was there four years. And I used to spend my holidays with some people in Germiston. I know Johannesburg well."

"Well, let me buy you a South African brandy. Come on, man, why not?" The black man smiled and indicated casually that his bottle of beer had already been put before him. "No, no, man, that'll do for a chaser; you're going to have a brandy with me, eh?" Manie Swemmer's big body curved over the bar as he agitated for the attention of the barman. He jolted the black man's arm and almost threw Willie's glass over. "Sorry— come on, there—two brandies—wait a minute, have you got Senator? D'you want another beer, Willie?" The kid might drink brandy on his own but he wasn't going to get it from his father.

"You'll get a shock when you have to pay." The black chap was amused. He had taken a newspaper out of his briefcase and was glancing over the headlines.

"Brandy's expensive here, eh? The duty and that. When I was up on the Copper Belt as a youngster we had to drink it to keep going. Brandy and quinine. It was a few bob a bottle. That's how I learnt to drink brandy."

"Is that so?" The black man spoke kindly. "So you know this country quite a long time."

Manie Swemmer moved his elbow within half-an-inch of a nudge— "I'll bet I knew it before you did—before you were born!"

"I'm sure, I'm sure." They laughed. Manie Swemmer looked excitedly from the man to his son, but Willie was mooning over his beer, as usual. The black man—he told his name but who could catch their names— was something in the ministry of Local Government, and he was very interested in what Manie Swemmer could tell him of the old days; he listened with those continual nods of the chin that showed he was following carefully; a proper respect—if not for a white man, then for a man as old as his father might be. He could still speak Afrikaans, Manie Swemmer discovered. He said a few sentences in a low voice but Manie Swemmer was pretty sure he could have carried on a whole conversation if he's wanted to. "You'll excuse me if I don't join you, but you'll have another brandy?" the black man offered. "I have a meeting in"—he looked at the watch—"less than half-an-hour, and I must keep a clear head."

"Of course! You've got responsibility, now. I always say, any fool can learn to do what he's told, but when it comes to making the decisions, when you got to shift for yourself, that's the time you've either got it up here, or . . . It doesn't matter who or what you are . . ."

The man had slipped off the bar stool, briefcase between chest and arm. "Enjoy your holiday . . ."

"Everything of the best!" Manie Swemmer called after him. "I'll tell you something, Willie, he may be black as the ace of spades, but that's a gentleman. Eh? You got to be open-minded, otherwise you can't move about in these countries. But that's a gentleman!"

"Some of them put on an act," said Willie. "You get them wanting to show how educated they are. The best thing is don't take any notice."

"What's the name of that feller was talking to me?" Manie Swemmer asked the white barman. He wanted to write it down so he'd be able to remember when he told the story back home.

"You know who that is? That's Thompson Gwebo, that's one of the Under Minister's brothers," the barman said. "When he married last November they had their roast oxen and all that at his village, but the wedding reception for the government people and white people and so on was here. Five tiers to the cake. Over three hundred people. Mrs. Davidson did the snacks herself."

They began to chat, between interruptions when the barman was called away to dispense drinks. Two or three beers had their effect on Willie, too; he was beginning to talk, in reluctant spates that started with one of his mumbled remarks, half-understood by his father, and then developed, through his father's eager questions, into the bits and pieces of a life that Manie Swemmer pieced together. "This feller said . . ." "Which one was that, the manager or your mate?" "No, the one I told you . . . the one who was supposed to turn up at the track . . ." "What

track?" "Stock car racing . . . there was this feller asked me to change
the plugs . . ."

In a way, it was just like the old days up there. Nobody thought about
going home. Not like Buks Jacobs' place, the pub empty over dinner-
time. This one was packed. The white men were solid at the bar again,
but the blacks at the tables—the labourers—were getting rowdy. They
were joined by a crowd of black ducktails in jeans who behaved just like
the white ones you saw in the streets of Johannesburg and Pretoria. They
surged up and down between the tables and were angrily hit off, like flies,
by the labourers heavily drunk over their beer: one lifted his bottle and
brought it down on the back of one of the hooligans' hands; there was a
roar. A black lout in a shirt with 007 printed across it kept stepping back
against Manie Swemmer's back in the brand-new tropical jacket. Manie
Swemmer went on talking and ignored him, but the hooligan taunted in
English—"Sorry!" He did it again: "Sorry!" The drunken black face with
a fleck of white matter at the corner of each eye breathed over him. If it'd
been a white man Manie Swemmer wouldn't have stood for it, he'd have
punched him in the nose. And at home if a native—but at home it
couldn't happen; here he was, come up to have a look, and he'd been in
some tough spots before—Good Lord, those gyppos in Egypt, they didn't
all smell of roses, either. He knew how to hold himself in if he had to.

Then another native—one in a decent shirt and tie—came over and
said something angrily, in their own language, to the hooligans. He said
to the barman in English, "Can't you see these men are making a nui-
sance of themselves? Why don't you have them thrown out?"

The barman was quick to take the support. "These people should be
outside in the beer garden!" he said to the company at large. "Go on, I
don't want trouble in here." The hooligans drifted away from the bar
counter but would not go out. Manie Swemmer had not noticed the
decently dressed native leave, but suddenly he appeared, quiet and busi-
nesslike, with two black policemen in white gloves. "What's the com-
plaint?" One shouldered past Willie to ask the barman. "Making a nui-
sance of themselves, those over there." There was a brief uproar; of
course natives are great ones for shouting. But the black hooligans were
carted away by their own policemen like a bunch of scruffy dogs; no
nonsense.

"No nonsense!" said Manie Swemmer, laughing and putting his hand
over Willie's forearm. "D'you see that? Good Lord, they've got mar-

vellous physiques, that pair. Talk about smart! That's something worth seeing!" Willie giggled; his Dad was talking very loud; he was talking to everyone in the place, joking with everyone. At last they found them-selves at dinner, after half-past nine it must have been. There were shouts of laughter from other late diners, telling stories. Manie Swemmer began to think very clearly and seriously, and to talk very seriously to Willie, about the possibility of moving up here, himself. "I've still got a lot of my life ahead of me. Must I see out my time making money for Abel Barends? In Bontebokspruit? Why shouldn't I start out on my own again? The place is going ahead!"

The jolly party left the dining room and all at once he was terribly tired: the journey, the arrival, the first look around—it left him winded, like too hearty a slap on the back. "Let's call it a day, son," he said, and Willie saw him to the room.

But the key would not open the door. Willie investigated by the flare of a match. "S'bolted on the inside." They rapped softly, then hammered. "Well I'm damned," said Manie Swemmer. "The Indian." He had been going to tell him about how many years Y.S. Mia had had a store near the farm.

They went down to the reception desk. The redhead thrust her tongue in a bulge between lower lip and teeth, in consternation. "Have you knocked?" "The blooming door down!" said Manie Swemmer. "Mind you, I thought as much," the girl said. "He was on his high horse when he came back and saw your bed and things. I mean I don't know what the fuss was about—as I said to him, it isn't as if we've put an African in with you, it's a white man. And him Indian himself."

"Well, what're you going to do about my dad?" Willie said suddenly.

"What can I do?" She made a peaked face. "Mr. Davidson's gone off to Kapiri Mposhi, his mother's broken her hip at eighty-one. I can't depend on anyone else here to throw that chap out. And if he won't even answer the door."

Manie Swemmer said nothing. Willie waited, but all he could hear was his father's slow breathing, with little gasps on the intake. "But what about my Dad?"

She had her booking list out again. They waited. "Tell you what. No. —There's a room with four beds out in the old wing, we keep it, you know—sometimes now, these people come in and you daren't say no. They don't want to pay for more than one room for the lot. It was booked, I mean, but it's after eleven now and no one's showed up, so I should think you could count on it being all right . . ."

Manie Swemmer put his big forearm and curled hand on the reception desk like a dead thing. "Look," he said. "The coolie, all right, I didn't say anything. But don't put me in with an African, now, man! I mean, I've only just got here, give me a bit of time. You can't expect to put me in with a native, right away, first thing."

"Oh I should think it would be all right," she said in her soothing, effusive way, something to do with some English accent she had. "I wouldn't worry if I was you. It's late now. Very unlikely anyone'd turn up. Don't you think?"

She directed him to the room. Willie went with him again. Across the garden; the old block, the way it was in the old days. There was no carpet in the passage; their footsteps tottered over the unevennesses of cracked granolithic. When Willie had left him, he pulled down the bedding of the best-looking bed to have a good look at the sheets, opened the window, and then, working away at it with a grunt that was almost a giggle, managed to drive the rusty bolt home across the door.

THE LIZARD

(for Robin H.)

Elaine Gottlieb

. . . A HABIT of observing, surmising, decorating the sky. A look under things. No, it is not a sickness in itself, though the doctors assume this need to write is an indication of abnormality. Perhaps. But not in the way they imagine. I started writing long before I could use the typewriter. It was my grandmother's typewriter that started me, her crippled portable for which she showed an unreasonable affection, an affection she granted numerous inanimate objects. I started writing in my head, and my hearing began to fade soon afterwards. The doctors try to find a correlation. I do not believe them, but I make an attempt to remember. I see myself beside my grandmother's pool in Miami. Twenty years ago?

Perhaps I was thinking: I am a leaf, a drop of water, an instinct. I knew words like *instinct,* knew all kinds of words: tetragrammaton, analgesic, inconsiderate. My mother thought it ridiculous that an eleven-year-old took the dictionary to bed with him. I would hear her laughing about it with Nat (who never read anything).

Late at night when they went out and left me alone (suspecting babysitters' intentions) I heard house sounds and outside sounds. As if the house were full of voices that started in the walls, trying to intrigue me with stories or plays, episodes about other people elsewhere, in which I was asked to play a leading role, though generally I declined, watching instead their hasty shadows on the ceiling. And sometimes, after they had finished their performance, I would hear a night bird sing my name, or call out: Glorious . . . glorious . . . or palm fronds would rattle against my window like the low clapping of a polite audience.

When I sat alone beside my grandmother's pool I heard little things buzz about me, and other things made timid advances through the grass or in the bushes. At first, everything was green plants, water, sky, a fence, the house, what I knew, what everyone knew. Then it began to open up . . . the world within the world.

The brown one was the first. It was almost the color of the coconut palm, and it seemed to trickle down and lie in a pool of itself on a stone at the base of the tree; then it was the hue of the stone and I would not have seen it if it hadn't snapped at a grasshopper. Then, slipping through the grass, a yellow one, smaller, faintly green, almost transparent; its spine nearly visible. An orange tinge near the throat, and as if trapped by my gaze, transfixed beneath the cactus bush.

I lay with my cheek to the flagstones of the pool, alternately watching the immobilized lizards and the lacing of light through the water. I became aware of a small blue lizard, almost purple, resting near the fence. At least I supposed it rested; I couldn't see it breathe. Sometimes my mother lay as still as that on her bed, with pads over her eyes. She rested a great deal, when she was not at her receptionist job or out somewhere with Nat or having a party in our dim unfinished-looking house. The chairs were always in the middle of the floor; I don't remember anymore where they should have been. The couch was soiled and slightly worn; my mother occasionally mentioned doing something about it, but always forgot. Blinds shut us in; light seemed to disturb her. On the wall in the foyer there was a painting of a black girl lying down, doing something I could not understand at the time, though in retrospect it appalls me. Yet even then I wondered about it. I did not want to, yet could not help looking at it. My mother had coaxed my father into leaving it there when they separated. She always told people how much it cost . . . as if she had won a bet.

In front of me the lizards seemed sunstruck, or stunned (by some exceptional news?). I touched one; it burned. But was its mind cool? Were the fluctuations of the day absorbed in its spiney shield? I went to sleep and when I awoke all the lizards had gone except one I didn't remember having seen before. It was larger than the others, green as Florida, and with muscular-looking legs. I couldn't see any ears and its eyes were lost in the mottled pattern of its skin. But as I was about to touch it the eyes flicked open, opaque, defensive. I turned over on my stomach and squinted.

I thought, had the impression, wanted to believe, was all ready to believe that I saw the lizard doing an exercise. But it wasn't like the floor touching and jogging and belt-shaking of my grandmother. It seemed more like a pose or a dance to me. I looked back because I knew that if my grandmother saw me, if she called out in her bottom-of-the-bottle voice (did all women speak to their children like that?): What are you doing there? What are you watching? . . . always suspecting something that might please me and not herself . . . I might have to show it to her. And then she would say: Why, it's just a dirty old lizard dying!

Nevertheless the lizard wasn't dying. Its legs were in the air, but that meant something else. Nor would it want to be turned right side up: it had the privilege of being on whatever side it pleased! The lizard's eyes shone golden.

Half its body was in the air; it seemed to be bringing its tail down over its head as it lay on its back, the two forelegs implanted on the ground. I tried to think where I had seen something like it; my mother's only exercises were swimming, tennis, golf. Then I remembered my aunt Sylvia, my father's sister who came to see me and take me out now and then. She was much younger than my father, still at college, studying philosophy, I adored her laugh. She told fantastic stories.

I recollected having seen her stand on her head. And turn herself into a pretzel. She had started to teach me a few things. Oga? I thought. No . . . yoga. A lizard doing yoga.

I laughed and turned on my back. Then I brought my legs over my head, too. But my stomach was full of the peanut butter and jelly sandwiches that were all, my grandmother insisted, I ever wanted to eat. It wasn't true. She just never cooked anything good.

My grandmother came out to the pool. She didn't look like a grandmother. I wondered if she ever would. She had curly blond hair and a wig just like it. Sometimes I couldn't tell which was which.

Pretending to be asleep, I could see my grandmother pussyfooting at the edge of the pool, a kerchief on her hair . . . it must have been her hair, she wouldn't have worn it over a wig. She was in her favorite tiger-striped shorts and a yellow sweater with a high neck and little sleeves. I wondered whether her neck sweated while her arms cooled.

She had pulled a deck chair out of the house and was setting it up with a frown and little impatient gestures and a look of disgust. Once, she kicked it. I was glad she thought me asleep, because she always asked me to do things before doing them herself. After settling in the chair (with a: Darn!) she went back to the house and returned with her baby-blue telephone which had an extremely long wire that she could plug in anywhere. She seemed to be doing a dance with the wire; it coiled around her bare feet and she stepped in and out of it and twirled it around and shook it out like a lasso. Then she fell into the chair and perched the phone on her shoulder and spoke into it and typed at the same time. My grandmother wrote fashion news, edited a fashion paper. Many people knew her: they were always embracing her in stores and restaurants. Flattering her, and I knew why. So she would write something nice about them or their clothes or their restaurants. For some reason, probably because it meant free meals, she also wrote gourmet news. I couldn't bear the way she looked at those people who came out from workrooms or behind cash registers or kitchens or dressing rooms and exclaimed: Francie, you look gorgeous today! Or: Francie, you get younger every minute. . . . Because I could see that it wasn't true, though at the same time a tremor of pleasure would pass through my grandmother's body as she smiled her smile of absolutely young-looking, astringent and perfectly modeled teeth. (No wonder. She was always jumping into the bathroom to brush them.)

Sometimes she would ask my opinion on the clothes she wore, as if I were the authority's authority. Or a man. Because, as she explained to me, a man's reaction to clothes was more significant than all the fashion predictions put together.

Women want to know what men think of them, she would say, as if she had worked years at this conclusion.

I liked to see her dressed up. She smiled more then, and sometimes even took me on dates. Occasionally a nightclub act might feature acrobats or animals. I loved animals.

But I tried not to notice the expression on her face when a man was with us. Because though she smiled, her eyes looked funny, as if she had caught something in them. She would glance up and down at the same time, fluttering her lashes and speaking rapidly and confusing me as to whether she was a friend or an enemy. Whatever her intention, there was a tone, a look about her that disturbed me; I preferred not to watch, or if watching were necessary, to make my mind go elsewhere. I practiced sitting still, smiling and nodding, while my thoughts reviewed something I had read the day before, or made up improbable stories. Occasionally, she caught me. Hoagy, are you there? . . . Yes (but I wished I weren't). On the other hand, my mother was worse than my grandmother. Always punishing me. For not listening, not cleaning the house, not knowing what the teacher had assigned. Yet my grandmother seemed suspicious of every breath I took. I tried to be quiet and get in no one's way.

On the phone again, her voice rose. I didn't know which of her friends she was scolding, but suddenly I realized she wasn't scolding, though she spoke angrily, her throat tensed like a bow. I closed my eyes, pretending to be a lizard. Not the kind that did yoga, but still, silent, dreaming, a sun-filled lizard on a stone, dreaming it was the stone.

She spoke of a sweater, the way she only spoke of her clothes. . . . When women grew older, I thought, and didn't have husbands, maybe they fell in love with their clothes. Yet, how I hated the yesterday-smell of the closet, all those dresses pressed together in a conspiracy of stale talc and sweat. Why did she keep them? In her own room the closet was full of new clothes with the same body scent and perfume, though more potent, yearning.

. . . The blue sweater, she hissed, the darling Caribbean blue that matched my eyes, made me think of all the nice things that were ever said to me. . . . How I loved that color! And she takes it. Rosabel. My own daughter. Always stealing!

I winced at my mother's name, even though I saw that hunter's gleam in her eyes every time she visited my grandmother. Even so. And despite the fact that nothing pleased Rosabel. She was my mother; I felt responsible for her. I wished I could unplug the phone. Slowly, so as not to distract, I let my head roll to a side. Then, slowly again, my body. The lizard, a dappled green, blinked metallic eyes. And I blinked back.

Now it pressed against the ground. Raising its head slightly, looking to one side, then the other. I thought of Sylvia doing the same. I thought I heard her tell me: Clear your mind of all but the lizard.

. . . It will free your spirit, she said to me.

I turned on my stomach, but too rapidly. My grandmother noticed me at once.

Hoagy! she said. Didn't I tell you to do your arithmetic? Where is your math book?

I ran through the chilly house. Looking for my math book, I passed her inflatable furniture. The previous year she had become incensed at a moving van that charged too much to deliver a small piano, had then proceeded to sell everything in the living room and substitute the inflatable, disposable, or foldable. I thought of sticking pins in the plastic or luring the dog in to try a few bites. But she only allowed the dog on the sun porch.

I found my book under the big double bed that had been my mother's when she lived there, as a girl. She was still a girl when she married. A child of sixteen, my grandmother had reminded me. Eloped, but fortunately, Francie added, with a wealthy man. Later she could not understand why anyone would give up a wealthy man (who was wild about her!).

Though it was obvious, Francie liked to add, Rosabel didn't know how to make herself interesting to men. All she ever spoke of was her job, how everyone tried to rape her. Why didn't she learn something about politics or dianetics or cybernetics?

I didn't like the bedroom. At night I would open the venetian blinds all the way so the moon and the palm trees and the smell of jasmine and oranges could enter. Then, with all forms hushed, I could forget the intrusion of the tank-shaped sauna with the radio on top . . . that made me think of robots; and facing it, the vanity with its tiny drawers in which everything from snapshots the color of tea stains to lost beads and dried up raisins had been stuffed. Or next to the bed, catty-cornered (she loved catty corners) the tall dresser in which she kept a medical encyclopedia (to diagnose herself), a roll of absorbent cotton, a muddy pink toy poodle, the color of syringes, and blue satin sheets. In the bookcase built into the headrest of the bed I found children's books so old they must have been her own. All over the house there were peanut butter jars of darkening pennies that she never turned into any bank, but kept as reminders of the days when pennies were useful. As each jar filled she would tell me: It's important. It will add up someday. They'll make lots of dollars for me . . . I was afraid to touch those jars. They threatened a nasty dollar-sized jangle.

And how I dreaded that dark closet where clothes at night seemed about to dislodge the door, the way a vampire, I imagined, might rise from a sewer. The door had a way of opening by itself, with a: pop! . . . revealing weary dresses, boxes, dirty towels and shoes on the floor, folded snack tables, whatnot. I trembled at the vulnerability of my own small trousers and shirts hanging with them. Was it the odor . . . like an armpit . . . that stifled me?

Walking circuitously to the pool, I carried my math book, notebook, and pencil. Briefly, over the telephone and above her glasses, Francie looked up; then she subsided into her work and dialed someone else.

The lizard was still there. It was actually balancing on its paws, perpendicular, tail in air. The math book fell from my hands.

Hoagy! my grandmother warned. Get that book before you kick it into the pool!

I retrieved it absently, lay on my stomach, propped the book before me, opened the notebook, and tried to start my work. But my glance kept wandering to the lizard, still balancing. It came down soporifically in the sunshine. I lifted the pencil and began a letter:

Dear Sylvia, I am looking at a lizard who I think has magic powers. . . .

—I can't get your son to do a single solitary thing he's supposed to do for school, Francie complained when my mother and her friend Nat came for me after dinner.

Oh, he's a brat, Rosabel said without altering her expression or tone of voice, while her fat white leg hung over and clung to the arm of the inflatable chair.

Nat sat on the other chair, looking as if he had driven himself through his last game of tennis. His hair fringed his forehead, and his sport shirt met his chest with a stain of geographical shape. Black hairs springing from behind the opening of his shirt shone dewily. Some of the hairs were grey. He was older than Rosabel. It seemed to me that he would have suited Francie better, despite my mother's pretty face. Actually, he had known Francie first.

Rosabel always looked cool. Even when her voice changed (like when she scolded me), her face remained serene. My grandmother, on the other hand, seemed constantly suffused by some hidden source of heat. She wriggled, grimaced, coughed, smiled aborted, nervous smiles, and had, at the same time, an expression in her eyes that made me wonder what could console her.

Nat brought to mind a Christmas ornament still hanging from a chandelier, shining its last dull shine, and about to fall down. Both Francie and Rosabel thought him handsome, despite the pneumatic waist, the oily skin, indifferent eyes.

I don't know why she doesn't let her hair down, Francie said to Nat.

She has such beautiful hair. Thick, curly. Mine was never like that. All my life I've tried to make it grow; it just won't. Rosabel, why don't you let your hair down? You look forty years old.

I'm not eighteen.

She doesn't take advantage of her natural endowments. If I had hair like that, and skin, and features. . . . Think of the people I meet. Millionaires. But what difference does it make?

You still look pretty good, Nat grunted.

Francie thanked him without enthusiasm, adding: Forty years old. . . as Rosabel got up. I looked at her hard to see what Francie meant.

Hair wouldn't make much difference, I thought, if Rosabel didn't have such a big ass. I had noticed that older women usually had big asses. Francie too, though the rest of her was slender. Slacks didn't suit either of them. My mother always wore something to half-cover her ass. This time she wore a blue sweater with silky hairs swaying.

Why don't you take off your sweater? Francie asked.

Because it's mine and I don't want you to claim it, Rosabel said from inside the refrigerator door.

Hers like heck, Francie commented to Nat. She never used the real curse words with which my mother shrank the atmosphere at home.

You two girls ought to stop fighting about that sweater, Nat said in his soft, exasperated voice.

Francie, sidling up to Nat, twisted her body a little as she held her hands out with the fingers spread, and batted her eyes: Now Nat, you know you love both of us. Why don't you get Rosabel a sweater so she'll give mine back to me?

The refrigerator door banged shut and my mother came listing back to the room, a cold lamb chop in her hand. —I'm on a diet, so I get hungry, she said to the chop, turning it around daintily.

And by the way, she added, her small mouth gleaming with fat, the sweater is mine, Dad bought it.

For me! Francie exclaimed. —He promised it to me the last time I went to his office. What I really wanted was a car because I heard he bought his wife one. He never bought me a car. But I couldn't bring myself to say it. I only talked about the clothes I'd seen that day. Especially the imported sweater. He just looked out the window. Finally, I cried. He never could stand me crying. So he said: O.K. The sweater.

You go to his office? Nat asked.

Why not? He invites me out sometimes for a drink or dinner. We're friendly; I still get money from him. Any time he feels like it he can come back to me. He knows that. He's the only man I ever really . . . But he played around.

Yeah, said Nat. I know.

Dad delivered it to me, Rosabel asserted. You were off to Jamaica. He said I could keep it.

You're lying. Just like him.

Listen girls, said Nat, I'll buy you another.

Oh, in that case, Rosabel told Francie, you can have this thing. And she pulled it off as if she loathed it.

Francie clasped the sweater to her, adding: It has your perfume!

Rosabel went back to the refrigerator. I watched her butt swing like a buoy in a storm.

I told my grandmother the sweater looked great on her.

You're a doll! Francie grabbed me awkwardly; I didn't feel embraced. Her body seemed to have no substance. But I smiled, embarrassed. My mother saw the smile when she returned from the kitchen, with another chop. And though her voice was moderate, she frowned, which made me feel guilty. But it was Francie she accused:

Why are you always sneaking Hoagy away from me?

You're glad to get rid of him.

I was out of the house. You always come when I'm out, when you know I'll be out. Like a thief. In the afternoon.

Well, who was there to ask? Am I his grandmother or not? What about the time in St. Thomas when you kidnapped him from the hotel playground? I was frantic. You could have asked.

Me ask? I'm his mother.

I had the police out . . . Francie appealed to Nat. He shrugged as usual.

Francie let out a sigh and stood up to view herself in the mirror, caressing the hairs of her sweater. Then she asked if anyone wanted coffee.

You'll make it? Nat asked. I thought you only ate in restaurants. Where'd you take lucky Hoagy tonight?

The Italian restaurant up the street. He had spaghetti. In every gourmet place it's either spaghetti or hamburger. I don't know why I bother. Except that I can't take the time to cook anymore. Even though I was a housewife for ten years.

Come to think of it, Rosabel said.

It broke your heart to live alone with me, didn't it? Francie asked, moving toward the kitchen.

While they were drinking coffee I went outside to look at the pool in the moonlight. I told them I had left some little boats out there. But I didn't think of boats when the warm air came twining over my arms and all the sweetness of invisible blossoms approached me. I wanted to get down on my belly and scurry beneath some bush.

Where are you? I thought.

Suddenly I heard the two women shriek at each other, and at the window their shadows reached out and seemed to merge. But I knew it only seemed that way.

Mine! I heard.

Mine!

The moon, fragmented over the pool, reminded me of Sylvia's hair, how it fell on her shoulders the day we took a glass-bottomed boat. We saw the miraculous fishes then, quick as impulse, curved and flowing, in all the illusory colors of their flight.

I said to her: I'll be a sea horse.

She said to me: We'll ride the sea together.

And her laughter sounded down the fluttering depths, and up to the silver-blue, white-birded sky.

Near the cactus bush a transparent shape. I lifted it and in the moon-light saw the emptied husk of the lizard. I thought: I shall slip inside and burrow into the night.

Then I hid it behind a stone.

. . . I have no one, no one, Francie moaned as I returned to the house. . . . Nobody cares what becomes of me. Except maybe Hoagy. . . . And she rushed to lay her wet, flaky face against mine, while my mother, indissoluble, linked her arm in Nat's.

They ushered me out with the smell of Francie's tears upon me, and at my neck the urgent: I'll leave it all to you, Hoagy, everything I've got . . .

. . . I'm not sure I want it, I answered silently, looking up at the night sky, pretending not to hear, as the door closed and my mother and Nat walked ahead to the car, and I halted once, looking upward again, at miracles yet to come.

THE WAY BACK

Shirley Ann Grau

THE beaches of the South Atlantic were behind them, and the swampy stretches and the neon-frosted motels. The ground turned sandy, and rose slightly; the open stretches filled with palmetto. Then the palmetto began to be dotted with thin black pine trunks. Eventually the palmetto disappeared and the slash pine came in long clean rows, each tree neatly tapped for its turpentine.

"Do you want me to drive?" she asked once during the morning. "I can if you're tired, if you want me to."

"I'm fine," he said. "With the roads this empty it's no strain."

The wordless morning hours slipped by. Neither of them spoke. The speedometer needle shivered at ninety, there was a steady clacking under the hood, a fluttering now and then as the light car held the road precariously.

She shifted in her seat, facing the window more squarely. This way, she thought, I can see how fast the trees pass. They go like blurs, I can't see any one tree. They're there but I can't see them. Like the scrub grasses on the side of the road—sage grass, shadow grass. I can see even less of them. When I look down I can't even see that there is anything there. Makes me dizzy. I'd rather look at the trees. The trunks are a black blur, and the rows are so even that when they pass it's like I'm watching a wheel spinning. At least with the trees I can see the tops, I can still make out the tops and they still look like trees, passing.

But I can't make out one individual single tree. They all go by as a mass, like the miles on the road, or the seconds on my watch. . . . And I can't remember—out of the last two days—I can't remember a single moment separately. All lumped together, all one, all blended and fused, the outlines confused by tiredness and lack of sleep. The colors all mixed. The sensations all mixed. And nothing clear. Not one memory clear. Not one thing I can reach back for and say: This was so, and this. Except maybe the sound of surf, pounding. Or was it surf? It could have been breathing. Yes, it could have been breathing. And the pound of water, white-crested water on the sand, that could have been the thump of a heart under the sheltering arches of ribs. And which was it? All blurred together. Like the weed and the rock and the chitin that surf grinds up, flings up in spume. All one, all mixed.

Abruptly they came out of the pine country and into the little flat patches of strawberry farms. Square tiny plots, still covered this time of year by strips of plastic.

"They haven't dared open them up yet," he said, "did you notice?"

"How can you see them going this fast?"

"Sorry. Did I scare you?" He slowed, the needle dropped to sixty, the blurs outside took shape and form.

"Not really. . . . You mean all those plastic sheets? This is only January, there's bound to be another frost or two, don't you think?"

"The coldest weather is still ahead of us," he said.

"When they're expecting a freeze do you suppose they put out smudge pots and old tires like they do in the orange groves around Lakeland?"

"I don't know," he said, "but I could find out if you're interested."

"I'm not interested. I just asked."

"That's a difference I don't understand." The blue eyes left the road, the light blue eyes with their strained nearsighted look.

"You really should put on your glasses," she said.

"I don't like them."

"They do make you look different. It's surprising how much. Like another person almost."

"People sometimes don't recognize me with glasses."

"Well," she said, "they're big and round and black and they're sort of all over your face."

"Makes a difference."

"Lots of things do, I suppose."

The two-lane road widened with an abrupt flash of yellow lights to a six-lane throughway. The jarring asphalt turned to smooth light concrete; the car's squeaks and jangles stopped.

"How nice this is," she said.

"Haven't you ever noticed how highways always get beautiful near the state capital?"

"No," she said, "I never paid any attention."

"You didn't? Well, in any state. Any one at all. You always come into the capital on a beautiful big highway. Doesn't matter what the rest of the country looks like, Tobacco Road or not—and you ought to see some of those turpentine workers back there a way—but the state goes and builds a billion dollar highway five miles out of the capital in all directions."

"Is that how far we are?" she asked. "Five miles?"

"No," he said, "I just picked a number. It's nearer twenty, I guess."

"Twenty miles is twenty minutes."

"Thirty or more. The traffic gets worse."

"So that's how long."

"I hate for it to end," he said, "I hate to have it end."

"Things do," she said.

"But this shouldn't."

"Shouldn't, but it does."

"I guess so."

"You know," she said, "I hate long goodbyes. I'd just as soon have it be done quickly and be finished."

"Would you? I'd rather have it last."

"I just hate goodbyes."

"Funny gal you are."

"It always takes so long to end things, and there isn't anything to say. I never know what to say."

"Don't you? I wouldn't think you'd have any trouble."

"I talked a lot last night, didn't I? I'm sorry, I shouldn't have."

"I like to listen to you. I like anything with you."

"Yes,'" she found herself staring at the shiny knobs of the radio. "I do too." The knobs began to pulse, to grow and shrink. She felt her own head nodding, back and forth toward them, in their rhythm, yo-yo on a string. She let it bob up and down a few times, then at the top of a swing, yanked back and broke the connection. When she looked at the radio again, she saw nothing but two shiny knobs, quite still. Ordinary pieces of unmoving metal.

The traffic got heavier. He swung around trucks sharply, the transmission slipping with a sharp knock. "Damn car. . . . See what I mean? About the traffic. Just a steady line of produce trucks. Look, those are hothouse strawberries."

"Going to market."

"Where else?"

She gave his shoulder a pat and slipped farther across the seat, until she leaned her back against the door. "I'd better sit over here then, if we're coming into town."

"I hate to have you do that."

"Somebody might see."

"Yes," he said. "I just hate to have you do it."

"You might as well be sensible."

"Yes. Look, you see this turn, where the road branches and there's just that concrete divider in the middle, see how it comes up quick when you're almost right on top of it?"

"It looks dangerous."

"Most dangerous spot on the road. I've seen car after car smash right there."

"I can see how the concrete is all chipped."

They were coming into town. There were businesses and tourist courts on each side of the highway, and now and then a shopping center: squat buildings in long rows with cars nuzzling their flat sides.

"Cars always look like beetles," she said.

"Only the VW's."

"No, all of them look like beetles to me when they're in the lots like that. Beetles on a log."

"How funny."

"Yes," she said, "isn't it?"

"Look now, are you sure you'll be all right driving back?"

"Three or four hours. Of course I will."

"I wish I could drive you."

"You can't."

"I know, but I don't like it."

"It's really all right."

The road ahead was a long sweep of concrete now, smooth, only dipping and banking slightly on the turns. Perfect and mechanical the way new roads are.

"It looks like tape from an adding machine," she said suddenly and laughed at herself.

"Why is that funny?"

"It isn't, I guess."

"I'll call you tomorrow."

"Yes, I hope so."

"I mean, it's all right in the morning?"

"My husband's plane won't get in before noon."

"I'll call you."

"I'll wait for it."

He left the road to turn down the gentle descending bank of a cloverleaf. The hazy small sun jumped from one side to the other.

"We parked your car right over there."

"Seems such a long time ago."

"It was only night before last."

"But it looks so different now," she said. "I couldn't have found it again."

"You can't really get lost in a city this small."

"Everything looks different in the daylight."

"Look," he said, "are you going to be able to find your way out of town?"

"I found my way in. Only got lost once and I asked at a gas station, wherever that was, and they told me the rest of the way."

"Now look," he said, "you'd better follow me out. I'll take you to the highway east, the one you want. And I'll take you down a way, until you see the signs. Big green overhead signs, you can't miss them. Then I turn off to the right and you go straight. That's the road home for you."

"Just follow you."

"Yes," he said. "It's simpler, I think."

When he pulled up next to her car, she had the keys ready in her hand. "Don't get out," she said. "I can shift the bag without any trouble. And if you stay in the car, people are less likely to see you."

She stepped out. He, ignoring her, got out too and moved the bag from the back seat. They stood between the two cars, sheltered by the open doors like small wings on each side. For a moment there was only the hiss of tires fifty yards away on the road, and a sharp far-off squeal of brakes. Then something tapped her hair, brushed her cheek. She jumped, twisting around behind her.

"An acorn," he said.

She glanced up, and saw the high arching oaks in two solemn lines through the parking area. "I didn't notice them the other night. But I guess I was too excited."

"They were there."

Another acorn fell, bounced from the car top. He caught it, with a quick sidewise sweep of the hand, the way a boy catches a fly. "You see?"

She took it, her fingers brushing his palm. "Yes," she said, "I see." His eyes took color from the sky, she decided. Now they were cloudy grey, not blue at all. She held out her hand. "Goodbye."

He took the hand, formally. "I'll call you. You just follow me and I'll take you to where you can see the signs."

She nodded and got into the car, quickly, not looking back, not looking at him. She started the motor, bouncing her foot up and down so that clouds of exhaust rose in the heavy wet air. Then she backed out quickly and followed him to the road.

His ears stick out, she thought. I never noticed that before. He looks like somebody else from the back. So different. But then he looks different with glasses too. And different from face to profile. Maybe all people look like that. Maybe I do. I wonder, now. I wonder if I do. He looks different in bed too, his face gets longer and thinner. And how could that be possible. . . .

There was traffic all around them now. Two cars in a stream of other cars. She followed more closely.

His car is a white car and so is mine, but there's another white car following me and I can see still another one in my side mirror. A world full of white cars—and how do you tell one from the other? How could I tell his from any other one, if I lost it now? What would be special about it? And there wouldn't be anything, would there?

She shifted her grip on the wheel and felt something in her left hand. The acorn. She had been holding it all this time. An ordinary acorn, brown and green and dusty looking. Nothing special about it either. But she held it. And settled back to driving the smooth straight car-speckled strip.

Then she saw the signs. Far-off yet. But there. The place where he would turn off. Where the way back began. Right there.

But in a way, the road back didn't go back at all. Nothing was where you left it. Nothing was the same.

Except maybe the signs, the green and white signs. Approaching now. And this part of her life was nearly over.

And now it was all over, she thought, could she say what it had been? Could she say what had happened? What had really happened.

Some time had passed. A day. Little more than one day. Less than two. A bit of time. Passing. The endless river. Passing.

And what else. What else on the surface of that river. Not much when you thought about it. Some whispers. Muscles contracting. Shudders. Spasmodic shudders, that tore and twisted and wracked. But the muscles through which they had run were smooth and quiet again and carried no memory of the sudden convulsive movements. No more than had the time they floated and wasted. Impulse and time alike. Gone.

And what was left. What was really left. Something back inside your head. Way back in your head, inside the shelter of the skull, hidden by the bone. Encircled by the grey cells, fed by the blood.

But it wasn't anything at all.

No more than the acorn she held in her left hand. The green and brown acorn that had happened to bounce off the roof of the car.

She looked at it again. Dusty thing. With the possibilities of an oak tree. How unlikely. From something like that.

The road signs were very close now. She could read them clearly. He had turned his signal light on and was looking in the mirror. She lifted one hand to show that she understood. It was the hand with the acorn.

Following the soft downward curve of the road, his car swung to the right. She kept straight on, following the rising concrete. An overpass. Of course. The two white cars were peeling off like planes. She glanced to her right once, answered a wave. And watched out of the tail of her eye until the other car disappeared.

I will not turn my head, she thought. And did not.

I will not look back, she thought. Not for anything. I will just drive.

Quite suddenly she had trouble seeing. The concrete of the road turned the same color as the sky. Sharp gray with prickles of bright metal like needles stuck in it. Stinging like salt water in her eyes.

Concrete shouldn't dazzle. Not like that. And ground and sky aren't the same. Why should they be the same color? The car ahead of her, it had been black just a moment ago. But it was gray now too, the shadowy hollow gray of a photograph negative. And that other car, she could see it though it wasn't in sight anymore, the car that had turned off the road, to go another way. Another way back.

All the gray colors. All the shiny hard gray colors. Earth and sky and car alike. And why did it happen like that?

She scrubbed at her eyes, and that helped. She blinked and shook her head. Now she could see the sides of the road clearly—the dusty straggly bushes, the scrubby grass. The hard gray light was fading. Colors came back, the sky was just a rain sky, the road was just concrete, cars were just full of people going some place.

She clenched her left hand over the acorn. Holding like that, she could feel the life inside it. Feel it move and twist against her flesh.

My own pulse, she thought. It's my own pulse I'm feeling. That's all.

But that doesn't matter either. Because one is as alive as the other. Life is the same in me as in anything else. Trees did come out of acorns, no matter how unlikely that seemed. An acorn was just a tree's way back into the ground. For another try. Another trip through.

One life or another. And what came out of sex now. Love maybe. But that wasn't as sure as a tree. Or maybe a tree was as unsure as love. One capsule life or another.

She opened her hand and looked at the acorn again. Dusty green and brown. Tree colors. And the colors of love? Not colors at all. Lights like fireworks and spasms like death and absolute silence afterwards. Just silence and nothing moving. Just silence. That was all. The tree was still in the acorn, and love hadn't grown either.

The highway climbed another overpass. Cars cut in front of her. She grabbed the wheel hastily, swerved. The acorn fell. For a minute her fist felt empty and cold. Then the flow of her own blood warmed the spot. All the long drive back alone, she sat and listened to the singing of her veins, the pumping of her heart and the steady rhythm of her blood.

And those sounds and movements of her body kept her from remembering: that kind of loneliness was the next thing to death.

JOANNA
Martha Lacy Hall

> So even the Lattimore children have to die.
> There was a time we thought we were all immortal.
> —From "Isabel," by Richmond Lattimore

A FEW great raindrops began to smack the dusty windshield. Virginia pressed her finger against the chrome button, but the windshield washer was empty, and the blades of the wiper groaned against the dry glass. She slowed down and squinted, trying to see through the brown arcs. *Oh, for a good shower.*

> Dr. Foster went to Gloster
> In a shower of rain.
> Stepped in a puddle
> Up to his middle
> And never went there again.

She looked in the rearview mirror to see what she looked like reciting childhood verse on her way to her sister's funeral. Dr. Foster was part of a shift into the past that began yesterday, almost the moment her brother called. As they talked, it was as though someone kept switching television from the evening news to an old movie.

"I have some sad news for you, Virginia. Joanna was found dead this morning," her brother began.

"Oh, no. What happened?"

Then she was only half hearing Richard. Her eyes were fixed on the folds of a rust-colored dish towel that lay at the edge of the sink, but she was seeing Joanna at sixteen, dressing herself up in old clothes in Mama's big linen closet, pushing her red hair under an old felt hat of Daddy's, turning herself into a hobo. Virginia had watched the transformation in wonderment. Ten years younger than Joanna, she believed Joanna could do anything. Everybody in town talked about her talents, her gleaming hair, her green eyes, green as winter rye, they said. She was always acting in plays, singing, dancing, playing the piano, painting. She carved Mozart's head out of a bar of Ivory soap and set it beside the metronome.

But that day Joanna slipped out of the house and around to the back door and knocked loudly. It was 1934 and tramps knocked often, poorly dressed jobless men, begging to earn a meal—rake some leaves, clean out the gutters, chop some wood.

Mama walked to the door, Virginia right behind her, trying not to giggle. Mama didn't recognize Joanna and told the tramp she'd warm him a plate of greens and corn bread left from dinner that he could eat on the back steps. Mama never turned anyone away, but if Daddy wasn't home, she wouldn't let a stranger in. No white, God-fearing southern lady would. When she turned to go into the kitchen, Joanna, still disguising her voice, came boldly into the house. Mama screamed and grabbed Virginia, sure that after all her years of warnings she and one of her four daughters were about to be "assaulted." Racing up the hall into the library, she slammed the door and jammed it with the little Victorian chair, all the time screaming hysterically. Beside her, Virginia was trying to be heard, "Mama, Mama, it's only Joanna!" And outside the door Joanna was about to die laughing and was shouting, rattling the knob against a carved rose on the chair's back, "Mama, it's just me. It's me, Mama."

Finally, Mama, incredulous, heard both her daughters, whereupon her fear changed to outrage, and she opened the door and slapped Joanna in the face, hard. She never forgave Joanna. Never could she laugh about it. It became a symbol of Joanna's wrongheadedness, just as her red hair, like Daddy's, symbolized her hot temper. Joanna was *a McCall, not a Leger.* It was true.

So when Brother paused, Virginia had to force herself to realize he had said that Joanna had been lying dead on her kitchen floor, knocked on her back by a massive coronary, a bag of groceries spilled around her. She had been dead four days. There would be graveside services—tomorrow, Sunday afternoon, at four.

"V.A.? Are you okay?"

"Yes. Yes. Of course. I'm just . . . so sorry. I'll be there. Suppose I meet you at Nelda's after noon." Now she was seeing Joanna lying there like a doll, arms and legs spread out, the red hair now white, the finger-nails that she once laughingly put bright green polish on, white. "I'll be there."

Hanging up, she turned to her husband. "Joanna's dead. Brother went to see why she didn't answer the phone. Found her on the kitchen floor. A 'massive coronary,' he said."

Stephen's face sagged. "Oh. I'm sorry. I liked Joanna."

Virginia looked away. She knew his chin was trembling. He did that since his stroke. It had been called a light stroke, but now, even a sentimental TV commercial caused his eyes to well up, and he would have to swallow if he tried to talk. Stephen had been fond of Joanna when she was young and gorgeous and full of fun and ideas—everybody had. But he hadn't seen her in years, ten maybe. Neither of them had. Joanna didn't like Virginia. It was a fact that took many years for Virginia to learn to live with. It had been more than a decade since she'd lain awake most of the night, thinking about what happened to Joanna to make her hostile to her whole family, not only Virginia. And when Virginia quit trying so hard to understand, acceptance came. Accepting meant leaving Joanna alone. That was all Joanna seemed to want, finally. Privacy. And bourbon. Virginia, living in New Orleans, could stay away.

Joanna married Kip Rankin when she was eighteen, virtually skipping the porch-swing segment of her social development. When Mama and Daddy had found out that she was serious about Kip, a good-natured senior at Ole Miss, who played saxophone and rode his huge roan horse right up to the gallery and pulled Joanna up behind his western saddle, they had thrown up their hands.

The pretense of cheer faltered early at the wedding. Miss Winnie Rankin broke into loud weeping and was comforted by, of all people, Mama, who startled even eight-year-old Virginia by saying, "Miss Winnie, look at it like I do. I'm not losing a daughter, I'm gaining a son." This precipitated a still noisier outcry from Miss Winnie, who was full of proverbs. "Your daughter's your daughter all her life. Your son's your son till he gets him a wife," she said. As Joanna cut the cake she said, "There's no fool like an old fool." Virginia figured she meant Miss Winnie, who looked old. Daddy walked out on the gallery and stared out across the lawn, where Mama had set up tables for lunch.

When Joanna's free-wheeling ebullience persisted after she was "adult" and married to Kip, who went next door to kiss his mother goodnight every night until she died just before he did, old heads nodded over Joanna and watched impatiently for her to settle down to behavior prescribed for young wives in Sweet Bay. But she continued, as a married woman, to wear short-shorts and bounce with the rhythm of her baby grand as she beat out jazz and swing. She chain smoked, learned to drink bourbon with Kip and his friends, and developed a laugh you could hear a block away. She was just too much, they sighed. She was also as sensitive as a fresh wound. Nobody ever seemed to catch onto that. If the gypsies, who used to camp every spring out in the Heaslip's pasture, had stolen Joanna, what a life she could have lived.

Joanna's laughter lost its mirth. At thirty she was an alcoholic, by forty she was an eccentric recluse, and at fifty a widow. She would have been sixty had she lived another month. For years she had been one of the town's many drunks. She had locked her doors, literally, against her family, even her own grown sons. She locked Mama out—Mama now long dead of her own heart attack. She locked Daddy out, who lived twenty years a widower, but not before she made off with some of his favorite possessions—furniture, odds and ends. He had disinherited her before he put out his last Pall Mall and hacked his final emphysemic cough. He spent his last decade in bitterness, glad to be steadfastly furious enough with this child to "cut her out—a disgrace to us all." As he railed against Joanna he never evoked one recognizable image of her. She had become a monster, foreign, his fascinating, redheaded McCall-child.

Well, now she was dead. Virginia walked around Stephen, to the French doors, and stared out across the patio to the water dripping off a piece of slate into the fish pool, making rings that bumped into lily pads. Boomer, the Australian shepherd, trotted up to the door, something in his mouth.

"Stephen! Boomer's got a rat in his mouth. Oh, my God." A black leg and a long hairless tail hung out of the big dog's mouth. "Oh, God." She ran to the bathroom and slammed the door. When she came out, Boomer had disappeared. Now she began to fear that the rat might have been poisoned, and she dialed the vet. No answer. After half an hour Boomer came back onto the patio, apparently in good health, his great eyes, as always, disconcertingly humble, no evidence of the wretched sight. Virginia was fond of the dog, but now she could not bear to get near him.

A call came from her sister in Asheville, who had just received her call from Brother. Marjorie was weeping. "I'm so far away. Oh, poor Joanna.

Oh I know. I know. We couldn't help her. We all tried. Oh, how poor Mother tried. Virginia! Four days! Do you realize . . . ? Virginia, honey, please explain to everyone why I'm not there. Tell May Ella and F. O. and Helen Sanders, all of them, tell them that I simply cannot make the trip. I'm no longer young. Even if I'd been able to go, I've been caught without a decent black dress for a funeral in the family, I mean. Explain . . . I'll probably die way up here and nobody will find me. No. That will never happen to me. I have too many friends. I wonder if Nelda will rise from her couch and attend her own sister's funeral. I'll bet she won't. She'll have some excuse—and right there only ten miles away." Nelda was the eldest sister.

"Probably not. I'm going directly to her house. If she and Frank can go, we'll all go together. Don't worry about that. And I'll speak to people for you. But remember, I haven't been up there for years. I might not know them. They might not know me." After she hung up, she and Stephen decided that she should drive up to Mississippi alone.

Virginia went about her business all that day. They were having yard-work done, and she and Stephen were in and out of the house supervising the man who was putting in a new border of liriope, moving crape myrtles along the driveway, trimming the fig vine—all established from cuttings and roots from Mama and Daddy's place. She sat down on the brick wall by the fish pool, watching the fantails of the goldfish, waving like gossamer on a soft breeze, and thought of Daddy's fish pool under the big magnolia in the front yard. His fish were enormous and his lilies and hyacinths fragrant. When grandchildren began coming, he covered the pool with a framework of chickenwire. The pool was shallow, but Mama frequently reminded him of the Cable's child who "drowned at two years while playing in a galvanized washtub in the backyard. It only takes a teacupful." She usually added a word about the dangers of blisters on the heel, President Coolidge's son having died from an infected blister after a game of tennis. Both of these sad events belonged to history, but they were sufficiently horrifying examples of carelessness for Mama, who went to extremes to shield her children.

Joanna had malaria all during the summer that she was fifteen. A cousin, who was going away to college, gave her four big scrapbooks of movie stars—pasted pictures of thin women with narrow arched eyebrows, dressed in long satin gowns edged with great rolls of white fur. The men leaned on polo mallets or gold-headed walking canes. Joanna adored the books and she collected more pictures and more books. She pasted her pictures with flour paste that she stirred up in a teacup. Sometimes she would leave the cup on her windowsill until the paste soured and gray mold formed on it. She forbade Virginia ever to take the scrapbooks out of the window seat in her room. Virginia did sneak in and raise the lid and open the top book to study the sepia faces—Billie Dove, Francis X. Bushman, Mary Pickford, Douglas Fairbanks, Vilma Banky. But she never looked for long, fearing that Joanna would catch her. Maybe Joanna would have liked her better if she'd found out, and they could have had a big fight and become friends.

Joanna never had another childhood illness that Virginia could re-member, but she *cheated Death* one afternoon out in Buckley's pasture. A barnstorming pilot was taking passengers up for rides in his little Waco, and Daddy took Joanna to the pasture and paid two dollars for her to have a thrilling ten-minute ride. When the two of them came home, with Joanna's red hair blown six ways to Sunday, Mama accused Daddy of risking one of his children's lives. Joanna, she said, had simply *cheated Death*. They were two of a kind, McCalls through and through. Daddy called Mama an "anachronism" and returned to his office in a huff. But Joanna didn't seem to mind. Virginia asked her what it was like, and Joanna said, "Do you mean flying? Or cheating Death?" Virginia had thought they were one and the same.

Soon after Virginia crossed the state line she began to see the green Mississippi hills rolling off before her, a pleasant sight after the unrelieved flatlands of south Louisiana. On toward Jackson the interstate lay like white straps binding the hills ahead, too tightly, slicing through red clay that reminded Virginia of raw beef. How could the trees be so green in a drought? She looked for a pond or a creek—water was her metaphor. Without it she could hardly express herself.

At Pontchatoula she drove off the exit and into a service station where an attendant hosed off her windshield and polished it with brown paper towels. Virginia thanked the man.

Back on the interstate she drove on northward, past her hometown, where her dead sister's house now sat empty, and past the used car lot where the old family home had been—a big house that burgeoned to its wraparound galleries, for decades, with the explosive clutch of siblings, more confusion than comfort to their parents. And past Brother's, where he now monitored his poor health with his third wife in his in-law's old home, high-backed rockers lined up on the porch, surely still slip-covered in tan Indianhead piped in green. The interstate took her around it all.

On to the next town, and Nelda's house with Nelda's French bedroom upstairs, and Frank's gold coin collection in a safe "on the premises," so Marjorie said. Nelda and Frank had recently returned from a business trip to Switzerland.

Frank didn't hear Virginia's ring at the iron-grilled door from the terrace, so she let herself into the back sitting room. A black man sat on a straight chair near the door. He looked at her, expressionless. But Frank sprang to his feet, apologizing. He'd been watching a football game from a dark blue leather sofa. Two identical sofas faced each other across the big room—his and hers. "Virginia, I didn't expect you this soon." He seemed unaware of the man in the chair. She looked back at the man who ignored her and stared at the TV.

"I thought I'd better come on if we're to go by the funeral home. Is Nelda . . ."

"Nelda isn't going. She's feeling bad. There is no—ah—visiting at the funeral home, only the graveside service. You and I will go to the cemetery and meet Joanna's boys and their families. They all got in last night. They're sleeping at the Holiday Inn. They couldn't stay at. . . . I'd have had them all come here, but you know how it is with Nelda not feeling well. Richard took to his bed after he called you and Marjorie. I think all this just got him down too much, and his blood pressure ran up. He and Joanna . . . you know . . . he called a while ago." Frank's elliptical fragments seemed appropriate.

"I see."

Virginia's thoughts went back to Joanna's sons, men with children of their own. Joanna had been a devoted and loving mother to them when they were small. She told them wonderful tales at bedtime—fantastic serials that went on night after night. The boys had adored her. Which was worse, Virginia wondered, a loving drunken mother or a shrewish drunken mother. You could just hate a shrew but not a laughing den mother stumbling about among the Cub Scouts serving fantastic brownies.

Did Joanna ever write her children's stories down? She painted in oils almost until the time of her death. Virginia knew that. And when Joanna was a young teenager she ordered boxes of printed Christmas cards and handpainted them in watercolor. Ringing doorbells up and down the street she sold all her boxes in an afternoon and made eighteen dollars. A child capable of earning eighteen dollars during the Depression was not ordinary. Virginia could see Joanna now, setting up the card table in front of the fireplace in her room and arranging the paints, a Ball jar of water, and the dull little cards that Joanna brought to life as she filled in the red on holly berries and Santa suits and green on holly leaves and Christmas trees.

While Frank took Virginia's handbag, a black woman came downstairs and left with the man. Frank said to them, "Thank y'all for coming." He walked into the kitchen and announced Virginia's presence on the intercom. Nelda's familiar, young-sounding voice came back: "Oh, she's already here? Tell her to give me a few minutes."

Virginia sat down in a Chinese Chippendale chair that didn't hit her back right.

"Drink? How about a martini—want vodka and tonic? It's so hot outside." He smiled his peculiar smile. He had a tic in his right cheek that Virginia had noticed since she was a child.

"No, nothing." Virginia was thinking that Nelda would look her over and find her still strangely careless of fashion. She smiled. That had once depressed her. Soon she was summoned upstairs. Nelda was propped up in her French, hand-decorated bed, frothy white eyelet-edged sheet and pillowcases framing her frail person. She wore aqua satin pajamas and robe. Her white face and short hair style were all the whiter for her large dark-rimmed spectacles. Diamonds twinkled on her ears and hands and the pendant on her chest. Stephen couldn't abide Nelda. "Prima donna," he'd said, and, "They're all prima donnas." Meaning her whole family. That had depressed her, too.

She walked to the bedside and kissed Nelda's very soft cheek. Nelda had no visible eyebrows. She spoke words of welcome, adding, "You haven't been here in three years." Virginia wondered if she were accusing her of neglect. Her last visit, about a year before, had been an obvious intrusion.

"Francis is much more upset over this than I am. It came as no surprise to me. I've been expecting it for years. Joanna withdrew from family and all society years ago. I knew that sooner or later this very thing would happen. Now it has. The last time she came here—two or three years

ago—she went straight to the bar—it was ten o'clock in the morning—
and she revisited it several times before she left—before noon. She didn't
seem intoxicated. I've been interviewing a woman—a maid."

"Oh. Are you going to hire her?"

"I am not."

"Oh?"

"When they walk in here like that—I've been through all this too
often—they're all ruined. The Roosevelts started it. You can't remember
all that."

"Nor the defeat of the Armada. Nor Appomattox."

"What?"

"Has Hattie quit?"

"No, but she can't be here every hour of every day. I've got to have
somebody to fill in, Virginia. I'm an invalid. I seldom go downstairs.
Nobody realizes how bad my health is. Those ridiculous doctors in
Houston and New Orleans, all the rest, they refuse to listen to me. What
are those tests? Nothing. Absolutely nothing. Francis traipses from clinic
to clinic with me, but he doesn't know how bad I feel—or care."

Frank entered with a large silver tray and put it on the coffee table
before the oyster white moiré sofa where Virginia sat. On the tray were
two Madeira tea napkins, pimento-cheese sandwiches on Spode plates,
and two silver tumblers filled with ice and Coke. He smiled and murmured something and went back downstairs. Soon he returned with a
plate and set it on a white wicker bed tray for Nelda. Virginia tried to
imagine him slapping Nelda's face. Marjorie claimed she saw him do it
one night in Antoine's. Virginia looked at him and said, "Frank?"

"Hmm?"

"Did you make this pimento cheese? It's great." She wondered what
he'd have said if she'd said, "You remind me of a maitre d'," or, "a butler."

"I made it. Yeah. But I didn't think it was so good."

"It's delicious. I make it in my Cuisinart. Do you?"

"What is a Cuisinart?" asked Nelda.

"A food processor," said Virginia.

"A what? Oh—I don't know about that. Do we have one, Francis? I'm
sure we do since you can't resist any fad or gadget. I never go in the
kitchen—haven't been to a grocery store in ten years."

"Who shops?"

"Hattie. Or Francis."

"Well, it is depressing. You're better out of it," Virginia conceded.

"Yeah," said Frank. "V.A., have I given you my gumbo recipe? Did I ever send you a copy?"

"With the instructions to take a drink between steps? After the roux . . ."

"Yeah—well," he laughed, "I don't make a roux, you know."

"Oh, that's right. I remember now. I'll have to watch you make it sometime. I make a dark roux first, then turn it down and sauté the chopped green stuff in it."

"Yours is probably better. I just use a lot of tomatoes and stir in some thickening."

"Well, I seldom use tomato. I make a really dark bottom-of-the-bayou gumbo—lots of okra—whole baby okra."

"Francis, why don't you go on downstairs so Virginia and I can visit. You can visit with her at the cemetery."

Frank picked up the trays. "I'll go get dressed, and maybe I can see the rest of the Saints game. They're getting clobbered, as usual."

Nelda talked dispassionately of Joanna. Virginia listened, with one ear as Mama used to say, but she was thinking her own thoughts, scarcely hearing Nelda who was saying that Joanna lay in a plastic bag, unembalmable.

Virginia thought of the rich green Asian groundcover that the man was spreading about the beds in her own yard, about the squared box-woods he trimmed with his hand clippers, though she'd offered her electric ones. He spoke only Sicilian, so he demonstrated his contempt for electric shears by breaking off a woody sprig of box and chewing at it with his teeth till it was splayed out like an old paint brush. He held it out, and Virginia got the message, though his twenty-year-old daughter, who worked with him, laughed and translated. Virginia thought of Boomer at the French doors, swallowing the vile rat. Quickly she moved her thoughts on to the azalea bed across the backyard, flowering shrubs now cut free of strangling honeysuckle by the man and his daughter.

When Joanna was eleven she boarded the Illinois Central's Number Five one morning and rode forty miles northward to Claybrook for a visit with Mama's sister and her son, Junius. Mama's descriptions of Joanna's departure in navy pleated skirt, white middy blouse, thick red braids tied with navy ribbons, were so vivid that Virginia fancied she could remember going down to the train station with her. Maybe she had been there. Joanna took with her a *Delineator* magazine in which were pressed many bright tissue linings she had saved from Christmas card envelopes. She arrived safely in Claybrook and was driven to Aunt Virginia's white antebellum Greek Revival far out on Chattahoochie Avenue.

That night she and Junius made trains from shoeboxes strung together. Junius had saved boxes for her visit, and they pasted Joanna's colored papers over the square windows and fastened candle stubs in the boxes. They pulled their long, glowing train up and down the front walk until Aunt Virginia made them come in. Then they pulled the train up and down the length of a storeroom on the second floor. After the family had gone to bed, fire roared out of the storeroom, and Aunt Virginia, Junius, and Joanna escaped down a sturdy rose trellis. That day Mama and Daddy drove up the gravel highway to Claybrook to fetch Joanna. Whatever traumas resulted were unknown to Virginia. The family seldom talked about the fire. Aunt Virginia's husband, Junius, Sr., who didn't live at home, quickly built a fine ugly red brick house that had lights in the closets and sparkling glass doorknobs.

Nelda got out of bed and showed Virginia four new pairs of pumps she'd ordered from Neiman-Marcus—white, rust, bone, black. They were still in the boxes—each pump wrapped in tissue.

"Hmmm. They're beautiful." They were 5-1/2 AAAAAs.

Nelda's pale blue room had four large closets with double sliding doors. One door was open slightly, revealing three mink coats, of different lengths.

"Virginia, Francis is a very rich man. But he's stingy. I get the same allowance I got ten years ago."

"That must be tough. When the cost of food is so inflated."

"Oh, I don't pay for the food."

Virginia went into the dressing room and combed her hair, touched her mouth with lipstick. Nelda's lipstick was scarlet, like always. Her heavy silver dresser things lay in perfect order, with other articles of Waterford, Lenox.

Frank was immaculate in a cream suit when Virginia went downstairs. He looked handsome. It was hard to believe that he was nearly seventy. They went to the cemetery in Frank's Mercedes. He drove down the interstate, very fast. Virginia wished he would slow down. He was talking animatedly, boyishly, complimenting her on her career, her perfume— said he was proud of her. She thanked him, surprised.

"Oh, damn," he said. "I've passed the turn-off."

"Just get off at the next exit—the old Maysburg Road—and go back up on the old highway." How easily she remembered.

"Okay. That's right. No problem." And he went on chatting as though he were enjoying her company. He didn't talk about Joanna.

Then they were driving up the little curving hill to the old cemetery. Virginia was startled. She had not imagined the scene. Cars lined the road on both sides. A large crowd half circled a green funeral canopy. The Cadillac hearse looked absurd parked nearby. Virginia realized now that Joanna was to be buried across the road in the "new part" next to Kip, and not in the large plot under the holly in the old section, where their parents were buried.

For the first time, she felt a rush of emotions, too many, too fast to be sorted out. She could only think that she was not thinking clearly. *Joanna, what happened?* Frank parked as near to the canopy as possible. She waited for him to open the door. She was back where men opened doors, invariably. She took his cream elbow and said, "Let's just go sit on the back row of the chairs. I'm afraid I won't be able to remember names. . . . It's been so long. . . ."

"All right."

She sat down facing the bronze coffin with its blanket of red roses. Red! Red McCall. Joanna had been called that in high school. Mama was horrified and forbade it. She also put her foot down about Jo. And V.A. for Virginia. No nicknames. Virginia looked away, to the west, toward the tall holly that shaded the McCall His-and-Her granite stone, and back, into the face of a man she had grown up with. She stood up quickly and went to meet him, and then many old friends came to her and spoke kindly—very kindly. She recognized girlhood friends of Joanna, and some of her own. One stout matron, every mahogany-veneered hair in place, embraced her and said, "Virginia, you don't remember me, but I'm Carolyn Best—I was Carolyn Carr. It's been what? Twenty years?"

"Of course. Carolyn." Carolyn had told her there was no Santa Claus one fall afternoon as they played dolls on the back porch.

A paunchy bald man—Jim Ray Rollins. He'd taken her paste brush on their first day at school, and the teacher, her first cousin, couldn't "show favoritism" by retrieving Virginia's brush. She'd heard Jim Ray was president of his dad's bank now, and she had imagined that lower lip coming forward as he held somebody's money in his pudgy hand, above his shoulder, saying, "You can't have this. It's mine." When he took her hand she discovered three of his fingers were missing.

Then Joanna's sons and their wives and children were under the canopy with her. Greetings and embraces were hasty, for one of the two ministers began reading passages from the Bible. "In My Father's house are many mansions. If it were not so, I would have told you. . . ." A favorite passage of their mother's. Virginia had never even seen either of the ministers. They wore dark suits and vests despite the sweltering heat, and they took turns reading verses from their Bibles. There was no eulogy—not a word about Joanna. Virginia sighed carefully. She felt miserable and sad. She had thought the McCalls were such a family! That she was uniquely lucky to have three grown sisters: tall, vivid, adored. She had to be told after she was grown that Joanna resented her for displacing her as the baby of the family. Sibling rivalry. The cliché had sounded so silly to her. It still did. The red roses were swimming. Everything was.

The heat bore down on the green canopy. The heavy, humid air was becoming unbearably oppressive, and Virginia could hardly breathe. Her cover of sturdy calm and nostalgia had begun to fall from her like a heavy garment, and the heat forced the sickening reality against her. *Four days, Virginia. Four days. Oh, my God, Joanna.* She lowered her head and took shallow breaths of terrible air, flavored faintly with the familiar scents rising from her own breast.

She could not now lift her eyes to the coffin and the red roses, Red McCall's coffin stinking in the hot Mississippi sun on a Sunday afternoon in the new part of the cemetery that had no marble angels, when everyone should be at home singing around the piano under the ceiling fan in the old house. Her hand was stuck to the dark blue leather of her handbag.

One of the ministers was saying *amen.* It was done. She looked at her watch. They had been there fifteen minutes. As they rose from their chairs a sudden rain began to drum on the canvas. The back half of the crowd ran to the parked cars. The front half tried to crowd under the canopy. Some of the people began to hug her and remind her of who they were. Then Frank took her arm, and a man from the funeral home sheltered them under his big black umbrella to Frank's car.

Going home, Frank drove through the little town. He drove past the old homeplace, now lined with a skimpy row of used cars that sat where the backyard had begun. The big live oak with its gnarled play-house roots that spread to the street's edge was gone, and the magnolia, the chinaberry by the south porch where she had climbed and sat and dreamed, and the pecans and the figs and crabapples down at the back. The old Wheeler house, next door, still stood, humiliated, like a once-beautiful woman painted grotesquely for whoring, signs nailed to its gallery columns, all the sweet bays and magnolias gone. Frank didn't seem to notice where they were. Probably he passed this way often.

"Were many people there?" asked Nelda, when Virginia returned to the ice blue room. "Jessie McPherson?"

"Yes. She was there."

"Corinne Cooper? Helen Sanders?"

"Yes."

She called more names. "What was it like?" She held her cigarette vertically before her eyes, like a pencil.

"It was over quickly," said Virginia.

Driving home, Virginia passed the turnoff to the curving old Cata-mawa road, where, before they were married, she and Stephen used to take Sunday afternoon drives under the moss-hung trees. He would stop occasionally, and they would kiss. The road led to a convent where several of her Catholic friends had attended school. She smiled. They had all cursed like sailors, fascinatingly, and they had said they learned how from the nuns. She looked ahead, down the interstate lowering itself out of the gentle hills of Mississippi.

QUINCY

Jefferson Humphries

M RS. Elbert was driving the yard-
man home. It was midday and the sky was a pale blue so bright it stung
her eyes and made her squint and blink. In the rearview mirror of the old
white Chrysler she saw her brother Quincy, looking small and drawn and
bright pink and as if lightning had struck him and left everything intact
except his brain. The sight of him pulled her spirits down and seemed to
drag them through the red clay ditches on the sides of the road. He was
like a crime she suddenly remembered having committed, a black cancer
on her soul which could never be lifted. The thought of him subtly and
persistently tainted her every pleasure like a thimbleful of Ennis' acrid
sweat baked into a cake. She could not let herself despise Quincy because
after all it was not his fault he was eighty-eight years old and had lost his
sense. She was a Presbyterian and he was a burden God had visited on
her, not to test her strength and her virtue but to prove them. She
sometimes told herself it would have been better to live in a shack like
Ennis and have it fixed up nice and pleasant like some Negroes—Viney
for instance who cooked for them and who was white in everything but
her skin, who was clean and did not sweat—than to have been born a
Clanton and grown up in a lovely house in a blue-blooded family with
other blue-blooded people for friends and have been sent to college and
elected to Phi Beta Kappa and married a blue-blooded man and had two
blue-blooded daughters who had married rich if not blue-blooded doctors
and lived in big houses, one in Savannah, Georgia, and the other in
Alexandria, Virginia, and still have had to put up with Quincy. But she
knew having had such privileges and having been blessed so meant that
God favored her and had raised her up high so she could bear great
burdens and suffer nobly and bring virtue to the community. God raised
people to bear crosses and her cross was as heavy as several of anybody

else's. God had raised her up so she could suffer greater burdens and reap a greater reward when the time came.

She reached one long thin arm and adjusted the rearview mirror so that she could see herself. She had been a beautiful baby and a beautiful child and a beautiful young woman and a beautiful middle-aged woman and now she looked in the mirror and remembered having thought in her youth that beauty and old age were incompatible. But she was sure she came nearer beauty than any other woman her age she knew of, though she had watched with alarm her slender figure grow brittle and bony and the curves in her body turn to sharp and abrupt angles. God had never seen fit to make her fat, and for this she was grateful. Most of her friends had let themselves go and had been punished for it by getting fat. Fat was repugnant to her in very much the same way Quincy was repugnant to her. She was grateful that God had not deemed it necessary to visit that on her among her other heavy burdens. Quincy was eighty-eight years old and didn't know his own name. He didn't know the difference between morning and afternoon, and he scarcely knew the difference between day and night. If there was anybody who *ought* to go on and die, it was Quincy. But Quincy seemed impervious to time. Even now he sat, small, plump, and rubicund on the back seat, as nimble as a frog and with about as much sense as one, she thought to herself. If there was anybody who *needed* to be dead, it was Quincy. He had been a successful lawyer in New York but he had never married, and when he retired he had had no one to take care of him but their mother, with whom he had moved in. For seven years Quincy's retirement had not been easy. He had done nothing but take care of their mother, who in her old age had lost her mind as well. She hadn't known where she was. In the summer she would take up the notion that they had sent her to "Hiwayer" to get rid of her, and it had been impossible to convince her of how absurd this was. None of them had ever been to Hawaii or ever had any desire to go there or to send her or anybody else there. The only reason she had known it existed was because of some program she looked at on television which she called "Hiwayer Five." Mrs. Elbert thought the real name of the thing was "Hawaii Five-O." Quincy still looked at it. The old moron would sit in front of the television for hours at a time in one of the moth-eaten, narrow-lapelled, baggy suits and the inch-wide ties which he always wore. She had tried to tell him people didn't dress like that anymore when she had first come back and he had still had some sense, but now he was impervious to all suggestions. His hardheadedness was probably the reason God had punished him by making him into a moron. He would sit in front of the television and stare at it as if he had died there sometime before with his eyes open. She did not look at television, excepting the news and ballet and Shakespeare and other culturally enriching or current events programs. Mrs. Elbert was an intellectual. She was president of a study club and vice-president of the Presbyterian women's guild and had served two terms as president of the local historical society. She felt that if God had given you a good mind it was your Christian duty to cultivate it and do the best you could with it and not look at trash on the television. She had no doubt that among the first people God made to suffer for what they had done would be those responsible for the trash they showed on television. Immoral trash. And those responsible for the trash books they sold in the drugstore, which had pictures of practically naked men and women on them, and the films they showed, even on the television where little children could see, the ones she had happened to glimpse out of the corner of her eye at night when she was reading the Bible and happened to be passing by Quincy's television—it was impossible not to see it as the door to her room faced his and the television screen was situated squarely in the center of the door frame as one looked into Quincy's room from hers—why, they showed people stripped down to possible and doing things that made her blush and feel so weak she had to sit down on the end of her bed (from which the television screen remained visible, so that small figures moving in it reached out and jerked her gaze against its will in their direction, and even if they hadn't, Quincy turned the volume up so loud you could hear the thing anywhere in the house just like you were standing in front of it). They showed that *on television*, where children could see it all over the United States, and she knew it couldn't hold a candle to the things they showed in the movie houses and about which she had read in the paper. She had seen ads for movies with titles such as *Hot Nurses*, *Teen Lust*, *Hot Lip Hayride*, and there would be pictures of a man and a woman stripped down to possible locked in torrid embraces, or of a large-breasted, common-looking girl with her tongue sticking out. These ads made her blush and feel weak so that she had to sit down on the end of her bed. It was a shame, what passed for progress. The world had been a far better place when she was a girl.

She squinted out at the shacks they were passing. One yard was full of little nigger children of various sizes and shades and most of them were practically naked, playing in puddles of rainwater that had collected in the yard, bare earth save a few mangy patches of weeds and some chickens. There was a yellow girl standing in the doorway with her stomach swelled out, pregnant. Mrs. Elbert thought the girl was probably not even married. Viney, the cook, had told her that the colored mothers told their daughters not to use birth control, that the white people had devised birth control in order to gradually extinguish the Negro race. Why, you couldn't even try to help them but what they came up with some ignorant misunderstanding of it.

"Who was that colored girl, Ennis?" she asked.

"What you say, Miss Honey?" he replied.

The Negroes had called her Miss Honey since she had been a little girl. It was a link with her distant and televisionless childhood and made her feel young and pure and beautiful to hear herself so called by a Negro. It made her burden feel easier to bear.

"I said, do you know who that colored girl was we just passed, with all those children?"

The black idiot turned with an idiotic permanent half-grin on his face and looked out the back of the car. "Yebm," he said, "that's Tee Esther McAlpine."

"Who?" muttered Quincy absently. He didn't know where he was.

"He said it's a woman named Tee Esther McAlpine, honey," she shrieked at him. She always spoke in clearly enunciated tones and more loudly than most people; this, she had learned early in her life, was the way to attract people's attention. You had only to say interesting, cheerful, pleasant things in a clearly enunciated, pleasant, cheerful tone and people would listen to you. She was an accomplished public speaker and had given more programs at historical society meetings and study club meetings than anyone else. When speaking to Quincy, however, she raised her voice to a *cheerful*, ear-splitting shriek, as if making him regain his sense was only a matter of sufficient decibels.

"A woman?" he muttered to himself. "I didn't see any woman."

"Yebm. She ain been live there but a mont. She been run off her old place."

"Run off? What for, Ennis?"

"Dey said the man she live with run her off. Said she were sleeping roun the neighborhood and he wadn't gon live wid no woman he didn't know whose her churren was."

"Well, he was just exactly right," she said. "I don't blame him a bit." There was nothing about anybody in town that Ennis didn't know. He asked so many questions of her that sometimes she wanted to lie down and cry. Sometimes she felt like picking up something heavy and hitting him with it if he asked another question. Colored people had been more intelligent and known how to behave themselves better when she had been a girl. Ennis was what came of giving them all that welfare and food stamps and what all. Why, they'd passed a law in Washington that she had to pay Ennis—idiot Ennis—the minimum wage! It was absurd. And that was not all. She had to pay Social Security to the government for him. So that Ennis could draw Social Security. And all he would do with it would be to go buy some cheap wine and get too drunk to do any work for her or any of the other white people who had given the government the money so it could give it to black idiots like Ennis. That was all the government did, take money away from the nice people who could have done something with it and give it to the idiotic ones who didn't know what to do with it and weren't willing to work for it. Every week she had to figure out how much Social Security tax to send the government. It was complicated arithmetic and gave her the headache. But she did not really mind this. What she really minded was that Ennis would ask you anything and ask you *for* almost anything. Before Viney arrived in the morning, she had to fix Ennis' coffee. This morning while he drank his coffee she had showed him some photographs of her with her daughter and grandchildren in Savannah and he had, to her great chagrin, insisted on taking each picture in his filthy hands and holding it three inches from his grimy face and breathing his whiskey breath on it—Ennis always smelled like whiskey and did not pay the slightest attention to the *people* in the pictures but asked every conceivable question about the clothes they had on and about the objects in the background. He wanted to know where everything had come from, how it had been made, and what they were going to do with it. There was no point in explaining the futility, much less the rudeness, of these questions to him. He did not think like white people and could not be made to. But Quincy was even worse than Ennis because he didn't know where he was. He would run away sometimes and walk through town in his baggy, moth-eaten suit introducing himself and telling people who had known him for forty years that he had just moved here from New York City and didn't know anybody. One morning he had come in her room and said he wanted to pay his bill, as if she ran a hotel. Another morning before she had even dressed or fixed her hair he came in and asked if they served breakfast in this place. Once when they were showing company to the door he had asked her where she was going and she had shrieked at him that she was not going anywhere, that she was his sister and lived there. He could be destructive. One day Ennis had not shown up for work and Quincy took it upon himself to trim the shrubs. He went directly to Mrs. Elbert's prize gardenia bush and amputated all its fine long branches at the very moment when they were heaviest with delicate flowers, so white and sweetly redolent of Mrs. Elbert's youth. Mrs. Elbert prized the bush because it reminded her of a much larger one which had grown in their parents' yard, not a gardenia but one with flowers of even finer hue and scent. When she had seen the strewn limp branches with their blooms already turning brown in the heat, Mrs. Elbert had cried bitter tears. She had looked heavenward through the water in her eyes and prayed for patience. Another time Quincy had come in her room at night and said he thought it was only fair that she be told that he was an old man and had had several operations and could not be expected to be any sort of a husband to her. This made her blush and feel weak so that she had had to sit down on the end of her bed. He was even worse than their mother had been before she died, which was before Mrs. Elbert's husband had died and she had come back home to live with Quincy. She had not, thank God, had to live with her mother when she had lost her mind, but it could not have been any worse than living with Quincy now. He tainted even her smallest pleasures, such as having company. If anyone came to see them, Quincy would go up to them every few minutes and shake their hands and ask them if they knew who he was. It mortified her to have her friends see how she had to live, that her own brother had become a blithering idiot. Her friends all shook their heads and agreed that Mary Elbert bore a heavier burden than anyone else they knew of. Sometimes it just did not seem fair to have had a mother and a brother become morons *and* to have to live with the brother and put up with him twenty-four hours a day after she had lived a good life and raised two children in the Church and taken care of a husband with heart trouble until he died. At least he had died with his good sense intact.

The spring sun glanced fiercely off the white hood of the car into her eyes as they turned off onto the rutted dirt road which led to the clapboard shack, half of which was occupied by Ennis. It had no conveniences, not even hot water, and it just proved that he was common down to his soul that he was able to live that way. The other half was rented by a stringy colored woman named Florentine whom Ennis had shot with a slug bullet some years before when they were both drunk. When Florentine had been in the hospital she'd sworn to kill him when she got well. No doctor had given her any chance of survival—if she had been white she would have died as soon as the bullet hit her—but she had survived and moved right back in with Ennis and not killed him at all.

There was scarcely more than a blade or two of real grass in the front of the shack, the rest being weeds and hard-packed dirt. Rising from the starved, shocked-looking earth, however, was a low bushy tree in furious bloom—all over it were great stunningly white blossoms as if the roots had absorbed the glaring acid sun from the surface of the earth and forced it out of its own wood as buds and petals. It looked for all the world like the tree which had grown in her parents' yard. She was overcome with the sight. It made her feel weak and blush so that if she had been at home she would have sat down on the edge of the bed. She was so overwhelmed that she did not hear Ennis telling her to look out until she had driven into a thick post, all that remained of a gate that had once stood before the house.

Quincy fell off the back seat onto the floor. Ennis had seen what was coming and reached out to brace himself. Mrs. Elbert's small head, capped by two tightly wound buns of white hair, struck the windshield with such a terrific force that it looked as if a huge rock had flown up from the road and struck it from without. After the impact, she fell back into her seat as limp as a doll. The engine continued to roar. She did not move or speak. Ennis leaned over and looked at her. She had a pleased, almost beatific expression. A large, thin drop of blood trickled down to the end of her long nose and hung there. She seemed to smile.

Ennis reached over the seat and her, took the key in his palsied grip, and stopped the engine. A hissing steam rose from under the hood. All was quiet. A lark warbled gaily off in the crazily lush meadow of briars behind the house. Quincy stirred in the back.

"Oh my," he said, fumbling with the door handle. "Oh my gracious."

He fumbled and fumbled without success. He furrowed his brow, grimaced.

"Wait jus a minute, Mist Quincy," said Ennis. "You stay yer a minute. I come roun and git you out in a minute." Ennis stepped gingerly from the car and closed the door, locking it from behind him. "You stay, Mist Quincy, don't you move, hear?" he bellowed hoarsely through the glass.

The old man blinked and took a deep breath. "Oh my," he moaned desperately.

Ennis opened the front door and with the most studied care lifted Mrs. Elbert in his arms. He studied her face with controlled and piercing curiosity. She was breathing steadily. She appeared whole save for a tiny crimson stitch in the stippled membranous skin of her forehead.

Ennis climbed the two plank and brick steps to the porch and leaned gently against the parched grey door. He ducked his head and bore Mrs. Elbert into the cool darkness beyond.

It was cool and damp in the tree house. The sunlight was stained soft green by the leaves and there was a smell of woodshavings, brightly spiced by the hundreds of frail white blooms, open and wilting, giving off a sweetness of gradual death. A squirrel chattered through the leaves at Mary Elbert. She drew further back from the ladder to avoid being seen. Her starched petticoats rustled loudly. She held her breath. The squirrel scolded. She looked down on her older brother Quincy. His belongings were being loaded into the buggy which would take him to the train, which would bear him far, far away, to school, away from her. She looked around her at the corncob doll and dollhouse he had made for her, at his slingshot and his marbles, which he had just that morning told her she could have. He had told her that the tree house now was hers alone, and she must take care of it. That was when she had run from him. No one had been able to find her. No one knew where she was. Her mother called for her: "Mary! Mary! Come and tell Brother goodbye, dear!" Their father said, "There's no time. He spoke to her this morning. You'll write, won't you, Quincy?" She didn't hear his answer. Tears welled up in her eyes. She yanked one of the blue ribbons from her hair and flung it out at them. It caught briefly on a flower and descended but no one saw it. The buggy was leaving the yard. Mary wept. The squirrel scolded. The corncob doll watched her with its flat, expressionless gaze. She picked it up and threw it at the squirrel. It fell, striking the ground and breaking into several pieces. The squirrel ran to a neighboring tree. There was no sound but the breathing and weeping of Mary, high in the silent white flowers and the cool green leaves, no sound at all but the purest silence.

She awoke, head pounding, to the sight of Ennis' bloodshot eyes suspended inches above hers, the smell of his whiskey breath. "Ennis!" she barked, sitting bolt upright.

He recoiled and stepped backwards, removing his Western Auto cap and scratching his head nervously. "How you feel, Miss Mary? Is you feel anything broke?" he inquired.

"Fine. Fine," she said, feeling her head and neck carefully. She looked around the room. Two curtainless windows poured a styptic clarity into the dank closeness, framing motes of dust. There was a ragged hole in the wall opposite for a fireplace and above it a plank mantel. From a mason jar on the mantel erupted an incongruous riot of white blooms cut from the tree outside. The room was heavily redolent of old wood-ashes, bitter sweat, mildewed linen, burned cooking oil, and these nectarous floral avatars of her childhood. She spied a large hot plate on a table, and a toaster oven, gifts from her and other white benefactors. She realized she must be lying on his bed and abruptly stood up. A crunch of newspaper accompanied this motion: newspaper was neatly spread over the sheets on the sway-backed ancient mattress.

"Well, I . . ." she fumbled at her dress, smoothing it.

"Yebm, I speck you might be a lil so in the head. I takes me a bufferin when I has the so head."

Quincy's voice broke on them through the open door. "Sister! Oh Sister!" It sounded oddly distant, aerial.

Mrs. Elbert passed a small quantity of gas and cleared her throat as if observing some phonic symmetry. He had hardly ever called her "Sister" since he had left home for boarding school.

"Ennis. Catch him before he tries to run off."

They strode out onto the porch, Mrs. Elbert leading. Quincy was nowhere to be seen. He had left the car; the door hung open where he had gotten out.

The tinny theme music of a TV soap opera advertised the presence of Florentine behind them. "Laws, is dat Miss Mary?" she crooned, leaning against the screen door of her one room in a slip. She grinned. The few teeth remaining in her head were enormous. One was gold. A tiny blue television screen shone like a moon in the dark behind her. She had curtains, all of which were pulled.

"How are you, Florentine?" asked Mrs. Elbert peremptorily, flashing an empty smile and returning her furrowed gaze to the lush horizon.

Florentine pushed open the door. Its spring whined and it slapped the wood frame behind her. "Y'all looking for Mister Quincy?"

Neither of the others replied.

Florentine shifted her weight languidly from one huge pancake foot to the other. "I been stanin yonder watchin him."

"Where he at, woman?" Ennis snapped.

"Clomb up thater tree, what he done." Florentine nodded at the tree festooned with the white blossoms.

Mrs. Elbert gasped and she and Ennis ran into the yard and looked up.

Florentine shuffled to the edge of the porch, folded her arms, and squinted up into the tree. "Mr. Quincy too old to be clombin tree. I don't reckon he gon clomb it. But he done clomb it. That old white man hop up yonder easas a skwull. What you speck make a old white gentermuns ack thataway?"

At the very top of the tree, in his black suit and hat, Quincy clung to a thin branch. He smiled and behind his thick spectacles his eyes sparkled. "Sister!" he cried, and with the recklessness of a small boy leaned outward, swaying precariously.

Ennis maneuvered to catch him. He was not so very high, perhaps fifteen feet. He must have weighed no more than a hundred and thirty pounds. It could be done. Mrs. Elbert raised her hand to her mouth in horror. She stood next to Ennis whose arms were outstretched and trembling.

"Quincy!" she cried, "come down from there this instant."

Quincy flung out one arm and leg and most of the branch broke off in his other hand. For a long instant, he appeared to fly. An extraordinary vision danced in the heads of Florentine, Ennis, and Mrs. Elbert: an old gnomish gentleman clad in suit, white shirt and tie, clasping in one hand a branch of white blossoms, floated in the blue spring firmament, spangled with afternoon sun, leaving his hat in midair as he began to fall from under it. He gave a kick and twirled as he fell, fell, fell, seemed to take minutes falling. Florentine's eyes followed him downward like a cat's intent upon a pendulum as he kicked, twirled himself out of Ennis' reach and into his sister's.

It was too late to move. Mrs. Elbert began to shriek, "Murder alive!" but all that got out was "Murder a-." A loud thump followed as Quincy struck her in the chest. Their bodies on the ground made a popping, cracking thud, punctuated by the purest silence.

OPENING THE DOOR ON SIXTY-SECOND STREET

Maxine Kumin

THE year Jeffrey Rabinowitz was sixteen, his grandfather died at the Seder table. That is, he slumped over the ceremonial plate with its horseradish root and lamb bone and roasted egg, a sprig of parsley in his hand, and had to be helped into the living room to lie down on the horsehair sofa. An elderly doctor, summoned from his own Passover festivities in an apartment upstairs, had laid his ear to the old man's naked chest and pronounced the flutter of his heart to be only a little arrhythmia brought on by excitement. Nevertheless, Jeff's grandfather died on West End Avenue before the eight days of matzoh were over.

"Did you finish the service? I mean, after he slumped over like that?" Robin Parks wanted to know.

"I think we must have," Jeff said. "Because every year since I catch myself thinking, we opened the door for Elijah and the Angel of Death entered in. You know, it's the Angel of Death who's supposed to pass over the houses. Instead, he came for Grampa."

It was important to be on time; he was hustling her from the airport terminal, where he had gone to fetch her, to a cab.

"It was always such a joke, opening the door for Elijah. Dewey used to pull rank on me. Being the younger son meant I had to ask the four questions and he got to yank the door open with a flourish. Dewey always said we wouldn't know him if he came, Elijah. He'd never get past the doorman, he used to say."

"Well, he was right, I guess. Now everybody says it about Jesus. When I was little I used to wonder how Jesus could put a coat on."

"Why not?"

"Over his wings, I mean."

"I thought you meant he couldn't fold his arms back down."

"Well, that too. But Unitarians don't talk much about the crucifixion. Our Jesus didn't transfigure."

"Dewey had three apparitions of Elijah in his lifetime. Chariot and all."

"Was God driving?"

"I don't know. When he described it, though, I could see it too. It was a fiery buckboard, all right. Something like Pegasus pulling a hansom cab in Central Park."

The driver cheated a crosstown light and edged between two trucks. They were quiet a minute, considering.

"It must be awfully hard now," Robin said finally. "For your parents, I mean, having the holiday without Dewey."

"In a way, it's easier than his visions and things. They always hated surprises."

His parents were old, he told her. His mother was forty-five when he was born.

"But that's incredible! You're lucky you're not a mongoloid."

"Well, I missed it by a percentage point. My mother was married before. But they never had any children. I think we came as a great shock to her. And my father was one of those lingering bachelors who finally gave in. He can be very charming, but you always feel he was dragooned into the system. It's hard for him to cope with family life."   .

Before dinner there was schnapps in the living room—scotch in the palest violet glasses. Only the men partook. Robin inferred that women did not take their whiskey neat and shook her head when the tray went round.

Jeff's mother had blue hair and blue harlequin glasses. Her face was childish and well-kept with sweet small features, the skin finely wrinkled. Robin thought of a silk nightgown that wanted ironing. She wore four rings.

"It just lifts my spirits to have you young people around," she said, settling her plumpness with a little bounce. "I think a Seder is more *fun* when you can set a full table. Jeffrey and Dewey always brought their Christian friends home, we encouraged that, didn't we, Harris?"

"My wife prides herself on her Christian friends," Harris Rabinowitz pronounced equably. He too wore glasses and threw his head back so that the light glinted off them. What wonderful hair! Robin thought. All silvery and benign, that's where Jeff gets it.

"What Daddy means is that the holidays are hard when there's been a death," Mrs. Rabinowitz went on. "You know about Dewey, of course. He was the *best* baby. He went potty before he was a year old. Jeffrey here was impossible to train. You just never could catch him. He'd go in a corner behind the piano and grunt—I swear it was just to defy me. We used to say we'd have to send him off to college with Dydee service."

"Now Clara, does Macy's tell Gimbel's?" Harris Rabinowitz rumbled.

"Mother has a compulsion to tell all," Jeff said. His voice was even. Robin couldn't tell whether he despised or enjoyed her candor.

"Never mind, never mind," she said. "I'm sure Miss Parks wants to see us as we are."

Miss Parks has gone away, Robin's here, Robin thought fiercely, but touched thumbs in her lap.

"I suppose you're wondering where the hors d'oeuvres are," Jeff's mother said. "Usually we have hot and cold ones. But tonight there's so much ceremonial food. Jews don't know how to drink for pleasure, really. These little shot glasses belonged to my father, they're Bohemian glass, you know. It comes from being uprooted, this attachment to *things.*"

And before they went to the table Robin had heard the history of three paintings, a Bisque figurine, and a pair of silver candelabra. It was the kind of promotional revelation that Robin's grandmother, who was, after all, of the same generation, would have shunned. "Good taste speaks for itself, Binnie," Gran would say. "Only an upstart waves a price tag."

"Ready, everyone?" Clara Rabinowitz trilled. "I'm lighting the candles! Sheila dear, will you say the blessing?"

Sheila Sheprow, Jeff's hugely pregnant cousin, stood at the head of the table like the figurehead of a Norse sailing ship and extended her hands, fingers paired, over the candle flames. "Any day now," Art Sheprow beamed. Her pleasantly freckled face shone as if buttered. Her parents, the Poppers, lined up opposite Robin. Downstream at attention stood the other aunt and uncle, the Szalds. Peter Kramer, who grew pot in the aluminum-foil lined closet of the apartment on West End Avenue he shared with Jeff, took a white silk yarmulke out of his back pocket, kissed it, and put it on. Robin, who had not bowed her head with the others, caught Mrs. Rabinowitz's frown at this gesture.

"That's very sweet of you, Peter," she said just as Sheila cleared her throat, "but we're very informal here. You don't need a yarmulke on East Sixty-second Street."

The pot farmer took off his skullcap, folded and kissed it, and stuffed it back in his pocket. Art coughed tentatively. And Sheila sang the Hebrew blessing in the clear, unselfconscious tones of a small child.

There was a general edging and tugging of chairs; the assemblage was seated. "Now dear," Clara Rabinowitz instructed Robin, "that was to symbolize the joy we feel when we can celebrate this festival in our own homes. Next, Daddy will bless the first glass of wine. It's called the kiddush. Oh Harris, wait! Not everyone is served yet."

Harris semaphored with his eyeglasses up and down the table. After he had spoken his portion everyone lifted his goblet. Robin sipped. Thick and sweet, the wine tasted like fermented grape juice.

"You have to drink all of it, you know," Jeff whispered.

"How many of these are there?"

"Four in all."

But his mother had overheard. Again the wide smile which ended in a little downturning of earnestness. "The four cups symbolize the four promises of redemption, Miss Parks. I forget what each one is, exactly. But on this night even the poorest of the poor were to be provided with enough wine to take part in the ceremony."

"It sounds like Thoreau," Robin said. "You know, the thing about 'none is so poor that he need sit on a pumpkin.'"

But no one knew except Jeff.

They had just gotten into the *Dayenus* when the phone rang.

"'Dayenu'—how would you translate that, Harris?" Clara asked, while deliberate footsteps could be heard moving offstage to lift the receiver.

"Does Macy's tell Gimbel's?" he grumbled.

"'It would have been enough,' Auntie," Sheila Sheprow supplied. "'Sufficient unto the day thereof,' something like that."

It was the other Popper children—Sheila's two married sisters and their husbands—conjoined in San Francisco to wish the family *Good Yuntuf.* Everyone in turn, except for Peter Kramer and Robin, queued up at the living room extension. The senior Poppers hurried upstairs to monitor the flow of conversation from the bedroom.

Left to themselves, Robin peeked ahead in the *Haggadah*. Sixty pages to go, but a lot of it was music.

Peter furtively lifted a napkin, slid out a wheel of matzoh, and stood in a corner by the china cabinet munching. "Starved," he explained. "Anyway, we're very informal here."

"That bothered you."

He shrugged. "She has her meaningful rituals, I have mine."

"Why did you kiss it?"

"You have your crucifix and I have my Grandpa's yarmulke."

"But Peter! I'm a Unitarian."

"So? A Unitarian's nothing but a homesick Christian."

"There will be a short wait for all seats," Jeff said coming back. "Sheila is reviewing her pregnancy long distance. She's up to the seventh month now. How's it going, Robinowitz?"

"Miss Parks to you."

"That's just Mother's way of indicating that you haven't been divinely elected," Jeff said. "Don't let it get you." But he looked unhappy; diminished somehow inside the frame of his curly hair and beard.

She relented. "No, it's very interesting, really. I *like* it. And I like having your mother explain things."

Between bouts of exegesis the service proceeded communally with each member reading a part. The Szalds shared one pair of bifocals which they passed back and forth between them like a dish of olives. Kramer, discountenanced by the English, chose each time to deliver his portion in Hebrew. Mrs. Rabinowitz promptly translated by way of reproof.

Symbols exalted her. She explained the parsley—gratitude to God for the fruits of the earth—the horseradish root, a warty phallus that made Robin think of John Donne's mandrake poem—the bitter lot of the Jews in Egypt—the haroses, unexpectedly delicious—mortar for the bricks the Jews made when they were the Pharoah's slaves. And did Miss Parks know why the matzoh was scored in perforations? (Does Macy's tell Gimbel's?) To keep the dough from rising and swelling.

During the dinner itself, conversation found its urban level. The Szalds reported a mugging; they alternated details like a responsive reading. The Poppers brought up landlords. Art Sheprow defended rent strikes, bussing, and peaceful acts of civil disobedience to disrupt the war machine.

"Have you ever done it?" Robin asked him. "Sat in, I mean?"

"I'd like to. But I can't risk arrest with Sheila in this condition."

Harris Rabinowitz sighed obtrusively. Conviviality sat heavily on him.

"The *schwartzehs*, the *schwartzehs*," he said. "Between the *schwartzehs* and the dog-do the whole city is a slum. When I was a young man we went up to Harlem to hear jazz. Portaricka was a foreign country. A nice Jewish girl, if she had to work, went into teaching. Now she goes to CCNY and gets raped in the ladies room."

Robin, prepared to despise him, was startled when he turned to her in supplication. "Don't get me wrong, young lady. You think I'm just a *kvetch*, a complaining old man. You think I'm some kind of a right-wing fanatic. But I want to tell you, I loved this city before it turned into a jungle. I was born here, I grew up in the Bronx in what they call a semi-detached. I had all kinds of neighbors, Italians, Polish people, even some coloreds. I went with all kinds, we had respect. The trouble with today is, there's no respect."

After dessert, they returned to the *Haggadah*. Art Sheprow, slightly flushed, read the grace and the company supplied the responses. When he came to "The door is opened for Elijah," there was a pause. Mrs. Rabinowitz unfolded a handkerchief and dabbed her eyes.

"We don't have to do this part," Jeff warned.

"No Jeffrey, I *want* to. I want *you* to do it." To Robin, she said, "It makes us all remember Dewey. Dewey *saw* Elijah, you know. Oh, no one ever believed him, I didn't at the time, but maybe he knew something we didn't. Dewey was such a bright child! Up until the eighth grade he always got all A's on his report card. Of course every night he read the same fairy tales over and over in his bed; we should have guessed that he was troubled, boys don't generally read fairy tales, but he loved them so! He *identified*. He was the frog who was going to turn into a prince. When all along he was the prince already."

Robin felt like a Strasbourg goose force-fed the unwanted grain.

Jeff stumbled from the table like a man fighting his way out of a hidden swamp. The front door was opened; the normal raw sounds of traffic swept in.

"O Praise the Lord all ye nations," Art Sheprow recited dubiously. After "Hallelujah!" there was the sucking sound of the door refilling its space. The latch clicked and Jeff returned to his seat with a marvelous show of self-possession.

This is what Robin read on his face: I shat in my pants to the age of four on purpose behind the piano. I played stoopball and kept porno magazines under the mattress and got C's in Latin. I have opened the door on Sixty-second Street and closed it again on the usual arrangement of furniture. It is not part of the divine plan that Elijah appear to Jeffrey Rabinowitz.

They went on into the psalms. "Out of distress I called upon the Lord. He answered me with great enlargement," Sheila recited. "Oh my God!" she said, pushing her chair back. Now she was standing, saying, "Oh my God, my God, I'm wetting my pants!"

In that suspended moment Mrs. Szald took off the bifocals and handed them to Mr. Szald who put them into his breast pocket. In her haste to get out of her chair Mrs. Popper knocked over a wine glass and Art Sheprow unaccountably buried his face in his hands.

It was all happening slow motion like a baseball replay; an awkward out-of-sequence pushing back of chairs against the heavy pile of the carpet, stick figures captured in various stages of arising, and a pool of wet unmistakably darkening the Aubusson.

Clara Rabinowitz found the first words. "It's all right, Sheila dear, your water just broke. Your water just broke and you're going to have your baby tonight."

"Let me take your shoes," Robin offered. Sheila stepped out of her navy pumps. Little puddles spilled from them.

Mrs. Popper, seeking equilibrium, exclaimed, "Isn't it lucky you're going to Doctors Hospital? You're already on the East side, darling. Isn't that the luckiest thing?"

"Oh, get me a towel, somebody!" Sheila wailed.

"Come on, old man. You're not going to be sick or something," Jeff said, steering the father-to-be from the table.

Mr. Popper called a cab. Coats were located and handed around. Sheila tucked a hand towel into her panties.

And the door on Sixty-second Street opened for the second time.

THE FACE OF HATE

Mary Lavin

JOHNNY knew the other boy only by sight, but he hated his white, Protestant face and his sedate, Protestant step. It was 1957 in Belfast. Johnny was sixteen.

The two boys passed each other every morning of the week, except Saturdays and Sundays, at the same time, and almost exactly the same spot. It galled Johnny to think the little Protestant was, then, within a stone's throw of the Grammar School, while he had yet to get across the city to St. Mary's. He never managed to be in time even though he rattled hell out of his old bike. He slunk into class every morning with what one of the priests called punctual tardiness.

Saturdays were different. There was no school that day, although he still had to serve Mass and do a paper round. Yet, when the alarm clock went off, he could luxuriate in the knowledge that when he'd get home he could have his mug of tea in comfort with his feet under the kitchen table.

Sometimes of a Saturday afternoon he'd catch sight of the other fellow coming home from rugger, carrying his football boots in a calico bag like a sissy. Once when he pointed him out to his pal Jer, Jer asked how he knew it was the same fellow. It was Jer's conviction that all Protestant kids looked alike, all pasty faced, all with blazers, and all with school caps set straight on their pates like pudding bowls. Few Catholic kids could afford a blazer, and those who had caps wore them down over one ear in a shamefaced sort of way.

Johnny used to think no Protestant kid ever had to wear hand-me-downs, but one night when he and his father were sitting in the kitchen with her, his mother put him right on that score.

"There are poor Protestants as well as poor Catholics," she said.

"Not in Belfast!" his father butted in, from where he sat hugging the range, nursing a sore head after a day spent in the pub. The shipyard had laid off another two hundred men and not one Protestant among them.

"Yes, even in Belfast," his mother said stoutly. "You only think they're well off because they're thrifty and take care of their clothes. The clothes that come out of a Protestant Jumble Sale are as good as new. I've heard they get them cleaned and pressed before they give them away and don't even cut off the buttons! I've heard they polish the boots and put in new laces, and wash and darn socks so's they won't be unpleasant for others to handle. You wouldn't get many Catholics to show that consideration for the poor of their parish!"

"Ah," said his father peevishly. "Have sense! What's poverty in a Catholic is parsimony in a Protestant." He stood up and kicked off his boots by pressing down on the broken uppers of one with the heel of the other, scattering mud all over the clean floor. Then stepping carefully over a bucket of soapy water that was left unemptied so the front steps could be swilled down last thing, he went up to bed without a word of goodnight.

Johnny looked at the muddy marks on the floor and then down at his own boots with their knotted laces and toecaps bleached white by wet and weather.

"I'll do the doorstep for you, Ma," he said, but she snatched up the bucket and he saw she was looking regretfully at his jacket. The day she bought it she'd bought a card of buttons as well, but she'd never got round to sewing them on.

"Do you know something I heard the other day, son? In Germany, boys as well as girls are taught to sew. Would you believe that? Ah well, never mind! You'll be getting a brand-new suit next year when you're sitting for your examination. I've my heart set on it. I was not going to tell you until it was paid off, but I made the down payment on it today."

Johnny's face lit up. She'd been a good mother to him always, as she had been to Sheamus when his older brother was still at home. Never, even in their poorest days, had she forced either of them to wear articles of women's clothing, the way other mothers did. That very day he had seen a little kid in Primary School wearing a green coat with a flared tail to it. Thinking to amuse his mother, he started to tell her, but it didn't make her smile.

"The poor child. I hope you didn't let on to notice, son," she said. "His poor mother was probably at her wit's end to keep him warm in that draughty school. I suppose the heating will soon be shut off now the worst of the winter is over?"

"Shut off!" Johnny had to laugh. "It's been out of order since January." He held out his fingers to show his chilblains broken and running, and as he did, he thought of the smell of blistering paint from overheated radiators that wafted out the open door of the Grammar School as he pedaled past it, his hands fastened by frost to the handlebars of the bike. He could almost hear the hot water rumbling and gurgling in the pipes like human guts. But his mother was harking back to the child in the girl's coat.

"That poor child is likely fatherless," she said, shaking her head sadly. "Not that your own father ever has a stitch of clothes fit for passing on to a beggar after they come off his back, God help him. It's true he spends all he can lay hands on in the pub, but he makes no bones about wearing the same suit of clothes year after year until it falls off him in tatters." She sighed again, and changing the heavy bucket from one hand to the other, she opened the street door. Looking up and down to see no one was passing, she sloshed the sudsy water out over the doorstep. Johnny remembered a time when, like her neighbors, his mother used to scrub the doorstep every Saturday night and whiten it with lime. That custom, like many another, was given up when curfew was imposed on the city. When she came back and left down the bucket, she closed the door. "Tell me, son, would you happen to know the name of that little boy you were telling me about? It might have been one of Larry Lardner's children, God be good to him, the youngest one. I saw that wee Lardner child myself one day wearing a cardigan a bit gaudy for a boy. It must have been sent by one of his older sisters from England because I remarked at the time the good quality of the yarn. Oh, son, son, that wee fellow was only an infant in his mother's arms when his father was shot dead at their own hall door in front of them all. I was at the father's wake, and although the shroud hid the bullet holes, I could get the smell of singed cloth. Ah, well! There's no use talking about those things! It's only keeping the bitterness alive."

Johnny couldn't let that pass.

"It isn't us that's keeping it alive, it's them—the Protestants. You know that, Mother."

His mother made the sign of the cross. "May the Lord have mercy on the dead, no matter who they are, or what they did."

To please her Johnny crossed himself. He knew it must have gone against the grain with her to have made even that one reference to the atrocities that were the main topic of talk in other houses—talk to which the children listened avidly, and repeated next day in the schoolyard. Jer Murphy's mind was an armory of terrible tales about things done up in the Divas hills to fellows belonging to illegal organizations—fellows like Sheamus. But he didn't want to think about things like that when he was going to bed.

"Goodnight, Mother," he said, reaching for the flannel rag that hung on a string over the range, to wrap it around the hot brick she always insisted on his taking to warm the bed, although it only made his chilblains sting like nettle rash. He was startled to see there was a second brick set to heat. "Are you expecting Sheamus, Ma?" he cried. It was several months since his brother had dared come home.

His mother's face went ashen and she sprang to her feet, and looked in terror at the thinly curtained window. "Ssh, ssh," she cried. "I know nothing! It's only that I had a queer feeling he might steal in tonight for a wee while."

Her face flushed, and it was as if she was transfigured to a girl again. Then, catching up the poker, she nudged the brick off the range and into the coal hod and pushed the hod out of sight. "May God forgive me! If anyone came to the door that brick would be a cruel giveaway." She sank back wearily on the chair. "Go to bed you, Johnny, will you, like a good boy. I have a few more chores to do before I turn in."

Johnny knew what that meant. She'd sit up half the night in case his brother might appear. She often took these notions, and never seemed to learn from disappointments. There was nothing he could do about it. Her hopes and fears were inextricably tangled together. Well! Better that maybe, than her to lie tossing and turning, listening for a sound of gunfire, thinking her own son could be the next to take a bullet in the belly. Johnny wrapped up his brick and went to bed.

The next day was the Twelfth of July, a public holiday, and in spite of what their parents felt toward the Orange Order, Catholic kids often had a great day of it. Even when he was in Primary School, Johnny used to go up to Donnegall Square with Jer and his pals to watch the parade, sneering silently during it and jeering loudly on their way home through the empty streets. Lately, it wasn't much fun. Now Jer and the others were almost as tense as their elders. As he jumped out of bed and ran downstairs, Johnny half hoped it would rain. Then, when he went into the kitchen, he was astonished to find that his mother, for once, was not down before him. The blinds were not up and the range was not lit. Looking into the coal hod he saw the brick was in it, ash grey and cold. He let up the blind. It was a fine day, and, as he scorched off down the street in the sunlight, he was soon whistling. Pedaling home he was whistling louder still, and when he reached his own street and saw the brass knocker was shined, he knew his mother was up. All was well.

In the kitchen his mother was on her knees scrubbing the rungs of an upended chair, but she got up at once, and he knew by the smile on her face she'd managed an egg for his breakfast. The kettle was boiling on the range, and on the mantelshelf there was a big brown egg.

"Where is the yard brush, Ma?" he asked when he'd eaten. He wanted to do something for her.

"It's in a place you won't find it, son!" she said smiling again. "Go off out for yourself into the fresh air, it's little enough of it you get." She glanced at the window where a dazzling line of sunlight ran along a crack in the glass. "It's a lovely day, thanks be to God." Setting the chair back on its legs she knelt to scrub the seat of it, but after a minute she stopped and rested her elbows on it as if it were a prie-dieu in the chapel. "What are you going to do with yourself today, son?"

"I don't know," he said lamely. "I'll see what Jer and the others are doing." His mother pursed her lips. She looked up angrily at him.

"You know as well as I do that you'll go to watch the parade. Small wonder the Orangemen prance around the streets when all the Catholics in the city turn out to gape at them. They'd soon give up parading if there was no one to admire them in their sashes and their bowler hats, banging drums like babbies!"

"It's not to admire them we go, Ma," he said coldly.

But this too she knew. It was of this she went in mortal dread.

"Oh, son, I wish you'd stay away and set an example to the others. A single stone idly picked up out of the gutter and fired at one of them Orangemen and the next thing fired could be a shot." She stared down at the suds in the bucket that were winking out one-by-one, and he knew she was thinking of Sheamus. To please her he thought he'd get his books and study for a while anyway, and he started to hunt around for them on the window sill, the mantelpiece, on the floor.

"Sheamus always kept his books in the one place," his mother remarked absently, but Johnny felt sure she was comparing the two of them—comparing them to his disadvantage. She was probably thinking that even if Sheamus came to no harm, he had thrown away his only chance of a decent career. Sheamus had had brains to burn, but Johnny felt his mother had no such confidence in him, although the priests were putting him in for the same scholarship Sheamus had thrown away. Yet the old priest who took the Latin class had made a strange remark lately: he said that fellows with application often did better for themselves than fellows who only abused the brains that God had deigned to give them. Just then, he found the books. They were under a clutter of old racing calendars belonging to his father. His mother stared at him.

"Ah, Johnny, isn't it a pity it's not this summer you're sitting for the scholarship instead of a whole year from now?"

"You wouldn't wish that if you were in my shoes, Ma," he said quietly.

She saw the sense of that. "Your're right, son. Amn't I the foolish woman wishing the years away! It's only wishing your life away. Keep on the way you're going, keep out of mischief and God will reward us."

Johnny stuck to his books and only went out with Jer and the others an odd time, although his mother distrusted the others more and more. On the other hand Sheamus, during one of his rare forays home, had put in a good word for Jer.

"That Jer has guts," he said, in one of the awkward silences that were liable to fall on them sometimes as they all listened unconsciously for a sound in the street. "He's a good kid. His heart is in the right place."

Johnny could hardly believe his ears when his mother turned on his brother. Usually, when Sheamus slunk home, she did her best in a few minutes to lavish a lifetime of love on him. But now her face flamed with fury.

"Leave his heart out of it!" she cried. "No more than yourself, I don't suppose he knows why God gave him a heart in the first place, unless to pump hate into his veins."

Sheamus only laughed and tried to chivvy her up.

"Come on, Ma. You and me always had our differences over affairs of the heart. You didn't take it well if I as much as lifted my eye to a bit of a skirt of a Sunday after Mass, even if it was only one of the O'Grady girls down the street, one of those poor dried-up skins that will never get a man."

Johnny was going to laugh until he saw their mother's face.

"God help all mothers," she said. "I thought in them days you were a bit too young for that sort of thing." She hurried over the last words as if she had expressed herself too crudely. "I thought then, God pity me, that you were going to lead a normal life. I didn't know you were saving yourself up to be a target for the R.U.C.!"

Sheamus' visit that night ended badly. When he went away, Johnny knew their mother would lie awake until all hours, eating out her heart at having made them all miserable.

Slowly the summer wasted and went the way of all summers. And when the next summer came, it was not like other years because at the end of it Johnny would be sitting for the scholarship, and he had been given extra study to do at home during the holidays. He spent a lot of time at his books. His mother had insisted he give up the paper round though, and the priests let him serve a late Mass, so he had a good lie-in most mornings. After breakfast, when he'd sit down at the kitchen table with his books in front of him, his mother used to go around on tiptoes so as not to disturb him, and even his father, when he'd get up at noon, took himself off to the pub earlier than usual, not to disturb him. The new suit was paid for in full and hung in the cupboard awaiting the big day.

Saturdays were a bit different.

"You've done enough reading all week," his mother would say, especially if it were a sunny day. Giving glory to God for all His blessings, she'd tell him to go out and enjoy himself. "There's no use breaking down your health, son," she'd say.

Then, one week in midsummer, there was a bit of trouble in the street. The R.U.C. had raided two neighbors' houses including O'Grady's, and although nothing was found, everyone's nerves were on edge. Unfortunately that week the Twelfth of July fell on a Saturday, and the first thing Johnny noticed after his breakfast was that his mother had cleared a space on the table and spread out his books. She had set a bowl of flour at the other end of the table to make a cake of bread, and the range was stoked up for baking. The kitchen was murderously hot. Compared with the heat inside, even the sunlight outside seemed cool. Seeing him gazing out, his mother ran over and rattled up the window. Then she rushed over to the yard door and flung it open.

"That'll let in a nice breeze," she said, as if he were going to spend the day there. Was she playing innocent, he wondered? She couldn't but know he'd be going to the parade. He was no longer in-the-know about all Jer's plans, but he had a feeling there might be more in the wind this year than just gawking. Everyone in the street was ratty over the raid. They would not do anything bad—only maybe let off a few squibs or firecrackers. All the same, they'd be counting on him going with them.

As a cool, fresh breeze blew through the kitchen, Johnny opened his book. He'd stick at the work for a while. Poring over the book though, he was soon engrossed. It was his mother who was fidgety. She went back and forth continually from the table to the range before she at last settled down, poured a cup of water into the bowl of flour, and began to stir it with a big wooden spoon. Then, plunging her hands into the bowl, she furiously kneaded the dough. But she must have felt guilty.

"You ought to be out in the sun, I suppose," she said at last.

"Ah, that sun is too bright to last. It'll probably be pouring rain before long," Johnny said, thinking to forestall an inquisition. "There's no use making any plans in this rotten country."

His mother scraped the wet dough off her arm before she answered.

"It won't rain," she said dully. "I sometimes think the Orange Lodge must control the weather in Belfast as well as everything else! Oh, son, it's a wonder to me you have nothing better to do on a nice, fine Saturday, than stand about in the streets breathing in the dust stomped up by those goms of Orangemen. If I was young again—or your poor father for that matter—it's off up to the hills we'd be on a day like this. Yes! Every Saturday in summertime all us young people used to set off up to the Divas. And when the evenings got short we'd walk out along the Lagan to Shaw's Bridge. And not only us! The foremen in the shipyards always walked their greyhounds out along the Lagan." Johnny was impressed. He'd never been up the hills unless in a car, and he'd never gone far along the Lagan. He'd have thought the riverbanks were all built up with houses and factories. He looked at his mother. She was talking very excitedly. "Sometimes even in winter, we'd have such a wish to get out of the dirty city we'd go down to the quays, just for a smell of the sea. Tell me! Were you ever down there?"

"I was, Ma. I was down there a few times with Sheamus."

As if struck by a thought that had not before occurred to her, his mother was silent for a moment, staring down at her floury hands. "I suppose you miss your brother too," she said. Then she looked up and said a most extraordinary thing. "At your age, son, and with your looks, it's a wonder to me some nice girl hasn't put her eye on you. I'll bet there's plenty would be proud to be seen out walking with you of a fine Saturday." Johnny blinked. He was three years younger than his brother, and he hadn't forgotten how his mother had clamped down on Sheamus where girls were concerned. Ah, she was cunning! She didn't believe—she never did—that he would get the scholarship, and she was afraid that if he failed there'd be nothing to stop him going the way Sheamus went, unless—but he recoiled from the idea that she would make use of a girl— any girl—as a decoy to keep him at home. She didn't know him as well as she thought! He couldn't look a girl in the face without going through agonies. Once recently, when he got a puncture on the way home from school, and had to walk and wheel the bike, he saw one of the O'Grady girls standing at her door, and rather than pass her he turned back and went round the block to enter the street from the other end. He wouldn't have minded if it had been one of the older ones, but it was the youngest of them, and she was the one he dreaded. She seemed to be always standing in the doorway. Even when he whizzed past her on his bike, he often felt she was staring at him as if she were deliberately trying to make him feel a fool. People said she was the brainy one in the family. She played the fiddle too, and Jer said she'd have got a scholarship to the London Conservatory of Music only she dug with the wrong foot. She wasn't bad with her old fiddle. He'd heard her himself scraping away at it nights he'd pass the house after dark when the blind was down. But suddenly his mother came closer to him and broke into his thoughts. "That's another injustice the Protestants inflicted on us—the worst of all!" she said. "By not distributing jobs fairly they made it impossible for us Catholics to get married until it's too late for us to grow together in the bonds God intended, and have the size family He meant for us." She lowered her voice and there was an intimacy in it he had never before known her to show. "I was thirty before your father and me could afford to get married. That's why I only had you two boys. Protestants of course— no matter how much money they had—would never think it a loss to have only two children. They see to it they don't have anymore! They never hesitate to interfere with nature—May God forgive them!"

Her nearness suddenly irked Johnny.

"In a few years time we'll be doing the same as the Protestants," he said. "They're better educated than us, that's all. If you ask me, the priests and bishops have ended up making paupers of us!" he said.

His mother's face went ashen.

"Where did you hear talk like that? Who are you aping?" Jerking around, knocking over a chair in her anger, she turned her back to him.

Johnny looked in misery at her rigid shoulders. Now, he wouldn't be able to go out at all, or, if he did, the image of her ashy face would follow him wherever he went and take the good out of the whole day.

"Ma, I didn't mean to speak bad about the Church," he said. "I was only repeating what the Protestants say about us. It's only old guff!" When she didn't stir, he raised his voice. "If you ask me, Protestants are too mean to have kids." Then remembering something funny a crony of his father's had said one night when he had been sent to assist the two men home from the pub, he trotted it out. "Protestants are so mean they wouldn't give you the steam off their piss," he said. Too late he realized that the old crony was stinking drunk when he'd said that. For a moment his mother was struck dumb by what he'd said. Then her glance flew to the statue of the Sacred Heart on the shelf over the sink, and blessing herself, she soundlessly moved her lips. She was asking forgiveness for him from the statue!

That was too much! Johnny opened the door leading into the street, but all desire to go out had been drained from him. Instead, he leaned back against the jamb of the door and stared into space. Behind him, he heard his mother open the back door. She had evidently produced the yard brush from wherever she'd hidden it, because next minute he heard the sound of it. It had so few bristles left, she might as well have been beating the ground with a stick.

At first, standing in the doorway, Johnny gazed out vacantly, but when two girls appeared at the far end of the street, his attention fastened on them. They looked as if they were parting, but instead they remained standing beside a lamppost, talking and laughing. The lamppost was between him and one of the girls, so he couldn't see her face. The other was the young O'Grady one.

At sight of the girls, Johnny was mildly agitated, but so long as they stayed at the far end of the street, he felt safe to stay at his own door and take stock of them. Eileen—that was the name of the young O'Grady one—had put her arms around the lamppost and was swinging out from it

as if she were waltzing with it! Silly twit! The other one had a fiddle case,
but she'd left it down, and now Johnny saw she was Kitty Lardner. She
was probably too early for a music lesson and the O'Grady one was
keeping her company. What were they gassing about, he wondered?
What did girls gas about anyway? They were always at it. He looked away
in contempt.

A few minutes later when Johnny looked back, the girls were still
yapping away. A pair of gas-bags! The Lardner one now lifted up the
fiddle case, but then she left it down again and put her arms behind her
head like she was leaning back against a pillow, instead of standing in the
public street. Twits. Both of them! Had they nothing better to do than
jabber, jabber, jabber? If it weren't for his mother, he'd go back into the
house. They weren't worth wasting time on. The Lardner one was
skinny, and her hair was short and oily. The O'Grady one was at least
good-looking. He remembered Sheamus once saying she was the pick of
the O'Grady crop, and that she wouldn't be left on the shelf like her
sisters. At the time, that made him snigger, but now, remembering his
mother's words, Johnny felt sort of sorry for those older girls. They
weren't bad looking either. Wasn't one of them at one time sweet on
Sheamus? He tried to remember. Perhaps they mightn't be on the shelf if
fellows like Sheamus and their own brother weren't on the run, when
they ought by rights to be. . . . Johnny pulled himself up short. Ought to
be what? He must be getting soft in the head, he thought. He looked
around to find something that might take his mind off the girls, and
overhead, perched on a telegraph wire, he saw a row of small birds. As he
looked at them, one small bird took wing and flew away, followed in a
moment by another. Then three more took flight. The line was steadily
diminishing. Were they departing at random or mustering to some secret
call-up? Now five, no, six took off together, followed soon after by another loner until finally only two little birds sat on the wire. Johnny
decided that when those two flew away, he'd go inside and not stand any
longer like a gom in the doorway.

"What on earth are you staring at, Johnny Mack?" Johnny nearly
jumped out of his skin. Eileen O'Grady was standing beside him. How
had she come up the street without his knowing? He thought his knees
would go out from under him. Why had she passed her own door?

"I was only looking at the birds," he mumbled, confused and shamefaced. Remembering the day it was, and that she was Sean O'Grady's

sister, he felt he had to offer some explanation for being at home. "I was going to bring books back to the Library only it's a public holiday," he said. Then he threw in a small lie to make weight. "They're overdue. There'll be a fine to pay on them."

To his relief she seemed to find his explanation acceptable.

"You are the clever one of the family, aren't you—always reading—the one they say will get on in the world—always studying!"

Johnny reddened with pleasure at the compliment, but he felt he had to disclaim it.

"I don't know about that!" he said. "What's the use of any of us addling our brains when there'll be no job for us after we leave school. Maybe it's different for a girl," he added quickly when she seemed crest-fallen.

"It's no different at all," she said. "I've given up the fiddle. I'd get nowhere with it. I'm taking sewing lessons in the Tech, instead—night classes."

"Do you mind much?" Johnny asked timidly.

"Not much," she said, "I wouldn't object to being a dressmaker if I lived anywhere else but Belfast, where I'll be doing nothing from one end of the week to the other only mending old rags of clothes that ought by rights to be thrown out—I'll be turning frayed collars, relining baggy skirts, and putting false hems on smelly old coats and dresses. I know what it will be like, because I give my mother a hand. Look!" She held out her index finger. It was etched with needle pricks. But it was at her fingernails that Johnny stared; they were like small pink shells he'd seen on the seashore at Killard once when he went there on excursion organized by the school. Ashamed of his own dirty nails, he put his hands behind his back and tried with one fingernail to prize out the dirt from under the others, but his nails were stubbed from biting them and the black was lodged below the quick. He gave up. Anyway, she wasn't looking at him. Her eyes had a faraway expression. "I'd have left here long ago if it wasn't for my mother, knowing the dread that comes over her in the night if she hears a patrol car coming down our street." Johnny nodded. He knew all about that.

"Where would you go, if you could?—Is it to England?" She gave him a scathing glance.

"You must be joking! Honest to God, it's no wonder the English despise us, with everyone in Ireland thinking England the only place in the world jobs are to be got!" She pursed her lips in annoyance, like his mother did when she was threading a needle. But when his mother did it, the blood went from her lips and they wrinkled up, while Eileen O'Grady's lips got fuller and she looked as if she were going to blow make-believe kisses up into the sky.

"Where would you go, so?" he asked, curiosity getting the better of his shyness.

"Ah, I don't know!" She was suddenly dejected. "If I ever do get a chance of going, I suppose I'll end up in England like everyone else."

"Well, you're not taking off today, anyway!" Johnny said quickly, hoping to cheer her up. Her face did brighten.

"Can I ask you something, Johnny Mack? If the Library was open would you really be going there? Or were you just standing here mooning?"

For the second time Johnny recalled where her O'Grady sympathies lay. Did she expect he'd be going up with Jer to Donnegall Square to watch the parade? "If you want to know! I had a row with my mother," he said recklessly.

She seemed surprised. "About what?"

"I used a dirty word," Johnny said, and he felt his ears and neck flush painfully. To his surprise, a little smile fluttered around the girl's mouth.

"What did she say to you?"

"Nothing! But she looked at the statue we have over the sink and she blessed herself, and I knew she was apologizing to it." As he told her, his feeling of outrage came back. She only laughed.

"Oh, Johnny! All mothers are alike. One day when my brother used a bad word, my mother snatched the muffler off his neck and wound it round the head of our statue so it wouldn't hear." That was a good one! A broad grin came on Johnny's face, but the girl's voice had grown harsh. "As if God would listen to anyone in Belfast, Catholic or Protestant, with the evil they both do in His Name! Take my advice, Johnny Mack, and don't worry about your mother. It's a pity the Library isn't open. It must be nice in there. I often saw you going up the steps and I wished I had a ticket."

"Oh, a ticket is easy to get. You've only to ask for one at the desk and get it signed by a teacher," Johnny said. He couldn't get over her noticing him. Then his enthusiasm got the better of him. "Would you like me to get a ticket for you? I'd get it for you on Monday."

"Sometime perhaps," she said civilly, and Johnny came down to earth again. There was an awkward silence. Then the girl broke it. "It's a nice day, isn't it?" she said, perhaps casually, but it made Johnny feel good. He looked up at the sky where a few clouds had gathered, soft and fleecy, making the sky look bluer.

"Do you know what my mother told me before she got mad at me—she told me that when she was young, people thought nothing of going up the Divas of a fine Saturday. It must be lovely up there today," he said. The girl looked unbelieving. "Yes!" he said, "And when the days got short they used to walk out along the Lagan as far as Shaw's Bridge. Often!"

She looked less unbelieving, but she sighed.

"Those places were a lot nearer then, than now," she said. "Oh, I don't mean the hills have moved, silly. Or the Lagan! I mean the city has spread out. You'd have a dreary trudge now, before you'd reach a green field, or a bit of riverbank."

Johnny's spirits were dampened. Then he caught sight of the tip of a crane over the roofs of the houses on the other side of the street. "The docks haven't moved!" he said, laughing. "I read in a book that the gantries are the real cathedral spires of Belfast." He saw he had impressed her. "It's very nice down at the wharves. If the wind is blowing the right way you get a grand smell of the sea coming in off Strangford Lough." But once more he was overcome by embarrassment. What if she thought he was suggesting she'd go down there with him! It was with a sweet shock he heard what she said next.

"If I was going down there, I'd have to tell my mother," she said. "Wait a sec, Johnny!"

When she half-skipped, half-danced away Johnny reached behind him and gave the doorknob a gentle pull, so the lock clicked. He wasn't going to risk facing his mother again. After all, he was doing what she wanted. Anyway, Eileen was coming back and he ran to meet her. As they walked up the street together, he tried to fit his stride to hers, but it wasn't easy because her high heels made her take short, uneven steps.

"Which way will we go?" she asked when they reached the top of the street. By common consent they headed in a direction that would avoid the center of the city. Eileen was doing all the talking. As he listened to her, Johnny was so excited he couldn't hide it. Once, his ear caught a faint echo of the Orange drums in the distance and he looked uneasily at her, but she took no notice of the drums.

Soon the streets narrowed and the houses and shops got shoddier. At one corner their ears were assailed by a loud burst of drunken song coming through the louvered doors of a public house.

"What a way to spend the day!" Eileen said, but Johnny looked anxiously at the pub door thinking his father could be in there and could, at that moment, reel out into the street. It didn't seem honest to agree too wholeheartedly with Eileen.

"God help them," he said, giving the excuse his mother always gave for his father's drinking. "At least it's only themselves they're harming. They can't do too much damage even to themselves, with what little money they have in their pockets."

"Money has nothing to do with it," Eileen retorted. "Protestants are all sober, the poor ones as well as the rich ones." Johnny was startled by the way she rapped out the words.

"When did you ever see a poor Protestant?" he scoffed. "If it comes to that, it's worth their while staying off the drink when they're holding down all the decent jobs in the city."

"Those louts in that pub have their brains so rotted with booze they couldn't hold down a job, not if it was offered to them on a plate!"

"Nobody ever gave them anything on a plate. Or ever will, if you ask me," he said, but she had confused him. Where did her sympathies lie?

Then, a few yards further on, they came to another pub, and once more song wafted out, although this time, the sound was not altogether unpleasant, as if the singers were younger and better able to hold their liquor. Eileen even smiled, and when they'd gone past, she began to hum the tune.

"Do you know that song?" she asked. Very softly she sang it, her voice sweet and true, but frail. Johnny was almost afraid to breathe in case its cadences be blown away. Then a line that he had heard with indifference scores of times caught his attention and unaccountably irritated him.

> Albert Mooney says he loves her,
> All the boys are crazy on her.

An odd notion came into his head and he frowned. She stopped singing.

"What's the matter?" she asked.

"Albert is a Protestant name," he muttered.

"Oh, for God's sake! Do we have to drag religion into everything?"

He looked at her.

"You wouldn't go walking-out with a Protestant, would you?" he asked hoarsely.

Her contempt was blistering.

"I don't know any Protestants, Johnny Mack. I never spoke to one except maybe to an R.U.C. man that once stopped me in broad daylight to ask if I had a lamp on my bicycle."

That was the extent of his own acquaintance with them, but Johnny wasn't satisfied yet.

"Protestants are too bigoted to mix with us," he said.

"That's beside the point," she said coldly.

"They hate us," he said doggedly.

"How do you know?" she rapped. "How do we know what hate is if we don't have it in our own hearts?" She came to a stand again. "Do you realize, Johnny Mack, that in other countries—civilized countries—people don't know—they don't care—what religion you are? Do you think in England if a fellow liked a girl, he'd want to find out what church she belonged to before he'd speak to her? It's only in Belfast you get that muck." She began to walk on. Now, above the rooftops, rising among the cranes and gantries, they could see the mast of a ship and gulls wheeling inward in slow circles, peering down hungrily at the litter in the gutters. Raucously then, right over their heads, a huge gull screamed and tried to wrest a scrap of refuse from the beak of another, both of them flopping about in the air.

"They'll fall on us!" Eileen screamed and caught his arm. "Greedy things, thinking only of grub!"

Johnny had to laugh. "Even nightingales forage for food," he said.

She looked surprised.

"But nightingales aren't real, are they? You only get them in poetry."

"Oh, they're real all right!" Johnny said, "although you and I may never see one."

To his delight she gave his arm a squeeze.

"Oh, Johnny, it's nice to be out with a fellow who reads books and who . . ." She paused, and a blush came into her cheeks. "I may as well tell you, Johnny Mack, it was because I've seen you going into the library every week that I spoke to you today. I thought maybe you'd have more in your head than your brother, Sheamus, or my own gom of a brother." Before he could answer, however, her face clouded. "All the same I don't suppose you could have been brought up in the same house as Sheamus without flirting with some of his ideas?"

Flirting? To Johnny this was a word that had only one connotation. He was taken aback.

"Are we never going to come to those docks?" he exclaimed, to cover his feeling of awkwardness.

They were nearer to them than he thought. The next street was darkened by high warehouses and their way was frequently impeded by lorries and vans backing in and out of archways, loading and unloading. Now, along with the screams of gulls, there was the bawling of navvies and stevedores between whom dodged distraught clerks, with sheaves of lading bills flapping in draughts, from gateways and alleys. High in the sky, the long steel arms of cranes swung out, their giant-toothed buckets clanking angrily on their chains, as if ready to bite at random into anything that offered. From somewhere nearby, there stole a polluted smell of stagnant, land-locked water. This was not at all what Johnny had expected. Still, he hurried Eileen on. Then, quite suddenly, at the end of the street, they flashed out onto the quayside and instantly everything changed. The breezes were now laden with a clean, briny smell, and seen against the blue sky, the arms of the cranes appeared frail as the webbed wings of a dragonfly. When a crane let down its bucket, it was seen that its prey was precisely designated, a crate or container upon which it laid hold, as delicately and deliberately as human fingers, to swing it aloft with a rhythm so true it dispelled fear.

Taking a deep breath of the sea air, Eileen sat down on a bollard, edging over to make room for Johnny. It amused him to see how neatly she fitted on less than half the bollard, while he could only hope to rest one hip on the half left for him. Even then, he had to make struts of his feet to prop himself up.

"It's nice here all right, isn't it?" Eileen said.

Johnny felt giddy with joy.

"You didn't really mean what you said—that you'd leave here, if you got the chance, did you?" he asked.

"I did," she said soberly. "I'd go like a shot, wouldn't you?"

Johnny blinked. It had never entered his head that he would ever leave this city where he had been born.

"Well?"

"I don't know," he said. Her question had unsettled him and he stared miserably out over the lough. Far out, angered by the offshore winds, the waves were choppy, but when they reached the harbor wall below him they nuzzled their snouts in tangles of black seaweed and shivered with delight. "If it weren't for the curfew and the raids, Belfast wouldn't be such a bad place, would it?"

Eileen shook her head.

"I can't picture this place being any different from what it's been all my life," she said. She turned and faced him. "How would you like to spend the whole of your days watching your words, with your mother waiting her chance to throw a cloth over your head like you'd cover a canary to stop it singing?" She was deadly earnest, but Johnny thought it was the funniest thing he'd heard in a long time.

"I wonder if Protestant mothers throw mufflers over their statues of King Billy every time a Protestant kid lets out a swear?" he said, laughing.

"Protestants don't curse or swear. Not before women anyway," Eileen said primly.

"How do you know? You said you never spoke to one," Johnny said. And at that she did laugh. "Listen," Johnny said. "You know those Protestant houses with King Billy painted on the gable end—wouldn't it be great sport to sneak up some night and paint Billy green?"

Eileen giggled. "Turn him into Saint Patrick!"

"Wait till I tell you something Sheamus and his pals really did one night when they were kids. They painted the pillar box in our street green. The real joke of it was that next morning the R.U.C. men didn't notice anything wrong and Sheamus saw them going off duty in the morning, swanking along pompous as ever, swinging their batons and . . ."

Eileen guessed what was coming and gave a little shriek. "I know. Their backsides were all green!" Backside was not a word Johnny would have used in her presence, but inconsistency was what he had always expected from girls. He was getting happier and happier. "That's the way to teach them, you know," Eileen said. "Make monkeys out of them. We'll never do it by sniping!"

"Ah, we'll never teach them anything—not by any means," Johnny said. A sudden gloom had come down on him again. "Haven't we been trying for four hundred years?" He stooped and picked up a loose pebble from a heap of gravel at his feet. The feel of the stone in his fist worked upon him, and raising his arm, he flung it at a lamppost a few yards from where they sat. The stone pinged loudly against the metal reflector but did no harm.

"What made you do that? You could have broken that lamp," Eileen said angrily.

"So what! I'd love to smash every lamp in Belfast," Johnny said savagely. "Often when I'm walking along the street, going about my own business, I can see the R.U.C. staring at me like I was a mongrel that was going to lift his leg against one of their rotten lampposts."

When Eileen said nothing he looked at her, and to his astonishment there were tears in her eyes.

"I'm not surprised you upset your mother," she said. "Such language! I thought you were different."

Johnny wanted to cry out that, of course, he was different, but instead, he found himself reaching down for another stone, selecting it for its sharp edges, and this time, taking conscious aim, he fired it straight at the globe of the lamp. He missed again—only by accident—but an involuntary sigh of relief escaped him, and he saw that Eileen knew he regretted his action.

"Come on, Johnny, we'd better be getting back." She stood up. "I told my mother I'd be home early." She was now facing away from the lough, toward where between the warehouses, the hills of Divas could be seen, their green expanses darkened in places by the purple shadows of passing clouds.

"What a place to put a cemetery," she said inconsequentially, and although it had never bothered him before, Johnny looked with distaste at the vast cemetery that dominated Belfast. Then Eileen sighed. "I suppose we ought not grudge the dead their last resting place up there in the peace and quiet," she said sadly. "Do you know what I think, Johnny? The only real patriotism in the world is the feeling people have for the sod. My mother told me once that the emigrants, before they went onto the ship, used to take up a fistful of earth and keep it all their lives, to be sprinkled on their coffins in the foreign land they were going to. The land was here before any of us—Catholics and Protestants." Suddenly she faced back to the lough again, where a ship was heading out to sea. "Oh, Johnny, supposing we were on that ship! Supposing we were leaving here forever."

"Forever?" Johnny wondered was she joking.

"Well perhaps not forever," she said, "but till all the hatred is burnt out of the people's hearts." Johnny looked so lost she laughed. "Well maybe we might come back when there is no trace left of this wretched city, and when its dark, ugly churches of every creed and kind are heaps of stone with the green grass growing over them."

Ah! Now Johnny understood. It was a fantasy.

"In three thousand years from now?" he cried. "Oh, Eileen! We'd sail in like the Milesians." She nodded, but Johnny could see she was proud of his book learning.

"Come on, let's go home," she said again. "I didn't tell you, but when I went back for my coat and scarf, my mother said I could bring you home with me for tea if I wanted."

Johnny's heart began to thump so violently he thought his ribs would crack.

"We can go back through Donnegall Square. It'll be shorter, and the parade will be over by now."

Eileen hesitated.

"As long as we don't stop along the way," she cautioned. "Promise!"

Johnny promised. Together they stepped out happily, briskly, and although walking quickly, Johnny found it really hard to keep step with her tap-tappety heels.

"Why, in the name of God, do girls wear such crazy shoes," he exclaimed.

"Every fellow asks that! Here, let me link you," Eileen said. Immediately, one rhythm ran through them, and in no time, they were in the center of the city.

The parade was over. Even the onlookers had gone, leaving the pavement scattered with cigarette butts and toffee wrappers. The few stragglers still in sight were heading homeward or making for their local pub. All the pubs in the city would soon be throbbing with song.

When they reached the residential area, Johnny and Eileen slowed down and began to stroll more leisurely. Johnny gave a sidelong look at her, but Eileen was staring in front of her. The quiet road had been empty when they first entered it, but now at the far end three youths were coming toward them. In this locality they would probably be Protestants, Johnny thought, but what did that matter? When he looked at Eileen though, her face had gone white. He realized then that the advancing trio were walking abreast, arms linked, the full of the footpath. There would be no room for the two parties to pass. The three buckos were advancing upright and as purposeful as R.U.C. men.

"Bloody bastards!" Johnny muttered.

"Johnny! Please!" Eileen tugged at his arm. "Let's cross the street."

"And let the likes of them push us into the gutter?"

"Oh, Johnny, what does it matter? Please, please!" she pleaded. She tried to unlink him, but he pressed her tighter to him. He could hear the feet of the oncoming youths marching in unison like the feet of soldiers, and like soldiers, they were spruced up and their boots were glossy with polish. Johnny was miserably aware of his raveled gansey and tub-washed shirt, but above all, he was conscious of his cracked, unpolished boots. He raised his head and he simply couldn't believe his eyes: one of them was that bastard from the Grammar School—the one in the middle. As Eileen made another and almost frantic effort to drag herself free, he got confused. No. It was not the one in the middle that was his enemy. It was the one on the inside. Johnny's eyes slotted from face to face of the three, and it seemed to him that they all had the same face, the same hateful, sneering Protestant face. And it was at him they were sneering. For a moment, shame almost disarmed him. He nearly let Eileen pull him out of their way. But at that moment, the fellow on the outside doffed his cap to Eileen, and side-stepping like a dancer, fell back politely behind his companions, leaving place for her to pass. Eileen wrenched free from Johnny and went forward with lowered eyes.

Johnny felt his face go blood red. Now, with stinking Protestant politeness the bastard was waiting for him, too, to pass, but Johnny saw through him. Trying to show his superiority! That was it! He stood his ground. He would not pass. He looked quickly at the other two. But now he did not know which was the one he knew. Jer was right. All Protestants looked the same. And so he shot out his fist and smashed it into the nearest face. There was a thin sound like chicken bones breaking, and then Johnny broke into a run to catch up with Eileen.

But where was she? The street ahead was empty. Panic-stricken, he looked back. The fellow he'd hit was on the ground propped against the railings in a sitting position. The other two were ministering to him, a small pool of blood forming under their feet. Then he saw that Eileen was on the ground, too. Good God, what were they doing to her? He ran back madly, but when he pushed his way between the brutes, he saw Eileen was on her knees pressing a handkerchief to the face of the fellow he'd hit. Johnny gaped stupidly at her. After a moment or two one of the fellows helped her to her feet.

"You'd better go," the youth said to her, and bending, he picked up her handkerchief that was soaked with blood. "What will I do with this?" he asked. "Will I have it washed and send it back to you?" Eileen said nothing, but Johnny snatched the handkerchief from him and stuffed it into his pocket.

"We have soap and water too," he said hysterically, and he grabbed Eileen by the arm. But she broke away from him.

"Leave me alone," she gulped. "Go away!"

"What do you mean?" he demanded, ignoring the others. "Your mother told you to bring me home to tea."

She shook her head.

"It's too late, Johnny," she said. Then when he went to protest, she held up her hand. "I'm not talking about time by the clock!" she said. Johnny didn't know what she meant, but one of the other fellows sniggered, and to Johnny's relief, Eileen turned on him.

"What's so funny?" she demanded. She stared at the three youths in turn, including the fellow on the ground who was getting to his feet with a grin on his face. "You were sneering at us, weren't you?" she said. She pointed to Johnny. "You were out to provoke him. You stupid fools! You think you're great, don't you? With your drums and sashes and your Union Jacks!" Then she swung toward Johnny. "And you! You, with your Green, White, and Gold! Soon there'll be only one flag in Belfast. Here, give me that!" she cried, and reaching forward, she pulled the blood-stained handkerchief out of Johnny's pocket and spiked it on the railings. "This will be your flag," she cried, and without another look at any of them, she walked away, going as steadily as was possible in her cheap papery shoes.

THE LOST SALT GIFT OF BLOOD

Alistair MacLeod

Now in the early evening the sun is flashing everything in gold. It bathes the blunt gray rocks that loom yearningly out toward Europe and it touches upon the stunted spruce and the low-lying lichens and the delicate hardy ferns and the ganglia rooted moss and the tiny tough rock cranberries. The gray and slanting rain squalls have swept in from the sea and then departed with all the suddenness of surprise marauders. Everything before them and beneath them has been rapidly, briefly, and thoroughly drenched and now the wet droplets catch and hold the sun's infusion in a myriad of rainbow colors. Far beyond the harbor's mouth more tiny squalls seem to be forming, moving rapidly across the surface of the sea out there beyond land's end where the blue ocean turns to gray in rain and distance and the strain of eyes. Even farther out, somewhere beyond Cape Spear lies Dublin and the Irish coast; far away but still the nearest land and closer now than is Toronto or Detroit to say nothing of North America's more western cities; seeming almost hazily visible now in imagination's mist.

Overhead the ivory white gulls wheel and cry, flashing also in the purity of the sun and the clean, freshly washed air. Sometimes they glide to the blue-green surface of the harbor, squawking and garbling; at times almost standing on their pink webbed feet as if they would walk on water, flapping their wings pompously against their breasts like over-conditioned he-men who have successfully passed their body-building courses. At other times they gather in lazy groups on the rocks above the harbor's entrance murmuring softly to themselves or looking also quietly out toward what must be Ireland and the vastness of the sea.

The harbor itself is very small and softly curving, seeming like a tiny, peaceful womb nurturing the life that now lies within it but which originated from without; came from without and through the narrow, rock-tight channel that admits the entering and withdrawing sea. That sea is entering again now, forcing itself gently but inevitably between the tightness of the opening and laving the rocky walls and rising and rolling into the harbor's inner cove. The dories rise at their moorings and the tide laps higher on the piles and advances upward toward the high-water marks upon the land; the running moon-drawn tides of spring.

Around the edges of the harbor brightly colored houses dot the wet and glistening rocks. In some ways they seem almost like defiantly optimistic horseshoe nails: yellow and scarlet and green and pink; buoyantly yet firmly permanent in the gray unsundered rock.

At the harbor's entrance the small boys are jigging for the beautifully speckled salmon-pink sea trout. Barefootedly they stand on the tide-wet rocks flicking their wrists and sending their glistening lines in shimmering golden arcs out into the rising tide. Their voices mount excitedly as they shout to one another encouragement, advice, consolation. The trout fleck dazzlingly on their sides as they are drawn toward the rocks, turning to seeming silver as they flash within the sea.

It is all of this that I see now, standing at the final road's end of my twenty-five hundred mile journey. The road ends here—quite literally ends at the door of a now abandoned fishing shanty some six brief yards in front of where I stand. The shanty is gray and weather-beaten with two boarded-up windows, vanishing, wind-whipped shingles and a heavy rusted padlock chained fast to a twisted door. Piled before the twisted door and its equally twisted frame are some marker buoys, a small pile of rotted rope, a broken oar, and an old and rust-flaked anchor.

The option of driving my small rented Volkswagen the remaining six yards and then negotiating a tight many twists of the steering wheel turn still exists. I would be then facing toward the west and could simply retrace the manner of my coming. I could easily drive away before anything might begin.

Instead I walk beyond the road's end and the fishing shanty and begin to descend the rocky path that winds tortuously and narrowly along and down the cliff's edge to the sea. The small stones roll and turn and scrape beside and beneath my shoes and after only a few steps the leather is nicked and scratched. My toes press hard against its straining surface.

As I approach the actual water's edge four small boys are jumping excitedly upon the glistening rocks. One of them has made a strike and is attempting to reel in his silver, turning prize. The other three have laid down their rods in their enthusiasm and are shouting encouragement and giving almost physical moral support: "Don't let him get away, John," they say. "Keep the line steady." "Hold the end of the rod up." "Reel in the slack." "Good." "What a dandy!"

Across the harbor's clear water another six or seven shout the same delirious messages. The silver, turning fish is drawn toward the rock. In the shallows he flips and arcs, his flashing body breaking the water's surface as he walks upon his tail. The small fisherman has now his rod almost completely vertical. Its tip sings and vibrates high above his head while at his feet the trout spins and curves. Both of his hands are clenched around the rod and his knuckles strain white through the water-roughened redness of small boy hands. He does not know whether he should relinquish the rod and grasp at the lurching trout or merely heave the rod backward and flip the fish behind him. Suddenly he decides upon the latter but even as he heaves his bare feet slide out from beneath him on the smooth wetness of the rock and he slips down into the water. With a pirouetting leap the trout turns glisteningly and tears itself free. In a darting flash of darkened greenness it rights itself within the regained water and is gone. "Oh damn!" says the small fisherman, struggling upright onto his rock. He bites his lower lip to hold back the tears welling within his eyes. There is a small trickle of blood coursing down from a tiny scratch on the inside of his wrist and he is wet up to his knees. I reach down to retrieve the rod and return it to him.

Suddenly a shout rises from the opposite shore. Another line zings tautly through the water throwing off fine showers of iridescent droplets. The shouts and contagious excitement spread anew. "Don't let him get away!" "Good for you." "Hang on!" "Hang on!"

I am caught up in it myself and wish also to shout some enthusiastic advice but I do not know what to say. The trout curves up from the water in a wriggling arch and lands behind the boys in the moss and lichen that grow down to the sea-washed rocks. They race to free it from the line and proclaim about its size.

On our side of the harbor the boys begin to talk. "Where do you live?" they ask and is it far away and is it bigger than St. John's? Awkwardly I try to tell them the nature of the North American Midwest. In turn I ask them if they go to school. "Yes," they say. Some of them go to St. Bonaventure's which is the Catholic school and others go to Twilling

Memorial. They are all in either grades four or five. All of them say that they like school and that they like their teachers.

The fishing is good they say and they come here almost every evening. "Yesterday I caught me a nine pounder," says John. Eagerly they show me all of their simple equipment. The rods are of all varieties as are the lines. At the lines' ends the leaders are thin transparencies terminating in grotesque three-clustered hooks. A foot or so from each hook there is a silver spike knotted into the leader. Some of the boys say the trout are attracted by the flashing of the spike; others say that it acts only as a weight or sinker. No line is without one.

"Here, sir," says John, "have a go. Don't get your shoes wet." Standing on the slippery rocks in my smooth-soled shoes I twice attempt awkward casts. Both times the line loops up too highly and the spike splashes down far short of the running, rising life of the channel.

"Just a flick of the wrist, sir," he says, "just a flick of the wrist. You'll soon get the hang of it." His hair is red and curly and his face is splashed with freckles and his eyes are clear and blue. I attempt three or four more casts and then pass the rod back to the hands where it belongs.

And now it is time for supper. The calls float down from the women standing in the doorways of the multicolored houses and obediently the small fishermen gather up their equipment and their catches and prepare to ascend the narrow upward-winding paths. The sun has descended deeper into the sea and the evening has become quite cool. I recognize this with surprise and a slight shiver. In spite of the advice given to me and my own precautions my feet are wet and chilled within my shoes. No place to be unless barefooted or in rubber boots. Perhaps for me no place at all.

As we lean into the steepness of the path my young companions continue to talk, their accents broad and Irish. One of them used to have a tame sea gull at his house, had it for seven years. His older brother found it on the rocks and brought it home. His grandfather called it Joey. "Because it talked so much," explained John. It died last week and they held a funeral about a mile away from the shore where there was enough soil to dig a grave. Along the shore itself it is almost solid rock and there is no ground for a grave. It's the same with people they say. All week they have been hopefully looking along the base of the cliffs for another sea gull but have not found one. You cannot kill a sea gull they say, the government protects them because they are scavengers and keep the harbors clean.

The path is narrow and we walk in single file. By the time we reach the shanty and my rented car I am wheezing and badly out of breath. So badly out of shape for a man of thirty-three; sauna baths do nothing for your wind. The boys walk easily, laughing and talking beside me. With polite enthusiasm they comment upon my car. Again there exists the possibility of restarting the car's engine and driving back the road that I have come. After all, I have not seen a single adult except for the women calling down the news of supper. I stand and fiddle with my keys.

The appearance of the man and the dog is sudden and unexpected. We have been so casual and unaware in front of the small automobile that we have neither seen nor heard their approach along the rock-worn road. The dog is short, stocky, and black and white. White hair floats and feathers freely from his sturdy legs and paws as he trots along the rock looking expectantly out into the harbor. He takes no notice of me. The man is short and stocky as well and he also appears as black and white. His rubber boots are black and his dark heavy worsted trousers are supported by a broadly scarred and blackened belt. The buckle is shaped like a dory with a fisherman standing in the bow. Above the belt there is a dark navy woolen jersey and upon his head a toque of the same material. His hair beneath the toque is white as is the three-or-four-day stubble on his face. His eyes are blue and his hands heavy, gnarled, and misshapen. It is hard to tell from looking at him whether he is in his sixties, seventies, or eighties.

"Well, it is a nice evening tonight," he says looking first at John and then to me. "The barometer has not dropped so perhaps fair weather will continue for a day or two. It will be good for the fishing."

He picks a piece of gnarled, gray driftwood from the roadside and swings it slowly back and forth in his right hand. With desperate anticipation the dog dances back and forth before him, his intense eyes glittering at the stick. When it is thrown into the harbor he barks joyously and disappears, hurling himself down the bank in a scrambling avalanche of small stones. In seconds he reappears with only his head visible, cutting a silent but rapidly advancing V through the quiet serenity of the harbor. The boys run to the bank's edge and shout encouragement to him— much as they had been doing earlier for one another. "It's farther out," they cry, "to the right, to the right." Almost totally submerged, he cannot see the stick he swims to find. The boys toss stones in its general direction and he raises himself out of the water to see their landing splashdowns and to change his wide-waked course.

"How have you been?" asks the old man, reaching for a pipe and a pouch of tobacco and then without waiting for an answer, "perhaps you'll stay for supper. There are just the three of us now."

We begin to walk along the road in the direction that he has come. Before long the boys rejoin us accompanied by the dripping dog with the recovered stick. He waits for the old man to take it from him and then showers us all with a spray of water from his shaggy coat. The man pats and scratches the damp head and the dripping ears. He keeps the returned stick and thwacks it against his rubber boots as we continue to walk along the rocky road I have so recently traveled in my Volkswagen.

Within a few yards the houses begin to appear upon our left. Frame and flat-roofed, they cling to the rocks looking down into the harbor. In storms their windows are splashed by the sea but now their bright colors are buoyantly brave in the shadows of the descending dusk. At the third gate, John, the man, and the dog turn in. I follow them. The remaining boys continue on; they wave and say, "So long."

The path that leads through the narrow whitewashed gate has had its stones worn smooth by the passing of countless feet. On either side there is a row of small, smooth stones, also neatly whitewashed, and seeming like a procession of large white eggs or tiny unbaked loaves of bread. Beyond these stones and also on either side, there are some cast-off tires also whitewashed and serving as flower beds. Within each whitened circumference the colorful low-flying flowers nod; some hardy strain of pansies or perhaps marigolds. The path leads on to the square, green house, with its white borders and shutters. On one side of the wooden doorstep a skate blade has been nailed—for the wiping off of feet and beyond the swinging screen door there is a porch which smells saltily of the sea. A variety of sou'westers and rubber boots and mitts and caps hang from the driven nails or lie at the base of the wooden walls.

Beyond the porch there is the kitchen where the woman is at work. All of us enter. The dog walks across the linoleum-covered floor, his nails clacking, and flings himself with a contented sigh beneath the wooden table. Almost instantly he is asleep, his coat still wet from his swim within the sea.

The kitchen is small. It has an iron cook stove, a table against one wall and three or four handmade chairs of wood. There is also a wooden rocking chair covered by a cushion. The rockers are so thin from years of use that it is hard to believe they still function. Close by the table there is a wash stand with two pails of water upon it. A wash basin hangs from a driven nail in its side and above it is an old-fashioned mirrored medicine cabinet. There is also a large cupboard, a low-lying couch, and a window facing upon the sea. On the walls a barometer hangs as well as two pictures, one of a rather jaunty young couple taken many years ago. It is yellowed and rather indistinct; the woman in a long dress with her hair done up in ringlets, the man with a serge suit that is slightly too large for him and with a tweed cap pulled rakishly over his right eye. He has an accordion strapped over his shoulders and his hands are fanned out on the buttons and keys. The other is one of the Christ-child. Beneath it is written, "Sweet Heart of Jesus Pray for Us."

The woman at the stove is tall and fine featured. Her gray hair is combed briskly back from her forehead and neatly coiled with a large pin at the base of her neck. Her eyes are as gray as the storm scud of the sea. Like her husband it is difficult to define her age other than that it is past sixty. She wears a blue print dress, a plain blue apron and low-heeled brown shoes. She is turning fish within a frying pan when we enter.

Her eyes contain only mild surprise as she first regards me. Then with recognition they glow in open hostility which in turn subsides and yields to self-control. She continues at the stove while the rest of us sit upon the chairs.

During the meal that follows we are reserved and shy in our lonely adult ways; groping for and protecting what perhaps may be the only awful dignity we possess. John, unheedingly, talks on and on. He is in the fifth grade and is doing well. They are learning percentages and the mysteries of decimals; to change a percent to a decimal fraction you move the decimal point two places to the left and drop the percent sign. You always, always do so. They are learning the different breeds of domestic animals: the four main breeds of dairy cattle are Holstein, Ayrshire, Guernsey, and Jersey. He can play the mouth organ and will demonstrate after supper. He has twelve lobster traps of his own. They were originally broken ones thrown up on the rocky shore by storms. Ira, he says nodding toward the old man, helped him fix them, nailing on new lathes and knitting new headings. Now they are set along the rocks near the harbor's entrance. He is averaging a pound a trap and the "big" fishermen say that that is better than some of them are doing. He is saving his money in a

little imitation keg that was also washed up on the shore. He would like
to buy an outboard motor for the small reconditioned skiff he now uses to
visit his traps. At present he has only oars.

"John here has the makings of a good fisherman," says the old man.
"He's up at five most every morning when I am putting on the fire. He
and the dog are already out along the shore and back before I've made
tea."

"When I was in Toronto," says John, "no one was ever up before
seven. I would make my own tea and wait. It was wonderful sad. There
were gulls there though, flying over Toronto harbor. We went to see them
on two Sundays."

After the supper we move the chairs back from the table. The woman
clears away the dishes and the old man turns on the radio. First he listens
to the weather forecast and then turns to short wave where he picks up
the conversations from the off-shore fishing boats. They are conversations of catches and winds and tides and of the women left behind on the
rocky shores. John appears with his mouth organ, standing at a respectful
distance. The old man notices him, nods, and shuts off the radio. Rising,
he goes upstairs, the sound of his feet echoing down to us. Returning he
carries an old and battered accordion. "My fingers have so much rheu-
matism," he says, "that I find it hard to play anymore."

Seated, he slips his arms through the straps and begins the squeezing
accordion motions. His wife takes off her apron and stands behind him
with one hand upon his shoulder. For a moment they take on the essence
of the once young people in the photograph. They begin to sing:

> Come all ye fair and tender ladies
> Take warning how you court your men
> They're like the stars on a summer's morning
> First they'll appear and then they're gone.
>
> I wish I were a tiny sparrow
> And I had wings and I could fly
> I'd fly away to my own true lover
> And all he'd ask I would deny.
>
> Alas I'm not a tiny sparrow
> I have not wings nor can I fly
> And on this earth in grief and sorrow
> I am bound until I die.

John sits on one of the homemade chairs playing his mouth organ. He
seems as all mouth organ players the world over: his right foot tapping out

the measures and his small shoulders now round and hunched above the cupped hand instrument.

"Come now and sing with us, John," says the old man.

Obediently he takes the mouth organ from his mouth and shakes the moisture drops upon his sleeve. All three of them begin to sing, spanning easily the half century of time that touches their extremes. The old and the young singing now their songs of loss in different comprehensions. Stranded here, alien of my middle generation, I tap my leather foot self-consciously upon the linoleum. The words sweep and swirl about my head. Fog does not touch like snow yet it is more heavy and more dense. Oh moisture comes in many forms!

> All alone as I strayed by the banks of the river
> Watching the moonbeams at evening of day
> All alone as I wandered I spied a young stranger
> Weeping and wailing with many a sigh.
>
> Weeping for one who is now lying lonely
> Weeping for one who no mortal can save
> As the foaming dark waters flow silently past him
> Onward they flow over young Jenny's grave.
>
> Oh Jenny my darling come tarry here with me
> Don't leave me alone, love, distracted in pain
> For as death is the dagger that plied us asunder
> Wide is the gulf love between you and I.

After the singing stops we all sit rather uncomfortably for a moment. The mood seeming to hang heavily upon our shoulders. Then with my single exception all come suddenly to action. John gets up and takes his battered schoolbooks to the kitchen table. The dog jumps up on a chair beside him and watches solemnly in a supervisory manner. The woman takes some navy yarn, the color of her husband's jersey, and begins to knit. She is making another jersey and is working on the sleeve. The old man rises and beckons me to follow him into the tiny parlor. The stuffed furniture is old and worn. There is a tiny wood-burning heater in the center of the room. It stands on a square of galvanized metal which protects the floor from falling, burning coals. The stovepipe rises and vanishes into the wall on its way to the upstairs. There is an old-fashioned mantelpiece on the wall behind the stove. It is covered with odd shapes of driftwood from the shore and a variety of exotically shaped bottles, blue and green and red which are from the shore as well. There are pictures here too: of the couple in the other picture; and one of them with their five daughters; and one of the five daughters by themselves. In that far-off picture time all of the daughters seem roughly between the ages of ten and eighteen. The youngest has the reddest hair of all. So red that it seems to triumph over the nonphotographic colors of lonely black and white. The pictures are in standard wooden frames.

From behind the ancient chesterfield the old man pulls a collapsible card table and pulls down its warped and shaky legs. Also from behind the chesterfield he takes a faded checkerboard and a large old-fashioned matchbox of rattling wooden checkers. The spine of the board is almost cracked through and is strengthened by layers of adhesive tape. The checkers are circumferences of wood sawed from a length of broom handle. They are about three quarters of an inch thick. Half of them are painted a very bright blue and the other half an equally eye-catching red. "John made these," says the old man, "all of them are not really the same thickness but they are good enough. He gave it a good try."

We begin to play checkers. He takes the blue and I the red. The house is silent with only the click-clack of the knitting needles sounding through the quiet rooms. From time to time the old man lights his pipe, digging out the old ashes with a flattened nail and tamping in the fresh tobacco with the same nail's head. The blue smoke winds lazily and haphazardly toward the low-beamed ceiling. The game is solemn as is the next and then the next. Neither of us loses all of the time.

"It is time for some of us to be in bed," says the old woman after awhile. She gathers up her knitting and rises from her chair. In the kitchen John neatly stacks his schoolbooks on one corner of the table in anticipation of the morning. He goes outside for a moment and then returns. Saying goodnight very formally he goes up the stairs to bed. In a short while the old woman follows, her footsteps traveling the same route.

We continue to play our checkers, wreathed in smoke and only partially aware of the muffled footfalls sounding softly above our heads.

When the old man gets up to go outside I am not really surprised, any more than I am when he returns with the brown, ostensible vinegar jug. Poking at the declining kitchen fire, he moves the kettle about seeking the warmest spot on the cooling stove. He takes two glasses from the cupboard, a sugar bowl, and two spoons. The kettle begins to boil.

Even before tasting it, I know the rum to be strong and overproof. It comes at night and in fog from the French islands of St. Pierre and

Miquelon. Coming over in the low-throttled fishing boats, riding in imitation gas cans. He mixes the rum and the sugar first, watching them marry and dissolve. Then to prevent the breakage of the glasses he places a teaspoon in each and adds the boiling water. The odor rises richly, its sweetness hung in steam. He brings the glasses to the table, holding them by their tops so that his fingers will not burn.

We do not say anything for some time, sitting upon the chairs, while the sweetened, heated richness moves warmly through and from our stomachs and spreads upward to our brains. Outside the wind begins to blow, moaning and faintly rattling the window's whitened shutters. He rises and brings refills. We are warm within the dark and still within the wind. A clock strikes regularly the strokes of ten.

It is difficult to talk at times with or without liquor; difficult to achieve the actual act of saying. Sitting still we listen further to the rattle of the wind; not knowing where nor how we should begin. Again the glasses are refilled.

"When she married in Toronto," he says at last, "we figured that maybe John should be with her and with her husband. That maybe he would be having more of a chance there in the city. But we would be putting it off and it weren't until nigh on two years ago that he went. Went with a woman from down the cove going to visit her daughter. Well, what was wrong was that we missed him wonderful awful. More fearful than we ever thought. Even the dog. Just pacing the floor and looking out the window and walking along the rocks of the shore. Like us had no moorings, lost in the fog or on the ice floes in a snow squall. Nigh sick unto our hearts we was. Even the grandmother who before that was maybe thinking small to herself that he was trouble in her old age. Ourselves having never had no sons only daughters."

He pauses, then rising goes upstairs and returns with an envelope. From it he takes a picture which shows two young people standing self-consciously before a half-ton pickup with a wooden extension ladder fastened to its side. They appear to be in their middle twenties. The door of the truck has the information: "Jim Farrell, Toronto: Housepainting, Eavestroughing, Aluminum Siding, Phone 481-3484," lettered on its surface.

"This was in the last letter," he says. "That Farrell I guess was a nice enough fellow, from Heartsick Bay he was."

"Anyway they could have no more peace with John than we could without him. Like I says he was here too long before his going and it all took ahold of us the way it will. They sent word that he was coming on the plane to St. John's with a woman they'd met through a Newfoundland club. I was to go to St. John's to meet him. Well, it was all wrong the night before the going. The signs all bad; the grandmother knocked off the lampshade and it broke in a hunnerd pieces—the sign of death; and the window blind fell and clattered there on the floor and then lied still. And the dog runned around like he was crazy, moanen and cryen worse than the swiles does out on the ice, and throwen hisself against the walls and jumpen on the table and at the window where the blind fell until we would have to be letten him out. But it be no better for he runned and throwed hisself in the sea and then come back and howled outside the same window and jumped against the wall, splashen the water from his coat all over it. Then he be runnen back to the sea again. All the neighbors heard him and said I should bide at home and not go to St. John's at all. We be all wonderful scared and not know what to do and the next mornen, first thing I drops me knife."

"But still I feels I has to go. It be foggy all the day and everyone be thinken the plane won't come or be able to land. And I says, small to myself, now here in the fog be the bad luck and the death but then there the plane be, almost like a ghost ship comen out the fog with all its lights shinen. I think maybe he won't be on it but soon he comen through the fog, first with the woman and then seen me and starten to run, closer and closer till I can feel him in me arms and the tears on both our cheeks. Powerful strange how things will take one. That night they be killed."

From the envelope that contained the picture he draws forth a tattered clipping:

> Jennifer Farrell of Roncevalles Avenue was instantly killed early this morning and her husband James died later in emergency at St. Joseph's Hospital. The accident occurred about 2 A.M. when the pickup truck in which they were traveling went out of control on Queen St. W. and struck a utility pole. It is thought that bad visibility caused by a heavy fog may have contributed to the accident. The Farrells were originally from Newfoundland.

Again he moves to refill the glasses. "We be all alone," he says. "All our other daughters married and far away in Montreal, Toronto, or the States. Hard for them to come back here, even to visit; they comes only every three years or so for perhaps a week. So we be haven only him."

And now my head begins to reel even as I move to the filling of my own glass. Not waiting this time for the courtesy of his offer. Making myself perhaps too much at home with this man's glass and this man's rum and this man's house and all the feelings of his love. Even as I did before. Still locked again for words.

Outside we stand and urinate, turning our backs to the seeming gale so as not to splash our wind snapped trousers. We are almost driven forward to rock upon our toes and settle on our heels, so blow the gusts. Yet in spite of all, the stars shine clearly down. It will indeed be a good day for the fishing and this wind eventually will calm. The salt hangs heavy in the air and the water booms against the rugged rocks. I take a stone and throw it against the wind into the sea.

Going up the stairs we clutch the wooden bannister unsteadily and say goodnight.

The room has changed very little. The window rattles in the wind and the unfinished beams sway and creak. The room is full of sound. Like a foolish Lockwood I approach the window although I hear no voice. There is no Catherine who cries to be let in. Standing unsteadily on one foot when required I manage to undress, draping my trousers across the wooden chair. The bed is clean. It makes no sound. It is plain and wooden, its mattress stuffed with hay or kelp. I feel it with my hand and pull back the heavy patchwork quilts. Still I do not go into it. Instead I go back to the door which has no knob but only an ingenious latch formed from a twisted nail. Turning it, I go out into the hallway. All is dark and the house seems even more inclined to creak where there is no window. Feeling along the wall with my outstretched hand I find the door quite easily. It is closed with the same kind of latch and not difficult to open. But no one waits on the other side. I stand and bend my ear to hear the even sound of my one son's sleeping. He does not beckon anymore than the nonexistent voice in the outside wind. I hesitate to touch the latch for fear that I may waken him and disturb his dreams. And if I did what would I say? Yet I would like to see him in his sleep this once and see the room with the quiet bed once more and the wooden chair beside it from off an old wrecked trawler. There is no boiled egg or shaker of salt or glass of water waiting on the chair within this closed room's darkness.

Once though there was a belief held in the outports, that if a girl would see her own true lover she should boil an egg and scoop out half the shell and fill it with salt. Then she should take it to bed with her and eat it, leaving a glass of water by her bedside. In the night her future husband or a vision of him would appear and offer her the glass. But she must only do it once.

It is the type of belief that bright young graduate students were collecting eleven years ago for the theses and archives of North America and also, they hoped, for their own fame. Even as they sought the near-Elizabethan songs and ballads that had sailed from County Kerry and from Devon and Cornwall. All about the wild, wide sea and the flashing silver dagger and the lost and faithless lover. Echoes to and from the lovely, lonely hills and glens of West Virginia and the standing stones of Tennessee.

Across the hall the old people are asleep. The old man's snoring rattles as do the windows; except that now and then there are catching gasps within his breath. In three or four short hours he will be awake and will go down to light his fire. I turn and walk back softly to my room.

Within the bed the warm sweetness of the rum is heavy and intense. The darkness presses down upon me but still it brings no sleep. There are no voices and no shadows that are real. There are only walls of memory touched restlessly by flickers of imagination.

Oh I would like to see my way more clearly. I, who have never understood the mystery of fog. I would perhaps like to capture it in a jar like the beautiful childhood butterflies that always die in spite of the airholes punched with nails in the covers of their captivity—leaving behind the vapors of their lives and deaths; or perhaps as the unknowing child who collects the gray moist condoms from the lover's lanes only to have them taken from him and to be told to wash his hands. Oh I have collected many things I did not understand.

And perhaps now I should go and say, oh son of my *summa cum laude* loins, come away from the lonely gulls and the silver trout and I will take you to the land of the Tastee Freeze where you may sleep till ten of nine. And I will show you the elevator to the apartment on the sixteenth floor and introduce you to the buzzer system and the yards of the wrought-iron fences where the Doberman pinscher runs silently at night. Or may I offer you the money that is the fruit of my collecting and my most successful life? Or shall I wait to meet you in some known or unknown bitterness like Yeats's Cuchulain by the wind-whipped sea or as Sohrab and Rustum by the future flowing river?

Again I collect dreams. For I do not know enough of the fog on Toronto's Queen St. West and the grinding crash of the pickup and of lost and misplaced love.

I am up early in the morning as the man kindles the fire from the driftwood splinters. The outside light is breaking and the wind is calm. John tumbles down the stairs. Scarcely stopping to splash his face and pull on his jacket, he is gone accompanied by the dog. The old man smokes his pipe and waits for the water to boil. When it does he pours some into the teapot then passes the kettle to me. I take it to the washstand and fill the small, tin basin in readiness for my shaving. My face looks back from the mirrored cabinet. The woman softly descends the stairs.

"I think I will go back today," I say while looking into the mirror at my face and at those in the room behind me. I try to emphasize the "I." "I just thought I would like to make this trip—again. I think I can leave the car in St. John's and fly back directly." The woman begins to move about the table, setting out the round white plates. The man quietly tamps his pipe.

The door opens and John and the dog return. They have been down along the shore to see what has happened throughout the night. "Well, John," says the old man, "what did you find?"

He opens his hand to reveal a smooth round stone. It is of the deepest green inlaid with veins of darkest ebony. It has been worn and polished by the unrelenting restlessness of the sea and buffed and burnished by the graveled sand. All of its inadequacies have been removed and it glows with the luster of near perfection.

"It is very beautiful," I say.

"Yes," he says, "I like to collect them." Suddenly he looks up to my eyes and thrusts the stone toward me. "Here," he says, "would you like to have it?"

Even as I reach out my hand I turn my head to the others in the room. They are both looking out through the window to the sea.

"Why thank you," I say. "Thank you very much. Yes, I would. Thank you. Thanks." I take it from his outstretched hand and place it in my pocket.

We eat our breakfast in near silence. After it is finished the boy and dog go out once more. I prepare to leave.

"Well, I must go," I say, hesitating at the door. "It will take me awhile to get to St. John's." I offer my hand to the man. He takes it in his strong fingers and shakes it firmly.

"Thank you," says the woman. "I don't know if you know what I mean but thank you."

"I think I do," I say. I stand and fiddle with the keys. "I would somehow like to help or keep in touch but. . . ."

"But there is no phone," he says, "and both of us can hardly write. Perhaps that's why we never told you. John is getting to be a pretty good hand at it though."

"Good-bye," we say again, "good-bye, good-bye."

The sun is shining clearly now and the small boats are putt-putting about the harbor. I enter my unlocked car and start its engine. The gravel turns beneath the wheels. I pass the house and wave to the man and woman standing in the yard.

On a distant cliff the children are shouting. Their voices carol down through the sun-washed air and the dogs are curving and dancing about them in excited circles. They are carrying something that looks like a crippled gull. Perhaps they will make it well. I toot the horn. "Good-bye," they shout and wave, "good-bye, good-bye."

The airport terminal is strangely familiar. A symbol of impermanence, it is itself glisteningly permanent. Its formica surfaces have been designed to stay. At the counter a middle-aged man in mock exasperation is explaining to the girl that it is Newark he wishes to go to *not* New York.

There are not many of us and soon we are ticketed and lifting through and above the sun-shot fog. The meals are served in tinfoil and in plastic. We eat above the clouds looking at the tips of wings.

The man beside me is a heavy equipment salesman who has been trying to make a sale to the developers of Labrador's resources. He has been away a week and is returning to his wife and children.

Later in the day we land in the middle of the continent. Because of the changing time zones the distance we have come seems eerily unreal. The heat shimmers in little waves upon the runway. This is the equipment salesman's final destination while for me it is but the place where I must change flights to continue even farther into the heartland. Still we go down the wheeled-up stairs together, donning our sunglasses, and stepping across the heated concrete and through the terminal's pneumatic doors. The salesman's wife stands waiting along with two small children who are the first to see him. They race toward him with their arms outstretched. "Daddy, Daddy," they cry, "what did you bring me? What did you bring me?"

NO TRACE

David Madden

GASPING, his legs weak from the climb up the stairs, Ernest stopped outside the room, surprised to find the door wide open, almost sorry he had made it before the police. An upsurge of nausea, a wave of suffocation forced him to suck violently for breath as he stepped into Gordon's room—his *own* two decades before.

Tinted emerald, the room looked like a hippie pad posing for a photograph in *Life,* but the monotonous electronic frenzy he heard was the seventeen-year locusts, chewing spring leaves outside. He wondered whether the sedative had so dazed him that he had stumbled into the wrong room. No, now, as every time in his own college years when he had entered this room, what struck him first was the light falling through the leaded, green-stained window glass. As that light illuminated the objects in the room, he felt steeped in the ambience of the 1940s. Though groggy from the sedative, he experienced, intermittently, moments of startling clarity when objects stood out, separately.

Empty beer can pyramids.

James Dean, stark poster photograph.

Records leaning in orange crate.

Rolltop desk, swivel chair, typewriter.

Poster photograph of a teenage hero he didn't recognize.

He shut the door quietly, listening to an automatic lock catch, as if concealing not just the few possible incriminating objects he had come to discover but the entire spectacle of a room startlingly overpopulated with objects, exhibits, that might bear witness to the life lived there.

He glanced into the closet. Gordon's suitcases did not have the look of imminent departure. Clothes hung, hangers crammed tightly together, on the rack above. The odor emanating from the closet convulsed him slightly, making him shut his eyes, see Gordon raise his arm, the sleeve of his gown slip down, revealing his white arm, the grenade in his hand. Shaking his head to shatter the image, Ernest opened his eyes.

Turning abruptly from the closet, he moved aimlessly about the room, distracted by objects that moved toward him. Ernest recognized nothing, except the encyclopedias, as Gordon's. Debris left behind when Gordon's roommate ran away. Even so, knowing Gordon, Ernest had expected the cleanest room in DeLozier Hall, vacant except for suitcases sitting in a neat row, awaiting the end-of-ceremonies dash to the car. He had to hurry before someone discovered the cot downstairs empty, before police came to lock up Gordon's room.

The green light drew him to the window where the babble of locusts was louder. Through the antique glass, he saw, as if under water, the broken folding chairs below, resembling postures into which the explosion had thrown the audience. The last of the curiosity seekers, turning away, trampling locusts, left three policemen alone among knocked-over chairs.

I AM ANONYMOUS/HELP ME. Nailed, buttons encrusted the window-frame. SUPPORT MENTAL HEALTH OR I'LL KILL YOU. SNOOPY FOR PRESI-DENT. As he turned away, chalked, smudged lettering among the buttons drew him back: DOCTOR SPOCK IS AN ABORTIONIST. After his roommate ran away, why hadn't Gordon erased that? Jerking his head away from the buttons again, Ernest saw a ball-point pen sticking up in the desk top. On a piece of paper, the title "The Theme of Self-hatred in the Works of—" the rest obscured by a blue circular, a message scrawled across it: GORDY BABY, LET ME HOLD SOME BREAD FOR THIS CAUSE. MY OLD LADY IS SENDING ME A CHECK NEXT WEEK. THE CARTER. The circular pleaded for money for the American Civil Liberties Union. Ernest shoved it aside, but "The Theme of Self-hatred in the Works of—" broke off anyway. Gordon's blue scrapbook startled him. Turning away, Ernest noticed REVOLUTION IN A REVOLUTION? A TOLKIEN READER, BOY SCOUT HANDBOOK in a bookcase.

As he stepped toward the closet, something crunching harshly under-foot made him jump back. Among peanut shells, brown streaks in the green light. Gordon tracking smashed guts of locusts. Fresh streaks, green juices of leaves converted to slime. He lifted one foot, trying to look at the sole of his shoe, lost balance, staggered backward, let himself drop on the edge of a cot. If investigators compared the stains—. Using his handkerchief, he wiped the soles. Dying and dead locusts, *The Alumni*

Bulletin had reported, had littered the campus paths for weeks. Everywhere, the racket of their devouring machinery, the reek of their putrefaction after they fell, gorged. Sniffing his lapels, he inhaled the stench of locusts and sweat, saw flecks of—. He shut his eyes, raked breath into his lungs, lay back on the cot.

Even as he tried to resist the resurgent power of the sedative, Ernest felt his exhausted mind and body sink into sleep. When sirens woke him, he thought for a moment he still lay on the bare mattress in the room downstairs, listening to the siren of the last ambulance. The injured, being carried away on stretchers, passed by him again. The dean of men had hustled Ernest into a vacated room, and sent to his house nearby for a sedative. Sinking into sleep, seeing the grenade go off again and again until the explosions became tiny, receding, mute puffs of smoke, Ernest had suddenly imagined Lydia's face when he would have to telephone her about Gordon, and the urgency of being prepared for the police had made him sit up in the bed. The hall was empty, everyone seemed to be outside, and he had sneaked up the narrow back stairway to Gordon's room.

Wondering which cot was Gordon's, which his roommate's and why *both* had recently been slept in, Ernest sat up and looked along the wooden frame for the cigarette burn he had deliberately made the day before his own commencement when he and his roommate were packing for home. As he leaned across the cot, looking for the burn, his hand grazed a stiff yellow spot that stuck the top sheet to the bottom sheet. An intuition of his son's climactic moment in an erotic dream the night before—the effort to stifle the urge to cry choked him. "I advocate—." Leaping away from the cot, he stopped, reeling, looked up at a road sign that hung over the door: DRIVE SLOWLY, WE LOVE OUR KIDS. Somewhere an unprotected street. What's-his-name's fault. *His* junk cluttered the room.

Wondering what the suitcases would reveal, Ernest stepped into the closet. Expecting them to be packed, he jerked up on them and jolted himself, they were so light. He opened them anyway. Crumbs of dirt, curls of lint. Gordon's clothes, that Lydia had helped him select, or sent him as birthday or Easter presents, hung in the closet, pressed. Fetid clothes Gordon's roommate—Carter, yes, Carter—had left behind dangled from hooks, looking more like costumes. A theatrical black leather jacket, faded denim pants, a wide black belt, ruby studs, a jade velvet cape, and, on the floor, boots and sandals. In a dark corner leaned the hooded golf clubs Ernest had handed down to Gordon, suspecting he would never lift them from the bag. "You don't like to hunt," he had blurted out one evening. "You don't like to fish. You don't get excited about football. Isn't there *something* we could do together?" "We could just sit and talk." They had ended up watching the Ed Sullivan Show.

Ernest's hand, paddling fishlike among the clothes in the dim closet, snagged on a pin that fastened a price tag to one of the suits he had bought Gordon for Christmas. Though he knew from Lydia that no girl came regularly on weekends from Melbourne's sister college to visit Gordon, surely he had had some occasion to wear the suit. Stacked on the shelf above, shirts, the cellophane packaging unbroken. His fingers inside one of the cowboy boots, Ernest stroked leather that was still flesh soft. Imagining Lydia's hysteria at the sight of Gordon, he saw a mortician handling Gordon's body, sorting, arranging pieces, saw not Gordon's but the body of one of his clients on view, remembering how awed he had been by the miracle of skill that had put the man back together only three days after the factory explosion. Ernest stroked a damp polo shirt, unevenly stained pale green in the wash, sniffed it, realizing that Carter's body could not have left an odor that lasting. Now he understood what had disturbed him about Gordon's clothes, showing, informal and ragged, under the skirt of the black gown, at the sleeves, at the neck, as he sat on the platform, waiting to deliver the valedictory address.

Gripping the iron pipe that held hangers shoved tightly together, his body swinging forward as his knees sagged, Ernest let the grenade explode again. Gentle, almost delicate Gordon suddenly raises his voice above the nerve-wearying shrill of the seventeen-year locusts that encrust the barks of the trees, a voice that had been too soft to be heard except by the men on the platform whose faces expressed shock—at *what* Ernest still did not know—and as that voice screams, a high-pitched nasal screech like brass, "I advocate a total revolution!" Gordon's left arm raises a grenade, holds it out before him, eclipsing his still-open mouth, and in his right hand, held down stiff at his side, the pin glitters on his finger. Frightened, raring back, as Ernest himself does, in their seats, many people try to laugh the grenade off as a bold but imprudent rhetorical gesture.

Tasting again Gordon's blood on his mouth, Ernest thrust his face between smothering wool coats, retched again, vomited at last.

As he tried to suck air into his lungs, gluey bands of vomit strangled him, lack of oxygen smothered him. Staggering backward out of the closet, he stood in the middle of the room, swaying. Avoiding Gordon's, he lowered himself carefully onto the edge of Carter's cot by the closet. He craved air but the stained-glass window, the only window in this corner room, wouldn't open, a disadvantage that came with the privilege of having the room with the magnificent light. The first time he had seen the room since his own graduation—he and Lydia had brought Gordon down to begin his freshman year—he had had to heave breath up from dry lungs to tell Gordon about the window. Early in the nineteenth century when DeLozier Hall was the entire school—and already one of the finest boys' colleges in the Midwest—this corner room and the two adjacent comprised the chapel. From the fire that destroyed DeLozier Hall in 1938, three years before Ernest himself arrived as a freshman, only this window was saved. Except for the other chapel windows, De-Lozier had been restored, brick by brick, exactly as it was originally. "First chance you get, go look in the cemetery at the grave of the only victim of the fire—nobody knows who it was, so the remains were never claimed. Probably somebody just passing through." He had deliberately saved that to leave Gordon with something interesting to think about. From the edge of the cot, he saw the bright eruption of vomit on Gordon's clothes.

The chapel steeple chimed four o'clock. The racket of the locust's mandibles penetrated the room as if carried in through the green light. Photosynthesis. Chlorophyll. The D$^+$ in biology that wrecked Ernest's average.

Rising, he took out his handkerchief and went into the closet. When the handkerchief was sopping wet, he dropped it into a large beer carton, tasting again the foaming beer at his lips, tingling beads on his tongue in the hot tent on the lawn as the ceremonies were beginning. He had reached the green just as the procession was forming. "You've been accepted by Harvard Grad School." Gordon had looked at him without a glimmer of recognition—Ernest had assumed that the shrilling of the locusts had drowned out his voice—then led his classmates toward the platform.

Ernest was standing on a dirty T-shirt. He finished the job with that, leaving a corner to wipe his hands on, then he dropped it, also, into the box.

He sat on the edge of the cot again, afraid to lie back on the mattress, sink into the gully Carter had made over the four years and fall asleep. He only leaned back, propped on one arm. Having collected himself, he would make a thorough search, to prepare for whatever the police would find, tag, then show him for final identification. Exhibit of shocks. The police might even hold him responsible somehow—delinquently ignorant of his son's habits, associates. Might even find something that would bring in the FBI—membership in some radical organization. What was *not* possible in a year like this? He had to arm himself against interrogation. "What sort of boy was your son?" "Typical, average, normal boy in every way. Ask my wife." But how many times had he read that in newspaper accounts of monstrous crimes? What did it mean anymore to be normal?

Glancing around the room, on the verge of an unsettling realization, Ernest saw a picture of Lydia leaning on Carter's rolltop desk. Even in shadow, the enlarged snapshot he had taken himself was radiant. A lucid April sunburst in the budding trees behind her bleached her green dress white, made her blond hair look almost platinum. Clowning, she had kicked out one foot, upraising and spreading her arms, and when her mouth finished yelling "Spring!" he had snapped her dimpled smile. On the campus of Melbourne's sister college Briarheath, locusts riddled those same trees, twenty years taller, forty miles from where he sat, while Lydia languished in bed alone—a mysterious disease, a lingering illness. Then the stunned realization came, made him stand up as though he were an intruder. On this cot, or perhaps the one across the room, he had made love to Lydia—that spring, the first and only time before their marriage. In August, she had discovered that she was pregnant. Gordon had never for a moment given them cause to regret that inducement to marriage. But Lydia's caution in sexual relations had made Gordon an only child.

Glancing around the room he hoped to discover a picture of himself. Seeing none, he sat down again. Under his thumb, he felt a rough texture on the wooden frame of the cot. The cigarette burn he had made himself in 1945. Then *this* had been Gordon's cot. Of course. By his desk. Flinging back the sheets, Ernest found nothing.

He crossed the room to Carter's cot where a dimestore reproduction of a famous painting of Jesus hung on the wall. Pulling to unstick the sheets, he lay bare Carter's bed. Twisted white sweat socks at the bottom. He shook them out. Much too large for Gordon. But Carter, then Gordon, had worn them with Carter's cowboy boots. Gordon had been sleeping in Carter's bed. Pressing one knee against the edge of the cot, Ernest leaned over and pushed his palms against the wall to examine closely what it was that had disturbed him about the painting. Tiny holes like acne scars in Jesus' upturned face. Ernest looked up. Ragged, feathered darts hung like bats from the ceiling. Someone had printed in Gothic script on the bottom white border: J.C. BLOWS. Using his fingernails, Ernest scraped at the edge of the tape, pulled carefully, but white wall paint chipped off, exposing the wallpaper design that dated back to his own life in the room. He stopped, aware that he had only started his search, that if he took this painting, he might be inclined to take other things. His intention, he stressed again to himself, was only to investigate, to be forewarned, not to search and destroy. But already he had the beer carton containing Carter's, or Gordon's, T-shirt and his own handkerchief to dispose of. He let the picture hang.

Backing into the center of the room, one leg painfully asleep, Ernest saw a sticker stuck on the pane, and went to the window again: FRUIT OF THE LOOM. 100% VIRGIN COTTON. More buttons forced him to read: WAR IS GOOD BUSINESS, INVEST YOUR SON. How would the police separate Carter's from Gordon's things? FLOWER POWER. He would simply tell them that Carter had left his junk behind when he bolted. But Gordon's failure to discard some of it, at least the most offensive items, bewildered Ernest. One thing appeared clear: living daily since January among Carter's possessions, Gordon had worn Carter's clothes, slept in Carter's bed.

From the ceiling above the four corners of the room hung the blank faces of four amplifiers, dark mouths gaping. Big Brother is listening. 1984. Late Show. Science fiction bored Ernest. Squatting, he flipped through records leaning in a Sunkist orange crate: MILES DAVIS / THE GRATEFUL DEAD / LEADBELLY / THE BEATLES, their picture red x'ed out / MANTOVANI / THE MAMAS AND THE PAPAS / THE LOVING SPOONFUL. He was wasting time—Carter's records couldn't be used against Gordon. But then he found Glenn Miller's "In the Mood" and "Moonlight Serenade," a 78-rpm collector's item he had given Gordon. "Soothing background music for test-cramming time." TOM PAXTON / THE MOTHERS OF INVENTION / 1812 OVERTURE (Gordon's?) / THE ELECTRONIC ERA / JOAN BAEZ / CHARLIE PARKER / BARTOK.

Rising, he saw a poster he had not glimpsed before, stuck to the wall with a bowie knife, curled inward at its four corners: a color photograph of a real banana rising like a finger out of the middle of a cartoon fist.

Over the rolltop desk hung a guitar, its mouth crammed full of wilted roses. The vomit taste in his own mouth made Ernest retch. Hoping Carter had left some whiskey behind, he quickly searched the rolltop desk, found a Jack Daniel's bottle in one of the cubbyholes. Had Gordon taken the last swallow himself this morning just before stepping out of this room?

Finding a single cigarette in a twisted package, Ernest lit it, quickly snuffed it in a hubcap used as an ashtray. The smell of fresh smoke would make the police suspicious. Recent daily activity had left Carter's desk a shambles. Across the room, Gordon's desk was merely a surface, strewn with junk. The Royal portable typewriter he had given Gordon for Christmas his freshman year sat on Carter's desk, the capital lock key set.

Among the papers on Carter's desk, Ernest searched for Gordon's notes for his speech. Ernest had been awed by the way Gordon prepared his senior project in high school—very carefully, starting with an outline, going through three versions, using cards, dividers, producing a forty-page research paper on Wordsworth. Lydia had said, "Why Ernest, he's been that way since junior high, worrying about college." On Carter's desk, Ernest found the beginnings of papers on Dryden, *The Iliad*, *Huckleberry Finn*. While he had always felt contentment in Gordon's perfect social behavior and exemplary academic conduct and achievements, sustained from grammar school right on through college, Ernest had sometimes felt, but quickly dismissed, a certain dismay. In her presence, Ernest agreed with Lydia's objections to Gordon's desire to major in English, but alone with him, he had told Gordon, "Satisfy yourself first of all." But he couldn't tell Gordon that he had pretended to agree with his mother to prevent her from exaggerating her suspicion that their marriage had kept him from switching to English himself after he got his B.S. in Business Administration. Each time she brought up the subject, Ernest wondered for weeks what his life would have been like had he become an English professor. As he hastily surveyed the contents of the desk, he felt the absence of the papers Gordon had written that had earned A's, helping to qualify him, as the student with the highest honors, to give the valedictory address.

Handling chewed pencils made Ernest sense the taste of lead and wood on his own tongue. He noticed a large box on the floor by his foot but was distracted by a ball-point pen that only great force could have thrust so firmly into the oak desk. The buffalo side of a worn nickel leaned against a bright Kennedy half-dollar. Somewhere under this floor lay a buffalo nickel he had lost himself through a crack. Perhaps Gordon or Carter had found it. He unfolded a letter. It thanked Carter for his two-hundred-dollar contribution to a legal defense fund for students who had gone, without permission, to Cuba. Pulling another letter out of a pigeonhole, he discovered a bright gold piece resembling a medal. Trojan contraceptive. His own brand before Lydia became bedridden. Impression of it still on his wallet—no, that was the *old* wallet he carried as a senior. The letter thanked Carter for his inquiry about summer work with an organization sponsored by SNCC. Stuffed into another pigeonhole, he found a letter outlining Carter's duties during a summer voter campaign in Mississippi. "As for the friend you mention, we don't believe it would be in our best interests to attempt to persuade him to join in our work. If persuasion is desirable, who is more strategically situated than you, his own roommate?" Marginal scrawl in pencil: "This is the *man* talking, Baby!"

He lifted his elbow off Gordon's scrapbook—birthday present from Lydia—and flipped through it. Newspaper photo of students at a rally, red ink enringing a blurred head, a raised fist. Half full: clippings of Carter's activities. AP photo: Carter, bearded, burning his draft card. But no creep—handsome, hair and smile like Errol Flynn in "The Sea Hawk." Looking around at the poster photograph he hadn't recognized when he came in, Ernest saw Carter, wearing a Gestapo billcap, a monocle, an opera cape, black tights, Zorro boots, carrying a riding crop. When Ernest first noticed the ads—"Blow Yourself Up"—he had thought it a good deal at $2.99. Had Gordon given the scrapbook to Carter, or had he cut and pasted the items himself?

Ernest shoved the scrapbook aside and reached for a letter. "Gordy, This is just to tell you to save your tears over King. We all wept over JFK our senior year in his school, and we haven't seen straight since. King just wasn't where the action's at. Okay, so I told you different a few months ago! How come you're always light years behind *me*? Catch up! Make the leap! I'm dumping all these creeps that try to play a rigged game. Look at Robert! I think I'm beginning to understand Oswald and Speck and Whitman. They're the *real* individuals! They work alone while we run together like zebras. But, on the other hand, maybe the same cat did *all* those jobs. And maybe Carter knows who. Sleep on *that* one, Gordy, Baby." Boot camp. April 5. Suddenly, the first day back from Christmas vacation, Carter had impulsively walked out of this room. "See America first! Then the world!" That much Gordon had told them when Ernest and Lydia telephoned at Easter, made uneasy by his terse letter informing them that he was remaining on campus to "watch the locusts emerge from their seventeen-year buried infancy into appalling one-week adulthood," adding, parenthetically, that he had to finish his honors project. Marriage to Lydia had prevented Ernest's desire, like Carter's, to see the world. Not "prevented." Postponed perhaps. A vice-president of a large insurance company might hope to make such a dream come true—if only after he retired. Deep in a pigeonhole, Ernest found a snapshot of Gordon, costumed for a part in *Tom Sawyer*—one of the kids who saunter by the whitewashing scene. False freckles. He had forgotten. On the back, tabs of fuzzy black paper—ripped out of the scrapbook.

Mixed in with Carter's were Lydia's letters. "Gordon Precious, You promised—" Feverish eyes. Bed rashes. Blue Cross. Solitude. "Sleep Lydia." Finding none of his own letters, Ernest remembered writing last week from his office, and the sense of solitude on the fifteenth floor, where he had seemed the only person stirring, came back momentarily. Perhaps in some drawer or secret compartment all his letters to Gordon (few though they had been) and perhaps other little mementos—his sharpshooter's medal and the Korean coin that he had given Gordon, relics of his three years in the service, and matchbooks from the motels where he and Gordon had stayed on occasional weekend trips—were stored. Surely, somewhere in the room, he would turn up a picture of himself. He had always known that Gordon preferred his mother, but had he conscientiously excluded his father? No, he shouldn't jump to conclusions. He had yet to gather and analyze all the evidence. Thinking in those terms about what he was doing, Ernest realized that not only was he going to destroy evidence to protect Gordon's memory as much as possible and "shield Lydia," he was now deliberately searching for fragments of a different Gordon.

But he didn't have time to move so slowly, like a slow-motion movie. Turning quickly to Carter's swivel chair, Ernest bent over a large box where papers had been dropped, perhaps tossed. Gordon's themes, including his honors thesis in a stiff black binder: "ANGUISH, SPIRITUAL AND PHYSICAL, IN GERARD MANLEY HOPKINS' POETRY. Approved by: Alfred Hansen, Thorne Halpert (who had come to Melbourne in Ernest's own freshman year), Richard Kelp, John Morton." In red pencil at the bottom, haphazard scrawls, as if they were four different afterthoughts:

"*Dis*approved by: Jason Carter, Gordon Foster, Lydia Foster, Gerard Manley Hopkins." Up the left margin, in lead pencil: "PISS ON ALL OF YOU!"

The portable tape recorder Ernest had given Gordon last fall to help him through his senior year. He pressed the LISTEN button. Nothing. He pressed the REWIND. LISTEN. ". . . defy analysis. But let's examine this passage from Aristotle's 'De Interpretatione': 'In the case of that which is or which has taken place, propositions, whether positive or negative, must be true or false.'" "What did he say?" Someone whispering. "I didn't catch it." (Gordon's voice?) "Again, in the case of a pair of contraries—contradictories, that is. . . ." The professor's voice slipped into a fizzing silence.

Ernest stepped over to Gordon's desk, seeking some evidence of Gordon's life before he moved over to the rolltop desk and mingled his own things with Carter's. The gray steel drawers were empty. Not just empty. Clean. Wiped clean with a rag—a swipe in the middle drawer had dried in a soapy pattern of broken beads of moisture, making Ernest feel the presence behind him of another table where Gordon now, in pieces, lay. Under dirty clothes slung aside lay stacks of books and old newspapers with headlines of war, riot, murder, assassinations, negotiations.

"I'm recording your speech, son," he had written to Gordon last week, "so your mother can hear it." But Ernest had forgotten his tape recorder.

The headline of a newspaper announced Charlie Whitman's sniper slaying of twelve people from the observation tower of the university administration building in Austin, Texas. But that was two summers past. Melbourne had no summer school. Folded, as though mailed. Had Carter sent it to Gordon from— Where *was* Carter from? Had Gordon received it at home?

A front page news photo showed a Buddhist monk burning on a Saigon street corner. Ernest's sneer faded in bewilderment as he saw that the caption identified an American woman burning on the steps of the Pentagon. Smudged pencil across the flames: THE MOTHER OF US ALL. Children bereft, left to a father, perhaps no father even. Lately, many cases of middle-aged men who had mysteriously committed suicide hovered on the periphery of Ernest's consciousness. It struck him now that in every case, he had forgotten most of the "sensible" explanations, leaving nothing but mystery. Wondering whether those men had seen something in the eyes of their children, even their wives, that Ernest himself had been blind to, he shuddered but did not shake off a sudden clenching of muscles in his shoulders. "When the cause of death is legally ruled as suicide," he had often written, "the company is relieved of its obligations to—" Did Gordon *know* the grenade would explode? Or did he borrow it, perhaps steal it from a museum, and then did it, like the locusts, seventeen years dormant, suddenly come alive? Ernest had always been lukewarm about gun control, but now he would insist on a thorough investigation to determine where Gordon purchased the grenade. Dealer in war surplus? Could they *prove* he meant it to go off? "When the cause of death is legally ruled—" Horrified that he was thinking so reflexively like an insurance executive, Ernest slammed his fist into his thigh, and staggered back into the bed Gordon had abandoned.

His eyes half-opened, he saw his cigarette burn again on the wooden frame beside his hand. He recalled Gordon's vivid letter home the first week of his freshman year: "My roommate turns my stomach by the way he dresses, talks, acts, eats, sleeps." Ernest had thought that a boy so different from Gordon would be good for him, so his efforts, made at Lydia's fretful urgings, to have Carter replaced, or to have Gordon moved, were slapdash. He wanted his son to go through Melbourne in his old room.

Books on Gordon's desk at the foot of the cot caught his attention. Some dating from junior high, these were all Gordon's, including the Great Books, with their marvelous Syntopicon. As the pain in his thigh subsided, Ernest stood up, hovered over the books.

A frayed copy of *Winnie the Pooh* startled him. "To Ernest, Christmas, 1928. All my love, Grandmother." The year he learned to write, Gordon had printed his own name in green crayon across the top of the next page. As Ernest leafed through the book, nostalgia eased his nerves. Penciled onto Winnie the Pooh was a gigantic penis extending across the page to Christopher Robin, who was bending over a daisy. "Damn you, Carter!" Ernest slammed it down—a pillar of books slurred, tumbled onto the floor. He stood still, staring into the green light, trying to detect the voices of people who might have heard in the rooms below. Ernest heard only the locusts in the light. A newspaper that had fallen leaned and sagged like a tent: Whitman's face looked up from the floor, two teeth in his school graduation smile blacked out, a pencil-drawn tongue flopping out of his mouth. His name was scratched out and YOU AND ME, BABY was lettered in. Ernest kicked at the newspaper, twisted his heel into Whitman's face, and the paper rose up around his ankles like a yellowed flower, soot-dappled.

Ernest backed into the swivel chair, turned, rested his head in his hands on the rolltop desk, and breathed in fits and starts. He wanted to throw the hubcap ashtray through the stained-glass window and feel the spring air rush in upon his face and fill and stretch his lungs. Cigarillo butts, scorched Robert Burns bands, cigarette butts. Marijuana? He sniffed, but realized he couldn't recognize it if it *were*.

Closing his eyes, trying to conjure up Gordon's face, he saw, clearly, only Carter's smile, like a weapon, in the draft-card-burning photograph. *Wanting* to understand Gordon, he had only a shrill scream of defiance, an explosion, and this littered room with which to begin. He imagined the mortician, fitting pieces together, an arm on a drainboard behind him. And when he was finished, what would he have accomplished? In the explosion, Gordon had vacated his body, and now the pieces had stopped moving, but the objects in his room twitched when Ernest touched them. Taking a deep breath, he inhaled the stench of spit and tobacco. He shoved the hubcap aside, and stood up.

Bending his head sideways, mashing his ear against his shoulder, Ernest read the titles of books crammed into cinder-block and pine-board shelves between Carter's cot and the window: 120 DAYS OF SODOM, the Marquis de Sade / AUTOBIOGRAPHY OF MALCOLM X / MEIN KAMPF—. He caught himself reading titles and authors aloud in a stupor. Silently, his lips still moving, he read: BOY SCOUT HANDBOOK. Though he had never been a scout, Ernest had agreed with Lydia that, like a fraternity, it would be good for Gordon in future life. FREEDOM NOW, Max Reiner / NAUSEA, Jean-Paul Sartre / ATLAS SHRUGGED, Ayn Rand / THE SCARLET LETTER. Heritage, leather-bound edition he had given Gordon for his sixteenth birthday. He had broken in the new Volkswagen, a surprise graduation present, driving it down. Late for the ceremonies, he had parked it, illegally, behind DeLozier Hall so it would be there when he and Gordon brought the suitcases and his other belongings down. CASTRO'S CAUSE, Harvey Kreyborg / NOTES FROM UNDERGROUND, Dostoyevsky / LADY CHATTERLEY'S LOVER, Ernest's own copy. Had Gordon sneaked it out of the house? Slumping to his knees, he squinted at titles he had been unable to make out: Carter had cynically shelved Ernest's own copy of PROFILES IN COURAGE, passed on to Gordon, next to OSWALD RESUR-RECTED by, Eugene Federogh.

There was a book with a library number on its spine. He would have to return that. The Gordon he had known would have done so before commencement. Suddenly afraid the police might come in, catch him there, Ernest rose to his feet. Glancing through several passages, high-lighted with a yellow magic marker, he realized that he was reading about "anguish, spiritual and physical, in Gerard Manley Hopkins' poetry." He rooted through the large box again, took out Gordon's honors thesis. Flipping through the pages, he discovered a passage that duplicated, verbatim, a marked passage in the book. No footnote reference. The bibliography failed to cite the book that he held in his hand and now let drop, along with the honors thesis, into the beer carton onto Carter's fouled tee shirt and Ernest's handkerchief.

Why had he cheated? He never had before. Or had he plagiarized *all* those papers, from junior high on up to this one? No, surely, this time only. Ernest himself had felt the pressure in his senior year, and most of the boys in his fraternity had cheated when they really *had* to.

Whatever Gordon had said in his valedictory address, Ernest knew that certain things in this room would give the public the wrong image of his son. Or perhaps—he faced it—the right image. Wrong or right, it would incite the disease in Lydia's body to riot and she would burn.

Now he felt compelled to search thoroughly, examine everything care-fully. The police had no right to invade a dead boy's privacy and plunge his invalid mother into grief.

In Carter's desk drawers, Ernest searched more systematically among letters and notes, still expecting to discover an early draft of Gordon's unfinished speech; perhaps it would be full of clues. He might even find the bill of sale for the grenade. Across the naked belly of a girl ripped from a magazine was written: "Gordy—" Carter had even renamed, re-christened Gordon. "Jeff and Conley and I are holding a peace vigil in the cold rain tonight, all night. Bring us a fresh jar of water at midnight. And leave your goddamn middle-class mottos in the room. Love, Carter."

A letter from Fort Jackson, South Carolina, April 20, 1968. "Dear Gordon, I am being shipped to Vietnam. I will never see you again. I have not forgotten what you said to me that night in our room across the

Dark Gulf between our cots. As always, Carter." Without knowing what Carter meant, Ernest knew that gulf himself. He had tried to touch Scott, his own roommate, whose lassitude about life's possibilities often provoked Ernest to wall-pounding rage. He had finally persuaded Scott to take a trip West with him right after graduation. Scott's nonchalant withdrawal at the last minute was so dispiriting that Ernest had accepted his father's offer of a summer internship with the insurance company as a claims adjuster.

A 1967 letter described in detail the march on the Pentagon. "What are you doing down there, you little fink? You should be up here with the rest of us. My brothers have been beaten by the cops. I'm not against the use of napalm in *some* instances. Just don't let me get my hands on any of it when those pig sonofabitches come swinging their sticks at us. We're rising up all over the world, Baby—or didn't you know it, with your nose in Chaucer's tales. Melbourne is about due to be hit so you'd better decide whose side you're on. I heard about this one campus demonstration where somebody set fire to this old fogey's life-long research on some obscure hang-up of his. I can think of a few at Melbourne that need shaking up." Shocked, Ernest was surprised at himself for being shocked. He wondered how Gordon had felt.

As Ernest pulled a postcard out of a pigeonhole, a white capsule rolled out into his hand. For a common cold, or LSD? He stifled an impulse to swallow it. He flipped the capsule against the inside of the large box and it popped like a cap pistol. Comic postcard—outhouse, hillbillies—mailed from Alabama, December 12, 1966. "Gordy, Baby, Wish you were here. You sure as hell ain't all *there!* Love, till death do us part, Carter." In several letters, Carter fervently attempted to persuade Gordon to abandon his "middle-class Puritan Upforcing" and embrace the cause of world brotherhood, which itself embraced all other great causes of "our time." But even through the serious ones ran a trace of self-mockery. He found Carter's draft notice, his *own* name crossed out, Gordon's typed in. Across the body of the form letter, dated February 1, 1968, was printed in Gothic script: NON SERVIUM.

Reaching for a bunch of postcards, Ernest realized that he was eager not only to discover more about Gordon, but to assemble into some shape the fragments of Carter's life. A series of postcards with cryptic, taunting messages traced Carter's trail over the landscape of America, from early January, to the middle of March, 1968. From Carmel, California, a view of a tower and cypress trees: "Violence is the sire of all the world's values." Ernest remembered the card Gordon sent him from Washington, D.C., when he was in junior high: "Dear Dad, Our class went to see Congress but they were closed. Our teacher got mad. She dragged us all to the Smithsonian and showed us Lindbergh's airplane. It was called THE SPIRIT OF ST. LOUIS. I didn't think it looked so hot. Mrs. Landis said she saved the headlines when she was in high school. Did you? Your son, Gordon."

Ernest found a night letter from Lynn, Massachusetts. "Dear Gordon, Remembering that Jason spoke of you so often and so fondly, his father and I felt certain that you would not want to learn through the newspapers that our dear son has been reported missing in action. While no one can really approve in his heart of this war, Jason has always been the sort of boy who believed in dying for his convictions. We know that you will miss him. He loved you as though you were his own brother. Affectionate regards, Grace and Harold Carter." June 1, 1968, three days ago.

Trembling, Ernest sought more letters from Carter. One from boot camp summed up, in wild, impassioned prose, Carter's opinions on civil rights, the war, and "the American Dream that's turned into a nightmare." In another, "God is dead and buried on LBJ's ranch" dispensed with religion and politics, "inseparable." May 4, 1968: "Dear Gordy, We are in the jungle now, on a search and destroy mission. You have to admire some of these platoon leaders. I must admit I enjoy watching them act out their roles as all-American tough guys. They have a kind of style, anyway. In here you don't have time to analyze your thoughts. But I just thought a word or two written at the scene of battle might bring you the smell of smoke." Ernest sniffed the letter, uncertain whether the faint smell of smoke came from the paper.

He pulled a wadded letter out of a pigeonhole where someone had stuffed it. As he unwadded the note, vicious ball-point pen markings wove a mesh over the words: "Gordon, I'm moving in with Conley. Pack my things and set them in the hall. I don't even want to *enter* that room again. What you said last night made me sick. I've lived with you for three and a half years because I was always convinced that I could save your soul. But after last night, I know it's hopeless. Carter." Across the "Dark Gulf" between their beds, what could *Gordon* have said to shock Carter? Had Gordon persuaded him to stay after all? Or was it the next day that Carter had "impulsively" run away? Ernest searched quickly through the rest of the papers, hoping no answer existed, but knowing that if one did and he failed to find it, the police wouldn't fail.

"Gordy, Baby, Everything you read is lies! I'm taking time to write to you. Listen, Baby, this is life! This is what it's all about. In the past weeks I've personally set fire to thirty-seven huts belonging to Viet Cong sympathizers. Don't listen to those sons-of-bitches who whine and gripe and piss and moan about this war. This is a *just* war. We're on the right side, man, the *right* side. This place has opened my eyes and heart, baby. With the bullets and the blood all around, you see things clearer. Words! To hell with words! All these beady-eyed little bastards understand is *bullets*, and a knife now and then. These bastards killed my buddy, a Black boy by the name of Bird. The greatest guy that ever lived. Well, there's ten Viet Cong that ain't alive today because of what they did to my buddy, and there'll be another hundred less Viet Cong if I can persuade them to send me out after I'm due to be pulled back. Yesterday, I found a Viet Cong in a hut with his goddamn wife and kids. I turned the flame thrower on the sons-of-bitches and when the hut burned down, I pissed on the hot ashes. I'm telling you all this to open your eyes, mister. This is the way it really is. Join your ass up, get over here where you belong. Forget everything I ever said to you or wrote to you before. I have seen the light. The future of the world will be decided right here. And I will fight until the last Viet Cong is dead. Always, your friend Carter." May 21, 1968, two weeks ago.

Trying to feel as Gordon had felt reading this letter, feeling nothing, Ernest remembered Gordon's response to a different piece of information some kid in grammar school dealt him when he was eleven. Having informed Gordon that Santa Claus was a lie, he added the observation that nobody ever knows who his real father and mother are. Just as Ernest stepped into the house from the office, Gordon has asked: "Are you my real father?" In the living room where colored lights blazed on the tree, Lydia was weeping. It took two months to rid Gordon of the fantasy that he had been adopted. Or had he simply stopped interrogating them? But how did a man know *anything*? Did Carter ever sense he would end up killing men in Vietnam? Did Gordon ever suspect that on his graduation day . . . ?

After Carter's letter from Vietnam, reversing everything he had preached to Gordon, Gordon had let his studies slide, and then the plagiarism had just happened, the way things will, because how could he really care anymore? Then did the night letter from Carter's mother shock Gordon into pulling the grenade pin? Was "I advocate a total revolution!" Gordon's *own* climax to the attitude expressed in Carter's Vietnam letter? Or did the *old* Carter finally speak through Gordon's mouth? These possibilities made sense, but Ernest felt nothing.

His foot kicked a metal wastebasket under Carter's desk. Squatting, he pulled it out, and sitting again in the swivel chair, began to unwad several letters. "Dear Dad—" The rest blank. "Dear Dad—" Blank. "Dear Dad—" Blank. "Dear Father—" Blank. "Dear Dad—" Blank.

Ernest swung around in Carter's chair, rocked once, got to his feet, stood in the middle of the room, his hands dangling in front of him, the leaded moldings of the window cast black wavy lines over his suit, the green light stained his hands, his heart beat so fast he became aware that he was panting. Like a dog. His throat felt dry, his tongue swollen, eyes burning from reading in the oblique light. Dark spots of sweat on the floor.

FILLING THE IGLOO

Peter Makuck

DUNES and sawgrass, empty beach —Quinn has it all to himself.

Sitting on the camp stool, he lifts a can of Lite from the red and white Igloo, pops the top, takes a long pull, and sets it in the sand. With a pair of Zeiss 10X50s, he peers at a charter boat offshore to the south; the stern says "Mijoy #1." Glittering like confetti, gulls work the wake.

Quinn glasses the stilted pier that juts a quarter of a mile into the ocean; people are hunched at the rail behind a crazy web of sunlit monofilament. In less than a minute three, four, five fish flash in the long space between water and rail. He rubs his eyes and checks his rod held by the sandpike, the tip barely moving. "Hell anyway!"

Hoisting the binoculars again, he looks in the other direction: two fishermen in the surf, small with distance. And three other figures: his wife, Joni, her brother—Gerald's bow-legged gait is unmistakable—and Jimmy. Quinn takes a deep breath, looks at his Rolex and times the arrival.

"Dad, whatja get?"

Joni says, "Why not fish in front of the cottage?"

Quinn says, "Too many kids and bathers."

Gerald says, "Don't worry, we won't disturb you. " Pushing the long, graying, touched-up hair out of his eyes, he moves off toward the dunes. He wears a light blue bikini.

Quinn says, "What's with him? Didn't he have his morning joint yet?"

"Be nice, Jack. He's just depressed."

"Why?"

"Dad, you get anything?"

"No, but I'm not depressed."

"Uncle Gerald!" The boy runs off.

"You don't have to be sarcastic in front of Jimmy."

"Sarcasm is something I learned from your brother."

Joni folds her arms, tightens her lips.

"Sorry," says Quinn.

"He might go back to The City tomorrow."

"Why?"

"The ocean overwhelms him. He can't practice."

"What about Denise and the boys?"

"They'll stay."

He is looking through the binoculars again. Two fish on a single bottom rig catch the sun as they flip over the rail.

In the pier parking lot, crowded with pickups, vans, and RVs, a thin man in tan work trousers and shirt is lifting a cooler onto the tailgate of his pickup. "Any luck?" Quinn asks.

"Yup, lotta action this morning." The guy opens a green Coleman cooler which is all fisheye and slither, sad mouths and bloody gills. Big.

"What are they?"

"Spanish."

And the man is gone. Quinn squints where the truck disappears—a telephone pole in the heat waves, a snake stood on end.

The only access is through a long paintless shack which tilts drunkenly to one side; tattered curtains swim from screenless windows at the rear. Inside, he leans his new Diawa and Garcia combo against the counter. Reels, rods, and nets hang from the ceiling. Quinn looks at the trophies (ALL FISH CAUGHT ON THIS PIER)—an arching tarpon with big scales, leaping Spanish and king mackerel, blues, sheepshead, and others—all identified by hand-scrawled cards. There is an old woman in black with one tooth like the prong of a can opener. Quinn says he wants a ticket to fish. She says nothing. He asks how much it is. She lets the register answer with a ding and a readable $2.65. And what are they catching the Spanish on? Wide-hipped, rump like an ottoman, she shuffles in pink fluffy slippers, reaches down a cellophane packet, skates back, and drops it on the counter. "A jerk-jigger, hunh?"

The register speaks again: $3.40.

Outside on the pier a sign says: NO SHARK FISHING. A guy in rolled-up Levis, his nipples trapped in a net jersey, strides for the scale suspended near the water-sluiced cleaning tables; he is carrying a fish that is easily a yard long. He hooks it by the bright bloody gills and when the pointer stops quivering at twenty-eight pounds, there are long moans of envy. He drifts back down the pier in an actorish way, basking in his own private sunshine, wearing the look of someone who has just proved something. "Spanish mackerel's the same thang, jes' smaller," a father is telling his son. "But you gotta *cas'* fo' um."

Most of the casting takes place on the last third of the pier, and Quinn begins to make his way to where the action is. A sand shark buzzes with flies on the salt-bleached planks. Teenage boys fish to the best of transistor rock; the number is "Bad Moon Rising." The pier seems to gather all kinds: old and young blacks, a fat white woman whose head is hived with pink curlers, a jabbering Oriental family, a crewcut Marine with a white noxema nose. "Some crew," whispers Quinn. They are merely bottom fishing, content with an occasional mullet or flounder. Quinn follows two gazing girls dressed in loud, heedless color; their liquid brown bodies are beautifully packed into shorts and halters that bounce and sloop with each step as they follow the net-shirted guy with the mackerel.

There. Quinn will have about five feet of railing to himself. He stoops to his tackle box. The lure has a brand name; it is called "Gotcha"—a three-inch white plastic tube with a red day-glo tip, a treble hook fore and aft. One of his rail mates, a wrinkled old man with skin as brown as a penny, tells Quinn not to use leader. "Spanish kin spot it. And cut off the front hook. You won't foul, you git better action."

Quinn gets out his pliers. "Like this?"

"Dash rat." The old guy look at him. "You been here long?"

Quinn shakes his head. "Yesterday."

"Where you from?"

"Ohio."

"Like it heah?"

"I'm working on it."

He laughs. "Pier ain't *spose* to be work."

The sky and a few thin horsetail clouds are red with the lowering sun— the same red as the skin on his neck, legs, and arms. Suddenly the old man's rod becomes a drawn bow, the drag singing. The rod jerks and trembles. He reels in, tightens the drag. The monofilament, brightly beaded, shears the water nicely. The old man talks as he works the fish: "You wont to keep it away fum the spiles. No hurry. You can snap the line. . . ." The drag no longer clicks, and the mackerel's flanks flash in the green as it comes to the surface. "Two-three pounds," says the old man. "No need to lower no gaff or net." Over the railing it comes, flips on the planks. Quinn looks closely. "Spanish mackerel," he whispers. Iridescent blue along the dorsal, gray-silver flanks stippled with light gold. Pretty as ice-bedded trout in the ads. The old-timer points his chin off to the right. "See um jump?" At first, he doesn't, then yes, far off, lots of small arcs and splashes. A school. And the pier is a flurry of movement, yells.

There. Somebody further down the pier is swinging in another. Quinn is all thumbs with the knots. The plug is light and doesn't fly far. The next cast is better, and the plug spurts in its Z-pattern. In the clear water, two Spanish follow the lure, then swerve off at the last second. "Shit!" He blows the next cast. Then the plug flies in a long arc, ploops under, and begins to work—a great pull and the line is alive, the drag whining. The old-timer tells him not to tighten down yet. Quinn keeps it away from the spiles, the other lines, a nice three-pound Spanish that, as it leaves the water, snaps the line with a great last flutter.

"Get you a jerk-jigger fum mah box," says the old guy.

With one knee on the planks, he takes no time to chat with these two tourist girls asking questions.

Then, as he is about to stand up, there is a quick, sharp pain at the corner of his eye. His face snaps around in the wrong direction; it leans, stretches, and tries to lessen its pain. He loses his balance and sits, then gets to his knees. He yells, wraps the line around his fist to keep the boy from pulling. Blood is dripping from his jaw, channeling down his neck. The boy's face is as white as his sun-bleached hair, the mouth slack. "Easy nah," says the father, a man with a belly that flabs over belted green trousers. His upper face is shaded by a baseball cap; the teeth are crooked and stained with nicotine. "Boy here . . . forgit . . . look out." He speaks slowly, his voice such a twisted drawl that Quinn can barely catch a word of what he says. "Nah didja, boy?"

"No suh." Tears brim.

To Quinn, the father says, "Holt stee-yul" and cuts the line at the plug. Other faces drift back to their stations; a few stay. "Hit's gone through the skin twicet" says a voice with a black cowboy hat. The father just stands there, a dead cigarette dangling from his dry, discolored lips. He keeps slapping the Zippo against his thigh, trying the wheel again, hands cupped at the cigarette tip. Quinn dabs his handkerchief about the corner of his eye but the plug is in the way and as long as the hook stays in, it will bleed, leak into his eye if he fails to keep it closed.

"Let me look, I'm a doctor."

The voice belongs to a tuna-shaped man in a yellow sport shirt with blue and red sailboats on it. No, it can't be pulled back through because of the barbs; too much tearing. He speaks with a pipe clamped in the side of his mouth. Even when the doctor touches the plug lightly, Quinn pulls back. He instructs the father to disassemble his rod. Which the man does, then resumes work on the Zippo. Finally the doctor is ready; he will cut the barbs with pliers and simply slide the hook back out. "But, ah, Burt dear, you, ah. . . ." This voice comes from a woman in a tennis dress; she has frosted her hair, and she shakes a plastic glass with ice cubes and a green olive. A shadow crosses the doctor's face. He chortles nervously. "Well, actually I'm a dentist," he says. "I might get in trouble for this. Better let an M.D. take care of it. I'm, ah, I'm just on vacation here." And he describes in great detail the people he is with and the location of their cottage, "The Xanadu." There is a pause and the father speaks, blowing into the Zippo and tapping it as if it were a mike; he says there is a doctor on the other end of the island, Pantigo Inlet. "On the lay-ff, pas' the watahtowah, onie house on the point." The dentist relents, decides he can at least tape Quinn's handkerchief to his cheek in such a way as to keep things from getting too messy. "That M.D.'ll fix you right up. Besides you're going to need a tetanus shot."

Quinn gathers his things.

The boy says he is real sorry.

The father offers to drive him to the doctor's place. Quinn shakes his head and flinches, a tiny rivulet of blood sliding onto the cheek.

In the parking lot, a trio of young men are unloading a pickup with a camper top. One of them asks Quinn about the action on the pier, then notices the jerk-jigger dangling from the corner of his eye. "By gawd, yew got chew a big un!"

Quinn speeds beneath the looming, four-legged water tower that rises in the windshield like a childhood giant. The road forks: "Left for luck."

Pantigo Inlet Road. A house by itself at the point: faded green shingles, peeling storm shutters, wrap-around veranda. Quinn crunches to a stop on the white shell-paved road. Salt-stunted palmettos rattle their mocking fronds in the wind. There is a sign on a paintless yardarm: PERCY BYNUM, M.D.

Quinn sits on a high stool.

Blood drips from his jaw, and his hair is plastered with sweat. He stares at the floor, listens to the click of a cabinet door, the plink of a metal container, the rip of paper, and hiss of a faucet. The doctor, small and fiftyish and gray, adjusts a gooseneck lamp, rips open a hermetic bag of suture materials and places them on the tissue-covered table next to him. Quinn winces as the doctor squirts a cleaning solution on the wound and snorts, "Don't get me started on that pier. Do you know what this is?" He holds up a pair of stainless-steel pliers, his accent unmistakably northern. "Isn't a week goes by I don't use them to cut a hook." Quinn sees himself in the cabinet window. The jerk-jigger dangles from the skin at the corner of his eye and creates a Chinese effect. It looks like a drunken attempt at self-adornment. The doctor says, "Don't move now." There is snapping sound, and Quinn sucks in, bites his lip.

"There."

The jerk-jigger clanks into the stainless steel pan. The doctor irrigates the wound with what seems a burning lighter fluid. "I said to hold still!" He holds up a syringe. "This is a local."

The face leans close. The track of a razor has missed here and there. Patches of stubble. A dab of dried shaving cream behind the ear. The lips are cracked and the corners of the wide mouth hook down and betray a testiness. Quinn winces.

"Give it a minute." He shakes his head, sighs wearily.

"Do you live here all year round?" Quinn asks.

The doctor nods yes.

"What's it like?"

"Quiet is what it's like . . . Most of the time," he says, no relish in his voice, and looks at his shoes, brown penny loafers.

"How does somebody come out here to live anyway?"

The doctor's irises disappear, the gray hardens. "Dozens of reasons." His voice has an edge and his jaw muscles bunch when he pauses. "You inherit property, you think you like the quiet life, boats, fishing. Your wife runs off, kids grow up. Signs of angina. Dozens of reasons." He taps the temple area. "Feel this?"

Quinn says no. Very quickly the doctor takes three stitches as if he is anxious to see Quinn gone. Then he gives him a tetanus shot with directions to have his own doctor remove the stitches in a week or so. The doctor walks him out to the veranda and tells him how once he saw someone lose an eye on the pier, come into the office with it hanging from the socket like a loose button. He looks Quinn in the eye. "You're lucky, you're a very lucky man."

His son, Jimmy, and his nephews, Julian and Larry, crowd close to the sink board where Quinn stands with two Spanish mackerel on an opened newspaper.

Joni says, "They've just been hanging around, bored."

"Sure they're bored—no TV or video games."

"Jesus, Jack."

"Christ, how could they possibly be bored? There's an ocean they never see ten feet out the back door."

The boys, all wearing baseball hats and numbered jerseys, brush against his legs.

"Dad?"

"What?"

"What are you doing?"

"Sharpening my fishing knife."

"What are you going to do, Uncle Jack?"

"Cut the head off. Like . . . so."

Gerald, his brother-in-law, gives up a stoned giggle.

"Ah, gross!" says Julian.

"Sick."

"Really!"

Gerald says, "You probably *bought* them."

"Sure, sure," says Quinn, stung by the accuracy of Gerald's guess.

"Tell the boys about some of your adventures as a captain on that tuna boat—the, ah, *Chicken of the Sea,* wasn't it?"

"Right."

"Down around the Bermuda Triangle, wasn't it?"

Quinn turns and levels a cold look.

Gerald sighs, "Ah yes, Captain Quinn. But that was—hell, Ahab was still just a gleam in his father's eye."

Quinn says nothing.

Gerald has a neatly clipped moustache, styled hair, oversized glasses.

Quinn watches him and his wife, Denise, from the kitchen; they are out on the wooden deck now with cups of coffee, looking at the ocean go a deeper green with evening. Joni finishes the last dish and says, "Christ, you could have lost an eye."

Quinn says nothing.

"Jack, taking off by yourself is—"

"Is the same thing as when we're skiing at Aspen—"

" 'Everyone does their own thing,' " she mocks.

"Hey, I wanted us to have fish."

"Christ, we can *buy* fish."

"That's failure. It's what your brother would do. Not me."

After a few minutes, she says, "Are you going to take the boys fishing tonight?"

"If I don't, nobody else will."

"Jack, be *nice*. Be fair. Gerald's a musician. He wouldn't know a pole from a cooler."

"You mean he doesn't want to know."

"Jack." She says it plaintively.

"Well, why did they come? They could read novels in New York."

"We're family, remember. Jack, forget the pier for tonight. We'll have some drinks and play board games with the children."

Quinn says, "Sorry. Whatever might save this friggin' day isn't here in the cottage."

Joni watches him lift a last filet from the spine, a fine comb of V'ed bones. She laces her fingers together, turns the palms downward, popping the cartilage.

Gerald and Denise come off the deck into the living room and light cigarettes. Quinn doesn't smoke, and the Salem fog irritates his nostrils. Loud laughter comes through the wall from the other side of the duplex. He has only caught a glimpse of these other renters but doesn't like what he has seen: five cars in a space for two. This morning he had to knock on the door to ask them to move the car that blocked him in.

Gerald stretches out on the sofa, puts a pillow under his head and finds his place in *The Last Exit to Brooklyn*. He looks over his glasses at Quinn. "Off to the pier with the boys?"

"That's it."

"Well, break a leg."

"Thanks."

"Captain Quinn?"

"What?"

"Know what they say a pier really is?"

Quinn shakes his head.

"A disappointed bridge."

The boys are already in the Audi when Quinn steps onto the back porch. They are playing with the power locks, and the antenna goes up and down with an electric groan. They are bouncing, climbing on the seats. Quinn inhales deeply. "Jesus, Doc, *you're* the one who's lucky."

It is dark when they roll into the parking lot. Quinn has stopped at Fishin Fever for bait and a few different lures and now, damnit, he is ready for fish. At first the boys don't want to carry anything, but, by Christ, they will be responsible if he has anything to do about it. Julian lugs the Igloo, Jim carries the crab trap, Larry the tackle box.

The jukebox inside is blasting. The boys give a *yeah* of recognition and Jimmy, barely ten, begins to nod to the beat. The old woman in black is still there selling tickets, sandwiches. A terribly wrinkled old man is dickering about a senior citizen discount. A small TV flickers behind the counter; it shows the news, a soldier with a rocket launcher, a building collapse in a cloud of smoke and dust. When Quinn digs out his wallet and points to the children, the old woman points to a sign: CHILDREN UNDER TWELVE ADMITTED FREE. Quinn says, "My lucky day." The woman in black looks at him blankly.

There are few spaces along the railing. A T-shirted fat man stares at him then fishes in a baggie full of olive seaweed veined with bloodworms. The boys yell and kick at a dead sandshark on the planks. "Hey, Dad, look, a shark!"

Jesus.

"Bad Moon Rising" is blatting from a radio on a bench between two black boys holding rods and nodding their corn-rowed heads.

"Gross me out!"

"Really!"

They have reached a point just past the breaking surf where everything is a field of white foam; now it deepens and darkens. Quinn hurries to a ten-foot segment of vacant rail. It is a choice location with a spotlight shining down into the water so you can see what you are doing. He begins rigging up, using the three rods, cooler, tackle box, and crab traps to stake out their territory against invasion. Slowly, one by one, each of the boys has a rod to hold. They clamor, making noise, and keep jerking up their lines unnecessarily, letting them go slack. "Hey, look," says Julian, "There's a Ferris wheel." A mile down the beach a rotating white neon ring stands out against the dark; inside it is a green six-pointed star. There are other colored lights. A small carnival perhaps.

By the time Quinn has found some fish heads, baited the traps, and placed them near spiles on the other side of the pier, somebody is fishing on the fringe of his territory. The guy wears Levis and a black T-shirt from which his face rises like a moon. The T-shirt advertises Wild Turkey in white letters on the back.

"He's a turkey all right," mutters Quinn.

The guy has tangled lines with little Larry.

Two chesty teenage girls pause and move on; one of them says, "I guess it's her first love-type experience."

"Dad, can we go down to that carnival?"

"No!" says Quinn. "You wanted to fish, now *fish.*"

The boys grumble.

Wild Turkey is joined by a friend wearing a white sleeveless T-shirt, a tall bearded man with a belly and a hat saying Wayne Feeds. They are both using red-and-white bobbers. Shortly, both drags sing out and after a minute of loud reeling, two good-sized fish shiver over the rail and slap against the rough planks. Several other fishermen come over and say "Sea trout."

"*Dad,*" whines Jim, "how come *we're* not getting nothing?"

"Uncle Jack, is their bait same as ours?"

Quietly, Quinn says he doesn't know.

"Well, why don't we use the same thing?"

In a growl-whisper, he says, "Just shut up and fish. You don't even have your line tight."

"Gee-*wiz!*"

"Uncle, I'm going in to the bathroom, okay?"

Quinn says yes.

"Me too."

"Dad, can I have money for an ice cream?"

Quinn says no, they came to catch fish, not eat ice cream. The boys run, pound off down the pier like receding thunder. Quinn leans his rod against the rail and walks to the other side of the pier to check one of the crab traps. *Wild Turkey. Just like the jerks this afternoon. Wise-ass rednecks.* Quinn pulls his Rapalla from its leather and takes a step toward Wild Turkey. He deepens his voice: *You find another fishin place, man, or you're gonna be wearin your guts for suspenders. Got it?*

"Hey, hey."

Quinn is squatting next to the trap, scooting out the hermit crabs. "Hey!" It's Wild Turkey. He holds Quinn's rod.

"You got one," says Wayne Feeds, his eyes a-sparkle.

Wild Turkey says, "Rod was jumpin' like mad. Didn't want y'all to lose him, so I set the hook." He hands the rod to Quinn.

The line is alive, heavy with pull. The fish breaks water at the edge of the light pool: a silver flash. The wooden pier thunders when the boys, at a distance, see the fish flapping on the planks, and come running. "Dad, Dad, what is it?"

"Wow!"

Quinn deepens his voice, "Quiet down, you guys."

"But, *Dad*, what is it?"

Jesus.

Wild Turkey says, "It's a sea trout, boy."

"Tha's right," Wayne Feeds puts in. "Call 'im a gray or a speckled trout too."

Wild Turkey looks at Quinn and grins. "A day-um sight bigger in ours too."

"Right nice fish."

"Thanks," says Quinn and drops it into the cooler. His hands are slippery with slime. Just as he is ready to use his jeans, Wayne Feeds says, "Feels gewd, done it?" and throws him a blood-spotted hand towel. They laugh.

Quinn has to say thanks again.

"You get 'im on bloodworms?"

"Dad, hey Dad?"

"That's right," says Quinn. "Bloodworms."

"Dad?"

Wild Turkey laughs. "Now don't that beat hell?"

"Thing is, they ain't *spose* to go after no worms."

"Tonight's yo' lucky night."

A teenager walks by with a transistor: "Bad Moon Rising" again.

"Dad!"

"What, for Chris'sake!"

"Can, can we go over to the carnival?"

"Yeah, can we, Uncle Jack?"

Quinn looks down at them. He sighs.

"We'll be real careful."

"Really," says Julian.

"We'll walk on the beach."

Quinn says, "Go, go." He waves his hand. "I give up."

"Dad?"

"What?"

"Can we have some money?"

Jesus.

"So."

It is Joni. She places her hand on his shoulder. Gerald keeps walking out to the end of the pier where the anchor rigs are, the shark and king lines; his white shirt begins to float in the dark, a ghost. "Where are the boys?"

"See that Ferris wheel? Don't look at me like that."

"Like what? Am I supposed to be cross?"

"They just can't sit still," he says.

"How's your eye? Still sensitive?"

"It's okay."

Joni laughs. "Mister Macho."

"Bag it, huh. Sounds like your brother. He mad at me?"

Joni shakes her head.

"Just the world, huh?"

"What?"

"Nothing." Quinn quickly opens the Igloo. "Look!"

"Nice. What are they?"

"Sea trout."

"How do you know?"

"I just do. And I'm going to fill the Igloo too."

Loudly two guys thump down the pier; they are laughing, and one keeps saying, "Take a break, take a break!"

"You like the pier?"

"It's pretty out here." Joni looks toward a menhaden trawler, a source of drifting gold light in the darkness.

Under his breath, Quinn says, "These people are something else. Half the time I can't make out—" Quinn tenses and studies the tip of his rod, clicking the line tighter. "Waves move the bait around."

"Jack, Gerald's going back."

Quinn jerks his rod to a vertical position, then gently tugs line in the porcelain eyelets.

Joni says, "He's sick and is afraid it's a sarcoma."

Quinn settles back, still focused on his line. "That a disease or a New York fad?"

Joni crosses her arms and looks again toward the disappearing lights of the trawler.

"Come on," says Quinn, "I'm just kidding."

"It's nothing to kid about."

"No? What about the time he told you he was going blind?"

"This is different. He's lost weight."

"What's Denise doing?"

"I don't know."

"Maybe if she'd put down that novel once in a while. . . ."

"The problem is deeper than that."

"The problem is Gerald's mouth. He's too free with it. It's why he has no friends."

"He's honest, Jack. You've said so yourself. He's . . ."

But Quinn straightens on his bench, leans forward, and tries the line. Suddenly it tugs, pulls steadily. The drag buzzes and subsides; he begins to reel, peering into the dark for the first glimpse of what he has caught coming in. When he finally has the trout in the Igloo, his eye begins to throb at the root. He looks around for Joni and sees her with Gerald, his white shirt floating, growing small with distance.

Six or seven halos of Coleman light are spaced along the beach to the south. A revolving green star in a white circle. Quinn watches a single light speeding along the beach, bouncing, followed by another: bikers. Hell, he should have gone with the boys. Tomorrow he can play ball with them on the low-tide sand, try to close the gap with Gerald. Clouds travel overhead. Stars seem to pulse. Or is it his eye? People up and down the pier mumble clichés about the weather and fishing, but their voices are wonderful. Behind him two teenage boys curse and continue to reel in an assortment of fish. Wild Turkey has left, and an old woman who has taken his spot at the rail turns and tells Quinn she has caught nothing all evening. She wears a wide-brimmed straw hat and has a narrow birdlike face. She looks at the cursing boys and back at Quinn: "Say in the Book it raineth on the just and the unjust alike."

Her husband says, "Amen."

Quinn bites back a laugh.

Out of the blue she tells him they have a new preacher in their church, *needed* a new preacher. "I seen hogs house the devil."

Good Lord.

Quinn concentrates on his line. With the trout Wild Turkey has given him, he has almost enough for a meal. Lights, glittering on the smooth dark water in the distance, look like sweepings of broken glass, a small neat pile. He tightens his line. Seeing is almost enough. He is thinking about the doctor when an old woman ten feet up the rail hauls in a big blue. Then someone else. And another and another. Finally his own line comes alive and all along the pier the darkness flashes with bluefish swinging from dozens of poles.

SWEET TICKFAW RUN SOFTLY, TILL I END MY SONG

William Mills

FRED Carlisle first sensed the danger as a rhino might who has foraged too close to killer bees protecting the center of the hive. Like a humming or buzzing that was common enough until the sounds intensified and then caught his real notice. He knew his immune-response system was outnumbered and that his little cells of resistance were being subtly overcome, so he scratched the thick hair on his chest and headed to the refrigerator for another beer, just a little sooner than he normally would have. He was outnumbered by females five to one.

Ever since his wife had run off with the resident pediatrician (met through his own good offices, Carlisle being the head X-ray technician), he had taken up the guitar. With that special fecklessness of the newly divorced, he took to the beaches, or rather a longish sandbar on the river Tickfaw, with his sailor hat, six beers, and the guitar. He felt himself alternately the sad buffoon and the troubadour, depending often on the effect of the beer and the sun. The troubadour is not easy to bring off when one is absolutely alone. Parents see to it that their children get nowhere near. Or, consider the dark repulsion, the dank specter, that arises in the minds of young men and women alike when, already nearly denuded for the sun and water, they suddenly confront a solitary, hairy-chested fellow strumming his guitar and singing softly to the river. Why has he come out from the shadows where he surely must reside? Imagine though how this force field would change about if one other human, man woman or child, were sitting by the singer's side, listening. The children would be permitted to gather round, for now the piper's goat feet would appear to be only sandaled toes. The sleepy, sun-drowsed young men and women would then envy the artist for his resemblance to the happy figures in the soft drink ads on television—instead of reviling him as the kind of figure that might lurk around bus station restrooms.

One afternoon when Carlisle's loneliness was about to get him *all* the way down where he could not even sing alone, two young succulent junior divinities wandered near him. The younger (both were less than half his age) asked innocently, "What kind of guitar is that?" Before either could get away, he thrust his instrument toward his inquisitor. "Swedish. Do you play?"

"No," the younger one answered. "My father used to."

"He doesn't play anymore?"

"He lives someplace else now." She fondled the neck of the guitar. "His was Mexican. I thought most guitars came from Mexico and Spain."

"I got this one when I was in the army. I was on vacation and went to Sweden and saw it there." Both of the girls had those well-developed, muscular bodies that had taken Carlisle's breath away when he was stationed in Germany. Much to be said for active women, he thought.

Though Carlisle had no children, he thought he understood Lot's difficulties with his daughters. Like most men, as he had gotten older he had had to account for his lust for girls who had not yet crossed the Greenwich Mean Line of Womanhood. His meditations on this led him to the obvious conclusion that the lust was perfectly natural—and that it must be fought like the true confrontation with the Devil it was, a Devil that threatened town and family, the civilized life.

Carlisle did not have long to flail his lust out of mind (as his eyes roved the dark tans of their flat abdomens and as they shook their long hair insouciantly), for just then an earlier, less tanned model was hieing it over the sand a bit clumsily, her soft thighs having fallen sullenly from an earlier grace.

So it was that the river Tickfaw became the setting for this union of the divorced. Several weeks passed by and Carlisle had "taken up" with this *Schatz* of German descent, Karola Mummelthey, and her offsprings (a funny word), Veila and Veronica. His pitch on the beach had been a response to her pitch: the plumbing and appliances were breaking down because they had bought everything new when they had married but now it was sixteen years and a woman had no preparation for fixing such things, always thinking her job was elsewhere—and Carlisle's had been a dignified and appropriate "I have always been good with my hands."

By the time Karola's sister showed up with her husband for a two-day visit some three months later, Carlisle had become a cog in the domestic machine. He encouraged his mate to cook German food, for he perceived her as a German though she had in fact been born and reared in Des Moines. Such cooking was news to her, but Carlisle tried to infect her with the idea that it was going back to her roots. She sniffed at this, but fell into German potato salad, kraut, fresh pork sausages that were dubbed bratwurst, and whatever else fitted his notion of things German. (How many Chinese have arrived in the States and been invited to cook Peking Duck or other elegances and, never having eaten them themselves, had to turn to in quick fashion?)

Veila and Veronica were just tickled pink about having a man around who could fix bicycles and run them to Girl Scouts and the Y.W.C.A. and so on. Were pink for about two months until the newness wore off and Karola brought him in as a consultant disciplinarian.

The Mother: "Shouldn't they be in bed by nine-thirty?" or "Tell them they're too young to be wearing Tropicana Red lipstick."

The Disciplinarian: "OK, you girls do what your mother says."

What comes next, of course, is "You're not our daddy."

Carlisle sighed. Would that they could be with this phantom, Frederick Rodehorst. They had kept his name. He still sometimes sent money. Karola Mummelthey would have no more of Rodehorst. She had spent a week changing social security, credit cards, bank accounts. Then she found out she had no credit. Carlisle was glad he wasn't around when she found that out. Her old man could still rile what was left of that *Deutches Blut*. That was another thing: the surfeit of names around the house. Carlisle, Mummelthey, Rodehorst. What to do? A school friend comes by and says "Hello Mr. Rodehorst." Carlisle just lets it go. Too much trouble explaining everything. A lot of the time you just have to let things ride. But the girls speak up. "His name is not Rodehorst. It's Carlisle." The school friend tries to look shrewd. "Their daddy is in New York City." So the friend figures, right. She's got that under control. Then the girls' mother walks in and she gets the "Hello Mrs. Rodehorst."

"Honey, my name is Mrs. Mummelthey. My girls' name is Rodehorst, after their father." It's not long before the kid gets on her bicycle and tools right out of this madhouse where nobody seems to have his right name. Even having the same first name as Rodehorst bothered Carlisle. He could never be sure when Karola murmured "Oh Fred" during love time whether she had impaled herself on the nothink of ecstasy and was simply replying with the name she had murmured for sixteen years. He had once thought of asking her to murmur "Carlisle" but he knew that wouldn't cut it. Although it did have a German formality about it.

What's in a lot of names? Confusion. And the grid was upped just a hair when Karola's sister and her husband putted into the driveway in an ancient Citroen. Sheila's name was no longer Mummelthey. Rather Polowski after her husband, Oskar Polowski. A second generation Pole. He and Sheila still lived in Des Moines with their twelve-year-old daughter, Tammy Sue. Tammy Sue Polowski had pain-in-the-ass written across her face to be read in any language.

Both of them were interested to see about this "new man in Karola's life." She had no doubt written them. Carlisle was interested in them, too. With his intense desire to know about people and their native lands, he had read up on Poles. He had even asked Karola if she would cook some native Polish food, but she said enough was enough and that she had heard it wasn't any good. She wrinkled her nose.

Sheila Polowski was a year younger than Karola. And it may have been that year or the one child less, but she was taut as a drum and had a watchfulness about her that said her radar was always on full alert. She was a little splay-eyed, and it was hard to tell sometimes which eye to look at when she looked at you. Fred knew that she was good to look at. She had a nice habit of holding the tip of her tongue sort of out and then caressing her lower lip. This was when she looked at him. She was friendly and all right. So was Oskar. He was six-by-six, and when he shook Carlisle's hand it was like having a warm pot roast thud across his palm. He was in plumbing fixtures in Des Moines, so Carlisle had something to talk about with him straight away. Thirty minutes and a cold beer later, they were seated on the tub edge and commode respectively, discussing the new kind of trap which would put a stop to the leak.

During dinner that first evening (Mummelthey tipping her hat at least with crisp thin wiener schnitzel) their vacation plans came out, and it seemed they were leaving after one more night to go to New Mexico. Why New Mexico?

"TM," said Sheila softly. Oskar looked away, embarrassed.

"TM?" echoed Carlisle.

"Transcendental Meditation."

With the smoothness of a right-hand arpeggio on his guitar, Carlisle played the host (played the guest?). "Oh, I've wanted to talk to somebody who knew something about that."

Oskar looked just the slightest bit surprised, as if Carlisle had evidenced an interest in knitting bootees, but he kept his counsel as Sheila went on. "I've just really gotten into it, just scratched the surface, and that's why I'm going to this TM camp in Taos. But it's a way to get in touch with your inner self."

"I see. Sounds interesting."

Karola was nodding approvingly. She was a very affirmative person. If a friend or sister said she was going to join the Foreign Legion, she would nod vigorously, then later on ask what the Foreign Legion was? Someone was going to surf on a tidal wave . . . nod, nod. Going to grow babies from butterfly manure . . . nod, nod.

"Do you find it pretty helpful, Oskar?" inquired Carlisle.

"Oh, I haven't gotten into it yet," he said respectfully.

"Oskar is going to go hiking with Tammy Sue while Sheila goes to the camp," explained Karola. The two sisters had been discussing all this while Oskar and Carlisle had worked on the commode.

Oskar grinned a little sheepishly. "I never cared for that kind of stuff," meaning TM, no doubt, for he got a sharp little look from Sheila.

"I've tried to get Oskar interested in something to develop his potential, but it's hard to get a Pollack to change his ways."

Oskar didn't grin at this. Oh, well, thought Carlisle, another happy marriage. The Prussians were partitioning Poland again. Carlisle had read about the sorrow that was Poland. Everybody wanted a piece of it. Christ's Body, he thought. A Polish sausage, he thought.

Karola got up to make coffee, but Carlisle asked Oskar if he wouldn't like another drink and Oskar said yes, he would, and did Fred have any gin? Carlisle felt sympathetic to Oskar, and as the evening passed and they drank more and more, Carlisle pulled out his guitar and the two men hacked up a few old American favorites. Then Carlisle showed off his two German songs, "Der Wirtin Tochterlein" and "So Ist's."

"Fred's a lot more German than we are, Sheila," and with this Karola took Oscar's glass to refill it and he followed her to the kitchen.

"You really sing those very well," Sheila said, putting that tip of her tongue just between her lips and then wetting the bottom one. Carlisle thanked her. "I really envy your and Karola's life-style," she said. "You both seem so free."

"Absolutely true, absolutely," bubbled Carlisle. What a wonderfully free life he had. What nice folks the Polowskis are. How good booze was. "Yes, my little schatzy, there's no denying our great and free passion."

She looked deeply into Carlisle's eyes as if she were searching for some answer to a question.

"Sheila, let me get you a drink," urged Carlisle, getting up. She had not been drinking.

"No, I'm fine." But she got up with him to go to the kitchen.

"A great little sister you got here," Carlisle said to Karola, and as he did so, Sheila laughed and put her arm around his waist and gave him a little squeeze.

"Watch it, little sister," Karola said, teasingly. Oskar became related to the three of them from outside, a separate point looking at a triangle. Sheila continued to hold him around the waist, now a little longer than was seemly.

"Another drink, Oskar?" moving to the refrigerator, leaving Sheila to stand.

"No, I 'bout had enough. It was a long drive."

Before Karola dropped off to sleep, she delivered the domestic news report. "They're having trouble." And Carlisle sighed, not knowing what else to do.

At breakfast Oskar and Sheila wore faces with criss-crossed marks of sleepless anger. Carlisle felt a pang of sadness that he did not show, but he remembered lying in that special caldron feigning hourless sleep, either too proud or too indecisive to leave the bed. He could remember that, but just as truly, he felt outside (not really above) their troubles. He had done his time, hadn't he? Now there was the distance and amusement of the old soldiers watching the new recruits. You ain't seen nothing yet, buddy. There is an airy omnipotence that accompanies this distance if one's memory is not especially vivid.

Carlisle left everyone at the table talking about Des Moines and made a dead run for the apartment that he still kept near the hospital. This was his Saturday for duty, and he had to slip into a fresh set of whites. During the day he called Karola and suggested they go to a riverside seafood dine-and-dance establishment—working-class style. She remarked sort of secretly that, yes, it would probably be good if everyone got out and loosened up.

The work day went easily, Saturday always being for non-scheduled shots that could not be done during the regular week. One chick needed several shots of her skull. Later in the afternoon she came walking back in the office and asked him if she could see them. It was against the rules unless the physician wanted to show them to her, but she had big tits and he knew she wouldn't understand them anyway. She gasped, seeing beyond her lips and cheeks and hair for the first time. But what appalled her the most was the massive spots where her teeth were—she had some twenty fillings which generally were invisible even to her. Naturally she asked about the tumor, but Carlisle answered he didn't know how to interpret them. Partly a lie. Besides the risk of getting in trouble with the radiologist, it was better for her to be more concerned about the surface of things, instead of about the hazy presence that might well spell the transition from tits and lips to dust. Looking beneath the surface of things was not all it was cracked up to be. The patterns were there, the symmetry. But what was always of such interest to people spelled a lot of trouble.

Carlisle felt expansive driving to Mummelthey's. He had changed to a blue, chambray work shirt and white dungarees. He felt watery—maritime, bawdy and yo-ho-ho. Karola had felt the evening out would loosen everybody up, and Carlisle certainly agreed. They ordered piles of hot, steaming shrimp in the shells and hardshell crabs. Peeling and cracking all that succulence lent a fine sensuality to the day. They had cold mugs of beer and, immediately afterwards, chilled bottles of blanc de blanc. The Polowskis seemed to get into the spirit of things. The drinking helped. Sheila was enjoying the cool wine, now and then drinking deeply. Without any special effort, it seemed, Oskar talked mostly to Karola, and this left Carlisle with Sheila. Being a great believer in the release of anxiety through euphoria, induce it how you will, Carlisle kept her glass always filled. Dionysus soon led them to the big dark dance hall on the river. One of the things that Carlisle felt he could hold onto in a world that was as slippery as eels, a treacherous world where wealthy pediatricians raided the sources of their income, promising the wives Arpège and station wagons, was the body of a woman. He dearly loved the electric interface of locked male and female ventral sides, tits to chest, pelvis to pelvis, that atomic bond as he pulled a woman's lower spine, her tailbone, closer to him. And he did this night. Danced with Karola and danced a lot with Sheila. Oskar Polowski did not feel the Nureyev wings that Carlisle felt tonight. Apparently. While Oskar was dancing with Karola, Carlisle was left at the table with the wine-tuned Sheila. Can a chief X-ray technician find happiness with his girlfriend's sister from Des Moines, a second generation *Schatz?* Yes. And so could she. Later, as she murmured "Oh, wonderful," she grasped (in the dark) his male instrument. Not his guitar, either.

What a joy! Barnacle Carlisle having this happen to him in the dark. But what a fright! His girlfriend's sister. A fellow Mummelthey! The barnacled Nureyev danced on with Polowski née Mummelthey, thinking how surely the sibilancy of sin issued from the serpent's hiss. And her soft tongue that had moistened her lip now moistened his. A straightforward joy.

So far so good? All the people go home from their frolic, and the Polowskis wheel it for the heights of New Mexico next morning: one to transcend via the spirit, and the other using his two feet. A duality with one appendage, a daughter that has the look of an imp. All in a Citroen.

Back to the rhythm of the household. What's in an interlude? Only a memory—one that he hopes does not announce itself if he should talk in his sleep. Family life, roll on, roll on. A little discipline for the Rode-horsts (on request from their mother), nice candlelight suppers in the evening after a day spent working at his profession, searching for cloudy spots or irregularities beneath the surface of the people who have been sent to X-ray.

During a nice supper of sauerbraten and potato salad, one week after the Citroen left, the phone goes off. Veila calls to her mother to pick up the extension in the dining room. Carlisle tries not to let all of his attention leave the food, but he cannot help being distracted by Karola's end of the conversation. It is her sister.

"I know, I know," and is nodding. "Don't cry. It's going to be all right. Look at me." She nods some more. "You know I will . . . right, right, don't let anyone push you around . . . you don't have to put up with it . . . sure you can come here, you know you can. You just get on the plane and come right out here. Forget the car. Let him go climbing around in the mountains . . . o.k. . . . can't wait to see you again."

Mummelthey was very excited. "They're having trouble. I told you. Sheila has left him." Carlisle went on eating, trying to figure out how this was going to change his life. He knew things don't ever stay the same, as much as you want them to, and he wondered what boded his way now. Mummelthey repeated much of the conversation that he had already guessed.

"Maybe this is just a little fight," he offered. "She's not leaving him for anybody else, right?"

"No, of course not. He just won't support her emotionally in the way that she needs. He imprisons her."

"He seemed like a nice sort to me," volunteered Carlisle.

That line stopped her a moment. She really liked Oskar. Had always thought he was a Gibraltar for her sister. This only served to confuse her. But she came back finally with, "Oh, you men always stick together." What man did he stick together with, Carlisle wondered?

All the next morning while they waited for the plane, Carlisle was struck with the almost jubilant excitement that had come over Mummelthey. It didn't seem the appropriate sadness for a breakup. More a festive air. She had taken special care with her hair and face this morning and put on one of his favorite dresses, which really made her look quite sensual. In a modest way.

The remainder of the day was a great emotional drain, like the day of a funeral or going to the dentist. Both of the sisters thrived on it. And mixed in this alloy was Carlisle's own curiosity about what Sheila was thinking about since she had grabbed his dong at the dance. Maybe she had forgotten? Maybe that had helped her back here? No. Hummm. For a moment as he put his arm affectionately around her shoulders while Mummelthey fixed supper and she leaned thankfully against him with Mummel looking on happily, Carlisle thought, look, this is the twentieth century. Maybe he could just shepherd both women and their offsprings. Ménage à trois? Just then her little brat daughter walked in, glared at him, tugged at her mother's arm and pulled her loose from Carlisle. "Mother, why can't daddy come back with us?"

"Because we are going to live separately. But you can see him anytime you want. Karola, how far off is supper?"

"Twenty minutes."

"Could you make it thirty?"

"Sure. What's up?"

"I generally meditate at this time."

Everybody got still for an instant. Embarrassed.

"Sure, sure," nodded Mummelthey.

What's a fine, sensual *Schatz* who grabs dongs in the dark doing in an empty room all locked away? After she left, Carlisle suggested to her kid, "Why don't you meditate a little in your room like your mom?" The kid stuck her tongue out. She didn't have the same movement with her tongue as her mother, but she left anyway.

"Why did you do that?" demanded Mummelthey.

"Nothing. Just kidding." He got a narrowed look. Forget the ménage à trois.

After supper the three adults sat around the table. They talked divorce. It seemed like a woman's affair. They laid plans just as he remembered hearing his wife lay plans for his marriage.

"You can move in here until you get settled," Mummelthey offered her sister. Didn't ask Carlisle, *danseur extraordinaire* and guitarist.

"Oh, but Fred would feel too cramped with so many women," and then she did her number with the tongue between the lips, batting her eyelashes.

"I'll levitate you," thought Carlisle. "I'll send you transcending with my instrument." Aloud, though, "Of course not. Just one big happy family." Mummelthey knew he was lying, and she got piqued. He got up and got some gin. Veila came into the kitchen screaming that Veronica had slapped her because she and Tammy Sue Polowski wanted to be alone in her bedroom.

"If you girls don't learn to love one another, Fred is going to give you a licking," Mummelthey threatened. The screaming stopped and Carlisle sighed. He didn't like being represented as lawgiver or domestic enforcer. There was getting to be this new level of buzzing, buzzing around the old pad. Polowskis and Rodehorsts in the bedroom, and Polowskis and Mummeltheys in the kitchen.

"This will all blow over, Sheila," counseled Carlisle. "You'll probably be back in your lover's arms by week's end." This was not a popular thing to say, he discovered. They had already started laying plans for the divorce. They didn't want the wife left standing at the court bench.

"Oh you just don't know what living with him is like, Fred. He's not interested in the spirit, in the adventure of discovering one's identity. He just says he already knows who he is, Oskar Polowski." Her look was intense and her eyes smoldered. "He doesn't support me in developing who I am."

You've developed a pretty fast right hand in the dark, honey. First things first. A hand, a quick tongue, and then a quick soul. "What would you do that's any different than with Oskar?" This kind of talk killed any playful flirting that had been going on between Sheila and him. Analysis did it every time. Like an X-ray of Marilyn Monroe. Not too good to forget the surfaces of things.

"I can't get him interested in anything like meditation. He's so set in his ways."

"You mean he won't do what you want him to do." A shot across the bow.

"Fred," howled Mummelthey. "How cruel! You know that's not what she means." There'd be no cavorting tonight.

"Maybe so," he murmured. "I just hate to see you split. Maybe just lay out for a while. Forget the institution thing. How can you make love when you're an institution? Maybe if marriage could become a loose confederation of states rather than a federal institution, then maybe you could levitate, and . . ."

"It's not levitate, Fred," Mummelthey cut in.

". . . and Oskar could be into plumbing fixtures and hiking. And you just gird up the confederacy when it is threatened from without, but when the threats are gone, back to doing what you can, or like to do. If maybe folks just confederated by choice and by the threat of outside invasion just so they could have more time for balling and thinking and dreaming, then the confederation would stay loose. And if we spent as much vigilance staying loose as we do girding up for outside threats, there'd be plenty of time for just having fun." Fred Carlisle was suddenly embarrassed about his speech. And it had dashed all the divorce ceremonies for the moment, or at least the momentum. "I just hate to see you dissolve if you don't have to, and furthermore, I am going outside with my guitar. You girls continue to march."

It's not just that way, though, is it, he thought. A loose confederation was not just a dream, it could happen (look at Mummelthey and him, look at the 1780s in the States), but just as surely, it was only a point on a curve, like the sine wave on his oscilloscope at the lab. And just as surely there were the partitions of Poland. He took his guitar and sat out on the imitation redwood picnic table in the patio, strummed a few chords, and began to sing. The neighbor slammed his window down, but Carlisle kept on singing and thinking—sometimes of the beach on Tickfaw River, but mostly of a horny woman sitting on the ground in a lotus position trying to transcend time, and of Polowski high in the mountains in New Mexico.

THIS LIGHT IS FOR
THOSE AT SEA

Kent Nelson

A cold snap came early that year on
the Cape, and the inland leaves were killed still green upon the trees.
Owen Leland knew the weather would warm again, but the chill had sent
the migrating warblers winging eastward toward Bermuda and beyond,
where the northeast tradewinds would sweep them to the Antilles. The
season had been over anyway. After Labor Day the vacationers had
returned to their elements in Boston and New York, and the beach was
deserted. In early October, the days had turned milder again, but with
the leaves already brown and with the absence of birds, the effect was of a
dead summer.

It stayed warm for five weeks, each day flowing faultlessly into the next
as if there were to be no change in the season. The exodus of birds had
been nearly complete, and though he checked the thickets and wood
margins near the shore, he had found only a few catbirds and towhees and
an occasional hawk. A few ducks and shorebirds lingered, pausing on
their way down the flyway, but they were sparse. He wrote down what he
saw—species, number, habitat, for whatever good it might someday do.

Only the remnants of the summer remained. Boats had been drawn up
onto the grass and covered with canvas; the windows of houses were
boarded against burglars and storms. He missed the anonymity of the
hordes who used the beaches. He liked the children and the sounds of
cars and the white wedges of sails atilt upon the sea.

One morning he woke early to jog and as he pulled on his sweat-
clothes, he sensed the change. He did not know how his internal barometer worked: it was a feeling in the bones. The sea haze had gathered
around the black posts on the pier near the yacht club, and the lighthouse on Harney's Island threw an eerie beacon into the gauzy air. He left
Monica asleep and went downstairs to his studio for his shoes. The large

plate-glass window for southeast light was opaque with gray, without distance, and the birds he had collected and stuffed made awkward silhouettes against the half light. He looped his binoculars around his neck and stepped outside. This day, he knew, would be the beginning of winter.

He scanned with the binoculars and vacant beach, the circle of the glass moving stealthily along the curve of the bay as he turned his body. Nothing. Near the yacht club were some gulls too far away to identify, and past Harney's Island two white-winged scoters raced with frantic wingbeats over the uneven gray swells.

He should take a trip, he thought: call Stefan in Santa Fe. On a few days' notice and a whim Stefan could free himself for anything. Maybe they could go down to Texas to Laguna Atascosa and then come back up along the Rio Grande. The last time they had found the brown jays at Santa Marguerita, and had finished up with hummingbirds in Big Bend.

He set his binoculars on the wooden steps to the beach and started his warm-ups—windmills, jumping jacks, stretches, push-ups. The sand was loose on his skin, between his fingers, under his bare feet. He pressed his chin down. Five, ten. It did no good, these exercises or the running. It seemed as though his body could not assimilate the training anymore. Despite his discipline, his muscles did not tighten or tone. Every day he ran down to the maroon house, walked to the white-gabled Winston house with the catamaran in the dunes, then ran along the path that led through the scrub trees to the yacht club. Usually he rested there, either inside or, on warm days, on the pier that spiderlegged out into the bay. Then he ran back more slowly to think about trends in the various markets and to clear his mind of sleep.

When he had caught his breath from the calisthenics, he surveyed the strand again. A flock of sanderlings had in the interim settled in a short way down the sand, tiny gray and white bobbins working the wash of waves. Some black-backed gulls, which had become more common in the last few years, sat stoically on the pilings near the club. Nothing else. Then, in a sweep of the glasses across the dunes, he glimpsed a patch of color. It was a woman in a blue sweater, hazy auburn hair, magnified and focused against the tangled mat of dry grasses on the dunes.

The woman seemed to be looking at Harney's Island, or so he assumed from the direction she faced. He had heard that a family had rented the Winston house for the winter. He turned and put the glasses on the lighthouse to see what she saw. Nothing unusual: the light's circling through the fog. When he turned back, she had disappeared.

He did not like the feeling that the season was changing. He liked the veiled atmosphere of the mist, the muted tones of gray sliding over the sea, filtering sea salt into the pores, coloring the yacht club gray-green. To him it was a visible admission of processes.

He ran barefooted along the harder wet sand near the water so he could get traction. It was difficult at first until he found a rhythm of breathing. Then when he had felt the first sweat, it became easier—the loping stride, the grainy sand kicked up behind, the breath coming in deep, free draughts. His mind floated separate from his body. His breath sounded heavy in his ears, his muscles and limbs flowed, but all of that was still temporal.

He could fantasize how he wished things were. He could relive moments or fix in his mind the static image of a cresting wave. As a boy he had sat on the roof of his mother's house, looking over the rooftops to the Long Island Sound. Once, in Europe after college, he had extended his hand to a Swiss girl who had reached out to him from the window of a moving car.

He thought in French. *C'était seulement un moment. Personne ne m'a vu, et àpres ils sont morts.* The image carried him. He crossed a rickety bridge in Lausanne and walked in a crowd of people he did not know, who did not know him. Their colorless eyes stared straight ahead. To escape the horror, he took a bus. But the faces were the same. He hoped someone might discover him.

The running ached in his chest, the air hard to catch. Before he reached the maroon house he stopped and walked. His dream left him. A numbness slid along his right arm, tingled in his shoulder. It was strange, he thought, that without his awareness or will this absence had crept into his flesh. He shook his arm, raised it, pressed his hands together to rid himself of the numbness.

The cold water washed over his feet, and he waded into the light surf. He continued along in the shallows. Ahead of him the gray-green clubhouse drifted, and the horizontal line of the pier wavered despite the support of the heavy, black, creosoted posts.

Then he glimpsed the flash of a black and white wing. The bird's legs were extended behind the body as it flew. The bill was curved. Avocet, he thought. Then, no, it couldn't be. He did not have the glasses to check.

Several hundred yards away the bird wheeled and flew up the coast. Willet, he thought.

The numbness remained in his arm longer than seemed healthy. He remembered once in private school being knocked unconscious in a hockey game and having no memory of the hit. But this numbness was not connected to experience. He started running again, believing the numbness would dissipate. He came even with the gabled house with its white porch suspended.

There were no lights, no sign of life. He cut across the beach from the water, heading toward the opening of the path through the scrub brush and the dunes. Morning seemed evening, and the autumn gathered the hint of spring. The dunes rolled away before him, rising toward a land without horizon, as if he had suddenly come upon the terrain of Venus with its gasses and impenetrable clouds which held tightly against the sun.

His running was awkward on the hill, and his feet slipped backward in the dry sand. Out of breath, he climbed weakly to the top of a dune and rested. The sea was gone now, though he could still hear it beating behind the veil of fog. He turned full circle and found, close to him, the woman he had seen earlier from the beach steps of his house.

Her back was turned. Her reddish hair hung in springs down her back; her light-blue sweater, ribbed with a darker blue he had not seen from a distance, made her upper body seem shapeless, without waist. The slacks she wore and her hair gave him the impression of youth.

What startled him was his memory. He had been twelve years old, and a friend of his mother's with red hair had, for no reason that he could have known then, touched him, caressed him. She had asked him to do the same to her. How soft she had felt! How warm!

The woman turned. She was not so young as he had imagined—late twenties, perhaps. The dark red hair was the kind which gave no freckles to the skin. The wild gray-brown tangles of dry oak behind her highlighted the color, and he felt the contrast as a brilliant sigh. He was embarrassed for his emotion while she, on the contrary, was perfectly composed, not in mood, but in structure, like a still-life arrangement carefully calculated by the artist.

They held each other's gaze for too long, and he was afraid that in the process of deciphering he would lose the essence of moment. She smiled ambiguously; he returned a half smile. He wished for a touch and to go from there, from moment to moment, leading to some meaning. He felt awkward in the silence. The woman's gaze was too severe, or too willing, and he turned away and began to run down the embankment of the dune. He found the trail worn hard by the summer people, and he plunged through the scramble of oak. He was aware, as soon as he emerged, breathless, at the clearing in front of the yacht club, that the numbness in his arm was gone.

Inside he sat beside the plate-glass window overlooking the harbor. A few frail boats covered with canvas bobbed on their moorings. The tide was ebbing, though he had never followed the chart carefully. A different tide came every day, later or earlier, higher or lower than normal, depending on the moon or the weather. He noticed the smudges on the window glass, a wavy perfection in the corner, the tiny wing of a fly on the sill. His tea steeped in the cup in front of him.

And how did the birds know to go eastward to get south? They flew past Bermuda, nearly to Africa to catch the tradewinds, without which they would never be able to survive such a distance. How had they learned? They knew how to navigate without the sun or the stars, without voices or mathematics or theories of physics. He had himself seen thousands of warblers disappear the day before the first cold weather had arrived.

Harold, the caretaker, passed him, and Owen called him over.

"Yes, Mr. Leland?"

"Harold, do you know whether anyone is living in the Winston house?"

"I think the Winstons have rented it," Harold said, "but I don't know whether anyone has moved in yet."

Owen nodded his thanks and turned back to the window. The haze was lifting, and the boats were clearer, their rippled reflections gliding away from their hulls like colored smoke. In spots the sun burned through.

He stood up, having drunk only half his tea.

He almost expected the woman to be standing in the doorway when he turned to go, and he deliberately did not face the main entrance. Instead he pretended to examine the pictures of ships on the walls. Then he slipped out the back way, where the stairs led in a zigzag down to the pier.

She was there, leaning against one of the pilings where he could not have seen her from the window, her auburn hair lifting in the slight breeze.

Her eyes were closed and her face tilted upward to catch the direct glare of the emerging sun. She did not move when he walked past her over the creaking platform. She did not open her eyes or startle or turn away.

He had not meant to walk out on the pier that morning. He had a call to make to his broker, pressing matters, and he had wanted to run back as usual. But he started out briskly toward a blue yawl tied up at the end of the pier.

Harney's Island light was clearing, and through the scattered fog beyond, a small fishing boat was moving silently across the bay. The two fisherman in the boat were silhouettes, one in the bow, the other with his arm at a right angle on the tiller.

He stayed longer than he meant to by the blue yawl, admiring the teak deck and the patterns which the dew had made on the stainless steel fittings. He was certain the woman would leave. Yet when he turned to start home, she was still there. She was facing him, as though tracing his movement the way a blind person might follow sound. He walked slowly the length of the pier; she could not have failed to hear his footsteps on the weathered boards. When he was near enough, he saw her eyes were still closed.

He walked straight at her, not keeping to the far edge of the pier as he had done before. Ten feet from her he stopped. He was about to call to her, to yell, to ask who she was and why she was taunting him. But he could not bring himself even to whisper. Instead he ran to her with quick steps, kissed her hard on the mouth, holding her tightly so she could not have shaken him away.

The next moment he was running down the planks of the ramp. He cut the corner at the end of the pier, banked his body on the turn, and jumped down onto the sand. The beach loomed in front of him.

The woman would tell. The husband would come around, or the police. Failing that, there would be rumors. Someone must have seen him—Harold perhaps. Or she would ask one of the neighbors who the crazy man was who in the early mornings ran on the beach.

He sprinted on the way back, and soon raced himself to exhaustion. A shell cut his foot, and though he could feel sand working into the gash, he did not stop. He did not look around. No dreaming now: his breath came agonizingly slowly; a tightness ran under his shoulder blades on his left side; his legs turned leaden. In the distance his own house bobbed in front of him.

He had to face Monica, too.

When he reached the wooden steps, he put one hand on each of the stair rails and retched. All the running, the hours of running, and his body was pure pain. He sat down heavily and held his head in his hands for a long time.

If he could get Monica to go away for a while to visit some friends of hers who were always asking if she were bored on the Cape in winter. He hated her friends, but maybe one of them would rescue him by accident. He wanted to be alone, without the threat, without the distraction, without having to account to anyone. Or he could call Stefan.

The sun sifted through the breaking fog, disappeared and reappeared. A flock of gulls wheeled back and forth over the small fishing boat out on the bay, one, then another of them catching the sporadic sunlight in its white wings. Farther out, an alcid flew frantically with rapid wingbeats over the open water toward the lighthouse—a black guillemot, perhaps, or a murre. Then he scanned the pier. The woman was gone.

His quiet breathing resumed, and he stood up and looped the binoculars' strap around his neck. Then, just down the beach a hundred yards or so, he saw the same bird's black and white flight, the wing pattern of a willet. He trained the glasses. Pinkish head, long, thin, upturned bill, powder-blue legs, faded plumage. Avocet. This was a bird of western ponds, occurring sporadically in the southeast, almost never on the Cape, never in the fall. He watched it settle upon the shore, wade, dip its head and thrust its needle bill into the water.

Stefan might believe him. They had seen so many things together, and they had learned to trust one another's vision. And who else but Stefan could he tell? He had no proof. Even a photograph would have been pointless because there were no landmarks on the shore.

Monica sat at the small table in the breakfast nook writing a letter. "You took longer this morning," she said, looking up when he came in.

He thought she was scrutinizing his face, as if to see whether he were concealing something. "I talked to Harold for a while," he said. "Whom are you writing?"

"Carrie."

"To invite her or to visit her?"

"If I go away, you don't eat."

He did not say anything. He hung the binoculars on a peg in the vestibule and stood for a moment, caught up in the swirling pattern of sunlight on the wooden wall.

"Is it clearing?" she asked.

"It'll be fine by noon."

She gazed at him closely. "Did something happen?" she asked. "Did you see anything?"

He was surprised by her question because she so rarely asked him anything. "No," he said. "There isn't much on a misty day. The birds seem to disappear."

Monica was a tall woman and, sitting, her erect posture gave her the appearance of putting stock in custom and manner. She kept her eye on him as he crossed the room and stood beside her at the window. Her silence had a way of irritating him, as if she were reminding him through absence that she was there.

Monica was his second wife. His first wife had been killed in the crash of an Amtrak train near Philadelphia, though he had not even known she had left home. He had thought she was playing bridge somewhere on Beacon Hill. Where was she going? She had with her only an overnight bag. And how often had he waited for her to come home in the evening when she was with another man? How many times had he discovered some lie?

He had waited a year after his first wife's death, and then he met and married Monica in two months. At first she had made him feel alive with her devotion to the outdoors and her willingness to try anything. She had even gone on some of his collecting trips with Stefan and him, excursions plagued with insects, rough country, and hundred-degree heat. But gradually he felt she forced her way into his life and into the easy routine which his money allowed. She became enamored of social events which he refused to attend. She said he had the right to do as he pleased.

He assumed she was merely honoring one of his early wishes. "I require someone who will leave me alone," he had said once.

"You mean stay away from you?"

He had meant it purely in the sense of physical space. "It has nothing to do with closeness of spirit," he said. "I need to be able to breathe."

Now, five years later, she had adopted the attitude of physician toward him, solicitous of his health and mental safety. He accepted her concern. He had no energy to try to understand why some emotions diminished and others subsumed them. Perhaps it was simply that his definitions had changed. Certainly love was the wrong word to describe what held them together.

"Are you going to work today?" she asked.

"No." He did not look at her, but kept his gaze on the pier. "I think I'll do some taxidermy on the skins Stefan sent."

She bent toward her letter, and when he did not leave, she asked, "Owen, are you all right?"

She was not being critical, but her tone of voice made him feel guilty, as though, if he were not all right he was somehow to blame.

"What do you mean 'all right'?"

"It was just a simple question."

"I'm all right."

Had she seen him run? Maybe as a vanishing speck, the regular motion of arms and legs, diminished or expanded by distance. Or had she seen him throw up by the steps?

"Why don't you take a shower first before you go downstairs?" she asked.

He was tired from running and knew without understanding he should not retaliate. His rebellion would solve nothing. But the way she ordered him, the way she directed his movements by suggestion. . . . He told himself to walk away.

"Owen?"

"Yes?"

"Would you like . . . ?"

"I would like," he said softly, but with vehemence that surprised him, "to slit your throat."

The sun was fully through the haze, and the sea appeared as lazy and hot as on a summer day. He descended to the grass and walked under the deck to his studio. Perhaps his feeling about the changing season had been wrong. It would stay warm another few days.

His studio had a musty smell: clay, dampness of salt air, the hint of chemicals used on skins. He closed the door and locked it, knowing Monica would come after him, if not right away, then later.

She came almost immediately. "Owen, please."

He did not go to the door. Instead he went to the refrigerator for ice and took a glass from the cupboard. He carried the bottle of bourbon back to the sofa in the studio.

"You don't have to prove anything to me," she said.

He did not say anything or tell her to go away. He poured bourbon into his glass. The woman on the pier would be there constantly, every day when he ran, or whenever he scanned through the binoculars for birds along the shore. He would not be able to face her: one did not do such things as he had done.

Or perhaps she had found his oddness attractive and would think of him secretly. He was not the kind of man for an affair of the heart. He would be no good at deception. He drank a swallow of bourbon and stared at the stuffed birds around his room—a short-eared owl, a piping plover, a Cape May warbler. The musty smell of the studio had already been accommodated by his unconscious and normal breathing so that he did not notice it anymore.

Late in the afternoon he was drunk. He had gone through a half bottle of bourbon and a great deal of his past. He had wasted such an immense time in bitterness over his first wife—her affairs, her griefs and deceptions, always claiming she was right. Then the void. When she had been killed there was no one to blame, nothing to fight against. Stefan had got him interested in birds. Travel. A world of difference. Meeting Monica had been chance, the worst way to do anything. Marrying her was an act of blind faith. He still wished, after all these years, that he had known the name of the Swiss girl in Lausanne. Had she beckoned to him or merely waved?

He got up from the sofa and looked up the avocet in one of his many bird books.

Genus recurviostra. Length 15–18 inches. A long-legged, long-billed wader. Adult's head, neck, and breast fawn brown, back and underparts white; wings have a conspicuous black bar; bill curved upward; legs bluish. Range: breeds from southern Saskatchewan and Alberta to eastern Washington and California, and south to Oklahoma and Texas. Lays three to four mottled eggs in pond or shoreline depressions or on marsh fringes.

There was no doubt in his mind.

He left his exile and walked outside to the edge of the lawn and scanned the sea with his glasses. The horizon was clear now, a distant deep blue, shading toward white. With the dusk and the clearing of the fog, it had become much colder. The water was calm. Without the breeze to trick him with chill, he felt the cold seep into the seams of his clothes and work its way deeper into him.

How had the avocet got there? There had been no storm, nothing to explain it wandering. He was happy that he had seen the bird, because otherwise he might not have believed it himself. And yet did it make a difference?

A flock of gulls strove purposely up the coast, their flight steady and direct: no playing or feeding now. The light on Harney's Island circled the bay, and each time it flashed in his eyes, he was conscious of its power. It reached far away. How far? Were birds attracted to it like moths? He smiled to himself. This light, he knew, was for those at sea, and he was vaguely comforted that it was so close to him.

Toward the yacht club, a few boats stuck to the smooth surface of the harbor, their colors gone now in the winnowed daylight. The faint lights from the club and from the other occupied houses were beginning to separate from the dusk. A glow rose from the windows of the Winston house.

He wheeled suddenly and faced his own window above him. There was a light here, too, a huge frame of light which shined over him on the lawn. Monica would be having a rum and tonic, her winter drink, and she would want a fire.

He went inside. The bourbon had made him tired and hungry.

Monica was working at the counter, and he watched her for a moment while she avoided him and peeled a cucumber.

"Would you like something?" she asked, "or is that a dangerous question?"

"No. No, I think I'll call Stefan."

"You could build a fire," she said. "It's getting quite cold."

He sat and dialed Stefan's number, which he had long ago committed to memory, together with the numbers of the fire department and the police. As Stefan's telephone rang, he became self-conscious. Monica's back was turned, but she could hear every word.

He stood up and carried the telephone into the living room.

"Stefan?" The voice which answered was faint. "How are things in New Mexico?"

"Owen?"

"Yes. How are you?"

"In the middle of building a barn. It's still daylight here. We had water this summer, so there's money."

"Good, good. How are Kip and Carol?"

The conversation moved in the circuitous path that Owen had

wanted: fillers of time, dabs of memory and common experience. They came around to birding excursions, talk of Alaska and the Rio Grande.

There was a pause, and Owen said, "I saw . . . "

And then he was going to say, I saw an avocet, just today on the Cape here. An avocet, of all things. Not rare, of course, but out of range, out of season. Rare for this place and this time of year. But he stopped and faced the window where his reflection was fastened to the glass by the lamps Monica had turned on in the room.

Outside, Harney's Island light came around and flashed.

"What about a trip," Owen asked.

"Can't. This barn. I'd like to, though. You know that. Just can't with the work here."

When he hung up, Owen stood for a moment looking toward the Winston house. Then he moved back into the kitchen and put the telephone down.

"What did you see?" Monica asked.

Owen shook his head.

They ate in an atmosphere of ghostly small talk. Monica, he thought, had never looked more lovely. The effort to recoup their earlier loss gave her a special beauty. Her cheeks were flushed, and her hair was combed smoothly across her forehead. Her eyes seemed grayer and more serious than he remembered them.

When dinner was over, he washed the dishes. He dried them and wiped the formica counter and the stove, and turned off the fluorescent light above the sink.

Monica was reading when he slipped outside for some air.

It had become very cold, and a north wind bristled across the bay. He shivered and held his arm tightly across his chest. The food and the cold sobered him. He stared into the darkness of Harney's Island and the sea, and then the light came around and pierced directly to the depth of his brain, where it twisted abruptly and illuminated a wordless dream.

Monica appeared on the balcony. "Owen?"

"Yes?"

"Are you coming back in?"

He did not answer. Instead he turned slowly and began running. He ran down the steps to the beach and along the dark sand in the direction of the Winston house far down the shore.

DÉTENTE

Joyce Carol Oates

ALL of life is real enough; but it's unevenly convincing. Begin with a flat blunt bold statement. A platitude, a challenge, a wise folk saying. There are so many wise folk sayings. Hadn't the chairman of the Soviet delegation said, the other evening at the crowded reception, when everyone was being friendly and those who could not speak English were smiling eagerly, hopefully, squeezing their American hosts' hands with a pressure that seemed, well, too intense, hadn't the chairman, the tall patrician silver-haired Yury Ilyin himself, a former ambassador to the Court of St. James's, a former dean of the Gorky Institute, rumored to be an old, difficult, but highly respected friend and rival of the Soviet president—hadn't he said, in impeccable English, with a certain half-lazy irony that chilled Antonia, who had been confused and charmed by the man's social manners: "*Nothing is more distant than that which is thought to be close.* A Russian folk saying, very old. Very wise."

All of life is real but it's unevenly convincing. There are incalculable blocks of time, days and even weeks, even months, that pass dimly, in a sort of buzzing silence; you sleepwalk through your life. Then the fog lifts. Abruptly. Rudely. You didn't realize you were sleeping and now you've been awakened and the sunshine hurts your eyes, the voices of other people hurt your ears, you find yourself astonished at what stands before you.

His name was Vassily Zurov. She rehearsed it, in silence. A tall, slightly stooped man in his mid-forties, lean, cautious, less given to mute strained smiles than his Soviet colleagues, but passionate in his speech, with a habit of widening his eyes so that the whites showed above the dark iris, fierce and glowering. Now he jabbed the air, and struck his chest, his heart, speaking so rapidly that Ilyin had to signal him to slow down, out of consideration for the interpreter. His metal-rimmed glasses had gone askew on his long thin nervous nose. A lank strand of dark, lusterless hair had fallen across his rather furrowed forehead. He looked, Antonia thought, with that flash of irony and resentment that always preceded her reluctant interest in a man, like an old-fashioned divinity student. Wasn't there one in Dostoyevsky, in *The Possessed,* hadn't he been one of the demons. . . . If Antonia hadn't been told at last Saturday's briefing that all of the members of the Soviet delegation were probably members of the Communist Party, she would have thought nevertheless, A fanatic of some sort: look at that pale twisted mouth.

His language was, of course, incomprehensible. A massive, intimidating windstorm, a marvelous barrage of sounds, utterly alien. The Russian language: a language of giants, of legendary folk. Like something in a dream. Ungraspable. She stared and listened. She was a woman of some linguistic ability, she could speak fluent French and Italian, and could manage German, but though she had tried to learn some Russian in preparation for this conference she was forgetting it all: the slow stumbling childlike words, the somewhat preposterous sounds, the humble refuge in *Da, da.* She had forgotten everything. In fact it had turned out to be a perplexing chore for her simply to remember the pronunciations of the Soviet delegates' names. You must understand that these people are often quite sensitive, Antonia was told. It's important that we don't inadvertently insult them.

Vassily Zurov paused impatiently, and the interpreter—hidden at the far end of the room, inside a glass-fronted booth—said in a voice that managed uncannily to imitate, or perhaps to mimic, the Russian's florid style: *What is the function of art? From what does it spring in our hearts? Why do a people treasure certain works, which they transmit to the generations that follow? What significance does this have? Is it a human instinct? Is there a hunger for it, like a hunger for food, and love, and community? Without the continuity of tradition, what meaning is there in life? As our Chinese comrades discovered to their chagrin, after having tried to erase their entire heritage—*

But this was the interpreter's voice, this was another man's voice; and Antonia was having difficulty with her headphones. Somehow the mechanism would not work for her. When it worked, it was seemingly by accident: a few minutes later and the words sounding in her ears might be flooded by static. . . . *the writer's mission in our two great nations? Is there a historical inevitability in art that carries us all along.* . . . Vassily Zurov hadn't the diplomat's aplomb of Ilyin, or of several of the older, more distinguished members of the Soviet delegation; Antonia remembered, or half-remembered, from the briefing that he had not been allowed to visit the United States before. He had been, from time to time, in trouble with the authorities. Had he actually spent some time in a labor camp in the North, or had he been closely associated with a "liberal" magazine whose editor had been expelled from the Writers' Union and sent away. . . . Surreptitiously Antonia scanned the official list of the man's credits. It was part of a lengthy document prepared by the Soviet delegation's secretary, and listed only achievements that, she supposed, were impressive in another part of the world. *The Order of the Red Banner. Two Lenin Orders. Medals for Valiant Labour.* Two medals for prose fiction, 1971, 1975. Contributor to the journal *Literaturnoye Obozreniye.* Born in Novgorod, now a resident of Moscow.

How warmly, how guilelessly the man spoke . . . ! His voice was somewhat hoarse, as if he were fighting a cold. During his fifteen-minute presentation he had led the discussion—"What Are the Humanistic Values of Present-Day Literature?"—away from naming of specific authors and titles and dates, which Matthew Burke, the chairman of the American delegation, had initiated, and into an abstract, inchoate region of ideas. Such speculations about life, and art, and the meaning of the universe, had fascinated Antonia many years ago, before she had grown up to become a professional, and surprisingly successful, writer; listening to Zurov now, she felt herself quite powerfully moved. It was all so childlike, so ludicrously appealing. The man's initial caution had fallen away and he was speaking with the urgency of an artist who has come halfway around the world to meet with fellow artists and to discuss matters of the gravest importance.

A photographer for the U.S. Information Services was crouching before Zurov, preparing to take a picture. The man's head was hidden from Antonia by his camera: an eerie sight. Zurov paused, and the interpreter translated his words, blasting Antonia's ears in a flood of capricious static. She could not quite decipher what was being said. *Art is political. Art is apolitical . . . ?*

The photographer took a number of pictures, rapidly, and Zurov, distracted by him, began to stammer. Antonia blushed. It was an old habit, an old weakness—she blushed scarlet when in the presence of someone who was himself embarrassed. The earphones went silent.

Then Zurov mumbled a few more words, now staring down at the microphone before him, and the simultaneous translation overlapped his faltering voice: *Thank you, that is all I wish to say.*

From her attractive third-floor room in the Rosedale Institute Antonia called her friends Martin and Vivian in Chicago. How are the Adirondacks this time of year, isn't June rather early for the mountains, they said, how is the conference going, how do you feel, do you expect to accomplish anything or is it just some sort of diplomatic game. . . . She heard her voice replying to their voices and it sounded normal enough.

How do you feel, Antonia, they asked.

Much better, she said.

After a while they said: Well, he isn't here. And he didn't call.

He didn't call?

One of us has been home the past three nights and he didn't call, are you absolutely certain he was headed this way . . . ? You know Whit sometimes exaggerates. He has such a . . . he has such a surrealistic sense of humor.

I didn't know that, Antonia said.

She spoke so gently, no one could have said whether she was being ironic or not.

They talked for a few more moments, about the Russians, about the embarrassing political context—the president's highly-publicized stand on "human rights," the recent defection of a Soviet representative to the United Nations—and about mutual friends. As if to console her they offered news of Vera Cullen's divorce: Antonia thought the gesture a rather crude one.

What shall we say if he does call, or if he shows up . . . ?

I don't know, Antonia said.

Give us your number there and we'll tell him to call. If he said he was coming here he must be on his way, unless of course something happened. . . . Should we have him call you at the conference?

I don't know, Antonia said, pouring an inch or two of cognac into a plastic glass. The cognac was a gift—a rather premature one, she thought—from a red-faced, gregarious, portly Ukrainian who had been very attentive to her the previous evening, and at breakfast and lunch today. *All the way to my homeland,* he said, in careful English, and Antonia had not had the heart to correct him. His name was something like

Kolevoy. According to the biographical sheet he was a poet, a writer of
sketches, and a member of the board of the Soviet Writers' Union. . . . I
don't think so, she said.

How long has he been gone? When did he leave?

A few days before I did.

Did he take many clothes, did he take much money . . . ?

No, Antonia said. But then he never does.

A pleasantly vulnerable feeling. As if convalescent. But it's been seven
years now, Antonia thought reasonably. Surely I have recovered.

Numbness. Emptiness. She was not the sort of woman to refer everything to her femaleness, to her womb; the very thought bored her. Yet
something circled, bat-like, nervous and fluttering, about the miscar-
riage of seven years ago, in the first year of her second marriage. Such
things mean a great deal, she thought. Though probably they mean
nothing.

It *did* bore her, she would never think of it again.

The problems inherent in a bourgeois existence, she would explain to
Vassily Zurov, arise out of idleness. One must think about something in
order to fill up time. So we think habitually of sex and death, of loss, of
symbolic gestures, dismal anniversaries, failed connections. . . .

She was in retreat from her own life, which she might or might not
explain to Zurov. There would be, after all, the problem of language: a
common vocabulary. So far they had grinned at each other over glasses of
sherry, and talked through one of the several interpreters—You are a
poet? No? A writer of prose? Unfortunately your works are not available
in my country. . . .

She had not wanted to participate in the Rosedale Conference on the
Humanities, though the four-day meeting of Soviet and American writers, critics, and professors of literature did seem to her a worthwhile
event. There were the usual promising words, and she liked them well
enough to repeat them silently to herself, like a prayer: *unity, cooperation,
universal understanding, East and West, friendship, sympathy, common plight,
peace, hope for the future.* At the opening session the Soviet chairman
Ilyin had even spoken, in English, of the need for Soviets and Americans
to resist "our common enemy who seeks to tragically divide us." (The
American chairman Burke called his delegation to a meeting room afterward, in order to speculate aloud, with the assistance of a Soviet special-

ist from Harvard and rapporteur named Lunt, on the possible meaning of Ilyin's carefully oblique words; but the words remained indecipherable, a kind of poetry.) Antonia had not wanted to participate though two friends of hers, or were they perhaps only acquaintances—the poet and translator Frank Webber, and the novelist Arnold Barry—were to be in attendance. In the end she said yes, for no particular reason.

She was a small-bodied woman of thirty-six who looked a great deal younger, mainly because of her shoulder-length, sumptuous brown hair. Which was grotesquely misleading: she did not feel sumptuous, had not felt sumptuous for many years. In fact the word puzzled her. Struck her as faintly comic. Her pale green eyes were slightly prominent and always a little damp. Her skin was an almost dead white: she hated it, and was made uneasy by well-intentioned compliments on her appearance. And by frequent half-accusatory remarks about her "youthfulness"—on the first morning of the conference a young woman journalist told Antonia with a beaming smile that she had pictured her as much older—in fact elderly.

She was the author of two slender novels, both written in her early twenties. They were fastidious and self-conscious, set in the upper-middle-class Catholic milieu of her girlhood in Boston. Obliquely autobiographical, but not stridently so, they were admired by the few critics who took the time to review them, but they were not commercially successful, and were reprinted in paperback only after Antonia achieved eminence for other work—essays on literature, art, and culture in general, some of them iconoclastic and devastatingly critical. Yet for the most part the essays were appreciative; they were certainly methodical, models of unobtrusive research and scholarship. In the world she customarily called "real"—that is, the world outside her imagination, her ceaselessly thinking and brooding self, her book- and music-cluttered apartment on East 72 Street—she was constantly meeting distorted images of herself which came to her with the blunt authority of seeming more real than the Antonia she knew. Though she was dismayingly shy, so quiet at large social gatherings that she might be mistaken for a mute, there was the widespread idea, evidently, that "Antonia Mason" was shrill and argumentative and maliciously—but, so her admirers claimed, brilliantly—unfair. She had published in the past decade interpretive and generally positive essays on John Cage, Octavio Paz, Iris Murdoch, Robert Rauschenberg, contemporary German films, contemporary

American poetry, and other subjects, but it was for lengthy and perhaps somewhat sardonic assessments of the achievement of Tennessee Williams, Robert Motherwell, the works of feminist novelists, and those of the "New Journalists" that she was most remembered. It must, she supposed, mean something significant: of six brief reviews she might publish in the New York *Times* in a year it was the one sarcastically negative review that would excite comment. Acquaintances telephoned to congratulate her on speaking honestly, people as far away as Spokane and Winnipeg might write to thank her for having made them laugh, friends alluded to her wit and courage and intelligence—as if these qualities, if they were hers at all, were not present in her more serious work. Even her husband, Whitney, complimented her when she was a "fighter" (his word) in public. If she complained that popular culture seems to push individuals toward what is most aggressive, most combative, and least valuable, he brushed aside her remarks as disingenuous. "At heart you're really competitive, you're really a hostile person," he often said, narrowing one eye in a mock wink. "Which accounts for your astonishing *gentleness* . . . and your exasperating charity. And your proclivity to forgive."

She could not help forgiving him: he was her husband, after all, despite his infidelities. And she loved him. Or had loved him. Or, at the very least, had consoled herself during a rather bad time some years ago with the thought that she was capable of loving someone after all—she would devote herself to this new relationship with Whitney Albright, she would meditate upon it, plunge into it, make the old-fashioned sacrifices now being mocked by her contemporaries, and thereby save herself. So she was, quite apart from her promise as a novelist, and her uncontested brilliance as a cultural critic, a genuine woman: divorced but remarried, once again someone's wife. She was also someone's daughter and someone's sister. One of the Soviet delegates had referred to her as the "leading American woman of letters"—or so the translation had gone. Meanings hung on her like loose clothing.

Someone's estranged wife.

Someone's abandoned wife.

Is it so, Yury Ilyin's secretary, a plump, affable young man with thick glasses, asked Antonia and several other Americans, that each year in the United States there are between 700,000 and 1,000,000 children who run away from home . . . ? We find this hard to believe and wonder if the figure was not misreported.

It could not be said, however, that Whitney had "run away." For one thing adults do not "run away"; they simply leave. And the circumstances of his leaving were abrupt and dramatic enough to suggest that the action was going to be temporary—his reply to her reply, so to speak. (It was not the first time that Whitney had left her. Several years ago, when driving to the West Coast, where Antonia was scheduled to participate in an "arts festival" at one of the state universities in California, Whitney had left her in the St. Louis Zoo, in front of the ocelot cage. The circumstances were amusing, perhaps, though Antonia had not found them so at the time. For weeks she and Whitney had been careful with each other, gentle and solicitous and patient, and the long drive to California was meant to be a vacation, a sort of second honeymoon; perhaps the strain of being so unrelievedly nice precipitated a violent quarrel during which each accused the other of being incapable of love and "worthless" as human beings. Antonia had been admiring the ocelots, especially a lithe playful ocelot kitten named Sweetheart, and Whitney had liked them well enough—strolling through the zoo was something to do, after all, a way of killing time until late afternoon and cocktails—but he hadn't Antonia's concern about a penned-up ocelot that was crying angrily and plaintively to be released into the larger cage. The creature was hidden from sight, though by standing on the railing Antonia could *almost* see it. "My God," she said, nearly in tears, "listen to it crying, it sounds just like a child, have you ever heard anything so heartbreaking in your life. . . ." Whitney urged her to come away. After all, the cat must be quarantined for some reason: the zookeepers knew what they were doing. "But it's so cruel. It's so stupidly cruel," Antonia said. The ocelot's enraged full-throated miaows were really quite disturbing. Whitney said something further, Antonia said something further, and then they were shouting at each other, and could not stop. I suppose the goddam ocelot is a symbol or something, Whitney said, I suppose I'm meant to interpret all this in some personal way, a goddam fucking symbolic commentary on our marriage, and Antonia had screamed that it wasn't a symbol, it was a living creature, how could anyone listen to it howl like that and not feel pity and want to help. . . . In the end Whitney had walked away. Antonia did not follow him. An hour later, when she returned to their hotel, much calmer and ready to apologize if it seemed likely that he, for his part, would apologize, she discovered that he had checked out, had taken his suitcases, his share of the toiletries, and the car.)

It might be said that she was abandoned now, and had been so since Whitney disappeared twelve days before, after a quarrel at a friend's apartment; but she did not think of herself as abandoned. Talking with a group of Soviet writers, among them Vassily Zurov, she had answered a question about her marital status by saying with a smile that "such questions were no longer relevant"—she wanted to meet with them as a person, as a fellow writer, not as a woman. Perhaps the translation had been witty: they had all laughed, though not disrespectfully. Zurov said, "That's so, that's right," in fairly emphatic English.

Yet she could not resist, a while later, asking him if he was married. She asked him directly, not through an interpreter; his reply was a dismissive shoulder shrug.

Which, of course, she could not confidently translate, for perhaps he had not understood her question. And she hadn't the ability to ask it in his language.

He sat beside her in the Institute dining room, and hovered near at the cocktail gatherings, and frequently stared at her during the sessions, quite visibly not listening; his hair was bunched and spiky and disheveled by the earphones, with which he had a great deal of trouble. Once when several members of the Soviet delegation were laughing zestfully at a lengthy anecdote told to them by a stout, swarthy man from Georgia—it turned out to be, rather incredibly, about Stalin himself, Stalin as someone's old uncle, gruff but lovable—he pulled her aside and spoke emphatically, half in English, half in Russian, managing to communicate to her the need they had for exercise, for a walk around the lake before dinner, didn't she agree . . . ?

She agreed. And halfway around the lake, as they stood on a grassy knoll staring at the glittering water and the Institute's fieldstone buildings on the far shore, he took her arm gently and slipped it through his. She did not resist, though she did not lean against him. "It's lovely, isn't it," she said. "Just at sunset. Just at this moment."

"Yes," he said doubtfully. He was obviously quite excited: she saw a flush on his throat, working its way unevenly up to his face.

At the American delegates' briefing Antonia and her colleagues had been told that the Soviet delegation was, of course, under strict control. They would be watching each other closely, spying on each other. They would above all be intimidated by their chairman and his aides. Yet it didn't seem to Antonia that this was the case. Vassily was his own man: it seemed quite clear that he was no more explicitly subservient to his chairman than the American delegates were to Matthew Burke. Wasn't it all rather exaggerated, Antonia wondered, this drama of East and West, Communists and American citizens, the outmoded vocabulary of the Cold War, the strain, the tension, the self-conscious gestures of brotherhood, the ballet of détente. . . . Walking with Vassily Zurov she felt only a curious sort of elation. She could not help but be flattered by his interest in her; he was an attractive man, after all.

And it seemed to her that he was rapidly becoming more proficient in English.

At breakfast the next morning they sat together, alone together. She asked him about his stories: would they ever be translated into English, did he think? Were they political?

He asked her to repeat the question.

It would have been difficult for Antonia to determine precisely what, in him, attracted her so powerfully. For some time she had stopped thinking of men as men, she had stopped thinking of herself as a woman in terms of men, the whole thing had come to seem so futile, so upsetting. Adultery appealed intermittently, but only as a means of revenging herself upon Whitney; and as her love for Whitney waned her desire for revenge waned. There was, still, the incontestable value of adultery as a means of getting through a certain block of time: it was an activity charged with enough passion, enough recklessness, to absorb thought, to dissipate anxiety. If she allowed herself to be touched by a man, if she leaned forward to brush her lips against a man's lips, or to allow a man to kiss her, she would have no time to think of the usual vexing questions. Her husband. Her marriage. Her meandering "career." And there were the slightly tawdry, glamorous and melancholy questions of her girlhood: What is the meaning of life? Does God exist? Are we born only to die? Is there a means of achieving immortality . . . ? The Russians would not have jeered at such questions. Vassily Zurov would not have jeered.

At last he understood her question about his writing, and labored to reply in English. He leaned forward, gesturing broadly, staring fixedly at her as he spoke. "My stories are political, yes," he said with great care. ". . . As all art."

Antonia felt a sense of triumph.

"All art? Did you say all art? . . . But all art isn't political," she said.

She was speaking too rapidly, he begged her to repeat what she had said.

"Art isn't political," she said slowly. "Not in its essence."

He stared at her, smiling, uncomprehending. She saw a dot of blood in his left eye. He adjusted his glasses, still staring. Antonia said, holding her hands out to him, palm upward, in an innocent, impulsive gesture whose meaning she could not have explained, "Of course some forms of art are political. Some writers are basically political writers. But in its essence art isn't political, it's above politics, it refers only to itself. I'm sure you understand. I'm sure you agree. Politics necessitates choosing sides, it excludes too much of life, life's nuances and subtleties, art can't be subservient to any dogma, it insists upon its own freedom. Political people are always superficial people. I couldn't be forced to choose sides—it's brutal, it isn't even human—"

He shook his head, baffled. He asked her to repeat her remarks.

She said only, blushing, that art isn't political. In its essence it isn't political.

He replied half in English and half in Russian, with a barking laugh that startled her. He seemed to be saying that art *is* political.

"Everything," he said firmly. He lifted a glass of water and gestured with it, as if toasting Antonia; he took a sip; he then extended it across the table to Antonia as if he wanted her to drink from it—but she drew away, baffled and a little annoyed. He was so demonstrative, so noisy. "Everything," he said with a queer wide smile, a half-mocking smile, "is political. You see, the water too. In the glass like this. Everything."

She shook her head to indicate that she didn't understand. And now that others were coming to join them, now that their intimate, edgily flirtatious conversation was becoming public, she felt suddenly drained of energy, unequal to his vehemence. She hadn't any appetite: she would have liked to go back to bed.

Vassily greeted the others in Russian and waved for them to sit down. He fairly pulled one of the English-speaking Soviets into the seat beside him, so that he could help with the conversation with Antonia. She looked from one to the other, smiling her strained polite smile, as Vassily spoke in rapid Russian, watching her cagily.

The interpreter—listed as a poet in the dossier, but named by Lunt as an *apparatchik,* a party hack—beamed at Antonia and translated in heavily-accented but correct English: "Mr. Zurov inquires—you do not think that art is political? But it is always political. It seeks to alter human consciousness, hence it is a political act. He says also that a mere glass of water is an occasion for politics. He says—but you see, we were talking about this last night, Miss Mason, some of us were talking about this last night, and Mr. Zurov insists upon bringing it up—perhaps you did not read the local newspaper yesterday?—no? Mr. Zurov refers to the front-page article about the poisons that have drained into the mountain lakes in this area. He says—through the winter, rain and snow have been blown into the mountains from somewhere to the west where there are coal and oil combustion plants, and nitric and sulfuric oxides have been concentrated in the snow, which has now melted, do you see?—and there are now toxins in the lakes—he is not certain of the technical terms, perhaps others here would know—and the fish, the trout, have died in great numbers. And so—"

Vassily interrupted him, speaking excitedly, watching Antonia's face. The man then translated, with a slight bow of his head in her direction: "Mr. Zurov does not mean to distress you on this lovely sunny day. He says—forgive me! But perhaps you did not know, perhaps it needed to be pointed out, that the simple act of drinking a glass of water can be related to politics and to history, if only you know the context in which it is performed, *and the quality of the water,* but of course if you are ignorant and do not know or choose to know, you will imagine it is above politics and you are untouched. He says, however, to forgive him for being so blunt, but it is his way, it is his only way of speaking."

Impulsively Vassily reached out to seize Antonia's hand, for all to see. His smile was wide and anguished, showing irregular teeth. The gesture surprised Antonia but she hadn't the presence of mind to draw away. "Excuse me, Miss Mason? Yes? It is all right?"

"Of course it's all right," Antonia whispered. But she felt shaken: it was not an exaggeration to say that she felt almost ill. And there was the entire day to get through, the morning and afternoon sessions, and the usual lengthy dinner. . . . Staring at Vassily's slightly bloodshot eyes she knew herself on the very edge of an irreparable act: at the very least, she might burst into tears in public. But how trivial, how demeaning, even to care about such things! She drew her hand out of Vassily's dry, warm, eager grip. "Of course," she said faintly.

A long day of speeches. Prepared remarks. "Allow me to speak, I will be brief," said a thick-bodied swarthy critic and editor from a Soviet journal that translated, according to Antonia's notes, as *The Universe*. He then spoke, not quite spontaneously, for forty-five minutes. . . . Why do United States citizens know so little of Soviet literature, why is there so much racist and pornographic material for sale in your country, why do you allow a "free market" for the peddling of such trash? Though it was a blatant attack, barely disguised by diplomatic language, the American delegation replied in civil, careful language: one of the novelists, whose books Antonia could never bring herself to read, managed to say something fairly convincing about the First Amendment, human rights, freedom of the press, democracy, the fear of censorship in any form. "And it's important, I think, for us to know, in a democracy, what people seem to want. Pornography disgusts me as much as it disgusts anyone, but I think . . . I think it might be valuable, in a democracy, simply to know what great masses of people seem to want." Antonia's colleague spoke softly but with a sophistication that pleased her.

Yes, freedom is desirable, certainly it is desirable, but racist trash, pornographic trash . . . ? "Such 'literature,'" one of the Soviets said, "strikes us as no more than a means of extracting money from the market."

The issue of the dissident writers: tentatively, gingerly, brought up. But Yury Ilyin brushed it aside. Such a matter is not, strictly speaking, a literary or humanistic matter, it has to do with illegal activities, the right of a sovereign state to deal with its criminals, perhaps we will have time to discuss it later. With a chilly, impertinent smile Ilyin said he supposed the Americans were primarily interested in legitimate Soviet writers: otherwise why did the Rosedale Institute extend its generous invitation to this group to visit the United States and to meet with outstanding American writers, their colleagues and equals in the field of literature . . . ?

Vassily was sitting hunched over, peering short-sightedly at the table before him, or at his clasped hands. He had taken off his glasses; with his spiky, rumpled hair he looked like a man surprised in his sleep. Antonia had the impression that he was about to interrupt Ilyin. His pale mouth worked, his forehead was deeply furrowed. He had been, some years ago, a "dissident" writer himself—or at any rate he had gotten into trouble with Party officials. Perhaps he had even been sent away for a while, to a mental asylum or a labor camp. The rapporteur from Harvard, Lunt, hadn't offered much background information for Vassily Zurov, he was one of several "mysterious" members of the delegation, little known in the West, with only a few short stories translated and anthologized. . . . Suppose we become lovers, Antonia thought idly. Then he will tell me everything. Then he will tell me all his secrets.

Prolonged remarks, ostensibly "spontaneous." Frequent references to "the great Mayakovsky"—a poet of mediocre gifts, surely?—and to the concept of "socialist realism," which Antonia had supposed to be out-moded; but perhaps it was not, not entirely. Marxist metaphysics explained succinctly by a youngish Moscow novelist who was also First Secretary of his Writers' Union: we have first matter, there is no contesting that, and then comes spirit, and then comes "spirituality" (but there is no exact word for that concept in Russian) which is the activity of highly organized matter. . . . Antonia tried to take notes, it would be her turn to speak in a few minutes, she was becoming unusually nervous. *The activity of highly organized matter.* But perhaps the translation was only an approximate one? How could one know? How could one be certain?

Maxim Gorky, who is the "father of Soviet literature." Lenin, who stated clearly that the main function of the printed word is organizational. Jack London, Theodore Dreiser, Stephen Crane. Steinbeck. Chekhov. Dostoyevsky, now being reexamined. Vassily, who had spoken little, said a few words about "your great American poet William Carlos Williams." When it was Antonia's turn she spoke briefly of the "post-modern" novel, its movement inward, toward lyricism, toward poetry, away from the statistical world, the objectively historical or political world. . . . She twisted her pen nervously as the Soviets gazed at her with great interest. But when she finished only a single question was directed to her, by the Ukrainian Kolevoy, and it was clearly meant to be courteous, to show his appreciation of her words.

She wondered how those frail words were being translated.

Another photographer was taking pictures, crouching discreetly in the aisle, moving forward on his haunches. He took a number of pictures of Ambassador Ilyin, who gave the impression of ignoring him.

Antonia watched Vassily and wondered what he was thinking. What he had endured. Her delegation had been told that they must not mention certain things to the Soviets—under no circumstances should they inquire about certain books, written by Soviets but published outside the country, nor should they inquire about dissidents whose work they might know. Labor camps, prisons, mental asylums: don't bring the subjects up. Antonia had read that during Stalin's reign several hundred poets, playwrights, and prose writers were murdered by the secret police, in addition to the other thousands, or millions. . . . And in the sixties there was the highly-publicized case of Joseph Brodsky, put on trial for being an idler and a parasite without any socially useful work, sentenced originally to five years of forced labor in the North. And, more outrageous, even, the joint trial of Siniavsky and Yuli Daniel, who dared claim artistic freedom, the right to follow wherever one's imagination leads. . . . If Antonia remembered correctly the men were both sentenced to several years' hard labor in a "severe regime camp." There was also the example of a young man named Galanskov, the editor of a Moscow literary magazine of "experimental" tendencies, first sentenced to a mental institution, then to a concentration camp where he was allowed to die. Perhaps she would ask Vassily about him: it was quite likely that they were acquainted. . . . When she thought of how little she risked, in publishing her essays, even the autobiographical novels, she was stricken with a sense of guilt.

Matthew Burke was speaking, perhaps too slowly, on the "humanistic tradition" in the West. Yury Ilyin then spoke of the "humanistic tradition" in his country. Antonia's head began to ache. She rarely suffered from headaches, this was really quite extraordinary, it seemed to have to do with the simultaneous translation: the phenomenon of hearing Russian spoken and hearing, immediately, its English translation, the words often overlapping, one voice louder than the other and then suddenly subsiding in a buzz of static, only to surface again a few seconds later. And what was the reality behind the words, to what did they refer . . . ? In her world she had grown accustomed to the relative impotence of words: they might have *meaning*, but they rarely had *effect*. But in the Soviet world even the most innocent of words might have an immediate, profound effect. . . .

Ilyin was concluding the morning's "very fruitful discussion." He was speaking of brotherhood, of universal understanding, the hope for global peace. Antonia watched him guardedly, as did the others. One simply could not trust the man. He followed a script, a scenario, possibly prepared in advance; it was clear that most of the members of his own delegation did not know what to expect from him. Though he had proudly identified himself earlier as being the son of "peasant stock" he was clearly an aristocrat in spirit, barely tolerant of his colleagues, and contemptuously formal with the American chairman, whom he challenged often and addressed as "dear Matthew." They had said of him a few days before that he was an anti-Semite. He was a neo-Stalinist. They had said . . . oh they had said wicked things, but Antonia hadn't wanted to listen, she hadn't wanted to believe, after all the conference was designed to bring people together, weren't they all involved in literature, in the humanities, wouldn't it serve the cause of "world peace" if she and Eliot Harder and Arnold Barry sat at the same table in the Institute's handsome dining room with their Soviet friends Vitaly and Boris and Grigory and Vassily and Yury himself. . . . A popular Leningrad poet named Kozanov, whose work Antonia had been reading with admiration, had been withdrawn from the delegation at the last moment and his place given to the mysterious Kolevoy, according to Lunt; an obvious party hack. What this means about Kozanov I wouldn't want to speculate, Lunt said with a conspiratorial drop in his voice, it might mean nothing or it might indicate bad news, very bad news. But I wouldn't want to speculate.

Ambassador Ilyin ended the session by expressing the hope that the United States would someday come to the enlightened realization that total freedom, in the arts as in any other sphere of life, is a very ignorant, one might almost say a very naïve, condition. "We aspire, after all, to the level of civilized man, we wish to leave barbarism behind," he said with a smile.

In Antonia's room she said, far too rapidly, to Vassily: "I'm not here to practice diplomacy, I'm a cultural critic, I think of myself as an amateur even at that, I don't have the stamina, the nerves, for this sort of thing—"

He had come to bring her gifts—a necklace, a slender bottle of vodka, a box of candies with a reproduction of the Ural Mountains on its cover, three slim, rather battered volumes of his short stories, in Cyrillic. Now he stood perplexed and uncomprehending. "What is—? You are angry? You are not—" Here he paused, squinting with effort. "—not leaving?"

"I came here to talk about literature, I didn't come to hear debates about politics, it's very upsetting to me, to all of us, I mean the American delegation—I mean—"

Vassily seized her hands, staring urgently at her.

"You are not leaving?"

He kissed her hands, stooping over. She stared at the top of his head, at the thinning hair at the crown, feeling a sensation of . . . it must have been a wave of . . . something like love, or at least strong affection, emotion. He was so romantic, so passionate, he was an anachronism in her own world, she did love him, suddenly and absurdly. She could not understand his words—he was speaking now in Russian, excitedly—but there was no mistaking the earnest, almost anguished look in his eyes. She felt a sensation of vertigo, exactly as if she were standing at a great height with nothing to protect her from falling.

In an impulsive gesture she was to remember long afterward she reached out to hold him, to bring his head against her breasts. He was crouched over, one knee on the edge of her bed, gripping her tightly, murmuring something she could not understand. She felt him trembling; to her amazement she realized that he was crying. "You're so sweet," she murmured, hardly knowing what she said, wanting only to comfort him, "you're so kind, so tender, I love you, I wish I could help you, you don't know anyone here, you must be homesick, the strain of these past few days has been terrible, I wish we could go away somewhere and rest, and hide, I wish there were just the two of us, I've never met a man so kind, so tender. . . ." He held her close, desperately; she could feel his hot anxious breath against her breasts; he seemed to be trying to burrow into her, to hide his face in her. "I know you've suffered," she said softly, stroking his hair, stroking the back of his warm neck, "you can't be happily married, I know your life has been hard, they've tried to break you, I wish I could help you, I wish we could be alone together without all these other. . . ."

They would be lovers, Antonia thought wildly. Perhaps she would return with him to Moscow. Perhaps she would have a baby: it wasn't too late, she was only thirty-six. It wasn't too late. Stroking his neck and shoulders, embracing him awkwardly (she was thrown slightly off balance by the way they were standing), she felt tears sting her eyes, she was in danger of sobbing uncontrollably. Love. A lover. A Communist lover. Whitney would jeer at her: how can you be so deluded? You can't possibly love this man since you don't know him, you can't possibly love anyone since you're incapable of love. . . .

"You're so far from home," she murmured, confused. "We're all . . . we're all homesick. . . ."

He straightened to kiss her, and at that moment the telephone rang, and it was over. He jumped away from her, and she away from him, as the phone rang loudly, jarringly; and it was over.

Disheveled, flush-faced, Vassily backed out of her room like a frightened, guilty child, muttering words of apology she could not understand.

They were never alone together again.

The next morning, enlivened by a spirit of adventure, she and Vassily and one of the interpreters went for a rowboat ride before the session at nine o'clock, but the wind was chilly, Antonia regretted not having worn her heavy sweater and scarf, and even before the accident—though perhaps it could not be called an "accident," it was simply a consequence of their stupidity—she found Vassily's exuberant, expansive manner jarring. His dark blue shirt was partly unbuttoned, showing graying kinky hair; he looked at her too earnestly, too openly, with a fond broad smile that showed his crooked, rather stained teeth. Quite obviously he was in love with her: the interpreter laughed gaily, shaking his head as if he were being tickled, possibly not translating everything Vassily said. She began to worry about being late for the final session, she brushed her hair out of her watering eyes repeatedly, smiling a strained smile, wondering if this little adventure—there was a notice in the Institute lobby, on the bulletin board, warning against "unauthorized" boat rides on the lake—might get them into trouble.

"We should head for shore," Antonia said. Vassily was rowing, and he was so uncoordinated, so awkward, that the oars were splashing water onto her legs and ankles. Her feet felt damp. "Tell him," she pleaded with the interpreter, "to head for shore. It's getting late."

The interpreter, one of the more genial members of the Soviet delegation, spoke a few words in Russian, and Vassily replied with a gay shoulder shrug, and a torrent of Russian, and the interpreter leaned over to Antonia to translate, somewhat apologetically: "Vassily says to tell you that we are all running away. An escape into the mountains. Into the woods. He says to tell you that he is very fond of you, he is very fond of you, perhaps you are aware of the fact, previous to this he has traveled in Northern Africa but not in Northern America, this is his first voyage, he is very grateful, he does not want the conference to end. . . . Just a joke, you know, a jest, running away into the mountains, Vassily is known for his humor, perhaps you have noted it."

Then Antonia noticed that her feet and ankles were wet because the boat was leaking.

There was a brief period of alarm, and consternation, though never any panic—for how could the three of them drown, so close to shore, in full view of anyone who chose to watch them from the Institute? The water was very cold. Antonia half-sobbed with the shock of it, and the discomfort, and the absurdity. Despite Vassily's spirited rowing they did not quite make it to the dock: they were forced to abandon the sinking rowboat in about three feet of freezing water, less than a dozen yards from safety. "I will save you—No danger—I will save—" Vassily cried, his teeth chattering from the cold. He tried to make a joke of it, though he was clearly chagrined. The interpreter cursed in Russian, his face gone hard and murderous, his skin dark with blood.

Vassily helped Antonia to shore, and insisted upon taking off his shirt to drape over her shoulders. Some of their colleagues came out to help; Lunt hurried to Antonia with a blanket, and one of the women connected with the Institute fussed over Vassily and the interpreter, who insisted, laughing, that they were all right, it was nothing, they would go change their clothes and that was that.

Antonia, blushing, saw a photographer on the veranda of the main lodge, his camera held up to his face, obscuring his face, as he took pictures. She pulled away from Vassily with an embarrassed murmur.

That was shortly before nine o'clock: by twelve-thirty, when the conference officially ended, her relationship with Vassily had ended as well.

The final session was tense, nearly everyone looked strained, or quite ordinarily exhausted; even Ilyin, taking up a great deal of time with an elegant expression of gratitude for the hospitality of the Institute, looked tired. Then, rather abruptly, certain issues resurfaced: a member of the Soviet delegation insisted upon speaking in response to Eliot Harder's statement of the other day concerning "freedom" of speech and of the marketplace, saying with ill-disguised contempt that one could package and sell human flesh, no doubt there would be some eager consumers, if you hold to a marketplace ideology where everything is for sale, every-thing is to be peddled, if you believe that in a "democracy" it is valuable to know what people want, what they will buy, why not package and sell human flesh, what is to stop you . . . ?

Another Soviet spoke of racist propaganda he had discovered in the American press. He had visited the United States many times, he said, as a guest of the government and of certain universities, and he had acquired astonishing publications, in order to study the mood of the United States, and it had shocked and disgusted him, anti-Negro propa-ganda published openly, in fact subsidized by leading capitalists, and there is the notorious instance of the American Nazis, defended by many, and their publications widely distributed, though perhaps it is not to be wondered at, for the United States has not suffered a war, it has not experienced a war like Russia experienced not long ago, when every family lost at least one member and many families of course were destroyed by the Germans under the madman Hitler, and in any case it is widely known, it is a matter of common knowledge, that the United States has no memory, it is the fashion to forget, to forgive and forget as the saying goes, and no doubt members of this American delegation would defend that point of view. . . .

Frank Webber insisted upon speaking, and in a trembling voice asked about the dissident writers, naming several names unfamiliar to Antonia, and going on to say, passionately, not quite coherently, that the human-istic tradition insists upon freedom of expression, freedom of the imag-ination, the enemy of the spirit is the totalitarian state, the supreme sovereign state, we have no tradition in the West of bowing down to authority, our writers and poets think for themselves, they are never censored, they speak out against the suppression of their fellow artists in all parts of the world. . . . It is complained by the Soviets, Webber went on, gripping his microphone, that we pay attention only to the dissident writers, we ignore the "real" writers, but no one would deny that the so-called dissident writers speak most truthfully, most forcefully, with the greatest aesthetic command, and in any case they would prefer to be published at home, they do not *want* to have their manuscripts smuggled out of their country, they do not *want* to be exiled or jailed. . . .

Matthew Burke intervened, and tried to restore calm, and Antonia sat
staring at her hands, wondering why she was here, what pretext had she
had for coming here, she remembered Vassily's head gripped against her
breast, she remembered the warmth, the urgency, the incredible un-
speakable tenderness of their embrace, but what had it to do with anything else, how could it help them . . . ? Vivian had called to tell her
that Whitney had called *them*, he did intend to drop by later in the week,
so far as they could judge he sounded in good spirits, he didn't sound at all
drunk, or bitter, once he got in Chicago they could persuade him to call
her, perhaps she could even fly out, would she be willing, should they
raise that possibility to Whit when he arrived . . . ?

Now Ilyin was speaking, now Ilyin had the floor and would not relinquish it. He spoke of Soviet anger over the fact that the American
president always surrounded himself with Soviet "authorities" who were
anti-Soviet, he spoke with irony of the fact that at the leading American
universities contemporary Russian literature is represented by such writers as Solzhenitsyn, who is no longer a Soviet citizen, and Nabokov, who
was an American, who is classified as an American, and now—the very
latest—they are taking up the cause of the mentally disturbed Sokolov,
and the criminal Siniavsky, and others whose works are worthless. . . .
There is no genuine feeling of brotherhood between the Americans and
the Russians, Ilyin said, or such outrages would not be permitted. Those
who are called dissidents are criminals, nothing more. They are ordinary
criminals. Why are such matters a concern for the United States, where
criminals are dealt with harshly enough . . . ? It is none of your business,
Ilyin said, and Antonia looked over to see Vassily staring at his hands, his
clasped hands, and all around the table the Soviets sat motionless, silent.
At the very moment that Frank Webber rose, not to protest but simply to
walk out of the room, Antonia thought weakly, with a sickening cer-
titude, We must leave, we must all leave, we can't sit here listening to
this, but of course she did not move, she sat motionless as all the others.

"Problems of human rights are problems of sovereign states," Ilyin
said, the interpreter said, droning in Antonia's ears, "not to be dealt with
by outsiders. You would think that the Americans, priding themselves on
their freedoms, would know enough to allow other states theirs. Why do
you imagine that your views of human rights and freedom should be ours?
Why do you even want to think so? . . . It is astonishing, I have always

found it astonishing, even rather amusing, the tragic misconceptions of my American colleagues."

After Ilyin finished there was a brief silence, and then Matthew Burke repeated, gamely, with a strained courtesy Antonia found touching, a number of the points already made, and there were final remarks having to do with the "communication channels" that had been opened, and with the hope that the conference would be only the first of many. The Soviet chairman, speaking in exactly the same voice he had used a few minutes before, thanked the Rosedale Institute for their gracious and generous hospitality, and the American delegates for their generous friendship, and of course Matthew Burke who had labored to bring all this about, and he believed he spoke for the Soviet delegation in expressing the hope that they would all meet again, perhaps in another year, to discuss literary matters, and matters of humanistic interest, in order to bring together our two great nations, and to work for universal peace and brotherhood, and understanding. . . .

Despite her dark glasses the bright sunshine hurt her eyes; her headache was really becoming quite painful. Yet she managed to say good-bye to everyone. There was a great deal of handshaking on all sides, and the presentation of gifts—mainly books, but also bottles of cognac and vodka, and boxes of candy, and, for Mrs. Burke and the other women connected with the conference, handsome hand-carved brooches, bracelets, and necklaces.

The limousines hired to drive the Soviet delegation to New York were waiting, the airport limousine for Antonia and several others was waiting, it was necessary to say good-bye for the final time, to repeat again how wonderful the conference had been, how fine it was to become acquainted. Vassily stood near, smiling at her, though no longer with that hopeful, loving gaze; his expression had gone resigned and perhaps even a little sardonic. Though she saw that he knew everything, he sensed her dismay, her sorrow, she continued to smile at him as she smiled at the others, shaking hands, her eyes narrowed behind the dark lenses, alarmingly damp. If she should cry, if tears should appear on her cheeks, everyone would misinterpret it. . . .

"You will come visit us soon?—someday?" Vassily asked, squeezing her hand roughly. "A guest of my government?"

"That's possible," Antonia said, edging away.

She remembered him clutching at her, his hot damp face against her breasts. She had felt such extraordinary, almost dizzying affection for him. . . . It had been real enough. She would not deny it though it would grieve her to remember it. And then again Vassily struggling with the oars, and sitting mute at the conference table while his chairman spoke. Of course he had to sit mute, Antonia knew, of course he couldn't speak up, he couldn't walk out, perhaps he doesn't really disagree with his chairman, he's a member of the Party after all, I can't attempt to judge him by my standards. . . . He squeezed her hand, still. Clearly he wanted to embrace her but did not dare. He was asking whether she might come to his country—to give lectures, to meet with fellow writers? She saw that he would not release her until she gave the right answer, and so, with a gentle twist of her lips, and returning the pressure of his fingers for a brief spasmodic instant, she said, "Da."

BLUES FOR MY FATHER,
MY MOTHER, AND ME

Richard Perry

ON Saturday, my mother calls. Dudley Strong is ill. No, nothing serious, a little pleurisy in his side. But he is moodier than usual. He sleeps fitfully and has bad dreams. Twice in the last week he woke screaming for Marcus. Perhaps if I came, not long, she knows I'm busy.

I try to stay away from my parents. I saw them last nine months ago at my brother's funeral. My mother didn't talk to me when I was a kid. My father always preferred my brother. I used to believe it was because Marcus was the older, but whatever the reason, it hurts. Still, it hasn't stopped me from making a life for myself. I've got a job, an apartment, and a couple of friends. A woman or two seem to enjoy my company. Sometimes I get a little lonely, but show me some people who don't.

I'll leave to see my parents in the morning. I have not been out today. I stayed in the darkroom, processing film I shot a week ago in Soho. Only two of the photographs developed revealed a smiling face. The smell of chemicals lines my throat. I swallow hard and something opens up inside, and I'm missing my brother.

"It's been tough," Marcus said. "I'm not crying, but it seems like for a long spell now, I've just been marking time. I'm ready to devote myself to what I have to do. I see that lasting change takes lasting struggle."

We were having a drink in the West End Bar on Broadway. It was one of the few times he allowed me a glimpse of what his life was like then, in the summer of 1971. He said he was dreaming all the time of Bobby Johnson, of Schwerner, Chaney and Goodman. Mississippi had ripped something out of Marcus. He'd been so confident, so brash. Mississippi had found his soft spot, taught him the meaning of fear, self-doubt, and failure. For a long time after he came North he was disconnected, floated from Harlem to Newark to Greenwich Village searching for the "radical" solution. His eyes were empty and his shoulders slumped. I worried, but there was nothing I could do. Then he got a regular job and found a shrink, and I thought he'd turned the corner.

The last time I saw him was six months before he died. He'd joined a group that planned to blow up the Statue of Liberty and the Stock Exchange. I thought he'd given up on all of that; I said he was crazy. He said I was part of the problem. That there could be no revolution without risk. That it was men like him who offered a way out, and that if I insisted on standing in the middle, then the middle was where I'd fall.

At the end he was sounding just like my father, and we were shouting. It's not good to imagine that your brother died angry at you. For a while I blamed myself.

My parents are another story. All the way up on the bus from New York to Kingston, I turned it over in my head. Sure they make me guilty, like anybody's parents can, but my reasons for staying away are better than most. The air in my parents' house is laced with their mutual hate, and I can't breathe it. I can't even figure out if something happened to make them the way they are, or if each just grew into despising the other. Sometimes I go through my childhood week by month, trying to recall some word, some gesture or expression that would tell me. But I never find anything. The way they are just is, that's all.

But it's such a waste. What's more important than family? I look at young couples in the street and I talk under my breath to them, telling them not to blow it. Don't fuck up the children, I say. Love one another. I'll never have my own kids, so I get very touchy about the subject. Maybe that's why I miss Marcus so, because now I can't have him. And it eats me up that we parted the way we did. I hate guilt. I'm guilty because I've mostly stayed away from my parents the last eight years. They're seventy-seven and seventy-four. They'll die soon. I don't know how I'll handle it. I feel like there's something awful in me that their deaths will activate, some unprotected place that, once bruised, will never heal. But I don't want to think about that now. I settle back in my seat and try to let the bus wheels hum me to sleep. After a while I sit up, stare out the window at the bright December sky.

I stand in front of the house I grew up in. It's small, two storied, has a porch my father screened himself. I am remembering waiting here for him to come home from work, wondering if he'd be drunk or sober. The foods he wore on his waiter's uniform, his music. My mother holding silence to her shoulders like a shawl. My brother, sure of himself from the time he understood the meaning of self. And me, a stranger in this house, lost, really, until I discovered cameras and the magic of darkrooms.

But I don't live here anymore. I'm twenty-seven and I've got my own place. I go up the porch steps, through the living room. I'm met by the smell of baking, the figure of my mother at the kitchen sink.

"Mama?"

She turns: the broad nose, the impossibly angled cheekbones. "Jason?"

"How you doing?"

"Didn't expect you so soon."

I cross the room, take her in my arms. "You gain a few pounds, lady?"

"You know I ain't never been no size. Too old to get some now."

"Old? Come on. What's old?"

She pulls back from me, begins, as if I have violated her, to adjust her clothing. "Old," she says, "is what you get when you don't die."

There's a silence, building with a rush, that and the dull ache she triggers in my chest with distance. She has fully rearranged herself. "Dad upstairs?"

"Last I looked."

"Guess I'll go see him."

She doesn't look at me. It's as if I've come and gone already. I go back through the living room, climb the stairs.

At the top I pause in the door of the room I shared with my brother. Both beds are tightly made as if we would sleep in them again, as if we would lie again in darkness and share our dreams. I miss my brother. I turn down the hall toward my parents' door, open it enough to stick my head into the darkened room.

"Dad?"

"Marcus?"

"Jason." I step into the smell of menthol.

"I must have been dreaming," he says. "I keep dreaming about him."

"How you feeling?"

"Not so good." His head flops toward me, features forming in the dimness as my eyes grow accustomed to the dark. His face is withered and grizzled; he needs a haircut and a shave. "Got this cold in my side. . . ."

"Want me to open a window?"

"The light," he grunts, "hurts my eyes. Sit. Rest yourself."

His guitar lies across the only chair. I lean the instrument against the wall, drag the chair to the bed. "Been playing?"

"Playing?"

"Guitar."

"Naw."

". . . Beautiful day outside."

"I guess so. When you seen your brother?"

Daylight leaks past the drawn shades, weak and tentative, the way light must enter the mausoleums of dead men. "Marcus is dead."

"I won't see another spring," he says. "I won't last the winter."

"Don't talk like that. Mama says it's only pleurisy."

"Your *mama.*" He spits the word out and struggles to lift his head from the pillow. There's a charge in the room, electric; I recognize the hate. "Your mama," he says, eyes small and ugly in the dimness, "she the reason for me going to prison. She the one told." He is looking not at me, but at the window where the light creeps through. "She hated Garvey. Hated Black. All she care about is that lily white Jesus of her'n. He had the way. He had the plan. That's why they got him. He died for us," my father says fiercely, and for a moment I don't know if he's talking about the black Garvey or the white Christ.

"Dad, I don't believe Mama did that."

"Never did believe she could do nothing, did you? Ask her."

"Did you?"

"Didn't need to."

"Then how . . . ?"

"Because," my father says, "she told me."

I sit here, sinking beneath menthol and despair. A long time ago, my father worked for Marcus Garvey, had been his driver and personal gofer, and then my father left for a job in a meat-packing plant. When Garvey was sent to prison on charges of mail fraud, my father became part of a group that plotted to break him out. Someone had betrayed them, and my father spent three years in jail.

Now he is telling me that his wife had been the traitor. Was this the reason for the way they were? If so, why hadn't he left; was his punishment of her in the staying? Why hadn't he considered *his* life, his misery? My father was fifty when I was born, my mother forty-seven. Marcus was fourteen months my senior. Why had they had us then?

Why had my mother betrayed him?

Why is he telling *me?*

Had Marcus known?

I sit, disgusted, feeling sorry for myself, waiting for my father to continue. But it's as if I'm no longer here, as if he's slipped back into the half-demented world I've disturbed with my presence. I try not to be bitter, but I can't help it. He's probably, in the bright place of his memory, sitting on the porch, playing checkers with his oldest son, while I stand in the dark outside the circle they make, watching. I listen to the labored snarl of his breathing, and I am thinking that I should get up and leave this house, leave him, forever.

"And you know what?" my father says.

"What?"

"Marcus ain't dead."

"Dad. . . ."

"Move out the way. Let me up."

"Dad. . . ."

"Move out the way, boy."

I move. It's the voice of his prime, full of power and authority, and I respond reflexively as I did when a child. He throws the blanket from his body, and then he looms above me, reeking of menthol. "Now where is my clothes?" he says, and, after a moment's indecision, makes his way like a drunken man to the closet. He is struggling to pull a pair of pants on over his pajamas. He is trying to put both feet into the same leg.

"Dad. Where you going?"

"Get my son."

"Where?"

"Want to come, come. Don't, don't."

I'm shaking. I cross to him, reach and grab his arm. "Come back to bed."

"Told you I'm going to get my son. Best let go of me." His voice is menacing, in his eyes a disbelief that I dare dictate to him, that I dare touch his body with impunity. I'm shaking. He is my father, no matter what he did to me, no matter how he felt about me, or feels now; he is my father. But I know what I have to do.

"Come back to bed. Marcus is dead."

"Ain't."

"He's dead," I shout. "I identified the body. They emptied shotguns in his face. Now come on back to bed."

"Going to see my son," he thunders. "Get out my way."

So it has come to this again. I watch him, towering above me, pants in a puddle at his feet. I think back nearly eight years to June, 1964, to the night before the morning Marcus and I left for Mississippi, when my father found out and waited up for Marcus and vowed to block Marcus' passage with his body, vowed to break his son's bones if need be, if that's what it took to keep him from going South. And Marcus coming into the room, frenzied, shaking my bed, and me awakening, thinking he my father finally come to seek revenge. *I didn't tell,* I said. The lamp turned over, the bulb exploded like a pistol shot and Marcus was astride me in the dark, screaming *traitor,* both fists flailing at my face. My father stood in the doorway, didn't move. So this is his revenge, I thought. . . .

And all because, months before, when I saw them about to fight, I threw my body between my parents, and when my father, crazed with drink and rage, kept coming, I hit him. Not out of loyalty to my mother, but out of fear and a longing for peace. But I could never explain that to him; he wouldn't let me, only grunted when I tried. And now he was pushing me all the way out into the darkness by disconnecting me from my brother's love, his precious elder son who was going to Mississippi to risk his life for a thing as frail as freedom. My father's revenge was beautifully conceived and structured, the perfect poetry of a madman's shattered heart.

I was nineteen, but I understood this. I understood it in the way that young men suddenly realize that the earth does not exist to do their bidding, and that they are not immune to death. The understanding allowed me to accept when the policemen the neighbors called said that one of us, me or Marcus, had to cool off for the night in jail, and my father picked me. It also drove me from this house, all the way to Mississippi, with Marcus, who finally believed me. I hadn't planned to go. I thought my father was right, those folks would kill you. It didn't make any sense to me to risk my life like that. But I went because there was no place else to go and I learned to believe in nonviolence and I hoped and turned the other cheek until three men with axe handles beat between my thighs until my flesh was purple, until their daughters were safe, until what they'd done meant that I would have no children. I hate those men. But that I was there in the first place is still my father's fault.

He has accomplished the putting on of his pants, is struggling into a shirt, lurching for the door, the shirt unbuttoned, his feet bare. I grab his arm and spin him and slap him across the face.

The last time I hit my father he touched his face and stared at his fingers in disbelief. Now, with a growl, he cocks his fist and swings at my head. But my father is an old, sick man this morning, and I step inside the punch and embrace him. He is grunting, hammering at my back with both hands, but the blows don't hurt. I hold him tighter, his chin on my shoulder, and I feel the madness spending its strength. His hands fall to his side; his knees buckle. I half carry, half drag him to the bed and lay him across it. I bump against the end table, setting in motion the empty vase which totters and falls, smashes against the floor. I leave it, peel the pants off, get him under the blanket. Then I just stand looking down at him, and I am frightened at what I feel: vengeance, pain, shame, love.

"You didn't," he says, "have to hit me." His face is turned, his eyes hidden.

"I'm sorry."

"Marcus. . . ."

"I'm *Jason.* Not Marcus."

"He's dead," my father says. "And I won't last the winter."

Something wells in me. I would never have thought my father could make me cry. I reach and touch his shoulder. "Sure you will. You'll outlive all of us."

"I ain't got no quarrel. . . . I done lived a long time." He faces me, eyes alive with hurt. "You all I got left now. You the last Strong man. The name is yours. You got to carry on."

I don't trust myself to speak. My father doesn't know; I never told him. Marcus was the last Strong man.

"Mouth's dry. Could you get me some water?"

I'm shaking, spent, everything moving two ways inside me. I go downstairs. My mother sits at the table, eyes like a threatened bird's, shoulders hunched. "What was all that fuss?"

"Oh . . . Dad got upset. He'll be all right. He wants some water."

She stares at me, as if trying to discover what water has to do with it, and then her gaze veers toward the counter and the cooling bread. "Ain't him I'm worried about."

I sigh, abused by their mutual hate, their private drama. "What's wrong, Mama? What is it?"

"What's he saying about me?"

I wave away the question. "He's sick. You can't listen to everything he says."

"He told what I did?"

I nod.

"I didn't *mean* for him to go to prison," she wails. "I was scared, that's why I told. The man said nothing would happen if it got stopped in time."

"Mama. . . ."

"I didn't *mean* it."

I close my eyes. "I know."

"And let me tell you something. My baby would've lived wasn't for him not being home. He the cause of my child dying."

The room begins to turn. I reach behind me for a wall; it's not there. I make it to the safety of the counter, hold to it with both hands. "What child?"

"It don't make no difference now."

"*Mama.* What child?" The room is turning, my mother's face the only still point. "Mama!"

She is rocking, holding herself, eyes fixed upon the floor. "We had a girl, your daddy and me. That's right. Was why he quit Garvey in the first place, we needed money. When Garvey went to jail for stealing, your daddy blamed himself as if his quittin' was the cause. Your daddy in prison and I'm left alone with a three-month baby, see? My milk went bad. From worrying. My baby died." She looks at me and blinks. "You had a sister. Been forty-seven had she lived. In August."

"Jesus, Mama. Did you tell him?"

"Tell him what?"

"How you *feel*," I whisper.

"Tell him? He knew."

She is curious, vaguely annoyed, and I hear the click as she dismisses my foolishness. "And then," she says, "to have him think I meant it. He had to have something on me, cause he know he the cause that baby dying. The way he know he the cause of Marcus ending up the way he did. It was what your daddy taught him. *Black* that, *black* this. He had to have something on me, to make us even."

It's more than she's spoken to me at one time in all my life. Winter sits on her face, gray and deadly, and when she speaks again her voice has lost its energy, gone flat. "This morning I went to take him his breakfast. He said he didn't like the way I looked at him. That I looked at him like he was a piece of dirt. And I told him . . . if the shoe fits, wear it."

"Maybe," I start, then say it anyway. "Maybe you shouldn't have said that."

Her eyes meet mine, then slide past to the window where the sun comes through. But I catch in the instant of our meeting her accusation, this and the knowledge that as she's suspected, nothing has changed. And as I begin to speak, to say that the path to peace did not lie in confrontation, I stop, thinking, who knew? Perhaps the *only* path to peace was confrontation, and my mother nods and says, almost triumphantly, "Sticking up for your father. Wasn't you, it was Marcus."

"I'm not taking sides. I just know he's suffering."

"Oh? *He's* suffering." And she looks at me and her face says I'm a grown man, yet stupid, have sight, but still can't see. "I birthed Marcus," she says, and blinks.

"I know. Listen. It'll be all right. He'll get over it."

"Maybe so. . . . But will I?"

I don't say anything. I move to the sink, fill a glass, then remember there is always a bottle of water in the refrigerator. Her voice arches behind me.

"Boy, let me tell you. You don't know the half. The *years*. But I won't cry no more. I won't."

I turn. Tears stream down her face. "Mama . . ." I step toward her; she holds her hands up.

"Go tend your father. He the one sick."

"What can I do? *Tell* me."

"Take your father his water."

I don't know where it comes from, but the thought explodes that someplace people are happy, someplace someone laughs. And all of it swells and bears down on me. The years of silence, of pain, and lost connections. I've had enough, not because I'm strong, but because I need and I'm grieving. I'm grieving for my parents, and for my brother, and I grieve for me. "There's nobody left but us now, Mama. Can't we make it better? Can't we try?"

She stares at me. If there's a feeling in her eyes, I can't read it. I look at her, all wrapped up in stubbornness and revenge, and I feel a sharp and searing rage. Then it drains, leaving me hollow, nothing to hold to. I wish my brother were here. I take a deep breath, try to get things to flow one way inside me. I go back upstairs, help my father to sit up, prop pillows behind his back.

"Did you dig a well?" he asks.

I consider strangling him. He drinks the water and smacks his lips. "Thankee, thankee. Now get me that guitar if you please."

I get the guitar. He picks a chord, tunes the instrument. "He really dead?"

"Dad," I say wearily.

"All right." He smiles a mocking, privileged smile. "What you want to hear?"

I want to say it doesn't matter. I want to say play a funeral dirge. Play the National Anthem. "Anything, Dad. Anything."

"You know 'Blues For The Boogie Man'?"

"No."

"How about 'I Have Had My Fun If I Don't Get Well No More'?"

"Yeah."

"Well, let's do it."

He begins to sing. I sit for a while, throat lined with menthol, feeling lost and tired and unconnected. I want to shout, to scream. I want to go to sleep in a sunlit room; I want to be held by someone who loves me. My father does something intricate on the guitar, makes it sound like laughing and crying at the same time, and I realize that though I've remembered the music, I've forgotten how good he is. Now I begin to focus on his song. It's an old song, one I recall from childhood; it is connected also to summer nights in Mississippi when I was afraid and wanted to leave there. Those voices in the South were deep and powerful, or high and sweet, and no matter how bad you felt they helped you make it through until the morning. My father's voice is thin, but not without strength, not without a stubborn desire to have the record show that although he was out there in the wilderness, half-mad, battered and barely alive, he was hanging tough. I'm feeling blue and washed out, but now at least I know. Everybody has a story; there's always a reason why. My parents had told their stories to me. I had seen the tales as burdens, dusty, unclaimed baggage whose weight they now insisted I should bear. But perhaps I am wrong. Perhaps each telling is a gift, a way of connecting to the only flesh they share.

I don't know, but as I listen to my father sing, I sense a developing of hope. And I realize that I will make it, that some of my parents' toughness is in me, that if they have never bestowed upon me a perfect love, they have bequeathed to me my spirit. My parents' lives were hard, but they were not wasted; they'd lived them the best way they knew. Neither was a life that I wanted to live, but I didn't have to. And I didn't have to let their lives color mine.

Even as I think this I feel something slip inside, go out of me, deepen the darkness of my father's room. None of what I want can be achieved without struggle. I'm tired, and more than a little afraid, and besides, there's all that history. I will always be my parents' child; some things I'll never forget. And I don't know if I'm strong enough to remember without yielding to bitterness and the urge to revenge, even when I know each prevents me from connecting.

My father sings. I hear steps on the staircase and my mother comes along the hall, stands in the doorway. She doesn't say anything, but she is here. As I am. My father sings. I go to my knees where the vase lies shattered, and I begin to pick up the pieces.

TRUTH AND LIES

Reynolds Price

GUESSING the signal Sarah Wilson flashed the car lights once. Nothing came or moved, only a rabbit close to the car, tan and quick in momentary light, eye congealed in terror. So she signaled again. Then dark and alone she said, "I will not break down. If she comes, if she's who I think she is, I will not give her that satisfaction." She shut her eyes to test her strength, to probe again the hole at the core of her chest. Then she hung her hands on the wheel, gripped till her ring ground loud on the grinding of crickets outside, and spoke again, "Don't let me break down now." That much was prayer to whatever might help—offered up through clear August night or ahead through glass to weeds of the railroad bank ten yards away where a girl had risen and stood now giant on the tracks and seeing the second light ran towards it. The crickets stopped as she split the weeds (safe down the bank from nights of practice), and her face stayed hid (a smile surely curled in the rims of her mouth). But she shrank as she came. That much made her bearable and when she crossed the last few feet and opened the door and lit the light, she reached her natural size, and Sarah Wilson could look and say, "Ella. I hoped it would not be you."

There had been no smile. There was none at their recognition. "Yes ma'm. It's Ella."

"And it's been you all this time."

Ella straightened into the dark, then leaned again. "I don't know how much time you mean, Mrs. Wilson."

"Oh I mean since before you were born, I guess."

"I am eighteen, Mrs. Wilson. It has been me since last December twentieth. Whoever was before me, I don't know her name."

That was true and saying it, hearing it, drained what was left of Ella's smile, Sarah Wilson's starting courage. So they hung in dull creamy light, picking each other's familiar faces for something to hate or forgive. But nothing was there, not yet, nothing they had not known and seen hundreds of times the past four years—Ella Scott's that had narrowed and paled beneath darkening hair to the sudden hot papery looks that all her sisters wore from the time they slouched through Sarah Wilson's class into a mill to watch loud machines make ladies' hose till the day they won boys who set them working on babies and the looks dried in as the skin drew yellow to their bones. And Sarah Wilson's that had never won praise even twenty years ago when she came here from college, had only won Nathan Wilson and then watched his life with no sign of cracking, yielding except on her lips that did not close, that stretched back always to speak (speech being something that held back terror).

Sarah Wilson said, "*I* know. Sooner or later I know every name. But I didn't know yours till he came in at seven drunk and fell on the bed asleep and I undressed him and found this note." She took up a folded note from the seat, opened, studied it again—*I have got something to tell you and will be on the tracks tonight at eight o'clock.* No name. Then she looked to the girl. "Well, your writing has improved." Then "Ella, if you don't mean to run *now* and never come back, never see Mr. Wilson or me again, will you get in here and talk to me? You know I don't mean you harm."

"I know that, Mrs. Wilson." Ella still leaned in the open door, a hand on the seatback. "I don't think I mean you no harm either so if you need to talk—yes ma'm, I can listen."

Sarah Wilson's throat closed at that. Then she could say against her will, "I don't need anything you've got to give," but she smoothed the cloth of the empty seat and Ella slid in. "Shut the door please. We have got to ride. We'll burn up here."

Ella nodded—ahead at the glass. "Yes ma'm. But I got to be home by ten o'clock. Papa's home tonight and he wants me back."

"Whoever you're with?"

"Papa knows who I'm with, who I come to meet anyhow."

"And he didn't stop you or warn you?"

"Mrs. Wilson, you know I have paid my way since I was sixteen." The engine ignited, the lights struck dust, weeds, the crest of the bank. "I have stood in that dimestore thousands of hours ringing up Negro quarters for some plastic nothing that lasts as far as the door. Papa just owns the lock on the house—or rents it. He don't own me, if he ever did. Looks like nobody owns me now." She faced Sarah Wilson and managed a smile.

But Sarah Wilson missed it. She had taken the wheel and turned them slowly towards the road, and they went two miles in silence—flanking the tracks at first and, beyond, the huddle of mill-owned huts where Ella would sleep, then across on a road that narrowed soon to a damp dirt swath through tobacco, cotton, black pine. They did not look beyond open windows. It was all their home, their daily lives. Ella stared forward. Sarah Wilson drove and felt the questions stack in her forehead, but the air swept cooler over them, bearing the cold sound of crickets again, and when they had passed a final house (its single light well back from the road) and nothing lay ahead but eight miles of burnt field, wild woods, Sarah Wilson started. "Ella, I think you have told me the truth so far and I'm grateful, but I'm asking you to answer some things I need to ask. You may say it's none of my business—"

"—It's your business, yes ma'm. And I come on this ride of my own will, so you got a right to ask anything, but I got a right not to answer what hurts."

Sarah Wilson set that against what questions were waiting, said to herself, "She is nothing but an ignorant child Nathan tinkered with. I knew her, taught her before she had power to hurt a flea much less break my life. Don't let me hurt her now." She waited a minute to strengthen that purpose. Then she started from the edge. "You say it's been you since December twentieth. That was the Christmas program."

"Yes ma'm. After Mr. Wilson carried you home, he come back to check on us and close the auditorium. Everybody was feeling good and it took a while to clean up the stage, and by then it had started sleeting. None of the others were headed for the mill, so Mr. Wilson took me."

"—And started his Christmas drunk."

"No ma'm. Mr. Wilson don't drink where I am. I never have seen him take a drink. I have smelt it on him and known what it was—I have got brothers—but he has been nice about that with me."

"Well, he started it after he left you then and brought it to me next morning for Christmas. The drinking is something he saves for me."

"Yes ma'm. I noticed that was it. Marvin is that way—Aleen's husband. He'll be gone whole days at a time, but let him get tight and he heads for home and hands Aleen a drunk like his pay." It had come to her naturally—Aleen's trouble. But once it was out, she guessed it might slow Mrs. Wilson, win her a rest, so she faced the open window.

And it worked. Aleen was the first Scott girl, Ella's senior by nine or ten years. Once a student left Sarah Wilson's class, she lost count of dates, age, their work. But she often retained the thought of their faces. Years later they would rise in her sight when she saw in the paper their weddings, children, by now even deaths (faces full for that year with premature life knocking beneath still formless noses, jaws), and Aleen's came to her now as it had a month before when she read *Mrs. Marvin Maynard has returned to her home after two weeks in Baptist Hospital* and guessed the trouble. So slowing a little she said to Ella, "I saw Aleen was sick again. Same trouble?"

"Yes ma'm. The third time. They fixed her though so she couldn't go through it again because her heart is affected now. This one lived four days, but they said he would never be right. Then he died, which I guess was a blessing."

"Poor Aleen. Tell her I sent my sympathies to her."

"Yes ma'm. Aleen has not had a easy life. I thought it would work this time. She took things easy, wanted it so bad. To calm things down, she said."

But the hole fell open again in Sarah Wilson's chest. Her foot weighed down on the gas, and she said, "You slept with Mr. Wilson that first night, didn't you?"

"Yes ma'm."

"And you've gone on sleeping with him—eight months nearly?"

"Yes ma'm, I have."

"And you don't think that's a sin?"

"Yes ma'm, I do."

"Then why didn't you stop? Just stop?"

"I don't know. Because Mr. Wilson was nice to me, I guess. I don't mean to say he gave me things. He didn't—oh a Pepsi now and then, and we drove twenty miles for that so nobody wouldn't recognize him—but he talked to me. He told me once he needed me to listen. So I just listened."

"To what?"

"You know it already—the times he had when he was a boy and being in the Army and coming here to teach and jokes his classes play on him—"

"—And marrying me."

"No ma'm. He don't speak of you. The one time I mentioned your name, he said 'Stop.' I was just saying how good you had been when you were my teacher, talking me into finishing high school and helping me get that job."

"So you could hang around four more years to sleep with my husband." She held back because they had come to a junction, then stopped, thought, turned to the left, then, "Was he the first man you slept with, Ella?"

The road they were on was paved again, concrete joints thudding under the wheels at a regular count of three, and shortly they met a car. Its light struck Ella's turned face and its horn tore loudly beside them. Ella swung towards it and followed it past—four ducking heads, two laughing girls, two boys. Then facing backwards she started, flat and sudden, turning as she went, "I ain't *slept* anywhere near your husband. All him and me has had is a dozen or so twenty-minute spells on this dirty seat." She slung her thumb towards the dark back seat, looked to confirm the vacant place, rushed on—"No ma'm, he was not the first. He was just the nicest. Still is. He is the only person in my whole life who asks me what I want to do—and waits for me to decide. What we have done is what I wanted to do, and look what it's been so far"—her thumb stabbed again—"a lot of quick dirt. But I'm not turning loose. Not now. Not with the little I've got. No ma'm." Still half backwards she laid her head on the top of the seat, her eyes towards Sarah Wilson but shut, dry.

Sarah Wilson managed to drive through that, and when Ella finished they were on the outskirts of Kinley, Sarah Wilson's birthplace, hardly a town. She drove through it slowly, the car lights dully slapping two strips of wooden buildings that lined the road, three general stores, post office, gas pump; then, set back, the squatty houses that held what was left of the dozen white families who owned the stores, the farms, still owned the best part of whoever lived in the broken ring that lay in the dark, farther out behind this road (tenants, field hands, nurses, cooks). Beyond that far ring was Sarah Wilson's home, the place she dreaded. She was numb to the rest of Kinley, and she passed it thinking only, "I have gone too far. I will turn at the station and carry her home and ask her to quit."

The station was at the end of town. Only two trains a day came now except for the freights that gathered pulpwood, and the evening train was surely gone, so the station should have been dark. But when she turned in, a last light showed in the passenger office, then vanished. She swung the car round on a cushion of pine bark, and just as she straightened to pull away, a man appeared in the station door and came down the steps, old and careful, not seeing till he reached the bottom. But then he waved and hurried towards them. It was Mr. Whitlow, the station master, and though he had been here always, Sarah Wilson had not seen him in the twenty-five years since he sold her the tickets that took her from Kinley to teacher's college. So she waited now and he came to Ella's side and said, "Train's left. Nothing on it but Negroes. Were you looking for somebody?"

Ella said "No" and looked to Sarah Wilson.

Sarah Wilson said, "It's Sarah Shaw, Mr. Whitlow—Sarah *Wilson*. I haven't seen you in twenty-five years."

He stared across and said, "Sarah Shaw. Has it been that long? Why don't you come to see us sometime?"

She said, "I keep busy. I do come down every once in a while to see Holt, but since Aunt Alice died I don't come much. She was the last I had down here."

He said, "I know it. I saw Holt today, walking past here. Straight as a rail and about as hard. Too mean to die. Is anybody out there with him now?"

"Not a soul and he says that's how he wants it. The others are gone— dead or in Richmond."

"Just Holt and the devil." He touched Ella's shoulder. "Sarah, is this your girl?"

"No sir. We don't have children. This is Ella Scott. She was my student four years ago."

"Was she a good one?"

"Good enough to finish. She finished this spring and is leaving for Raleigh, to business school."

He said "Good for her," looking past Ella to Sarah Wilson.

But Ella said, "I am thinking about it."

He studied her and said, "Go. If you've got good sense you'll get out of here. Your teacher yonder had the sense to leave. If she had stayed here she'd have died in misery twenty years ago. Trouble was she came more than halfway back. *Love* won't it, Sarah?"

"I don't remember that far back. Maybe it was. How is your sister?"

He leaned farther in. "Sarah, I didn't mean you harm. Sister's alive— old like me. Not old enough to shut up though." He held his arm across Ella, his hand palm down, and Sarah Wilson took it a moment. "You did what you had to, Sarah. I hope you have got satisfaction in life. God knows you deserved it."

She thanked him and he withdrew his hand, touched Ella again and took four steps. Then before they moved he turned and said, "I never did ask could I help you tonight?"

Sarah Wilson said, "No. Thank you, sir."

He said, "Well, I guess you know what you're looking for" and went across the road towards his home and his sister, using the beam of Sarah Wilson's lights as path.

She noticed that—that he walked in her lights—so she waited and watched him, then realized that the lights were dimmed and pressed her foot to raise them, but he was gone, sooner than she counted on. She thought, "That is somebody else I will never see again," and the new way was suddenly there—what to do, how to fight, maybe win, maybe save their lives. She looked to the clock, then to Ella. "We have got forty minutes. We might as well see this through."

Ella said, "I have said all I mean to say, Mrs. Wilson. Don't ask me no more questions tonight." She stared at her lap.

"I'm not. I'm not. What I know already will keep me sick long enough. But you say you have listened to Nathan so much. Now sit there and listen to me, to what you don't know, what Nathan wouldn't tell you if he talked ten years."

Ella stared on downwards, rocking the heel of one hand in her groin. She had said her say. Forty minutes was left and she could not walk eight miles tonight. She said, "I'm listening."

Beyond the station a dirt road cut back into the dark. It was one way—the old way—to Ogburn. It was also the way to Sarah Wilson's chance. She aimed them there and at once they were in total night, loud weeds pressing from the ditches, low pines choked with kudzu pressing above, boxing their lights. They sped through that till the sides opened out and the lights fell flat on fields of gapped dry corn that in nine hours would take the sucking sun again. The corn, the land were Holt Ferguson's, would be his for the next quarter-mile—and the dark oak grove, the house set back which they came to slowly on Ella's side. It was blacker than the sky behind it and so stood clear—a long low house hunched against the road. Sarah Wilson stopped, not pulling to the edge, and leaned towards Ella to look. Then she drew back and made a small sign with her hand to the house. She hung that hand on the wheel and began, meaning it to be the truth, her life that would speak for itself. "You can't see it now. There's no reason why you ever should, but when I was your age, I would sit in my room and press my head for relief, and what would come was the fact that I had this house, that if somebody would have me, we could come here and make as good a life as my parents had had. I thought this house was as surely mine as the soles of my feet. But I didn't even own the bed I was born in—a white iron bed behind that far big window on the right." She pointed again, no hope of Ella seeing. "The house belonged to my father then—built for his marriage on land that his father left—and that was their bedroom, his and my mother's. They slept there six years before I came. There was one boy before me who died, but I lived easily and I was the last. I never knew why. I used to ask Mother for brothers, company, and she would say, 'Sarah, I thought we were happy. Why aren't you satisfied?' I would think and decide I was. We were not rich—Father made eighty-five dollars a month as station agent plus half-shares on his farm—but we had what we needed, we valued each other, never stopped talking except from fatigue. Then when I was twelve they did try again on another child and that killed Mother. She lived four months after losing the child, but it poisoned her heart and she died one morning by the front porch swing. I had fallen at school and torn my skirt, and the teacher had sent me home to change. It was early November and warm, and she was out in the swing in her robe. Jane Phipps, her nurse, was sitting on the steps and Jane saw me first. I must have looked bad—dirty and torn—so Jane yelled, 'Sarah, what have you done?' and Mother stood up. I ran towards her to show I was safe, and she dropped at my feet. Thirty years ago and I know every second, could draw it if I could draw. Nobody told me. I saw it. I saw the next three years too but I barely remember them. They were the happiest—after the shock, when Father and I were here alone. I've thought about that—not remembering those years—and I know it's *because* we were happy. I have never forgotten one painful thing. So we had three years. I say *we*. I was happy and I thought Father was. I thought we were sufficient to one another, but when I was fifteen one June morning, I was sweeping the yard and a Negro boy ran up and said, 'Yonder—they are rolling your father home.' I ran for the road and met them on that last curve. They had him on a two-wheeled mail cart—black Ben Mitchell and Mr. Whitlow who was Father's help. They stopped when they saw me and Ben waited in the shafts while I looked. Father couldn't speak. He had had a stroke, forty-eight years old. It didn't kill him, not more than half. But that was when Holt saw his chance— Holt Ferguson, Aunt Alice's husband. She was Father's half-sister—his mother's child—so the Shaw land was Father's. Well, when Father could sit up and halfway talk, Holt came and said he and Alice would move here and keep house and farm as long as they could be of service. I was in the room. Father thought ten seconds, then he turned to me and said, 'Sarah, how about it?' It killed me to think he would welcome them when we had done so well alone, so I said the house and land were his, that he could ask in gypsies or Negroes, that I would be gone in two more years. He caught at his breath but managed to tell me to calm myself, then he turned to Holt and said, 'Come ahead. We need you. I thank you and so will Sarah when she understands.' But I never understood—only that the Fergusons came and from that day I recall every waking minute till now. I have slept very little. Father and I had the right side of the house, but we crept around and cleaned up after ourselves like cats. So did Holt and Aunt Alice—I give them that. She never did an unkind deed in her life, and Holt was working till late most nights. It was the boys I minded. They were younger than me and the house was their home in fifteen minutes, every rock in the yard. I grieved myself to sleep every night, but I never spoke another word to Father about asking them here. I got through the worst by telling myself, 'This place is Father's and will someday be mine.' And when Father was working—he limped around part-time—I fought for my own, thinking I knew what was my own. But I didn't, not till Father died. He lived till I was seventeen. Then the second stroke came and took him at the station on the *floor*, with no time to tell me what he had done. What I knew was what Aunt Alice told me after the funeral—that no plans were changed, that Father had arranged it with Holt, I was going to college and should think of this as home. So I lived through that last summer, sleeping in the bed I was born in, thinking I would go and come back and teach and marry—I was not in love; I had friends but no one I needed—and give the Fergusons the old Shaw place and start my life. September came and Tim, Holt's oldest boy, drove me to the station. I bought a roundtrip ticket from Mr. Whitlow, and when we could hear the train in the rails, I said to Tim, 'I will see you Christmas.' He said, 'I'll meet you. You might not know the house.' I said why and he said, 'After we put on that new kitchen.' I said it was odd Holt hadn't told me, and over that whistling train Tim said, 'I guess since it's his, he didn't think to tell you.' That was the first I knew. There was nothing to do but ride that train and wait for a letter. It came a week later—from Aunt Alice begging my pardon, saying Holt and the boys

thought I knew, that she was supposed to tell me but failed. Father had
sold Holt everything. He had seen he was dying, he must have remembered me saying those things, and he saw only one way to get me to
college. Holt had got it—house and land—for the price of college and
his word to give me a home if I needed one. I didn't then. I redeemed
what was left of that roundtrip ticket. Then I went four years without
seeing Kinley. In the summers I stayed at school and worked to pay for my
clothes. I make it sound bad. It did seem the worst of all my luck, but
once I got breath I was not that unhappy. God knows I wasn't happy but I
had work to do and friends to visit in my few vacations. One was Martha
Hawkins in Ogburn. I went to her on Christmas night of my last year in
college. I had spent three days in Kinley, here. Aunt Alice asked me,
saying I had broken her heart, so I came. I had had four years to show my
feelings and I made up my mind to do my share of healing wounds. So had
they. We grinned through a lot of food and presents, but I thanked God
hourly that I had arranged to leave Christmas day for Martha's. When I
left, Aunt Alice said they hoped I would come here to live and teach. I
thanked her and said I would take the best offer wherever that was. Then
again Tim drove me away, to Ogburn. That time he hardly spoke, so I
rode alone with what I had after those three days, twenty-one *years*—a
suitcase of clothes, three Christmas gifts, three-fourths of a college di-
ploma. Not one other thing and I knew it. Well, I took the first offer, not
the best. It came from Nathan Wilson. Martha was giving a party that
night, and when I walked in, he was the first thing I saw—Nathan—and
within an hour I was telling him this same story. *Because* he was drunk. I
don't make a policy of sharing trouble, but drunk as he was, he read my
face and when we were half alone, he said, 'Who knocked the props from
under you?' and I told him. He said, 'She was right. You must come here
and live and make peace or you'll die on the run.' I had seen from the first
that he was running—drunk two states north of his home—but I asked
him what he was running from and he told me. Himself of course and
what he had done to people that loved him—his dead mother and the
first girl that offered him her life. But you know all that if you've listened
like you say. I listened then—listen now if he asks me to—and when we
were done, I had offered him my life too. Not that night, not openly,
though before I slept I could feel he had stuck himself in my mind like a
nail, being like me—running from wrecks, needing someone to halt
him, plug up his chest. The next afternoon he came back to Martha's and

begged my pardon for anything out of the way he had done—*out of the way* when he was already what I needed. We took a ride that afternoon and he said there was something he *had* meant—that I must come here to teach, and he offered me a job. He had come to Ogburn as principal three years before. Being what he was, he made me think he was right, and I accepted, already back in my mind, making peace. Then he drove me to Kinley to tell Aunt Alice. She said to Nathan, 'If you are the reason, I am grateful to you.' I laughed but he *was* and I was so grateful I married him. He had come to see me most weekends, and by May when he asked me, I knew everything I would ever know—that his past was people he had let down and left—but I needed him and I thought he needed me. He never said so but he acted like need, still does—coming to me tonight like a child, not even trying to hide your note. So I said Yes, eyes open, and we married in June, here. Holt gave me away which was not easy, but we said it was part of our new beginning. *Beginning* when in two years it had died on my hands—Aunt Alice dead and Holt alone going harder and harder, Nathan and I crammed in rooms in Ogburn teaching all week, then taking long dark Saturday rides to buy his liquor, watching him pour it down secret from everyone but me, watching him tear on past me in this race I can't stop, can't slow, taking the best part of me with him through his hot quick dirt as you call it. But not killing it—the need I have to gouge out the drinking and women and calm him. The women anyhow. They started six years after our marriage when we finally knew we could not have children. It wasn't me that wanted them—things going so badly—but during those years I would sometimes say, 'Nathan, when will you stop?' and he would say, 'When I have a child to hide from.' He had never had to hide a thing from me. Then we found it was him at fault. There was one more hole through the middle of him. He was really no *good*—"

Ella said "Stop." She had heard every word looking down, not moving, giving Sarah Wilson that chance, but she pointed now to the lighted clock—the dim lights were on. "I have got twenty minutes. What are you trying to tell me please?" Then she faced Sarah Wilson.

It took her a while to know. "I have just now told you. Nathan Wilson is no good to you, no good on earth to anyone but me. What do you want out of half a man, young as you are?—when the half has been mine twenty-one years, is grown to me and must never tear loose. *Will* not."

"I was not *tearing* nothing—I wish I had been—I do not love your pitiful husband. What I said tonight—about not turning loose—I said it wild. You made me say it, digging so ugly. Mr. Wilson is yours and I thank God for it. But I need to see him one more time."

"No Ella, please. Just end it now."

"You are too late, Mrs. Wilson. Two days too late. I have turned loose already, *torn* loose. I have ended the little we had, myself." She took up the note from the seat beside her, held it between them "But I told him here I had something to say."

"Then say it to me. I'll see that he knows."

"He knows, he knows. Oh—" Ella shut her eyes, clamped her teeth, said, "Say to Nathan, to Mr. Wilson, that Ella has done what she promised to—" Breath and force refused, sucked back into her, grated her throat. Her hand wadded in on the note, her head faced the black grove, the house. Then noise came in chunks from the pit of her neck.

That saved Sarah Wilson, gave her strength to crank the car, turn it, aim for Kinley, the highway, the quick way to Ogburn—thinking she had won and numb from winning, from not breaking down. Past Kinley she steered on quickly through fields darker now, insects thicker and dazed by the heat, no other car in sight and only one man in the eight fast miles— a Negro stalled, beside his old truck in open white shirt, one hand on a fender, the other flapped once like a wing as they passed, signing for help he did not expect (as if she could help an angel of light after this night's work, could speak again, even think, before morning). Yet they were nearly back and soon she would have to speak—whatever awful last thing to Ella, to calm her, thank her, find the end of her message to Nathan. Sarah Wilson slowed to plan her speech but too late—her lights had nudged the first ranks of mill huts coiled so dense they would flash in a trail if one spark dropped, dark in the windows but each throwing naked hall light into dwarf dirt yards through open doors. She checked the time. Five more minutes and Ella's father would wait in one door, ready to lock. Not wanting to know which house was Ella's, she took the tracks, and when Ella looked up puzzled she said, "I will put you out where I met you—here." They were there again at the foot of the bank and Sarah Wilson stopped. Before they were still Ella reached for the door. Sarah Wilson touched her, her cool bare arm. That was the thanks. Then she said, "Ella, wait. I did not mean to press you to tears. What I meant to do was tell you my life and let that speak as a warning to you. But I went too far, telling that secret. That is *our* grief, mine and Nathan's. I had no right to give it to you. I beg your pardon and, bad as what you have done may be, I thank you for promising to leave him now. I'll hold you to it. So give me your message and go on home where your father is."

Ella opened the door, slid from beneath Sarah Wilson's hand, then leaning in as she had at the first—but her hair caved down on her bloated eyes—she said clearly, "I have not promised you nothing, Mrs. Wilson. I won't need to see your husband again, but that's not because of a promise to you or because of what you thought up tonight. The promise I made was to Nathan Wilson, and I went to Raleigh this week and kept it— went on the *bus* and ditched a baby in a Negro kitchen for two hundred dollars. Tell him that and tell him I said I will pay him back my half when I can work." She said that three feet from Sarah Wilson's face. Then she turned and walked towards the tracks, leaving the car door open. She went slowly purposely to show she was free, that whatever her debts she owned herself.

Yet slow as she was, she reached weeds and bank before her meaning reached Sarah Wilson's mind, entered through still open mouth, spread through palate, skull. Her head had turned forward while Ella spoke, and it stayed there rigid, seeing Ella walk, then quicken in the weeds and take the bank running, stumbling on top to her hands and knees but rising at once, sinking on the far side slowly again. Sarah Wilson shut her eyes, struggled to shut her mouth, but it hung apart—taut not slack as if it would speak of its own will, free and pure. Yet no words came, only the strength to move the car, give it signals to take her home—at least to where Nathan slept (if he slept, if he was not gone), breathing aloud on the bed they shared.

The car obeyed and turned beneath her towards Ogburn. There would be one mile of air to breathe before the town streets exhaling day, the houses she knew, that knew her, knew all but this night and would soon know this—if it was true, had been and would last beyond morning. That hope, simply, sent her on—that it *all* was lie, would end when Nathan woke and eased her. But the car reached Ogburn. It did not slow. It mounted the hump where paving began and threw light left on the first open yard, scalding a rabbit with sudden discovery. Tan and quick it was sucked towards Sarah Wilson, beneath her wheel. In the bones of her hand—her fine bones gripped to swerve—she felt its brittle death. Too late she braked, slewed in the street, halted. Then her mouth spoke freely its waiting threat. "How could I, why should I tell the truth when I thought I could save what was left of our life—that had *stopped.*" Her lips sealed down. Grunts like steam rammed her heart, her teeth.

THE ST. ANTHONY CHORALE
Louis D. Rubin, Jr.

WHEN I went to Staunton to work on the newspaper there I had the feeling, which I never afterwards quite lost, that I was moving to a far-off place, remote and different from what I had known. It is quite possible that if I had first gone there in any other season than wintertime it might not have seemed that way. As it happened, though, when the bus from Lynchburg turned off the highway east of the mountains to begin its climb over the Blue Ridge it was soon traveling along a steeply graded road with ice and snow everywhere about, and I had the sense that I was engaged in traversing a high wall, a barrier that shut off the Valley of Virginia from the rest of the world. But it was not only the mountains and the winter; I saw later that it was also the way that I was at the time.

I was twenty-three years old then, and this was a little more than a year after the war ended. I had gone for a job interview in Lynchburg, and from there I took the bus for another interview in Staunton—pronounced, I reminded myself so as to be sure not to make a mistake, as if it were spelled Stanton, with no *u* in it. Once the bus left the main highway and turned westward the ascent was steady, and soon there came hairpin turns and sharp climbs. From the window I could look down along the slopes of mountains and down ravines for long distances, and see only snowy hillsides and snow-covered trees.

It was a gray day and the clouds were low and heavy, a grayish white against the sky, so that it was difficult at a distance to tell just where the horizon ended and the clouds began. I wondered whether the deserts of Africa were any more desolate in appearance. The bus was a long time making its way over the summit and descending the western slope of the mountains, and even after it reached the floor of the valley and turned toward Lexington and Staunton there were mountains in sight east and west, and snow in every direction.

The impression of the city of Staunton that I took that day was that it was a raw, windy place, somewhat as I imagined towns might be like in the Far West. The wind was blowing very sharply, and though by then it was no longer snowing, fine grains of powdered snow from the mounds heaped along the sidewalks were flying about in the air. The sky had cleared a little, so that there were patches of blue. The buildings and stores of the city seemed old, as if built before the turn of the century or earlier. I saw very few trees along the street. Everything appeared open and exposed to the wind from off the mountains.

The newspaper office, which I found without difficulty, was the kind of old wooden building that I thought of as belonging to Civil War times. It had a show window, just like a store, with the words *Staunton News-Leader—Staunton Evening Leader* in black-shaded gold script on the plate glass, and above the second story a false front with scrolled woodwork and cornices. By comparison with the newspaper that I had worked on in New Jersey, and with others of my acquaintance, it was a very small plant, with business office, newsroom, composing room, pressroom all located on the ground floor.

Even so, I accepted the job when the publisher offered it to me. I had not been told whether or not there would be an opening for me in Lynchburg as a reporter on the considerably larger newspaper there. The job in Staunton was as city editor, with a $50 weekly salary—$12 more than I had been earning in New Jersey before my engagement had been broken and I had quit and come back home. To be made a city editor, after no more than six months of full-time newspaper work, was an elevation in status. True, there was only a single reporter on the staff, and the city editor handled all the telegraph, local and sports news, made up the pages, and even edited the church news. Nonetheless it could be considered a promotion, and after all that had happened I was in no condition of mind to pass up anything that might enhance my estimate of my own worth.

The Sunday before I left New Jersey for the South I had gone up to Newburgh to see my uncle. He was my father's older brother and origi-nally from South Carolina, too. He lived by himself in a hotel room, and had a collection of phonograph records. He had begun his career as a newspaper reporter and now wrote radio scripts. He lived in a place like Newburgh, he said, because he detested living in New York City but had to be near enough to it to confer with the network on his script writing. Each morning, before beginning the day's stint at the typewriter, he would place music on his phonograph for an hour. In particular he liked the symphonies of Johannes Brahms.

What we usually did when I went up to visit him was to talk and listen to music. He had never met my fiancée, and did not offer an opinion about whether the cancellation of our plans to be married was a good thing or not. He merely listened. Talking to him about what happened made me feel less panicky, even though I was unable to bring myself to speak of the humiliation I felt. I made out as if the breaking of the engagement had been a mutual decision, but I think he suspected what had happened. When it was time for me to return to New Jersey he rode the ferryboat with me across the river to Poughkeepsie, and we walked out along the station platform to await my train. When the train had pulled into the station and I was stepping aboard the coach, he said, "Don't worry, bud, it'll all come out in the wash."

After I agreed to take the job in Staunton I went back to Richmond on the bus to collect my belongings. My parents were pleased. They had understood why I had given up my job in the North, but would have preferred that I move directly from it to another. As for myself, I too had begun dreading the possibility that I might have to ask them for help, as if I were still a child. When I had gone up to work in New Jersey I had felt that at last I was going to be earning my own living and otherwise becoming, for the first time in my life, a successful young man, practical and self-sufficient, able to make my own way. And for almost six months, despite my small salary, I had been able to convince myself that it was so—until my plans had collapsed and I had lost any reason for being up there.

The next morning I departed for Staunton, not on the bus but riding on a train, in a comfortable coach with a reclining seat. I had lunch in the dining car. Up ahead the locomotive whistled musically for the crossings. As I watched the piedmont Virginia countryside pass by the window, I thought that it was a considerable improvement over the previous train trip I had made, when I had come home to Richmond from New Jersey. The train that night had been late in leaving Washington and then had been delayed for several hours because of a wreck on the line just south of Fredericksburg. I had to sit for a long time at night in an old, overheated coach with uncomfortable, hard plush seats, trying to read but more often staring out into the darkness, thinking how I was going back to where I came from, and not even able to return there without trouble. My hopes for success as a newspaper reporter in New Jersey and then, as I had confidently expected, in New York City itself were gone. So, too, the notion that I might quickly be able to emulate my uncle and move from newspaper writing into, if not radio scripts, perhaps plays, or, as seemed more appropriate to my interests, poems and stories. Instead I was back in the South, far away from where plays were produced and books published, and I had accomplished nothing. It had been after three in the morning before the train finally arrived in Richmond, and I had taken a taxi home and then had to beat on the front door for a long time before my father at last heard me and came down to let me in. "Well," he had said.

But now, en route to Staunton—pronounced without the *u*, I kept reminding myself—the immediate future at least seemed no longer so uncertain, for I was riding aboard a fast train westward to the mountains, to be the city editor of a daily newspaper, however small.

In Staunton, the place I found to stay was on the top floor of an old three-story house which had been divided up into rooms for rent. The room was large, with windows on two sides, a double bed, a desk, an easy chair, and a wash basin. Compared with the tiny room I had rented in New Jersey for the same price, it was far more satisfactory. It was located just at the eastern edge of the business district, a block south of the campus of a women's college, and about five blocks from the newspaper office, up a steep hill. The city of Staunton was very hilly and had considerably more trees along the streets than I had thought when I first saw it. The snow had melted a little when I arrived to stay, but it was still along the sidewalks and on the lawns and the rooftops. The people at the newspaper said that we would be likely to get several more heavy snows, for it was only February and the weather did not customarily break until about the first week in March.

However, in my new job the weather would be of comparatively little importance to me, for from the time I began work, in the late afternoon, until I left the office after one o'clock in the morning, almost the only time I ventured outside the building was when I went out to eat dinner. I came to work about four o'clock in the afternoon, checked the night

Associated Press budget to see what was expected over the teletype that evening, learned from the woman who was the paper's only reporter what she would have in the way of local news, then began laying out the front page and editing copy. As the evening's news from the outside world began arriving on the teletype, I edited it up and wrote headlines. The teletype copy was in all-capital letters, and it was necessary to mark it for capital and lower case for setting on the linotype. About six o'clock I went out to dinner. On the way I usually stopped at a newsstand to buy a magazine or a paperback book to read at dinner. An hour later I was back at work, editing copy steadily. Sometimes I took news over the telephone from a correspondent, and sometimes the reporter had an evening city council meeting or another such late story, but usually everything was on hand by ten o'clock, except for breaking news on the AP teletype. If I had a story to send out over the AP, I scheduled it on the wire, and when the bells rang to signal me to begin sending, I punched it out on the teletype keyboard.

When most of the copy had been set into type and I had edited and placed headlines on all the news that was to go into the paper, I went into the composing room and saw to the page layout, making cuts and changing about type to fit. There were only two or three pages of fresh type, which was all that the plant's four linotype machines could handle in an evening. Much of the type we carried was picked up from the afternoon paper, with the headlines reset into the morning paper's typographical style and the time references changed. By midnight we were usually ready to pull a proof of the front page, and after I checked it over for errors I went to work editing up some of the assortment of copy that was mailed in by rural correspondents in outlying areas, which would be set into type early the next day. The edition came off the press about one o'clock in the morning, and I was free to leave once I had finished editing up all the correspondents' copy and a few filler stories.

Several blocks away, not far from the railroad station, there was an all-night restaurant, and when I finished work I went there for what in effect was my supper. Since I knew no one, I sat by myself at the counter, reading the paper or a magazine while I waited for my order to be filled. After eating I walked up the long hill to my room. By then it was close to two o'clock, but I was far from feeling sleepy yet, so I read for a while and listened to the radio. Because of the altitude I could pick up stations in the Midwest much more clearly than those to the east or the south. From two to three in the morning I listened as I read to a classical music program on a Chicago station called the Starlight Concert. By three o'clock I was usually sleepy enough to turn off my reading lamp and go to sleep.

The truth is that during all of this time, from the very night I had come back to Richmond from the North, throughout the several weeks of job hunting, and now in the first weeks of my new job, I was waiting for a letter. Exactly what its contents were to be I should have been unable to say, even though I wrote drafts of it to myself in my mind from time to time. It was from the girl to whom I had been engaged to be married, and what it was supposed to announce was that everything was not irrevocably over between us.

It was not that I did not possess all the proof to the contrary that should have been needed to convince me. During the weeks after I left New Jersey I had come to realize in retrospect that the breaking of the engagement had not been a sudden decision, but planned out well in advance. I saw too that her parents, both of whom I had liked very much, had undoubtedly been in on the secret, and the three of them had plotted how and when it was to be done. In my naïveté I had failed to read signs that were being flashed at me. No doubt her parents, who I was sure liked me, had been chagrined at my inability to realize what was taking place. The thought of that was so humiliating that I could not bear to think about it.

Yet despite the fact that such realization was intermittently coming to me, I was managing to keep from dwelling upon it most of the time, shoving it back into the periphery of my consciousness, as it were, by assuring myself that it did not matter, that one day soon the letter would arrive that would change everything. There need not be an outright confession of error and remorse, a plea to resume as before, to have the ring returned to her, to plan the wedding. What would suffice was a letter which took up as if nothing had happened, implicitly assumed a continuing relationship, expressed pleasure and interest in my new job, even hinted perhaps of a desire to come for a visit sometime to see me in my new surroundings.

Because of the late hours I was now working, when I woke up in the morning it was seldom earlier than eleven o'clock. I went out to a restaurant to get my breakfast while others were eating lunch. Then I stopped in at the newspaper office to see whether there was any mail for me. Afterwards there were three hours or so remaining before time to begin work. Usually I went back to my room, since there was no place else for me to go. I hoped that there would be mail, for then I could answer it. If not, usually I read until time to begin work. The city library was located near my room, and several days a week I stopped in there to find new books, usually taking three and four at a time to my room. What I liked most were archeology and Civil War history. The library was housed in the former residence of Stonewall Jackson's cartographer, the famous Jed Hotchkiss, and there were many books about the war.

During my first few weeks in the new job I was busy learning what was involved in getting out the newspaper. Not even in the afternoon, in my room, did I often think to feel bored or lonely. My first Sunday in town, when there was no paper to get out that evening, I had felt the time hanging heavy for a little while, but I wrote letters. I rather liked being there by myself in my room, listening to the New York Philharmonic concert on the radio, with the snow falling steadily beyond the window-pane. I could hear the truck traffic on the Valley Pike, which ran just below my window, laboring up the hill, and the road maintenance crews scraping the snow and spreading sand and salt on the icy grade. Later on I heard the westbound Chesapeake and Ohio train whistling on its way through town. After dinner I wrote a letter to my uncle. He had responded to my account of my new job with the observation that it would be good training, though his guess was that after a time I would find it tiresome to be doing only a routine of desk work each day. I told him that while he might well be right, for now at least I found the editing quite interesting. I did not add that what I liked most of all was just that routine, and that the more hours a day it demanded of me, the more grateful I was for it.

The day when the letter arrived was at the very end of February. It came in response to one that I had finally written, on a pretext having to do with the return of a book I had borrowed from a library some time ago and left behind me in New Jersey. It was one of several letters waiting in my mailbox at the office, and my first, reflexive response was to shove it quickly to the bottom of the stack of envelopes I was holding, as if by postponing the reading of it, even for a few minutes, I might also postpone its meaning as well. For at that instant I was quite certain of what it would say, and I realized too that I had known all along. After a moment I tore open the envelope and hastily scanned the words, written in the familiar penmanship, on a double sheet of notepaper.

What was said was little more than a repetition of what had been said to my face a month earlier, together with the comment that my own letter had seemed to be written in anger, and that she was happy to see that I was indeed angry, which I had every right to be, she said. "The little bitch!" I said aloud, and looked around me to assure myself that no one had heard me speak. "The little bitch," I repeated under my breath. For not only had I not written in anger, but I saw that by pretending that I had been angry she was assuaging any feelings of guilt she might have had at having hurt me. What I had accomplished by writing was to provide her with an opportunity to enjoy feeling distressed at having to decline my love. I thrust the letter into my pocket and left the office. "The damn spoiled little bitch!" I said aloud as I walked up Coalter Street, after first looking to see that no one was within hearing distance. "Now I really *am* mad. Mad as hell!"

Yet as I was saying these things, I knew I was deceiving myself not at all. The truth was that I should have liked to be angry, to resent the way I had been put aside, as one might put aside a novel when one finished enjoying it, or, more appropriately, I thought, as a child might put aside a set of finger paints once the novelty of being able to make pretty configurations with one's fingers had worn off. But I could not make myself feel anger—only a sense of humiliation.

I felt grateful that the barrier of the mountains existed, protecting me from further involvement. The condition to which I should aspire, I felt, was an emotional and moral numbness, a complete freezing of emotional engagement, so as to make myself impervious. If I could cultivate an attitude of unconcern and indifference to my present circumstance, then ultimately I might be able to bring my memory to a similar invulnerability.

And for a while it seemed to be working. I found that if I went to the office a littler earlier than usual, and if I worked a little later after the paper had gone to press, I could stretch my working hours so that they filled most of my waking hours, leaving only a brief period between the time I arose in the very late morning and went out to get breakfast, and the time I began the night's work, when my thoughts were not occupied by the requirements of my job. And after I had put the paper to bed and gone by for a sandwich at the all-night restaurant, I was sufficiently tired so that when I went to my room I could read about the Civil War or the exploration of the Upper Nile and listen to music on the radio until almost dawn without feeling restless and lonely. After a few days I came to know something close to actual contentment at the way I was managing. I even decided that there would be no need for me to go home to Richmond on weekends. I would simply stay in my room and read. For the first time since I had come back South, I felt that I was close to being master of my emotions. I did not require anyone else's company.

How long I might have continued in this way if the winter had held on, I cannot say. But there came a day when the ice and snow were gone, the streets and lawns were wet from the melting, and the temperature was suddenly up in the sixties. Almost overnight the Valley changed from a stronghold of frozen rock into a swiftly thawing garden. Everything around me now began turning toward color and warmth. To the west of my room, and visible from my window, was a low mountain called Sally Grey, which had loomed over the little winter city in barren woods and stark granite. So perfectly had it seemed to match the frame of mind to which I aspired that I would sit and look at it for long intervals, as if through focusing my thoughts upon it I might acquire its hardness. But now the bare crest was giving way to a faint but unmistakable green, and the trees along the slopes, which had seemed so sterile and rigid, were fringing into a blurred growth that softened and obscured the harsh outlines of the hillside. And late at night, when I finished my work and went by the all-night restaurant, I discovered to my dismay that the darkness, which had seemed so chilled and barren that I was glad to retreat to my room where I could read and listen to music, had now acquired a depth and resonance that I found threatening to my feeling of immunity.

Yet the night proved to be as much my ally as my enemy. For it was, after all, very late when I finished at the newspaper and had eaten my supper, I had been at work for ten hours and more, so that I was not obligated to reflect that under more fortunate circumstances I should have been enjoying the company of a girl—if I had a girl. Rather, by the time I was done with work it was an hour when I could only have expected to be alone anyway, so that I did not need to be ashamed at my solitary condition or believe that if only I were more attractive and desirable than I was I would not be left to myself.

Thus on a Saturday night in March, after the paper had been printed and I had stopped by the restaurant, I found the night so warm and inviting that instead of proceeding home to my room I decided to walk down to the railroad station two blocks away. It was, after all, no longer Saturday night at all but very early on Sunday morning, so that I need not feel, as I had so often done, that there was something wrong because I did not have a date.

The station was deserted except for a clerk in the ticket office of the lighted but unoccupied waiting room. I walked out along the platform to the west of the station, where the rock cliff that lay just beyond the double track slanted off. To the west I could hear a train whistle blowing. It must be a freight train, I decided. I would wait and watch it come through town before I went back to my room. I took up a seat on an empty baggage cart. Except for the whistle of the train, the town was still; I could hear an occasional automobile go by along Beverley Street three blocks away, but that was all.

Listening to the train drawing nearer, until eventually I could begin to hear the iron wheels reverberating along the rails, I felt a note of satisfaction in my solitariness that made the night seem not merely amiable but even harmonious, as if I were a part of it. To be seated there by myself in the darkness, past two in the morning, with no one else nearby and very few of the inhabitants of the community that lay around me even awake, seemed entirely appropriate. I felt a measure of pride in my separateness, a sense of resolution in being as I was, alone in the nighttime in a mountain town where I knew almost nobody and was known to few. The road that had brought me there, I thought, had been deceptive and erratic. It had not been remotely what I had imagined or intended for myself. Yet here I was, on a faintly warm night in the very early spring (or the tail end of winter, according to the calendar), with the city asleep around me and the C & O freight train blowing for the crossings as it neared town.

Finally the night freight came banging into the city, the locomotive headlight probing through the darkness like a baton, until as it drew close the light thrust into view, in swift counterpoint, objects I had not hitherto made out: a row of boxcars on a siding, semaphores, telegraph poles, switch blocks, a warehouse alongside the tracks. It played upon the jagged rock wall of the cliffside across the way, breaking it into a mosaic of planes and recesses. The locomotives—there were two of them, their drive wheels performing in unison—rolled powerfully up and past, and I could see for a moment the firemen and engineers in their cabs, high above the tracks, illuminated by the red glow of the open firebox doors. Then a freight car, and another, and another; one after the other clanged past, chains rattling and the flanged wheels singing as they cruised along, their song punctuated with a chorus of creaks and bangs and bumps as the cars held to the rails, in cadenced processional, a hundred cars and more, until at last the sound lightened and the caboose swung past.

As I turned to watch it go I saw a trainman standing on the rear platform, lantern in hand, with the red and green lamps above him. He waved to me and I waved back, and I watched as the caboose receded rapidly past the columns of the station platform and into the darkness, the signal lights solemnly glowing, and then around the bend of the rock cliff and out of sight. And all I could hear was the movement of the wheels in the distance, growing fainter as the train cleared the city limits and headed eastward. Further and further away, off to the east, the whistle sounded ever more distantly for the crossings. I sat on in the darkness, all by myself again, in no hurry to leave, listening pleasantly.

"The sleeping city," I said to myself, half aloud. I might write a poem entitled that. And only myself awake to listen. Lyrical whistle of the freight train, miles to the east and receding eastward. But then I heard another and, as it seemed, answering whistle, dirgelike and much fainter. The freight train could not possibly have moved so far away so rapidly. It must be the westbound passenger train, which came through the city each morning at about three o'clock. I looked at my watch in the darkness. It was indeed after three. If I waited for the passenger train to come and go, it would be almost four before I got back to my room and to bed. And what of that? What was to hinder my staying here for as long as I wished, till broad daylight if I chose? Tomorrow I could sleep even later than usual. Besides, tomorrow was Sunday—more properly, it had now been Sunday for more than three hours. I might do whatever I wanted; there was no one to object. Since I worked when others slept, the night was fairly my own.

I could now hear two trains whistling; there was no doubt of it. They were both far away, but one was coming toward Staunton. There was a noise behind me, not far from where I sat. I turned and saw a man engaged in loading some sacks of outbound mail onto a cart. When he was done he began pulling it up the concrete station platform. The train whistle was closer now, and presently I could hear the monotone of the wheels on the rails. Far down the platform, almost past the station, a man and a woman were standing, with suitcases alongside. That was where the pullmans would be stopping.

Now the passenger train came gliding into the station, the headlamp abruptly materializing from around the rocky bend. The locomotive moved up and past me, immense and stern, its high drive wheels performing their revolutions very slowly. It pulled to a stop a hundred yards ahead. Opposite me on the rails was a darkened coach. I watched down the track as the porters swung down with their yellow footstools. Even at that hour there were some passengers debarking. The man and woman I had seen waiting now stepped aboard, with the pullman porter following them, carrying their luggage; the arriving travelers walked off toward the station.

The train did not stay long. After only a few minutes I heard the conductor calling "All aboard!" and saw him signaling with his flashlight to the engineer up ahead. The air brakes went off with a hot iron hiss. The locomotive coughed twice in staccato explosion, and the train began easing forward into a slow, sustained rolling. I watched as the day coaches went by, then the dining car, cold and dark and the windows fogged, each to a swifter rhythm than its predecessor. Then the pullmans: City of Ashland, Collis P. Huntington, Balcony Falls, Gauley Bridge. The last pullman swept past in clattering haste. The red and green lamps receded westward. I listened until they were well out of sight. Soon the locomotive was blowing for grade crossings to the west of town. It would not be long before the train would have cleared the valley and begun climbing into the Alleghenies. As for the freight train, it was out of earshot now, and doubtless thundering along the grades of the Blue Ridge, bound for Charlottesville and the Northeast.

I walked home in the dark, feeling tired now and quite pleased with myself. It was well on toward four o'clock in the morning, I had seen two trains arrive and depart, and now I was all alone again on the deserted streets of the mountain town. I felt that I had accomplished something, had asserted my sensibility. I was persuaded, too, that whatever my present inconsequence, I was inevitable. On just what grounds this assurance was to be based, and for what, I could not have said. Yet the certainty, as I thought it, made me walk faster and breathe hard as I climbed up the hill toward my rented room, all by myself, at four in the morning, acting out a silent melodrama of prideful fulfillment.

The next day, however, after I had gone out almost at noon to eat breakfast at the hotel restaurant, I felt no such assurance. My confidence, my optimism of the evening before now seemed not merely misplaced but pathetically absurd. For in the light of a warmish Sunday in mid-March I saw myself in a different perspective, as a self-important young man with neither talent nor assurance, who had thus far failed at everything he had ever undertaken to do. I worked at a nighttime job that made it almost impossible to meet other people and make friends and have dates with girls. And what was worse, I had been glad of it, because it enabled me to hide from myself the knowledge of my ineptitude and unattractiveness. Now, because it was Sunday and I possessed no such refuge for the ten or twelve hours before I could fall asleep again, I felt trapped and in panic.

I remembered how, the previous evening when the freight train had been calling in the night as if to me alone, I had fancied that I was going to write a poem about the sleeping city. What vanity! For I knew very well that on all occasions when I had attempted to write anything, I had been quite unable to produce three lines that were not empty, pompous, and flat. Whenever I actually sat down before my typewriter and tried to begin anything other than a routine newspaper article, all my confidence, and all the ideas I had in mind, swiftly went stale.

I read the Sunday New York *Times* in my room, then tried reading a book for a while, but could not escape my gloom. I decided to go out for a walk. Perhaps the spring weather would divert me. On Sundays only there was an eastbound local passenger train that came through town about two o'clock. I would go down to the station and watch it.

As I headed eastward on Beverley Street I saw several couples, my age or younger, strolling along, looking at the displays in the store windows, chatting happily. There were two couples who were holding hands. Students from the local women's college and their dates, I decided. A year ago and I had done as much.

I passed the Stonewall Jackson Hotel. Would I end up like my uncle, living in a hotel room somewhere? He didn't seem to mind. I envied him his spartan invulnerability, his hermitlike ability to live by himself and not care about anything except his work.

I walked on toward the depot. Waiting near the tracks were a young man and several girls who seemed to be a little older than college age; they did not look like students. I walked past them, near enough to be able to hear what they were saying. They were talking with each other in French, and laughing at each other's pronunciation. They must be teachers at the college, I thought.

I should have liked very much to get to know people like that. I would have delighted in using my French, as they were doing. But I had no excuse for venturing into their conversation. As if waiting for the train, I stood not too far distant, observing them from the corner of my eye. If only I had some reason, some plausible excuse, for joining them. I knew that someone more sure of himself, more sophisticated and less self-conscious, would need no occasion but would simply go up to where they waited and strike up a conversation.

The train came drifting into the station. I had been so preoccupied that I had paid it no heed. One of the girls was apparently going away on a trip, or else returning somewhere after a visit to the others; the man was carrying her suitcase. I watched them as they said good-bye. Then after the girl who was leaving had gone inside the coach and found a seat by a window overlooking the platform, they were waving. *"Bon-voyage!"* one of the girls on the platform kept calling, mouthing her words very deliberately so that her friend on the train might read her lips.

If I were to go aboard, I thought, I might take the seat next to the girl and strike up a conversation. And why should I not do so? I might ride as far as Charlottesville and then take the evening train back to Staunton. I was free; I had nothing to prevent me from getting aboard and going along on the journey eastward. The thought frightened me, and instead I merely looked on as the railroad conductor signaled to the engineer, the vestibule doors slammed shut, the airbrakes went off, and the train moved from the station.

The young man and the two remaining girls who had escorted the traveler to the station waved good-bye, then walked off toward town. As they went by, one of the girls glanced at me for an instant. Hastily I averted my eyes, and so as not to seem to be following them, I walked a block eastward along the station platform and then took a side street back toward my rented room.

When I reached my room I turned on the radio. The New York Philharmonic Sunday concert was just beginning. Dmitri Mitropoulos was conducting the *Symphonie Pathétique*, which I disliked. Yet I did not switch it off. As if to torture myself, to make my afternoon complete, I lay on my bed, face downward, and listened to the oh so melancholy music.

They had been conversing in French. How very cultured, how very toney! And I, eavesdropping, watching them from a few yards away, had been standing there like a gawky fool and wanting to join them. The sensitive soul indeed. How very romantic! The lonely young man in the mountains! The thought of my pathetic posturing made me wince.

A few months ago on a Sunday afternoon, and her father and I would probably have been playing chess and listening to this self-same concert. That *he* had been in on the plan! I writhed at the thought. During all that time, for at least a month and very probably two or three, she had her mind made up to send me packing, and had only been awaiting the Proper Moment. But in my invincible vanity I had proved so obtuse as not to see what should have been plain. So there had been the need to make it obvious, overt. And in discussing it, they had pitied me! The poor, naïve young man from down South. . . .

"Damn!" I said aloud, over the melancholy music. "Damn!" Who in hell was she, who were they, to pity me?

It was true. Who *were* they? For while it was undeniable that I was lonely and missed very much having a girl, it need not be *her*. I could see that now.

I leaped up from the bed and walked across the room to the east window. The Sunday afternoon traffic was moving along Route 11. I thought, by God, I will write her a letter and tell her exactly what I think of her spoiled, stinking self. I went over to my typewriter, placed a sheet of paper in the machine. I stared at it a minute, then ripped it out. Hold on now, I told myself, just because you see daylight you are not out of the woods just yet. It would be exactly what she would want—another sequel to the little game of Falling Out of Love. I had had all I wanted of games. I crumpled the sheet of paper into a ball, threw it across the room at the wastepaper basket. It hit the wall, bounced in.

It must have been the people at the train station. I thought of how I should enjoy cramming their French conversation and their silly chatter down their cultivated throats. But that was not what I was angry about, was it? No, I had wanted to join them. My anger was for myself. Yet how could I expect to be other than what I was?

I lay in bed, and gradually became aware that the *Symphonie Pathétique* was concluded, and the commentator, Deems Taylor, was talking about the next number to be played by the orchestra. His mellifluous, too urbane voice droned on. Johannes Brahms had long put off writing a fully symphonic work, and it was not until he was forty-three years old that he completed his first symphony. The *Variations on a Theme by Haydn,* though originally composed for two pianos, was really a trial run, so to speak, whereby Brahms had for the first time used the full resources of an orchestra to develop an extended symphonic creation. The theme he had chosen, said Deems Taylor, was a choral work by Haydn, the *St. Anthony Chorale.*

Then, without warning, all unprepared as I was to meet it, there came the most cadenced, masterfully gentle music, calm and reassuring, that I had ever heard. In unhurried progression, tranquil and controlled, yet by no means without strength or resonance, the theme spoke out confidently, sustained and borne alone by the horns and violins. I had always liked Brahms, but this composition possessed a sweetness and harmoniousness that seemed to soften and transform everything around me—the air, the room, the time of day. The music formed itself into an assertion, an acknowledgment of purpose, but without either panic or desperation. It climbed steadily forward, building to a more urgent reiteration, but only enough to make its point, without any clamor or abandonment of its dignity and congruence. It closed on three drawn-out, unhurried chords. ST. ANTHONY, I thought, as if punching out the letters on a teletype keyboard, STANTON. Without the *you* in it.

The variations that Johannes Brahms had made on the theme by Haydn continued, and I listened on. But because I was young and had almost until that moment been in love, as I lay on my bed and the music played I did not think to wonder why it was that the pleasure I drew from the music was so like that which I took from the trains. Neither did it occur to me, being neither traveler nor musician but only a newspaperman temporarily resident in a mountain town in Virginia, to consider the odd coincidence in names, or even to ask who St. Anthony was. That truth, if such it proved to be, would come. For now, for Sunday afternoon, I was content to lie and listen to the music.

THE COUSINS

Elizabeth Spencer

I COULD say that on the train from Milan to Florence, I recalled the events of thirty summers ago and the curious affair of my cousin Eric. But it wouldn't be true. I had Eric somewhere in my mind all the time, a constant. But he was never quite definable, and like a puzzle no one could ever solve, he bothered me. More recently, I had felt a restlessness I kept trying without success to lose, and I had begun to see Eric as its source.

The incident that had triggered my journey to find him had occurred while lunching with my cousin Ben in New York, his saying: "I always thought in some way I can't pin down—it was your fault we lost Eric." Surprising myself, I had felt stricken at the remark as though the point of a cold dagger had reached a vital spot. There was a story my cousins used to tell, out in the swing, under the shade trees, about a man found dead with no clues but a bloody shirt and a small pool of water on the floor beside him. Insoluble mystery. Answer: He was stabbed with a Dagger of Ice! I looked up from eating bay scallops. "My fault! Why?"

Ben gave some vague response, something about Eric's need for staying indifferent, no matter what. "But he could do that in spite of me," I protested. "Couldn't he?"

"Oh, forget it." He filled my glass. "I sometimes speculate out loud, Ella Mason."

Just before that he had remarked how good I was looking—good for a widow just turned fifty, I think he meant. But once he got my restlessness so stirred up, I couldn't lose it. I wanted calming, absolving. I wanted freeing and only Eric—since it was he I was in some way to blame for, or he to blame for me—could do that. So I came alone to Italy, where I had not been for thirty years.

For a while in Milan, spending a day or so to get over jet lag, I wondered if the country existed any more in the way I remembered it. Maybe, even back then, I had invented the feelings I had, the magic I had wanted to see. But on the train to Florence, riding through the June morning, I saw a little town from the window, in the bright, slightly hazy distance. I don't know what town it was. It seemed built all of a whitish stone, with a church, part of a wall cupping round one side and a piazza with a few people moving across it. With that sight and its stillness in the distance and its sudden vanishing as the train whisked past, I caught my breath and knew it had all been real. So it still was, and would remain. I hadn't invented anything.

From the point of that glimpsed white village, spreading outward through my memory, all its veins and arteries, the whole summer woke up again, like a person coming out of a trance.

Sealed, fleet, the train was rocking on. I closed my eyes with the image of the village, lying fresh and gentle against my mind's eye. I didn't have to try, to know that everything from then would start living now.

Once at the hotel and unpacked, with dim lamp and clean bathroom and view of a garden—Eric had reserved all this for me: we had written and talked—I placed my telephone call. "Pronto," said the strange voice. "Signor Mason," I said. "Ella Mason, is that you?" So there was his own Alabama voice, not a bit changed. "It's me," I said, "tired from the train." "Take a nap. I'll call for you at seven."

Whatever southerners are, there are ways they don't change, the same manners to count on, the same tone of voice, never lost. Eric was older than I by about five years. I remember he taught me to play tennis, not so much how to play because we all knew that, as what not to do. Tennis manners. I had wanted to keep running after balls for him when they rolled outside the court, but he stopped me from doing that. He would take them up himself, and stroke them underhand to his opponent across the net. "Once in a while's all right," he said. "Just go sit down, Ella Mason." It was his way of saying there was always a right way to do things. I was only about ten. The next year it was something else I was doing wrong, I guess, because I always had a lot to learn. My cousins had this constant fondness about them. They didn't mind telling what they knew.

Waking in Florence in the late afternoon, wondering where I was, then catching on. The air was still and warm. It had the slight haziness in the brightness that I had seen from the train, and which I had lost in the bother of the station, the hastening of the taxi through the annoyance of crowds and narrow streets, across the Arno. The little hotel, a pensione, really, was out near the Pitti Palace.

Even out so short a distance from the center, Florence could seem the town of thirty years ago, or even the way it must have been in the Brownings' time, narrow streets and the light that way and the same flowers and gravel walks in the gardens. Not that much changes if you build with stone. Not until I saw the stooped gray man hastening through the pensione door did I get slapped by change, in the face. How could Eric look like that? Not that I hadn't had photographs, letters. He at once circled me, embracing, my head right against him, sight of him temporarily lost in that. As was his of me, I realized, thinking of all those lines I must have added, along with twenty extra pounds and a high count of gray among the reddish-brown hair. So we both got bruised by the sight of each other, and hung together, to blot each other out and soothe the hurt.

The shock was only momentary. We were too glad to see each other. We went some streets away, parked his car, and climbed about six flights of stone stairs. His place had a view over the river, first a great luxurious room opening past the entrance, then a terrace beyond. There were paintings, dark furniture, divans and chairs covered with good, rich fabric. A blonde woman's picture in a silver frame—poised, lovely. Through an alcove, the glimpse of an impressive desk, spread with papers, a telephone. You'd be forced to say he'd done well.

"It's cooler outside on the terrace," Eric said, coming in with drinks. "You'll like it over the river." So we went out there and talked. I was getting used to him now. His profile hadn't changed. It was firm, regular, Cousin Lucy Skinner's all over. That was his mother. We were just third cousins. Kissing kin. I sat answering questions. How long would it take, I wondered, to get around to the heart of things? To whatever had carried him away, and what had brought me here?

We'd been brought up together back in Martinsville, Alabama, not far from Birmingham. There was our connection and not much else in that little town of seven thousand and something. Or so we thought. And so we would have everybody else think. We did, though, despite a certain snobbishness—or maybe because of it—have a lot of fun. There were three leading families, in some way "connected." Eric and I had had the same great-grandfather. His mother's side were distant cousins, too. Families who had gone on living around there, through the centuries. Many were the stories and wide ranged the knowledge, though it was mainly of local interest. As a way of living, I always told myself, it might have gone on for us, too, right through the present and into an endless future, except for that trip we took that summer.

It started with ringing phones.

Eric calling one spring morning to say, "You know, the idea Jamie had last night down at Ben's about going to Europe? Well, why don't we do it?"

"This summer's impossible," I said, "I'm supposed to help Papa in the law office."

"He can get Sister to help him—" That was Eric's sister Chessie, one way of making sure she didn't decide to go with us. "You all will have to pay her a little, but she wants a job. Think it over, Ella Mason, but not for very long. Mayfred wants to, and Ben sounds serious, and there's Jamie and you makes five. Ben knows a travel agent in Birmingham. He thinks we might even get reduced rates, but we have to hurry. We should have thought this up sooner."

His light voice went racing on. He read a lot. I didn't even have to ask him where we'd go. He and Ben would plan it, both young men who had studied things, knew things, read, talked, quoted. We'd go where they wanted to go, love what they planned, admire them. Jamie was younger, my Uncle Gale's son, but he was forming that year—he was becoming grown-up. Would he be like them? There was nothing else to be but like them, if at all possible. No one in his right mind would question that.

Ringing phones. . . . "Oh, I'm thrilled to death! What did your folks say? It's not all that expensive what with the exchange, not as much as staying here and going somewhere like the Smokies. You can pay for the trip over with what you'd save."

We meant to go by ship. Mayfred who read up on the latest things, wanted to fly, but nobody would hear to it. The boat was what people talked about when they mentioned their trip. It was a phrase: "On the boat going over. . . . On the boat coming back. . . ." The train was what we'd take to New York, or maybe we could fly. Mayfred, once redirected, began to plan everybody's clothes. She knew what things were drip-dry and crush-proof. On and on she forged through slick-paged magazines.

"It'll take the first two years of law practice to pay for it, but it might be worth it," said Eric. "J'ai très hâte d'y aller," said Ben. The little French he knew was a lot more than ours.

Eric was about twenty-five that summer, just finishing law school, having been delayed a year or so by his army service. I wasn't but nineteen. The real reason I had hesitated about going was a boy from Tuscaloosa I'd been dating up at the university last fall, but things were running down with him, even though I didn't want to admit it. I didn't love him so much as I wanted him to love me, and that's no good, as Eric himself told me. Ben was riding high, having gotten part of his thesis accepted for publication in the *Sewanee Review.* He had written on "The Lost Ladies of Edgar Allan Poe" and this piece was the chapter on "Ulalume." I pointed out they weren't so much lost as dead, or sealed up half-dead in tombs, but Ben didn't see the humor in that.

The syringa were blooming that year, and the spirea and bridal wreath. The flags had come and gone but not the wisteria, prettier than anybody could remember. All our mothers doted on their yards, while not a one of us ever raised so much as a petunia. No need to. We called each other from bower to bower. Our cars kept floating us through soft spring twilights. Travel folders were everywhere and Ben had scratched up enough French grammars to go around so we could practice some phrases. He thought we ought at least to know how to order in a restaurant and ask for stationery and soap in a hotel. Or buy stamps and find the bathroom. He was on to what to say to cab drivers when somebody mentioned that we were spending all this time on French without knowing a word of Italian. What did *they* say for Hello, or How much does it cost? or Which way to the post office? Ben said we didn't have time for Italian. He thought the people you had to measure up to were the French. What Italians thought of you didn't matter all that much. We were generally over at Eric's house because his mother was away visiting his married sister Edith and the grandchildren, and Eric's father couldn't have cared less if we had drinks of real whiskey in the evening. In fact, he was often out playing poker and doing the same thing himself.

The Masons had a grand house. (Mason was Mama's maiden name and so my middle one.) I loved the house especially when nobody was in it but all of us. It was white, two-story with big high-ceilinged rooms. The tree branches laced across it by moonlight, so that you could only see patches of it. Mama was always saying they ought to thin things out, take out half the shrubs and at least three trees (she would even say which trees), but Cousin Fred, Eric's father, liked all that shaggy growth. Once inside, the house took you over—it liked us all—and we were often back in the big kitchen after supper fixing drinks or sitting out on the side porch making jokes and talking about Europe. One evening it would be peculiar things about the English, and the next, French food, how much we meant to spend on it, and so on. We had a long argument about Mont St. Michel, which Ben had read about in a book by Henry Adams, but everybody else, though coaxed into reading at least part of the book, thought it was too far up there and we'd better stick around Paris. We hoped Ben would forget it: he was bossy when he got his head set. We wanted just to see Ver-sigh and Fontaineblow.

"We could stop off in the southern part of France on our way to Italy," was Eric's idea. "It's where all the painting comes from."

"I'd rather see the paintings," said Mayfred. "They're mostly in Paris, aren't they?"

"That's not the point," said Ben.

Jamie was holding out for one night in Monte Carlo.

Jamie had shot up like a weed a few years back and had just never filled out. He used to regard us all as slightly opposed to him, as though none of us could possibly want to do what he most liked. He made, at times, common cause with Mayfred, who was kin to us only by a thread, so complicated I wouldn't dream of untangling it.

Mayfred was a grand-looking girl. Ben said it once: "She's got class." He said that when we were first debating whether to ask her along or not (if not her, then my roommate from Texas would be invited), and had decided that we had to ask Mayfred or smother her because we couldn't have stopped talking about our plans if our lives depended on it and she was always around. The afternoon Ben made that remark about her, we were just the three of us—Ben, Eric, and me—out to help Mama about the annual lining of the tennis court, and had stopped to sit on a bench, being sweaty and needing some shade to catch our breath in. So he said that in his meditative way, hitting the edge of a tennis racket on the ground between his feet and occasionally sighting down it to see if it had warped during a winter in the press. And Eric, after a silence in which he looked off to one side until you thought he hadn't heard (this being his way), said: "You'd think the rest of us had no class at all." "Of course we have, we just never mention it," said Ben. So we'd clicked again. I always loved that to happen.

Mayfred had a boyfriend named Donald Bailey, who came over from Georgia and took her out every Saturday night. He was fairly nice-looking was about all we knew, and Eric thought he was dumb.

"I wonder how Mayfred is going to get along without Donald," Ben said.

"I can't tell if she really likes him or not," I said. "She never talks about him."

"She just likes to have somebody," Ben said tersely, a thread of disapproval in his voice, the way he could do.

Papa was crazy about Mayfred. "You can't tell what she thinks about anything and she never misses a trick," he said. His unspoken thought was that I was always misjudging things. "Don't you *see*, Ella Mason," he would say. But are things all that easy to see?

"Do you remember," I said to Eric on the terrace, this long after, "much about Papa?"

"What about him?"

"He wanted me to be different, some way."

"Different how?"

"More like Mayfred," I said, and laughed, making it clear that I was deliberately shooting past the mark, because really I didn't know where it was.

"Well," said Eric, looking past me out to where the lights were brightening along the Arno, the towers standing out clearly in the dusky air, "I liked you the way you were."

It was good, hearing him say that. The understanding that I wanted might not come. But I had a chance, I thought, and groped for what to say, when Eric rose to suggest dinner, a really good restaurant he knew, not far away; we could even walk.

". . . Have you been to the Piazza? No, of course, you haven't had time. Well, don't go. It's covered with tourists and pigeon shit; they've moved all the real statues inside except the Cellini. Go look at that and leave quick. . . ."

"You must remember Jamie, though, how he put his head in his hands our first day in Italy and cried, 'I was just being nice to him and he took all the money!' Poor Jamie, I think something else was wrong with him, not just a couple of thousand lire."

"You think so, but what?"

"Well, Mayfred had made it plain that Donald was her choice of a man, though not present. And of course there was Ben. . . ." My voice stopped just before I stepped on a crack in the sidewalk.

". . . Ben had just got into Yale that spring before we left. He was hitching to a *future*, man!" It was just as well Eric said it.

"So that left poor Jamie out of everything, didn't it? He was young, another year in college to go, and nothing really outstanding about him, so he thought, and nobody he could pair with."

"There were you and me."

"You and me," I repeated. It would take a book to describe how I said that. Half-question, half-echo, a total wondering what to say next. How, after all, did *he* mean it? It wasn't like me to say nothing. "He might just have wondered what *we* had?"

"He might have," said Eric. In the corner of the white-plastered restaurant, where he was known and welcomed, he was enjoying grilled chicken and artichokes. But suddenly he put down his fork, a pause like a solstice. He looked past my shoulder: Eric's way.

"Ben said it was my fault we 'lost' you. That's how he put it. He told me that in New York, the last time I saw him, six weeks ago. He wouldn't explain. Do you understand what he meant?"

" 'Lost,' am I? It's news to me."

"Well, you know, not at home. Not even in the States. Is that to do with me?"

"We'll go back and talk." He pointed to my plate. "Eat your supper, Ella Mason," he said.

My mind began wandering pleasantly. I fell to remembering the surprise Mayfred had handed us all when we got to New York. We had come up on the train, having gone up to Chattanooga to catch the Southern. Three days in New York and we would board the Queen Mary for Southampton. "Too romantic for anything," Mama had warbled on the phone. ("Elsa Stephens says, 'Too romantic for anything,'" she said at the table. "No, Mama, you said that, I heard you." "Well, I don't care who said it, it's true.") On the second afternoon in New York, Mayfred vanished with something vague she had to do. "Well, you know she's always tracking down dresses," Jamie told me. "I think she wants her hair restyled somewhere," I said. But not till we were having drinks in the hotel bar before dinner did Mayfred show up with Donald Bailey! She had, in addition to Donald, a new dress and a new hairstyle, and the three things looked to me about of equal value, I was thinking, when she suddenly announced with an earsplitting smile: "We're married!" There was a total silence, broken at last by Donald, who said with a shuffling around of feet and gestures: "It's just so I could come along with y'all, if y'all don't mind." "Well," said Ben, at long last, "I guess you both better sit down." Another silece followed, broken by Eric, who said he guessed it was one excuse for having champagne.

Mayfred and Donald had actually gotten married across the state line in Georgia two weeks before. Mayfred didn't want to discuss it because, she said, everybody was so taken up with talking about Europe, she wouldn't have been able to get a word in edgewise. "You better go straight and call yo' Mama," said Ben. "Either you do, or I will."

Mayfred's smile fell to ashes and she sloshed out champagne. "She can't do a thing about it till we get back home! She'll want me to explain everything. Don't y'all make me . . . please!"

I noticed that so far Mayfred never made common cause with any one of us, but always spoke to the group: Y'all. It also occurred to me both then and now that that was what had actually saved her. If one of us had gotten involved in pleading for her with Ben, he would have overruled us. But Mayfred, a lesser cousin, was keeping a distance. She could have said—and I thought she was on the verge of it—that she'd gone to a lot of trouble to satisfy us; she might have just brought him along without benefit of ceremony.

So we added Donald Bailey. Unbeknownst to us, reservations had been found for him and though he had to share a four-berth, tourist-class cabin with three strange men, after a day out certain swaps were effected, and he wound up in second class with Mayfred. Eric overheard a conversation between Jamie and Donald which he passed on to me. Jamie: Don't you really think this is a funny way to spend a honeymoon? Donald: It just was the best I could do.

He was a polite squarish sort of boy with heavy, dark lashes. He and Mayfred used to stroll off together regularly after the noon meal on board. It was a serene crossing, for the weather cleared two days out of New York and we could spend a lot of time on deck playing shuffleboard and betting on races with wooden horses run by the purser. (I forgot to say everybody in our family but Ben's branch were inveterate gamblers and had played poker in the club car all the way up to New York on the train.) After lunch every day Mayfred got seasick and Donald in true husbandly fashion would take her to whichever side the wind was not blowing against and let her throw up neatly over the rail, like a cat. Then she'd be all right. Later, when you'd see them together they were always talking and laughing. But with us she was quiet and trim, with her fashion-blank look, and he was just quiet. He all but said "Ma'am" and "Sir." As a result of Mayfred's marriage, I was thrown a lot with Eric, Ben, and Jamie. "I think one of you ought to get married," I told them. "Just temporarily, so I wouldn't feel like the only girl." Ben promised to take a look around and Eric seemed not to have heard. It was Jamie who couldn't joke about it. He had set himself to make a pair, in some sort of way, with Mayfred, I felt. I don't know how seriously he took her. Things run deep in our family—that's what you have to know. Eric said out of the blue, "I'm wondering when they had time to see each other; Mayfred spent all her time with us." (We were prowling through the Tate Gallery.) "Those Saturday night dates," I said, studying Turner. At times she would show up with us, without Donald, not saying much, attentive and smooth, making company. Ben told her she looked Parisian.

Eric and Ben were both well into manhood that year, and were so future conscious they seemed to be talking about it even when they weren't saying anything. Ben had decided on literature, had finished a master's at Sewanee and was going on to Yale, while Eric had just stood law school exams at Emory. He was in some considerable debate about whether he shouldn't go into literary studies, too, for unlike Ben, whose interest was scholarly, he wanted to be a writer, and he had some elaborate theory that actually studying literature reduced the possibility of your being able to write it. Ben saw his point and though he did not entirely agree, felt that law might just be the right choice—it put you in touch with how things actually worked. "Depending, of course, on whether you tend to fiction or poetry. It would be more important in regard to fiction because the facts matter so much more." So they trod along ahead of us—through London sights, their heels coming down in tandem. They might have been two dons in an Oxford street, debating something. Next to come were Jamie and me, and behind, at times, Donald and Mayfred.

I was so fond of Jamie those days. I felt for him in a family way, almost motherly. When he said he wanted a night in Monte Carlo, I sided with him, just as I had about going at least once to the picture show in London. Why shouldn't he have his way? Jamie said one museum a day was enough. I felt the same. He was all different directions with himself: too tall, too thin, big feet, small head. Once I caught his hand: "Don't worry," I said, "everything good will happen to you." The way I remember it, we looked back just then, and there came Mayfred, alone. She caught up with us. We were standing on a street corner near Hyde Park and, for a change, it was sunny. "Donald's gone home," she said, cheerfully. "He said tell you all goodbye."

We hadn't seen her all day. We were due to leave for France the next morning. She told us, for one thing, that Donald had persistent headaches and thought he ought to see about it. He seemed, as far as we could tell, to have limitless supplies of money, and had once taken us all for dinner at the Savoy, where only Mayfred could move into all that glitter with an air of belonging to it. He didn't like to bring up his illness and trouble us, Mayfred explained. "Maybe it was too much honeymoon for him," Eric speculated to me in private. I had to say I didn't know. I did know that Jamie had come out like the English sun—unexpected, but marvelously bright.

I held out for Jamie and Monte Carlo. He wasn't an intellectual like Ben and Eric. He would listen while they finished up a bottle of wine and then would start looking around the restaurant. "That lady didn't have anything but snails and bread," he would say, or, of a couple leaving, "He didn't even know that girl when they came in." He was just being a small-town boy. But with Mayfred he must have been different, she laughed so much. "What do they talk about?" Ben asked me, perplexed. "Ask them," I advised. "You think they'd tell me?" "I doubt it," I said. "They wouldn't know what to say," I added, "they would just tell you the last things they said." "You mean like, Why do they call it the Seine if they don't seine for fish in it? Real funny."

Jamie got worried about Mayfred in Paris because the son of the hotel owner, a young Frenchman so charming he looked like somebody had made him up whole cloth, wanted to take her out. She finally consented with some trepidation on our part, especially from Ben, who in this case posed as her uncle, with strict orders from her father. The Frenchman, named Paul something, was not disturbed in the least: Ben fit right in with his ideas of how things ought to be. So Mayfred went out with him, looking, except for her sunny hair, more French than the natives—we all had to admit being proud of her. I also had invitations, but none so elegant. "What happened?" we all asked, the next day. "Nothing," she insisted. "We just went to this little nightclub place near some school . . . begins with an 'S.'" "The Sorbonne," said Ben, whose bemusement, at that moment, peaked. "Then what?" Eric asked. "Well, nothing. You just eat something, then talk and have some wine and get up and dance. They dance different. Like this." She locked her hands together in air. "He thought he couldn't talk good enough for me in English, but it was OK." Paul sent her some marrons glacés which she opened on the train south, and Jamie munched one with happy jaws. Paul had not suited him. It was soon after that, he and Mayfred began their pairing off. In Jamie's mind we were moving on to Monte Carlo, and had been ever since London. The first thing he did was find out how to get to the Casino.

He got dressed for dinner better than he had since the Savoy. Mayfred seemed to know a lot about the gambling places, but her attitude was different from his. Jamie was bird-dogging toward the moment; she was just curious. "I've got to trail along," Eric said after dinner, "just to see the show." "Not only that," said Ben, "we might have to stop him in case he gets too carried away. We might have to bail him out." When we three, following up the rear (this was Jamie's night), entered the discreetly glittering rotunda, stepped on thick carpets beneath the giant, multiprismed chandeliers, heard the low chant of the croupier, the click of roulette, the rustle of money at the bank, and saw the bright rhythmic movements of dealers and wheels and stacks of chips, it was still Jamie's face that was the sight worth watching. All was mirrored there. Straight from the bank, he visited card tables and wheels, played the blind dealing-machine—chemin-de-fer—and finally turned, a small sum to the good, to his real goal: roulette. Eric had by then lost a hundred francs or so, but I had about made up for it, and Ben wouldn't play at all. "It's my Presbyterian side," he told us. His mother had been one of those. "It's known as 'riotous living,'" he added.

It wasn't riotous at first, but it was before we left, because Jamie, once he advanced on the roulette, with Mayfred beside him—she was wearing some sort of gold blouse with long peasant sleeves and a low-cut neck she had picked up cheap in a shop that afternoon, and was not speaking to him but instead, with a gesture so European you'd think she'd been born there, slipping her arm through his just at the wrist and leaning her head back a little—was giving off the glow of somebody so magically aided by a presence every inch his own that he could not and would not lose. Jamie, in fact, looked aristocratic, overbred, like a Russian greyhound or a Rumanian prince. Both Eric and I suspended our own operations to watch. The little ball went clicking around as the wheel spun. Black. Red. And red. Back to black. All wins. People stopped to look on. Two losses, then the wins again, continuing. Mayfred had a look of curious bliss around her mouth—she looked like a cat in process of a good purr. The take mounted.

Ben called Eric and me aside. "It's going on all night," he said. We all sat down at the little gold and white marble bar and ordered Perriers.

"Well," said Eric, "what did he start with?"

"Couldn't have been much," said Ben, "if I didn't miss anything. He didn't change more than a couple of hundred at the desk."

"That sounds like a lot to me" said Eric.

"I mean," said Ben, "it won't ruin him to lose it all."

"You got us into this," said Eric to me.

"Oh, gosh, I know it. But look. He's having the time of his life."

Everybody in the room had stopped to watch Jamie's luck. Some people were laughing. He had a way of stopping everybody and saying: "What's *that* mean?" as if only English could or ought to be spoken in the entire world. Some man near us said, "Le cavalier de l'Okla-hum," and another answered, "Du Texas, plutôt." Then he took three more in a row and they were silent.

It was Mayfred who made him stop. It seemed like she had an adding machine in her head. All of a sudden she told him something, whispered in his ear. When he shook his head, she caught his hand. When he pulled away, she grabbed his arm. When he lifted his arm, she came up with it, right off the floor. For a minute I thought they were both going to fall over into the roulette wheel.

"You got to stop, Jamie!" Mayfred said in the loudest Alabama voice I guess they'd ever be liable to hear that side of the ocean. It was curdling, like cheering for 'Bama against Ole Miss in the Sugar Bowl. "I don't have to stop!" he yelled right back. "If you don't stop," Mayfred shouted, "I'll never speak to you again, Jamie Marshall, as long as I live!"

The croupier looked helpless, and everybody in the room was turning away like they didn't see us, while through a thin door at the end of the room, a man in black tie was approaching who could only be called the "management." Ben was already pulling Jamie toward the bank. "Cash it in now, we'll go along to another one . . . maybe tomorrow we can. . . ." It was like pulling a stubborn calf across the lot, but he finally made it with some help from Mayfred, who stood over Jamie while he counted everything to the last sou. She made us all take a taxi back to the hotel because she said it was common knowledge when you won a lot they sent somebody out to rob you, first thing. Next day she couldn't rest till she got Jamie to change the francs into travelers' checks, U.S. He had won well over two thousand dollars, all told.

The next thing, as they saw it, was to keep Jamie out of the Casino. Ben haggled a long time over lunch, and Eric, who was good at scheming, figured out a way to get up to a village in the hills where there was a Matisse chapel he couldn't live longer without seeing. And Mayfred took to hand holding and even gave Jamie on the sly (I caught her at it) a little nibbling kiss or two. What did they care? I wondered. I thought he should get to go back and lose it all.

It was up in the mountain village that afternoon that I blundered in where I'd rather not have gone. I had come out of the chapel where Ben and Eric were deep in discussion of whether Matisse could ever place in the front rank of French art, and had climbed part of the slope nearby where a narrow stair ran up to a small square with a dry stone fountain. Beyond that, in the French manner, was a small café with a striped awning and a few tables. From somewhere I heard Jamie's voice, saying, "I know, but what'd you do it for?" "Well, what does anybody do anything for? I wanted to." "But what would you want to *for*, Mayfred?" "Same reason you'd want to, sometime." "I wouldn't want to except to be with you." "Well, I'm right here, aren't I? You got your wish." "What I wish is you hadn't done it." It was bound to be marrying Donald that he meant. He had a frown that would come at times between his light eyebrows. I came to associate it with Mayfred. How she was running him. When they stepped around the corner of the path, holding hands (immediately dropped), I saw that frown. Did I have to dislike Mayfred, the way she was acting? The funny thing was, I didn't even know.

We lingered around the village and ate there and the bus was late, so we never made it back to the casinos. By then all Jamie seemed to like was being with Mayfred, and the frown disappeared.

Walking back to the apartment, passing darkened doorways, picking up pieces of Eric's past like fragments in the street.

". . . And then you did or didn't marry her, and she died and left you the legacy. . . ."

"Oh, we did get married, all right, the anticlimax of a number of years. I wish you could have known her. The marriage was civil. She was afraid the family would cause a row if she wanted to leave me anything. That was when she knew she hadn't long to live. Not that it was any great fortune. She had some property out near Pasquallo, a little town near here. I sold it. I had to fight them in court for a while, but it did eventually clear up."

"You've worked, too, for this other family . . . ?"

"The Rinaldi. You must have got all this from Ben, though maybe I wrote you, too. They were friends of hers. It's all connections here, like anywhere else. Right now they're all at the sea below Genoa. I'd be there too, but I'd some business in town, and you were coming. It's the export side I've helped them with. I do know English, and a little law, in spite of all."

"So it's a regular Italian life," I mused, climbing stairs, entering his salotto where I saw again the woman's picture in a silver frame. Was that her, the one who had died? "Was she blonde?" I asked, moving as curiously through his life as a child through a new room.

"Giana, you mean? No, part Sardinian, dark as they come. Oh, you mean her. No, that's Lisa, one of the Rinaldi, Paolo's sister . . . that's him up there."

I saw then, over a bookshelf, a man's enlarged photo: tweed jacket, pipe, all in the English style.

"So what else, Ella Mason?" His voice was amused at me.

"She's pretty," I said.

"Very pretty," he agreed.

We drifted out to the terrace once more.

It is time I talked about Ben and Eric, about how it was with me and with them and with the three of us.

When I look back on pictures of myself in those days, I see a girl in shorts, weighing a few pounds more than she thought she should, lowset, with a womanly cast to her body, chopped-off reddish hair, and a wide, freckled, almost boyish grin, happy to be posing between two tall boys, who happened to be her cousins, smiling their white tentative smiles. Ben and Eric. They were smart. They were fun. They did everything right. And most of all, they admitted me. I was the audience they needed.

I had to run to keep up. I read Poe because of Ben's thesis; and Wallace Stevens because Eric liked his poetry. I even, finding him referred to at times, tried to read Plato. (Ben studied Greek.) But what I did was not of much interest to them. Still, they wanted me around. Sometimes Ben made a point of "conversing" with me—what courses, what books, etc.—but he made me feel like a high school student. Eric, seldom bothering with me, was more on my level when he did. To one another, they talked at a gallop. Literature turned them on, their ideas flowed, ran back and forth like a current. I loved hearing them.

I think of little things they did. Such as Ben coming back from Sewanee with a small Roman statue, copy of something Greek—Apollo, I think—just a fragment, a head, turned aside, shoulders and a part of a back. His professor had given it to him as a special mark of favor. He set it on his favorite pigeonhole desk, to stay there, it would seem, for always, to be seen always by the rest of us—by me.

Such as Eric ordering his "secondhand but good condition" set of Henry James's novels with prefaces, saying, "I know this is corny but it's what I wanted," making space in his Mama's old upright secretary with glass-front bookshelves above, and my feeling that they'd always be there. I strummed my fingers across the spines lettered in gold. Some day I would draw down one or another to read them. No hurry.

Such as the three of us packing Mama's picnic basket (it seems my folks were the ones with the practical things—tennis court, croquet set: though Jamie's set up a badminton court at one time, it didn't take) to take to a place called Beulah Woods for a spring day in the sun near a creek where water ran clear over white limestone then plunged off into a swimming hole. Ben sat on a bedspread reading Ransom's poetry aloud and we gossiped about the latest town scandal, involving a druggist, a real estate deal where some property went cheap to him, though it seemed now that his wife had been part of the bargain, being lent out on a regular basis to the man who sold him the property. The druggist was a newcomer. A man we all knew in town had been after the property and was now threatening to sue. "Do you think it was written in the deed, so many nights a week she goes off to work the property out," Ben speculated. "Do you think they calculated the interest?" It wasn't the first time our talk had run toward sexual things; in a small town, secrets didn't often get kept for long.

More than once I'd dreamed that someday Ben or Eric one would ask me somewhere alone. A few years before the picnic, romping through our big old rambling house at twilight with Jamie, who loved playing hide-and-seek, I had run into the guest room where Ben was standing in the half-dark by the bed. He was looking at something he'd found there in the twilight, some book or ornament, and I mistook him for Jamie and threw my arms around him crying, "Caught you!" We fell over the bed together and rolled for a moment before I knew then it was Ben, but knew I'd wanted it to be; or didn't I really know all along it was Ben, but pretended I didn't? Without a doubt when his weight came down over me, I knew I wanted it to be there. I felt his body, for a moment so entirely present, draw back and up. Then he stood, turning away, leaving. "You better grow up," was what I think he said. Lingering feelings made me want to seek him out the next day or so. Sulky, I wanted to say, "I *am* growing up." But another time he said, "We're cousins, you know."

Eric for a while dated a girl from one of the next towns. She used to ask him over to parties and they would drive to Birmingham sometimes, but he never had her over to Martinsville. Ben, that summer we went to Europe, let it be known he was writing and getting letters from a girl at Sewanee. She was a pianist named Sylvia. "You want to hear music played softly in the 'drawing room,'" I clowned at him. "'Just a song at twilight.'" "Now, Ella Mason, you behave," he said.

I had boys to take me places. I could flirt and I got a rush at dances and I could go off the next to the highest diving board and was good in doubles. Once I went on strike from Ben and Eric for over a week. I was going with that boy from Tuscaloosa and I had begun to think he was the right one and get ideas. Why fool around with my cousins? But I missed them. I went around one afternoon. They were talking out on the porch. The record player was going inside, something of Berlioz that Ben was onto. They waited till it finished before they'd speak to me. Then Eric, smiling from the depths of a chair, said, "Hey, Ella Mason"; and Ben, getting up to unlatch the screen, said, "Ella Mason, where on earth have you been?" I'd have to think they were glad.

Ben was dark. He had straight, dark brown hair, dry-looking in the sun, growing thick at the brow, but flat at night when he put a damp comb through it, and darker. It fit close to his head like a monk's hood. He wore large glasses with lucite rims. Eric had sandy hair, softly appealing and always mussed. He didn't bother much with his looks. In the day they scuffed around in open-throated shirts and loafers, crinkled seersucker pants, or shorts; tennis shoes when they played were always dirty white. At night, when they cleaned up, it was still casual but fresh laundered. But when they dressed, in shirts and ties with an inch of white cuff laid crisp against their brown hands: they were splendid!

"Ella Mason," Eric said, "if that boy doesn't like you, he's not worth worrying about." He had put his arm around me coming out of the picture show. I ought to drop it, a tired romance, but couldn't quite. Not till that moment. Then I did.

"Those boys," said Mr. Felix Gresham from across the street. "Getting time they started earning something 'stead of all time settin' around." He used to come over and tell Mama everything he thought, though no kin to anybody. "I reckon there's time enough for that," Mama said. "Now going off to France," said Mr. Gresham, as though that spoke for itself. "Not just France," Mama said, "England, too, and Italy." "Ain't nothing in France," said Mr. Gresham. "I don't know if there is or not," said Mama, "I never have been." She meant that to hush him up, but the truth is, Mr. Gresham might have been to France in World War I. I never thought to ask. Now he's dead.

Eric and Ben. I guess I was in love with both of them. Wouldn't it be nice, I used to think, if one were my brother and the other my brother's best friend, and then I could just quietly and without so much as thinking about it find myself marrying the friend (now which would I choose for which?) and so we could go on forever? At other times, frustrated, I suppose, by their never changing toward me, I would plan on doing something spectacular, finding a Yankee, for instance, so impressive and brilliant and established in some important career, that they'd have to listen to him, learn what he was doing and what he thought and what he knew, while I sat silent and poised throughout the conversation, the cat that ate the cream, though of course too polite to show satisfaction. Fantasies, one by one, would sing to me for a little while.

At Christmas vacation before our summer abroad, just before Ben got accepted to Yale and just while Eric was getting bored with law school, there was a quarrel, I didn't know the details, but they went back to school with things still unsettled among us. I got friendly with Jamie then, more than before. He was down at Tuscaloosa, like me. It's when I got to know Mayfred better, on weekends at home. Why bother with Eric and Ben? It had been a poor season. One letter came from Ben and I answered it, saying that I had come to like Jamie and Mayfred so much; their parents were always giving parties and we were having a grand time.

In answer I got a long, serious letter about time passing and what it did, how we must remember that what we had was always going to be a part of ourselves. That he thought of jonquils coming up now and how they always looked like jonquils, just absent for a time, and how the roots stayed the same. He was looking forward, he said, to spring and coming home.

Just for fun I sat down and wrote him a love letter. I said he was a fool and a dunce and didn't he know while he was writing out all these ideas that I was a live young woman and only a second cousin and that through the years while he was talking about Yeats, Proust, and Edgar Allan Poe that I was longing to have my arms around him the way they were when we fell over in the bed that twilight romping with Jamie and why in the ever-loving world couldn't he see me as I was, a live girl, instead of a cousin-spinster, listening to him and Eric make brilliant conversation? Was he trying to turn me into an old maid? Wasn't he supposed, at least, to be intelligent? So why couldn't he see what I was really like? But I didn't mail it. I didn't because, for one thing, I doubted that I meant it. Suppose, by a miracle, Ben said, "You're right, every word." What about Eric? I started dating somebody new at school. I tore the letter up.

Eric called soon after. He just thought it would do him good to say hello. Studying for long hours wasn't his favorite sport. He'd heard from Ben, the hard feelings were over, he was ready for spring holidays already. I said, "I hope to be in town, but I'm really not sure." A week later I forgot a date with the boy I thought I liked. The earlier one showed up again. Hadn't I liked him, after all? How to be sure? I bought a new straw hat, white-and-navy for Easter, with a ribbon down the back, and came home.

Just before Easter, Jamie's parents gave a party for us all. There had been a cold snap and we were all inside, with purplish-red punch, and a buffet laid out. Jamie's folks had this relatively new house, with new carpets and furnishings and the family dismay ran to what a big mortgage they were carrying and how it would never be paid out. Meantime his mother (no kin) looked completely unworried as she arranged tables that seemed to have been copied from magazines. I came alone, having had to help Papa with some typing, and so saw Ben and Eric for the first time, though we'd talked on the phone.

Eric looked older, a little worn. I saw something drawn in the way he laughed, a sort of restraint about him. He was standing aside and looking at a point where no one and nothing were. But he came to when I spoke and gave that laugh and then a hug. Ben was busy "conversing" with a couple in town who had somebody at Sewanee, too. He smoked a pipe now, I noticed, smelly when we hugged. He had soon come to join Eric and me, and it was at that moment, the three of us standing together for the first time since Christmas, and change having been mentioned at least once by way of Ben's letter, that I knew some tension was mounting, bringing obscure moments with it. We turned to one another but did not speak readily about anything. I had thought I was the only one, sensitive to something imagined—having "vapors," as somebody called it—but I could tell we were all at a loss for some reason none of us knew. Because if Ben and Eric knew, articulate as they were, they would have said so. In the silence so suddenly fallen, something was ticking.

Maybe, I thought, they just don't like Martinsville anymore. They always said that parties were dull and squirmed out of them when they could. I lay awake thinking, They'll move on soon; I won't see them again.

It was the next morning Eric called and we all grasped for Europe like the drowning, clinging to what we could.

After Monte Carlo, we left France by train and came down to Florence. The streets were narrow there and we joked about going single file like Indians. "What I need is moccasins," said Jamie, who was always blundering over the uneven paving stones. At the Uffizi, the second day, Eric, in a trance before Botticelli, fell silent. Could we ever get him to speak again? Hardly a word. Five in number, we leaned over the balustrades along the Arno, all silent then from the weariness of sightseeing, and the heat; and there I heard it once more, the ticking of something hidden among us. Was it to deny it we decided to take the photograph? We had taken a lot, but this one, I think, was special. I have it still. It was in the Piazza Signoria.

"Which monument?" we kept asking. Ben wanted Donatello's lion, and Eric the steps of the Old Palace, Jamie wanted Cosimo I on his horse. I wanted the Perseus of Cellini, and Mayfred the Rape of the Sabines. So Ben made straws out of toothpicks and we drew and Mayfred won. We got lined up and Ben framed us. Then we had to find somebody, a slim Italian boy as it turned out, to snap us for a few hundred lire. It seemed we were proving something serious and good, and smiled with our straight family smiles, Jamie with his arm around Mayfred, and she with her smart new straw sun hat held to the back of her head, and me between Ben and Eric, arms entwined. A photo outlasts everybody, and this one with the frantic scene behind us, the moving torso of the warrior holding high the prey while we smiled our ordinary smiles—it was a period, the end of a phase.

Not that the photograph itself caused the end of anything. Donald Bailey caused it. He telephoned the pensione that night from Atlanta to say he was in the hospital, gravely ill, something they might have to operate for any day, some sort of brain tumor was what they were afraid of. Mayfred said she'd come.

We all got stunned. Ben and Eric and I straggled off together while she and Jamie went to the upstairs sitting room and sat in the corner. "Honest to God," said Eric, "I just didn't know Donald Bailey had a brain." "He had headaches," said Ben. "Oh, I knew he had a head," said Eric, "we could see that."

By night it was settled. Mayfred would fly back from Rome. Once again she got us to promise secrecy—how she did that I don't know, the youngest one and yet not even Ben could prevail on her one way or the other. By now she had spent most of her money. Donald, we knew, was rich; he came of a rich family and had, furthermore, money of his own. So if she wanted to fly back from Rome, the ticket, already purchased, would be waiting for her. Mayfred got to be privileged, in my opinion, because none of us knew her family too well. Her father was a blood cousin but not too highly regarded—he was thought to be a rather silly man who "traveled" and dealt with "all sorts of people"—and her mother was from "off," a Georgia girl, fluttery. If it had been my folks and if I had started all this wild marrying and flying off, Ben would have been on the phone to Martinsville by sundown.

One thing in the Mayfred departure that went without question: Jamie would go to Rome to see her off. We couldn't have sealed him in or held him with ropes. He had got on to something new in Italy, or so I felt, because where before then had we seen in gallery after gallery, strong men, young and old, with enraptured eyes, enthralled before a woman's painted image, wanting nothing? What he had gotten was an idea of devotion. It fit him. It suited. He would do anything for Mayfred and want nothing. If she had got pregnant and told him she was a virgin, he would have sworn to it before the Inquisition. It could positively alarm you for him to see him satisfied with the feelings he had found. Long after I went to bed, he was at the door or in the corridor with Mayfred, discussing baggage and calling a hotel in Rome to get a reservation for when he saw her off.

Mayfred had bought a lot of things. She had an eye for what she could wear with what, and she would pick up pieces of this and that for putting costumes and accessories together. She had to get some extra luggage and it was Jamie, of course, who promised to see it sent safely to her, through a shipping company in Rome. His two thousand dollars was coming in handy, was all I could think.

Hot, I couldn't sleep, so I went out in the sitting room to find a magazine. Ben was up. The three men usually took a large room together, taking turns for the extra cot. Ever since we got the news, Ben had had what Eric called his "family mood." Now he called me over. "I can't let those kids go down there alone," he said. "They seem like children to me—and Jamie . . . about all he can say is Grazie and Quanto." "Then let's all go," I said, "I've given up sleeping for tonight anyway." "Eric's hooked on Florence," said Ben. "Can't you tell? He counts the cypresses on every knoll. He can spot a Della Robbia a block off. If I make him leave three days early, he'll never forgive me. Besides, our reservations in that hotel can't be changed. We called for Jamie and they're full; he's staying third-class somewhere till we all come. I don't mind doing that. Then we'll all meet up just the way we planned, have our week in Rome, and go catch the boat from Naples." "I think they could make it on their own," I said, "it's just that you'd worry every minute." He grinned; "our father for the duration," was what Eric called him. "I know I'm that way," he said.

Another thing was that Ben had been getting little caches of letters at various points along our trek from his girl friend Sylvia, the one he'd been dating up at Sewanee. She was getting a job in New York that fall which would be convenient to Yale. She wrote a spidery hand on thick rippled stationery, cream colored, and had promised in her last dispatch, received in Paris, to write to Rome. Ben could have had an itch for that. But mainly he was that way, careful and concerned. He had in mind what we all felt, that just as absolutely anything could be done by Mayfred, so could absolutely anything happen to her. He also knew what we all knew, that if the Colosseum started falling on her, Jamie would leap bodily under the rocks.

At two o'clock in the morning it was too much for me to think about. I went to bed and was so exhausted, I didn't even hear Mayfred leave.

I woke up about ten with a low tapping on my door. It was Eric. "Is this the sleep of the just?" he asked me, as I opened the door. The air in the corridor was fresh: it must have rained in the night. No one was about. All the guests, I supposed, were well out into the day's routine, seeing what next tour was on the list. On a trip you were always planning something. Ben planned for us. He kept a little notebook.

Standing in my doorway alone with Eric, in a loose robe with a cool morning breeze and my hair not even combed, I suddenly laughed. Eric laughed, too. "I'm glad they're gone," he said, and looked past my shoulder.

I dressed and went out with him for some breakfast, cappucino and croissants at a café in the Signoria. We didn't talk much. It was terrible, in the sense of the Mason Skinner Marshall and Phillips sense of family, even to think you were glad they were gone, let alone say it. I took Eric's silence as one of his ironies, what he was best at. He would say, for instance, if you were discussing somebody's problem that wouldn't ever have any solution, "It's time somebody died." There wasn't much to say after that. Another time, when his daddy got into a rage with a next-door neighbor over their property line, Eric said, "You'd better marry her." Once he put things in an extreme light, nobody could talk about them anymore. Saying "I'm glad they're gone," was like that.

But it was a break. I thought of the way I'd been seeing them. How Jamie's becoming had been impressing me, every day more. How Mayfred was a kind of spirit, grown bigger than life. How Ben's dominance now seemed not worrisome, but princely, his heritage. We were into a Renaissance of ourselves, I wanted to say, but was afraid they wouldn't see it the way I did. Only Eric had eluded me. What was he becoming? For once he didn't have to discuss Poe's idea of women, or the southern code of honor, or Henry James's views of France and England.

As for me, I was, at least, sure that my style had changed. I had bought my little linen blouses and loose skirts, my sandals and braided silver bracelets. "That's great on you!" Mayfred had cried. "Now try this one!" On the streets, Italians passed me too close not to be noticed; they murmured musically in my ear, saying I didn't know just what; waiters leaned on my shoulder to describe dishes of the day.

Eric and I wandered across the river, following narrow streets lined with great stone palaces, seeing them open into small piazzas whose names were not well known. We had lunch in a friendly place with a curtain of thin twisted metal sticks in the open door, an amber-colored dog lying on the marble floor near the serving table. We ordered favorite things without looking at the menu. We drank white wine. "This is fun," I suddenly said. He turned to me. Out of his private distance, he seemed to be looking down at me. "I think so, too."

He suddenly switched on to me, like somebody searching and finding with the lens of a camera. He began to ask me things. What did you think of that, Ella Mason? What about this, Ella Mason? Ella Mason, did you think Ben was right when he said . . . ? I could hardly swing on to what was being asked of me, thick and fast. But he seemed to like my answers, actually to listen. Not that all those years I'd been dumb as a stone. I had prattled quite a lot. It's just that they never treated me one to one, the way Eric was doing now. We talked for nearly an hour, then, with no one left in the restaurant but us, stopped as suddenly as we'd started. Eric said, "That's a pretty dress."

The sun was strong outside. The dog was asleep near the door. Even the one remaining waiter was drowsing on his feet. It was the shutting-up time for everything and we went out into streets blanked out with metal shutters. We hugged the shady side and went single file back to home base, as we'd come to call it, wherever we stayed.

A Vespa snarled by and I stepped into a cool courtyard to avoid it. I found myself in a large yawning mouth, mysterious as a cave, shadowy, with the trickling sound of a fountain and the glimmer in the depths of water running through ferns and moss. Along the interior of the street wall, fragments of ancient sculpture, found, I guess, when they'd built the palazzo, had been set into the masonry. One was a horse, neck and shoulder, another an arm holding a shield, and a third at about my height the profile of a woman, a nymph or some such. Eric stopped to look at each, for as Ben had said, Eric loved everything there, and then he said, "Come here, Ella Mason." I stood where he wanted, by the little sculptured relief, and he took my face and turned it to look at it closer, then with a strong hand (I remembered tennis), he pressed my face against the stone face and held it for a moment. The stone bit into my flesh and that was the first time that Eric, bending deliberately to do so, kissed me on the mouth. He had held one side of me against the wall, so that I couldn't raise my arm to him, and the other arm was pinned down by his elbow, the hand that pressed my face into the stone was that one, so that I couldn't move closer to him, as I wanted to do, and when he dropped away suddenly, turned on his heel and walked rapidly away, I could only hasten to follow, my voice gone, my pulses all throbbing together. I remember my anger, the old dreams about him and Ben stirred to life again, thinking, *If he thinks he can just walk away,* and knowing with anger, too, *It's got to be now,* as if in the walled land of kinship, thicker in our illustrious connection than any fortress in Europe, a door had creaked open at last. Eric, Eric, Eric. I'm always seeing your retreating heels, how they looked angry; but why? It was worth coming for, after thirty years, to ask that. . . .

"That day you kissed me in the street, the first time," I asked him. Night on the terrace; a bottle of chianti between our chairs. "You walked away. Were you angry? Your heels looked angry. I can see them still."

"The trip in the first place," he said, "it had to do with you partly. Maybe you didn't understand that. We were outward bound, leaving you, a sister in a sense. We'd talked about it."

"I adored you so," I said. "I think I was less than a sister, more like a dog."

"For a little while you weren't either one." He found my hand in the dark. "It was a wonderful little while."

Memories: Eric in the empty corridor of the pensione. How Italy folds up and goes to sleep from two to four. His not looking back for me, going straight to his door. The door closing, but no key turning and me turning the door handle and stepping in. And he at the window already with his back to me and how he heard the sliding latch on the door—I slid it with my hands behind me—heard it click shut, and turned. His face and mine, what we knew. Betraying Ben.

  :   Walking by the Arno, watching a white and green scull stroking by into the twilight, the rower a boy or girl in white and green, growing dimmer to the rhythm of the long oars, vanishing into arrow shape, then pencil thickness, then movement without substance, on. . . .

  :   A trek the next afternoon through twisted streets to a famous chapel. Sitting quiet in a cloister, drinking in the symmetry, the silence. Holding hands. "D for Donatello," said Eric. "D for Della Robbia," I said. "M for Michelangelo," he continued. "M for Medici." "L for Leonardo." "I can't think of an L," I gave up. "Lumbago. There's an old master." "Worse than Jamie." We were always going home again.

  :   Running into the manager of the pensione one morning in the corridor. He'd solemnly bowed to us and kissed my hand. "Bella ragazza," he remarked. "The way life ought to be," said Eric. I thought we might be free forever, but from what?

At the train station waiting the departure we were supposed to take for Rome, "Why do we have to go?" I pleaded. "Why can't we just stay here?"

"Use your common sense, Ella Mason."

"I don't have any."

He squeezed my shoulder. "We'll get by all right," he said. "That is, if you don't let on."

I promised not to. Rather languidly I watched the landscape slide past as we glided south. I would obey Eric, I thought, for always. "Once I wrote a love letter to you," I said. "I wrote it at night by candlelight at home one summer. I tore it up."

"You told me that," he recalled, "but you said you couldn't remember if it was to me or Ben."

"I just remembered," I said. "It was you. . . ."

"Why did we ever leave?" I asked Eric, in the dead of the night, a blackness now. "Why did we ever decide we had to go to Rome?"

"I didn't think of it as even a choice," he said. "But at that point, how could I know what was there, ahead?"

We got off the train feeling small—at least, I did. Ben was standing there, looking around him, tall, searching for us, then seeing. But no Jamie. Something to ask. I wondered if he'd gone back with Mayfred. "No, he's running around Rome." The big smooth station, echoing, open to the warm day. "Hundreds of churches," Ben went on. "Millions. He's checking them off." He helped us in a taxi with the skill of somebody who'd lived in Rome for ten years, and gave the address. "He's got to do something now that Mayfred's gone. It's getting like something he might take seriously, is all. Finding out what Catholics believe. He's either losing all his money, or falling in love, or getting religion."

"He didn't lose any money," said Eric. "He made some."

"Well, it's the same thing," said Ben, always right and not wanting to argue with us. He seemed a lot older than the two of us, at least to me. Ben was tall.

We had mail in Rome; Ben brought it to the table that night. I read Mama's aloud to them: "When I think of you children over there, I count you all like my own chickens out in the yard, thinking I've got to go out in the dark and make sure the gate's locked because not a one ought to get out of there. To me, you're all my own, and thinking of chickens is my way of saying prayers for you to be safe at home again."

"You'd think we were off in a war," said Eric.

"It's a bold metaphor," said Ben, pouring wine for us, "but that never stopped Cousin Charlotte."

I wanted to giggle at Mama, as I usually did, but instead my eyes filled with tears, surprising me, and a minute more and I would have dared to snap at Ben. But Eric, who had got some mail, too, abruptly got up and left the table. I almost ran after him, but intent on what I'd promised about not letting on to Ben, I stayed and finished dinner. He had been pale, white. Ben thought he might be sick. He didn't return. We didn't know.

Jamie and Ben finally went to bed. "He'll come back when he wants to," said Ben.

I waited till their door had closed, and then, possessed, I crept out to the front desk. "Signor Mason," I said, "the one with the capelli leggero—" My Italian came from the dictionary straight to the listener. I found out later I had said that Eric's hair didn't weigh much. Still, they understood. He had taken a room, someone who spoke English explained. He wanted to be alone. I said he might be sick, and I guess they could read my face because I was guided by a porter in a blue working jacket and cloth shoes, into a labyrinth. Italian buildings, I knew by now, are constructed like dreams. There are passages departing from central hallways, stairs that twist back upon themselves, dark silent doors. My guide stopped before one. "Ecco," he said and left. I knocked softly, and the door eventually cracked open. "Oh, it's you." "Eric. Are you all right? I didn't know. . . ."

He opened the door a little wider. "Ella Mason—" he began. Maybe he was sick. I caught his arm. The whole intensity of my young life in that moment shook free of everything but Eric. It was as though I'd traveled miles to find him. I came inside and we kissed and then I was sitting apart from him on the edge of the bed and he in a chair, and a letter, official looking, the top of the envelope torn open in a ragged line, lay on a high black-marble-topped table with bowed legs, between us. He said to read it and I did, and put it back where I found it.

It said that Eric had failed his law exams. That in view of the family connection with the university (his father had gone there and some cousin was head of the board of trustees), a special meeting had been held to grant his repeating the term's work so as to graduate in the fall, but the evidences of his negligence were too numerous and the vote had gone against it. I remember saying something like, "Anybody can fail exams—" as I knew people who had, but knew also that those people weren't "us," not one of our class or connection, not kin to the brilliant Ben, nor nephew of a governor, nor descended from a great Civil War general.

"All year long," he said, "I've been acting like a fool, as if I expected to get by. This last semester especially. It all seemed too easy. It is easy. It's easy and boring. I was fencing blindfold with somebody so far beneath me it wasn't worth the trouble to look at him. The only way to keep the interest up was to see how close I could come without damage. Well, I ran right into it, head on. God, does it serve me right. I'd read books Ben was reading, follow his interests, instead of boning over law. But I wanted the degree. Hot damn, I wanted it!"

"Another school," I said. "You can transfer credits and start over."

"This won't go away."

"Everybody loves you," I faltered, adding, "Especially me."

He almost laughed, at my youngness, I guess, but then said, "Ella Mason," as gently as feathers falling, and came to hold me a while, but not like before, the way we'd been. We sat down on the bed and then fell back on it and I could hear his heart's steady thumping under his shirt. But it wasn't the beat of a lover's heart just then; it was more like the echo of a distant bell or the near march of a clock; and I fell to looking over his shoulder.

It was a curious room, one I guess they wouldn't have rented to anybody if Rome hadn't been, as they told us, so full. The shutters were closed on something that suggested more of a courtyard than the outside as no streak or glimmer of light came through, and the bed was huge, with a great dark tall rectangle of a headboard and a footboard only slightly lower. There were brass sconces set ornamentally around the moldings, looking down, cupids and fawns and smiling goat faces, with bulbs concealed in them, though the only light came from the one dim lamp on the bedside table. There were heavy, dark engravings of Rome—

by Piranesi or somebody like that—the avenues, the monuments, the river. And one panel of small pictures in a series showed some familiar scenes in Florence.

My thoughts, unable to reach Eric's, kept wandering off tourist-fashion among the myth faces peeking from the sconces, laughing down, among the walks of Rome—the arched bridge over the Tiber where life-sized angels stood poised; the rise of the Palatine, mysterious among trees; the horseman on the Campidoglio, his hand outstretched; and Florence, beckoning still. I couldn't keep my mind at any one set with all such around me, and Eric, besides, had gone back to the table and was writing a letter on hotel stationery. When my caught breath turned to a little cry, he looked up and said, "It's my problem, Ella Mason. Just let me handle it." He came to stand by me, and pressed my head against him, then lifted my face by the chin. "Don't go talking about it. Promise." I promised.

I wandered back through the labyrinth, thinking I'd be lost in there forever like a Poe lady. Damn Ben, I thought, he's too above it all for anybody to fall in love or fail an examination. I'm better off lost, at this rate. So thinking, I turned a corner and stepped out into the hotel lobby.

It was Jamie's and Ben's assumption that Eric had picked up some girl and gone home with her. I never told them better. Let them think that.

"Your Mama wrote you a letter about some chickens once, how she counted children like counting chickens," Eric said, thirty years later. "Do you remember that?"

We fell to remembering Mama. "There's nobody like her," I said. "She has long talks with Daddy. They started a year or so after he died. I wish I could talk to him."

"What would you say?"

"I'd ask him to look up Howard. See'f he's doing all right."

"Your husband?" Eric wasn't that sure of the name.

I guess joking about your husband's death isn't quite the thing. I met Howard on a trip to Texas after we got home from abroad. I was visiting my roommate. Whatever else Eric did for me, our time together had made me ready for more. I pined for him alone, but what I looked was ripe and ready for practically anybody. So Howard said. He was a widower with a Texas-size fortune. When he said I looked like a good breeder, I didn't even get mad. That's how he knew I'd do. Still, it took a while. I kept wanting Eric, wanting my old dream: my brilliant cousins, princely, cavalier.

Howard and I had two sons, in their twenties now. Howard got killed in a jeep accident out on his cattle ranch. Don't think I didn't get married again, to a wild California boy ten years younger. It lasted six months exactly.

"What about that other one?" Eric asked me. "Number two."

I had gotten the divorce papers the same day they called to say Howard's tombstone had arrived. "Well, you know, Eric, I always was a little bit crazy."

"You thought he was cute."

"I guess so."

"You and I," said Eric, smooth as silk into the deep silent darkness that now was ours—even the towers seemed to have folded up and gone home—"we never worked it out, did we?"

"I never knew if you really wanted to. I did, God knows. I wouldn't marry Howard for over a year because of you."

"I stayed undecided about everything. One thing that's not is a marrying frame of mind."

"Then you left for Europe."

"I felt I'd missed the boat for everywhere else. War service, then that law school thing. It was too late for me. And nothing was of interest. I could move but not with much conviction. I felt for you—maybe more than you know—but you were moving on already. You know, Ella Mason, you never are still."

"But you could have told me that!"

"I think I did, one way or another. You sat still and fidgeted." He laughed.

It's true that energy is my middle name.

The lights along the river were dim and so little was moving past by now they seemed fixed and distant, stars from some long dead galaxy maybe. I think I slept. Then I heard Eric.

"I think back so often to the five of us—you and Ben, Jamie and Mayfred and me. There was something I could never get out of mind. You remember when we were planning everything about Europe Europe Europe, before we left, and you'd all come over to my house and we'd sit out on the side porch, listening to Ben mainly but with Jamie asking some questions, like, 'Do they have bathtubs like us?' Remember that? You would snuggle down in one of those canvas chairs like a sling, and Ben was in the big armchair—Daddy's—and Jamie sort of sprawled around on the couch among the travel folders, when we heard the front gate scrape on the sidewalk and heard the way it would clatter when it closed. A warm night and the streetlight filtering in patterns through the trees and shrubs and a smell of honeysuckle from where it was all baled up on the yard fence, and a cape jessamine outside, I remember that, too—white flowers in among the leaves. And steps on the walk. They stopped, then they walked again, and Ben got up (I should have) and unlatched the screen. If you didn't latch the screen it wouldn't shut. Mayfred came in. Jamie said, 'Why'd you stop on the walk, Mayfred?' She said, 'There was this toadfrog. I almost stepped on him.' Then she was among us, walking in, one of us. I was sitting back in the corner, watching, and I felt, If I live to be a thousand, I'll never feel more love than I do this minute. Love of these, my blood, and this place, here. I could close my eyes for years and hear the gate scrape, the steps pause, the door latch and unlatch, hear her say, 'There was this toadfrog. . . .' I would want literally to embrace that one minute, hold it forever."

"But you're not there," I said, into the dark: "You're here. Where we were. You chose it."

"There's no denying that," was all he answered.

We had sailed from Naples, a sad day under mist, with Vesuvius hardly visible and damp clinging to everything—the end of summer. We couldn't even make out the outlines of the ship, an Italian-line monster from those days, called the *Independence*. It towered white over us and we tunneled in. The crossing was rainy and drab. Crossed emotions played around amongst us, while Ben, noble and aware, tried to be our mast. He read aloud to us, discussed, joked, tried to get our attention.

Jamie wanted to argue about Catholicism. It didn't suit Ben for him to drift that way. Ben was headed toward Anglican belief: that's what his Sylvia was, not to mention T. S. Eliot. But Jamie had met an American Jesuit from Indiana in Rome and chummed around with him; they'd even gone to the beach. "You're wrong about that," I heard him tell Ben. "I'm going to prove it by Father Rogers when we get home."

I worried about Eric; I longed for Eric; I strolled the decks and stood by

Eric at the rail. He looked with gray eyes out at the gray sea. He said: "You know, Ella Mason, I don't give a damn if Jamie joins the Catholic Church or not." "Me either," I agreed. We kissed in the dark beneath the life-boats, and made love once in the cabin while Ben and Jamie were at the movies, but in a furtive way, as if the grown people were at church. Ben read aloud to us from a book on Hadrian's Villa where we'd all been. There was a half-day of sun.

I went to the pool to swim, and up came Jamie, out of the water. He was skinny, string beans and spaghetti. "Ella Mason," he said, in his dark croak of a voice, "I'll never be the same again." I was tired of all of them, even Jamie. "Then gain some weight," I snapped, and went pretty off the diving board.

Ben knew about the law school thing. The first day out, coming from the writing lounge, I saw Eric and Ben standing together in a corner of an enclosed deck. Ben had a letter in his hand, and just from one glance I recognized the stationery of the hotel where we'd stayed in Rome and knew it was the letter Eric had been writing. I heard Ben: "You say it's not important, but I know it is—I knew that last Christmas." And Eric, "Think what you like, it's not to me." And Ben, "What you feel about it, that's not what matters. There's a right way of looking at it. Only to make you see it." And Eric, "You'd better give up; you never will."

What kept me in my tracks was something multiple, yet single, the way a number can contain powers and elements that have gone into its making, and can be unfolded, opened up, nearly forever. Ambition and why some had it, success and failure and what the difference was, and why you had to notice it at all. These matters, back and forth across the net, were what was going on.

What had stopped me in the first place, though, and chilled me, was that they sounded angry. I knew they had quarreled last Christmas; was this why? It must have been. Ben's anger was attack and Eric's self-defense, defiance. Hadn't they always been like brothers? Yes, and they were standing so, intent, a little apart, in hot debate, like two officers locked in different plans of attack at dawn, stubbornly held to the point of fury. Ben's position, based on rightness, classical and firm. Enforced by what he was. And Eric's wrong, except in and for himself, for holding on to himself. How to defend that? He couldn't, but he did. And equally. They were just looking up and seeing me, and nervous at my intrusion I stepped across the high shipboard sill to the deck, missed clearing it and fell sprawling. "Oh, Ella Mason!" they cried at once and picked me up, the way they always had.

One more thing I remember from that ship. It was Ben, finding me one night after dinner alone in the lounge. Everyone was below: we were docking in the morning. He sat down and lighted his pipe. "It's all passed so fast, don't you think?" he said. There was such a jumble in my mind still, I didn't answer. All I could hear was Eric saying, after we'd made love: "It's got to stop now; I've got to find some shape to things. There was promise, promises. You've got to see we're saying they're worthless, that nothing matters." What did matter to me, except Eric? "I wish I'd never come," I burst out at Ben, childish, hurting him, I guess. How much did Ben know? He never said. He came close and put his arm around me. "You're the sister I never had," he said. "I hope you change your mind about it." I said I was sorry and snuffled a while, into his shoulder. When I looked up, I saw his love. So maybe he did know, and forgave us. He kissed my forehead.

At the New York pier, who should show up but Mayfred.

She was crisp in black and white, her long blonde hair wind shaken, her laughter a wholesome joy. "Y'all look just terrible," she told us with a friendly giggle, and as usual made us straighten up, tuck our tummies in and look like quality. Jamie forgot religion, and Eric quit worrying over a missing bag, and Ben said, "Well, look who's here!" "How's Donald?" I asked her. I figured he was either all right or dead. The first was true. They didn't have to do a brain tumor operation; all he'd had was a pinched nerve at the base of his cortex. "What's a cortex?" Jamie asked. "It sounds too personal to inquire," said Eric, and right then they brought him his bag.

On the train home, Mayfred rode backwards in our large drawing room compartment (courtesy of Donald Bailey) and the landscape, getting more southern every minute, went rocketing past. "You can't guess how I spent my time when Donald was in the hospital. Nothing to do but sit."

"Working crossword puzzles," said Jamie.

"Crocheting," said Eric, provoking a laugh.

"Reading Vogue," said Ben.

"All wrong! I read Edgar Allan Poe! What's more, I memorized that poem! That one Ben wrote on. You know? That 'Ulalume'!"

Everybody laughed but Ben, and Mayfred was laughing, too, her grand girlish sputters, innocent as sun and water, her beautiful large white teeth, even as a cover girl's. Ben, courteously at the end of the sofa, smiled faintly. It was best not to believe this was true.

> "'The skies they were ashen and sober;
> The leaves they were crisped and sere—
> The leaves they were withering and sere:
> It was the night in the lonesome October
> Of my most immemorial year. . . .'"

"By God, she's done it," said Ben.

At that point Jamie and I began to laugh, and Eric, who had at first looked quizzical, started laughing, too. Ben said, "Oh, cut it out, Mayfred," but she said, "No, sir, I'm not! I *did* all that. I know *every* word! Just wait, I'll show you." She went right on, full speed, to the "ghoul-haunted woodland of Weir."

Back as straight as a ramrod, Ben left the compartment. Mayfred stopped. An hour later, when he came back, she started again. But it wasn't till she got to Psyche "Uplifting her finger" (Mayfred lifted hers) saying, "Ah, fly!—let us fly!—for we must," and all that about the "tremulous light, the crystalline light," etc., that Ben gave up and joined in the general merriment. She actually did know it, every word. He followed along open-mouthed through "Astarte" and "Sybillic," and murmured, "Oh, my God" when she got to

> "'Ulalume—Ulalume—
> 'Tis the vault of thy lost Ulalume!'"

because she let go in a wail like a hound's bugle and the conductor, who was passing, looked in to see if we were all right.

We rolled into Chattanooga in the best of humor and filed off the train into the waiting arms of my parents, Eric's parents, and selected members from Ben's and Jamie's families. There was nobody from Mayfred's, but they'd sent word. They all kept checking us over, as though we might need washing, or might have gotten scarred some way. "Just promise me one thing!" Mama kept saying, just about to cry. "Don't y'all ever go away again, you hear? Not all of you! Just promise you won't do it! Promise me right now!"

I guess we must have promised, the way she was begging us to.

Ben married his Sylvia, with her pedigree and family estate in Connecticut. He's a big professor, lecturing in literature, up East. Jamie married a Catholic girl from West Virginia. He works in her father's firm and has sired a happy lot of kids. Mayfred went to New York after she left Donald and works for a big fashion house. She's been in and out of marriages, from time to time.

And Eric and I are sitting holding hands on a terrace in far-off Italy. Midnight struck long ago, and we know it. We are sitting there, talking, in the pitch-black dark.

THE ARTIFICIAL FAMILY
Anne Tyler

THE first full sentence that Mary ever said to him was, "Did you know I have a daughter?" Toby was asking her to dinner. He had just met her at a party—a long-haired girl in a floor-length gingham dress—and the invitation was instant, offered out of desperation because she was already preparing to leave and he wasn't sure he could ever find her again. Now, how did her daughter enter into this? Was she telling him that she was married? Or that she couldn't go out in the evenings? "No," said Toby. "I didn't know."

"Well, now you do," she said. Then she wrote her address down for him and left, and Toby spent the rest of the evening clutching the scrap of paper in his pocket for fear of losing it.

The daughter was five years old. Her name was Samantha, and it suited her: she was an old-fashioned child with two thick braids and a solemn face. When she and her mother stood side by side, barefoot, wearing their long dresses, they might have been about to climb onto a covered wagon. They presented a solid front. Their eyes were a flat, matching blue. "Well!" Toby would say, after he and Samantha knew each other better. "Shall we all *three* go somewhere? Shall we take a picnic lunch? Visit the zoo?" Then the blue would break up into darker colors, and they would smile—but it was the mother who smiled first. The child was the older of the two. She took longer to think things over.

They would go to the Baltimore Zoo and ride the tiny passenger train. Sitting three abreast on the narrow seat—Toby's arm around Mary, Samantha scrunched between them—they rattled past dusty-looking deer fenced in among the woods, through a tunnel where the younger children screamed, alongside a parade of wooden cartoon animals which everyone tried to identify. "That's Bullmoose! There's Bugs Bunny!" Only Samantha said nothing. She had no television set. Bugs Bunny was a stranger to her. She sat very straight, with her hands clasped between her knees in her long skirt, and Toby looked down at her and tried to piece out her father from the curve of her cheek and the tilt of her nose. Her eyes were her mother's, but surely that rounded chin came from her father's side. Had her father had red hair? Was that what gave Samantha's brown braids that coppery sheen? He didn't feel that he could ask straight out because Mary had slammed a door on the subject. All she said was that she had run away with Samantha after two years of marriage. Then once, discussing some earlier stage in Samantha's life, she pulled out a wallet photo to show him: Samantha as a baby, in her mother's lap. "Look at you!" Toby said. "You had your hair up! You had lipstick on! You were wearing a sweater and skirt! Look at Samantha in her party dress!" The photo stunned him, but Mary hardly noticed. "Oh, yes," she said, closing her wallet, "I was very straight back then." And that was the last time she mentioned her marriage. Toby never saw the husband, or heard anything about him. There seemed to be no visiting arrangements for the child.

Mornings Mary worked in an art gallery. She had to leave Samantha with a teenage babysitter after kindergarten closed for the summer. "Summers! I hate them" she said. "All the time I'm at work I'm wondering how Samantha is." Toby said, "Why not let *me* stay with her. You know how Samantha and I get along." He was a graduate student with a flexible schedule; and besides, he seized on every excuse to entrench himself deeper in Mary's life. But Mary said, "No, I couldn't ask you to do that." And she went on paying Carol, and paying her again in the evenings when they went out somewhere. They went to dinner, or to movies, or to Toby's rambling apartment. They always came back early. "Carol's mother will kill me!" Mary would say, and she would gather up her belongings and run ahead of Toby to his car. When he returned from taking her home his apartment always smelled of her: a clean, straw smell, like burlap. Her bobby pins littered the bed and the crevices of the sofa. Strands of her long hairs tended to get wound around the rollers of his carpet sweeper. When he went to sleep the cracked bell of her voice threaded through all his dreams.

At the end of August, they were married in a civil ceremony. They had known each other five months. *Only* five months, Toby's parents said. They wrote him a letter pointing out all their objections. How would he support three on a university grant? How would he study? What did he want with someone else's child? The child: that was what they really minded. The ready-made grandchild. How could he love some other man's daughter? But Toby had never been sure he would know how to love his *own* children; so the question didn't bother him. He liked Samantha. And he liked the idea of her: the single, solitary treasure carried away from the disaster of the sweater-and-skirt marriage. If he himself ever ran away, what would he choose to take? His grandfather's watch, his favorite chamois shirt, eight cartons of books, some still unread, his cassette tape recorder—each object losing a little more worth as the list grew longer. Mary had taken Samantha, and nothing else. He envied both of them.

They lived in his apartment, which was more than big enough. Mary quit her job. Samantha started first grade. They were happy but guarded, still, working too hard at getting along. Mary turned the spare bedroom into a study for Toby, with a "Private" sign on the door. "Never go in there," she told Samantha. "That's Toby's place to be alone." "But I don't *want* to be alone," Toby said. "I'm alone all day at the lab." Nobody seemed to believe him. Samantha passed the doorway of his study on tiptoe, never even peeking inside. Mary scrupulously avoided littering the apartment with her own possessions. Toby was so conscientious a father that he might have written himself a timetable: At seven, play Old Maid. At seven-thirty, read a story. At eight o'clock, offer a piggyback ride to bed. Mary he treated like glass. He kept thinking of her first marriage; his greatest fear was that she would leave him.

Every evening, Samantha walked around to Toby's lab to call him for supper. In the midst of reaching for a beaker or making a notation he would look up to find her standing there, absolutely silent. Fellow students gave her curious looks. She ignored them. She concentrated on Toby, watching him with a steady blue gaze that gave all his actions a new importance. Would he feel this flattered if she were his own? He didn't think so. In their peculiar situation—nearly strangers, living in the same house, sharing Mary—they had not yet started to take each other for granted. Her coming for him each day was purely a matter of choice, which he imagined her spending some time over before deciding; and so were the sudden, rare smiles which lit her face when he glanced down at her during the walk home.

At Christmastime Toby's parents flew down for a visit. They stayed four days, each one longer than the day before. Toby's mother had a whole new manner which kept everyone at arm's length. She would look at Samantha and say, "My, she's thin! Is her father thin, Mary? Does her father have those long feet?" She would go out to the kitchen and say, "I see you've done something with Toby's little two-cup coffeepot. Is this *your* pot, Mary? May I use it?" Everything she said was meant to remind them of their artificiality: the wife was someone else's first, the child was not Toby's. But her effect was to draw them closer together. The three of them formed an alliance against Mrs. Scott and her silent husband, who lent her his support merely by not shutting her up. On the second evening Toby escaped to his study and Samantha and Mary joined him, one by one, sliding through the crack in his door to sit giggling silently with him over a game of dominoes. One afternoon they said they had to take Samantha to her art lesson and they snuck off to a Walt Disney movie instead, and stayed there in the dark for two hours eating popcorn and Baby Ruths and endless strings of licorice.

Toby's parents went home, but the alliance continued. The sense of effort had disappeared. Toby's study became the center of the apartment, and every evening while he read Mary sat with him and sewed and Samantha played with cut-outs at their feet. Mary's pottery began lining the mantel and the bookshelves. She pounded in nails all over the kitchen and hung up her saucepans. Samantha's formal bedtime ritual changed to roughhousing, and she and Toby pounded through the rooms and pelted each other with sofa cushions and ended up in a tangle on the hallway carpet.

Now Samantha was growing unruly with her mother. Talking back. Disobeying. Toby was relieved to see it. Before she had been so good that she seemed pathetic. But Mary said, "I don't know what I'm going to do with that child. She's getting out of hand."

"She seems all right to *me*," said Toby.

"I knew you'd say that. It's your fault she's changed like this, too. You've spoiled her."

"*Spoiled* her?"

"You dote on her, and she knows it," Mary said. She was folding the laundry, moving crisply around the bedroom with armloads of sheets and towels. Nowadays she wore sweaters and skirts—more practical for house-work—and her loafers tapped across the floor with an efficient sound that made him feel she knew what she was talking about. "You give her every-thing she asks for," she said. "Now she doesn't listen to *me* any more.

"But there's nothing wrong with giving her things. Is there?"

"If you had to live with her all day long," Mary said, "eighteen hours a day, the way I do, you'd think twice before you said that."

But how could he refuse anything to Samantha? With him, she was never disobedient. She shrieked with him over pointless riddles, she asked him unanswerable questions on their walks home from the lab, she punched at him ineffectually, her thumbs tucked inside her fists, when he called her Sam. The only time he was ever angry with her was once when she stepped into the path of a car without looking. "Samantha!" he yelled, and he yanked her back and shook her until she cried. Inside he had felt his stomach lurch, his heart sent out a wave of heat and his knees shook. The purple marks of his fingers stayed on Samantha's arm for days afterward. Would he have been any more terrified if the child were his own? New opportunities for fear were everywhere, now that he was a family man. Samantha's walk from school seemed long and under-policed, and every time he called home without an answer he imagined that Mary had run away from him and he would have to get through life without her. "I think we should have another baby," he told Mary, although of course he knew that increasing the number of people he loved would not make any one of them more expendable. All Mary said was, "Do you?"

"I love that little girl. I really love her. I'd like to have a whole *armload* of little girls. Did you ever think I would be so good at loving people?"

"Yes," said Mary.

"I didn't. Not until I met you. I'd like to *give* you things. I'd like to sit you and Samantha down and pile things in your laps. Don't you ever feel that way?"

"Women don't," said Mary. She slid out of his hands and went to the sink, where she ran cold water over some potatoes. Lately she had started wearing her hair pinned up, out of the way. She looked carved, without a stray wisp or an extra line, smooth to the fingertips, but when Toby came up behind her again she ducked away and went to the stove. "Men are the only ones who have that much feeling left to spare," she said. "Women's love gets frittered away: every day a thousand little demands for milk and Band-Aids and swept floors and clean towels."

"I don't believe that," said Toby.

But Mary was busy regulating the flame under the potatoes now, and she didn't argue with him.

For Easter, Toby bought Samantha a giant prepacked Easter basket swaddled in pink cellophane. It was a spur-of-the-moment purchase—he had gone to the all-night drugstore for pipe tobacco, seen this basket and remembered suddenly that tomorrow was Easter Sunday. Wouldn't Samantha be expecting some sort of celebration? He hated to think of her returning to school empty-handed, when everyone else had chocolate eggs or stuffed rabbits. But when he brought the basket home—rang the doorbell and waited, obscured behind the masses of cellophane like some comical florist's-messenger—he saw that he had made a mistake. Mary didn't like the basket. "How come you bought a thing like that?" she asked him.

"Tomorrow's Easter."

"Easter? Why Easter? We don't even go to church."

"We celebrated Christmas, didn't we?"

"Yes, but—and Easter's not the question," Mary said. "It's this basket." She reached out and touched the cellophane, which shrank beneath her fingers. "We never *used* to buy baskets. Before I've always hidden eggs and let her hunt for them in the morning, and then she dyes them herself."

"Oh, I thought people had jellybeans and things," Toby said.

"*Other* people, maybe. Samantha and I do it differently."

"Wouldn't she like to have what her classmates have?"

"She isn't trying to keep up with the *Joneses*, Toby," Mary said. "And how about her teeth? How about her stomach? Do I always have to be the heavy, bringing these things up? Why is it you get to shower her with love and gifts, and then it's me that takes her to the dentist?"

"Oh, let's not go into *that* again," Toby said.

Then Mary, who could never be predicted, said, "All right," and stopped the argument. "It was nice of you to think of it, anyway," she said formally, taking the basket. "I know Samantha will like it."

Samantha did like it. She treasured every jellybean and marshmallow egg and plastic chick; she telephoned a friend at seven in the morning to tell her about it. But even when she threw her arms around Toby's neck, smelling of sugar and cellophane, all he felt was a sense of defeat. Mary's face was serene and beautiful, like a mask. She continued to move farther and farther away from him, with her lips perpetually curved in a smile and no explanations at all.

In June, when school closed, Mary left him for good. He came home one day to find a square of paper laid flat on a club sandwich. The sight of it thudded instantly against his chest, as if he had been expecting it all along. "I've gone," the note said. His name was nowhere on it. It might have been the same note she sent her first husband—retrieved, somehow, and saved in case she found another use for it. Toby sat down and read it again, analyzed each loop of handwriting for any sign of indecision or momentary, reversible anger. Then he ate the club sandwich, every last crumb, without realizing he was doing so, and after that he pushed his plate away and lowered his head into his hands. He sat that way for several minutes before he thought of Samantha.

It was Monday evening—the time when she would just be finishing with her art lesson. He ran all the way, jaywalking and dodging cars and waving blindly at the drivers who honked. When he arrived in the dingy building where the lessons were given he found he was too early. The teacher still murmured behind a closed door. Toby sat down, panting, on a bench beneath a row of coat hooks. Flashes of old TV programs passed through his head. He saw himself blurred and bluish on a round-cornered screen—one of those mysteriously partnerless television parents who rear their children with more grace and tact and unselfishness than any married couple could ever hope for. Then the classroom door opened. The teacher came out in her smock, ringed by six-year-olds. Toby stood up and said, "Mrs.—um. Is Samantha Glover here?"

The teacher turned. He knew what she was going to say as soon as she took a breath; he hated her so much he wanted to grab her by the neck and slam her head against the wall. "Samantha?" she said. "Why, no, Mr. Scott, Samantha didn't come today."

On the walk back, he kept his face stiff and his eyes unfocused. People stared at him. Women turned to look after him, frowning, curious to see the extent of the damage. He barely noticed them. He floundered up the stairs to his apartment, felt his way to the sofa and sat down heavily. There was no need to turn the lights on. He knew already what he would find: toys and saucepans, Mary's skirts and sweaters, Samantha's new short dresses. All they would have taken with them, he knew, was their long gingham gowns and each other.

SURFICTION

John E. Wideman

AMONG my notes on the first chapter of Charles Chesnutt's "Deep Sleeper" there are these remarks:

> Not reality but a culturally learned code—that is out of the infinite number of ways one might apprehend, be conscious, be aware, a certain arbitrary pattern, or finite set of indicators is sanctioned and over time becomes identical with reality. The signifier becomes the signified. For Chesnutt's contemporaries reality was "I" (eye) centered, the relationship between man and nature disjunctive rather than organic, time was chronological, linear, measured by man-made units—minutes, hours, days, months, etc. To capture this reality was then a rather mechanical procedure—a voice at the center of the story would begin to unravel reality: a catalog of sensuous detail, with the visual dominant, to indicate nature, "out-there" in the form of clouds, birdsong, etc. A classical painting rendered according to the laws of perspective, the convention of the window frame through which the passive spectator observes. The voice gains its authority because it is literate, educated, perceptive, because it has aligned itself correctly with the frame, because it drops the cues, or elements of the code methodically. The voice is reductive, as any code ultimately is; an implicit reinforcement occurs as the text elaborates itself through the voice: the voice gains authority because things are in order, the order gains authority because it is established by a voice we trust. For example the opening lines of "Deep Sleeper" . . .

> It was four o'clock on Sunday afternoon, in the month of July. The air had been hot and sultry, but a light, cool breeze had sprung up; and occasional cirrus clouds overspread the sun, and for a while subdued his fierceness. We were all out on the piazza—as the coolest place we could find—my wife, my sister-in-law and I. The only sounds that broke the Sabbath stillness were the hum of an occasional vagrant bumblebee, or the fragmentary song of a mockingbird in a neighboring elm . . .

Rereading, I realize "my remarks" are a pastiche of received opinions from Barthes, certain cultural anthropologists, and linguistically oriented critics and Russian formalists, and if I am beginning a story rather than an essay the whole stew suggests the preoccupations of Borges or perhaps a footnote in Barthelme. Already I have managed to embed several texts within other texts, already a rather unstable mix of genres and disciplines and literary allusion. Perhaps for all of this, already a grim exhaustion of energy and possibility, readers fall away as if each word is a well-aimed bullet.

More Chesnutt. This time from the text of the story, a passage unremarked upon except that in the margin of the xeroxed copy of the story I am copying this passage from, several penciled comments appear. I'll reproduce the entire discussion.

Latin: secundus-tertius
quartus-quintus.

"drawing out Negroes"—custom in old south, new north, a constant in America. Ignorance of one kind delighting ignorance of another. Mask to mask. The real joke. Naming: plantation owner usurps privilege of family. Logos. Word made flesh. Power. Slaves named in order of appearance. Language masks joke. Latin opaque to blacks.

Note: last laugh. Blacks (mis) pronounce *secundus*. Secundus = Skundus. Black speech takes over—opaque to white—subverts original purpose of name. Language (black) makes joke. Skundus has new identity.

"Tom's gran'daddy wuz name' Skundus," he began. "He had a brudder name' Tushus en' ernudder name' Cottus en' ernudder name' Squinchus." The old man paused a moment and gave his leg another hitch.

My sister-in-law was shaking with laughter. "What remarkable names!" she exclaimed. "Where in the world did they get them?"

"Dem names wuz gun ter 'em by ole Marse Dugal' McAdoo, w'at I use' ter b'long ter, en dey use' ter b'long ter. Marse Dugal' named all de babies w'at wuz bawn on de plantation. Dese young un's mammy wanted ter call 'em sump'n plain en' simple, like 'Rastus' er 'Casear' er 'George Wash'n'ton'; but ole Marse say no, he want all de niggers on his place ter hab diffe'nt names, so he kin tell 'em apart. He'd done use' up all de common names, so he had ter take sump'n else. Dem names he gun Skundus en' his brudders is Hebrew names en' wuz tuk out'n de Bible."

I distinguish remarks from footnotes. Footnotes clarify specifics; they answer simple questions. You can always tell from a good footnote the question which it is answering. For instance: *The Short Fiction of Charles W. Chesnutt,* edited Sylvia Lyons Render, Howard University Press, 1974: p. 47. Clearly someone wants to know, Where did this come from? How might I find it? Tell me where to look. Okay. Whereas remarks, at least my remarks, the ones I take the trouble to write out in my journal, * which is where the first long cogitation appears / appeared, [the ambiguity here is not intentional but situational, not imposed for irony's sake but necessary because the first long cogitation—*my remark*—being referred to both *appears* in the sense that every time I open my journal, as I did a few moments ago, as I am doing *now* to check for myself and to exemplify for you the accuracy of my statement—the remark *appears* as it does / did just now. (Now?) But the remark (original) if we switch to a different order of time, treating the text diacronically rather than paradigmatically, the remark *appeared;* which poses another paradox. How language or words are both themselves and *Others,* but not always. Because the negation implied by *appearance,* the so-called "shadow within the rock" is *disappearance.* The reader correctly anticipates such an antiphony or absence suggesting presence (shadow play) between the text as realized and the text as shadow of its act. The dark side paradoxically is the absence, the nullity, the white space on the white page between the white words not stated but implied. Forever.] are more complicated.

The story, then, having escaped the brackets can proceed. In this story, *Mine,* in which Chesnutt replies to Chesnutt, remarks, comments, asides, allusions, footnotes, quotes from Chesnutt have so far played a disproportionate role, and if this sentence is any indication, continue to play a grotesquely unbalanced role, will roll on.

It is four o'clock on Sunday afternoon in the month of July. The air has been hot and sultry, but a light, cool breeze has sprung up; and occasional cirrus clouds (?) overspread the sun, and for a while subdue his fierceness. We were all out on the piazza (stoop?)—as the coolest place we could find—my wife, my sister-in-law, and I. The only sounds that break the Sabbath stillness are the hum of an occasional bumblebee, or the fragmentary song of a mockingbird in a neighboring elm. . . .

The reader should know now by certain unmistakable signs (codes) that a story is beginning. The stillness, the quiet of the afternoon tells us

---

*Journal: unpaginated. In progress. Unpublished. Many hands.

something is going to happen, that an event more dramatic than bird-song will rupture the static tableau. We expect, we know a payoff is forthcoming. We know this because we are put into the passive posture of readers or listeners (consumers) by the narrative unraveling of a reality which, because it is unfolding in time, slowly begins to take up our time and thus is obliged to give us something in return; the story enacts word by word, sentence by sentence in "real" time. Its moments will pass and our moments will pass simultaneously, hand in glove if you will. The literary, storytelling convention exacts this kind of relaxation or compliance or collaboration (conspiracy). Sentences slowly fade in, substituting fictive sensations for those which normally constitute our awareness. The shift into the fictional world is made easier because the conventions by which we identify the real world are conventions shared with and often learned from our experience with fictive reality. What we are accustomed to acknowledging as awareness is actually a culturally learned, contingent condensation of many potential awarenesses. In this culture—American, Western, twentieth-century—an awareness that is eye-centered, disjunctive as opposed to organic, that responds to clock time, calendar time more than biological cycles or seasons, that assumes nature is external, acting on us rather than through us, that tames space by man-made structures and with the I as center defines other people and other things by the nature of their relationship to the "I" rather than by the independent integrity of the order they may represent.

An immanent experience is being prepared for, is being framed. The experience will be real because the narrator produces his narration from the same set of conventions by which we commonly detect reality— dates, buildings, relatives, the noises of nature.

All goes swimmingly until a voice from the watermelon patch intrudes. Recall the dialect reproduced above. Recall Kilroy's phallic nose. Recall Earl and Cornbread, graffiti artists, their spray paint cans notorious from one end of the metropolis to the other—from Society Hill to the Jungle, nothing safe from them and the artists uncatchable until hubris leads them to attempt the gleaming virgin flanks of a 747 parked on runway N-16 at the Philadelphia International Airport. Recall your own reflection in the fun house mirror and the moment of doubt when you turn away and it turns away and you lose sight of it and it naturally enough loses sight of you and you wonder where it's going and where you're going and the wrinkly reflecting plate still is laughing behind your back at someone.

The reader here pauses.
   stream a totally
irrelevant conversation:
   twenty-seven
double-columned pages by
accident

Picks up in mid-

I mean it started that way

started yeah I can see starting curiosity whatever staring over some-
bodies shoulder or a letter maybe
you think yours till you see not
meant for you at all

I'm not trying to excuse just understand it was not premeditated
your journal is your journal that's
not why I mean I didn't forget
your privacy or lose respect on
purpose
        it was just there and, well
we seldom talk and I was desperate we haven't been going too
well for a long time

and getting worse getting finished
when shit like this comes down

I wanted to stop but I needed
something from you more than
you've been giving so when I saw
it there I picked it up you understand not to read but because it
was you you and holding it was all
a part of you

you're breaking my heart

please don't dismiss

dismiss   dismiss what   I won't
dismiss your prying   how you de-
filed how you took advantage

don't try to make me a criminal
the guilt   I feel it   I know right

from wrong and accept whatever you need to lay on me but I had to do it I was desperate for something, anything, even if the cost

was rifling my personal life searching through my guts for ammunition and did you get any   did you learn anything you can use on   me   Shit   I can't even remember

the whole thing is a jumble I'm blocking it all out   my own journal and I can't remember a word

because it's not mine anymore

I'm sorry I knew I shouldn't   as soon as I opened it I flashed on the Bergman movie the one where she reads his diary   I flashed on how underhanded how evil a thing she was doing but I couldn't stop

A melodrama a god damned Swedish subtitled melodrama you're going to turn it around aren't you   make it into

The reader can replay the tape at leisure. Can amplify or expand. There is plenty of blank space on the pages. A sin really given the scarcity of trees, the rapaciousness of paper companies in the forests which remain. The canny reader will not trouble him/her self trying to splice the tape to what came before or after. Although the canny reader would also be suspicious of the straightforward, absolute denial of relevance dismissing the tape.

Here is the main narrative again. In embryo. A professor of literature at a university in Wyoming (the only university in Wyoming) by coincidence is teaching two courses in which are enrolled two students (one in each of the professor's seminars) who are husband and wife. They both have red hair. The male of the couple aspires to write novels and is writing fast and furious a chapter a week his first novel in the professor's creative writing seminar. The other redhead, there are only two redheads in the two classes, is taking the professor's seminar in Afro-American literature, one of whose stars is Charlie W. Chesnutt. It has come to the professor's attention that both husband and wife are inveterate diary keepers, a trait which like their red hair distinguishes them from the professor's other eighteen students. Something old-fashioned, charming about diaries, about this pair of hip graduate students keeping them. A desire to keep up with his contemporaries (almost wrote "peers" but that gets complicated real quick) leads the professor, who is also a novelist, or as he prefers novelist who is also a professor, to occasionally assemble large piles of novels which he reads with bated breath. The novelist / professor / reader bates his breath because he has never grown out of the awful habit of feeling praise bestowed on someone else lessens the praise which may find its way to him (he was eldest of five children in a very poor family—not an excuse—perhaps an extenuation—never enough to go around breeds a fierce competitiveness and being for four years an only child breeds a selfishness and ego-centeredness that is only exacerbated by the shocking arrival of contenders, rivals, lower-than-dog-shit pretenders to what is by divine right his). So he reads the bait and nearly swoons when the genuinely good appears. The relevance of this to the story is that occasionally the professor reads systematically and because on this occasion he is soon to appear on a panel at a neighboring university (Colorado) discussing "Surfiction," his stack of novels was culled from the latest, most hip, most avant-garde, new *Tel Quel* chic, anti, non-novel bibliographies he could locate. He has determined at least three qualities of these novels. *One*—you can stack ten in the space required for two traditional novels. *Two*—they are *au rebours* the present concern for ecology since they sometimes include as few as no words at all on a page and often no more than seven. *Three*—without authors whose last names begin with B, surfiction might not exist. B for Beckett, Barth, Burroughs, Barthes, Borges, Brautigan, Barthelme . . . (Which list further discloses a startling coincidence or perhaps the making of a scandal—one man working both sides of the Atlantic as a writer and critic explaining and praising his fiction as he creates it: *Barth Barthes Barthelme.*)

The professor's reading of these thin (not necessarily a dig—thin pancakes, watches, women for instance are *á la mode*) novels suggests to him that there may be something to what they think they have their finger on. All he needs then is a local habitation and some names. Hence the redheaded couple. Hence their diaries. Hence the infinite layering of the fiction he will never write (which is the subject of the fiction which he will never write). Boy meets Prof. Prof reads boy's novel. Girl meets Prof. Prof meets girl in boy's novel. Learns her pubic hair is as fiery red as what she wears short and stylish, flouncing just above her shoulders. (Of course it's all fiction. The fiction. The encounters.) What's real is how quickly the layers build, how like a spring snow in Laramie the drifts cover and obscure silently.

Boy keeps diary. Girl meets diary. Girl falls out of love with diary (his), retreats to hers. The suspense builds. Chesnutt is read. A conference with Prof in which she begins analyzing the multilayered short story "The Deep Sleeper" but ends in tears reading from a diary (his? hers?). The professor recognizes her sincere compassion for the downtrodden (of which in one of his fictions he is one). He also recognizes a fiction in her husband's fiction (when he undresses her) and reads her diary. Which she has done previously (read her husband's). Forever.

The plot breaks down. It was supposed to break down. The characters disintegrate. Whoever claimed they were whole in the first place. The stability of the narrative voice is displaced into a thousand distracted madmen screaming in the dim corridors of literary history. Whoever insisted it should be more ambitious. The train doesn't stop here. Mistah Kurtz he dead. Godot ain't coming. Ecce Homo. Dats all Folks. Sadness.

And so it goes.

NOTES ON CONTRIBUTORS

ELIZABETH BISHOP (1911–1979) was born in Worcester, Massachusetts, and attended Vassar, receiving her B.A. in 1934. Among her awards were the Pulitzer Prize for Poetry in 1956 for her book *North and South—A Cold Spring* and the National Book Award in 1970 for *Complete Poems.*

PAT ESSLINGER CARR has published six books, including *The Women in the Mirror,* which won the Iowa Fiction Award for 1977. She currently lives on a thirty-acre farm in the Ozarks and is working on a new novel.

JOHN WILLIAM CORRINGTON is the author of eight novels, three written with his wife Joyce, as well as three volumes of short fiction. His most recent fictions are *All My Trials* (1987) and *A Civil Death* (1987) with Joyce H. Corrington. His stories have been published in numerous journals and have been widely anthologized.

ROBB FORMAN DEW has published fiction in *The New Yorker* and *Virginia Quarterly Review.* Her 1982 novel, *Dale Loves Sophie to Death,* received the National Book Award for Best First Novel.

RITA DOVE has published three books of poetry with Carnegie-Mellon University Press, most recently *Thomas and Beulah* (1986), for which she was awarded the Pulitzer Prize for Poetry in 1987, as well as a collection of short stories, *Fifth Sunday* (Callaloo Fiction Series, 1985).

CHARLES EAST, former director of Louisiana State University Press, has since 1981 been editor of the University of Georgia Press's short fiction series, the Flannery O'Connor Award volumes. He has published fiction in *Mademoiselle, Virginia Quarterly Review,* and other magazines and is the author of *Where the Music Was* (Harcourt).

NADINE GORDIMER was born and still lives in South Africa. She has published nine novels, most recently *A Sport of Nature* (Knopf, 1987), seven short story collections, and, with the photographer David Goldblatt, *Lifetimes Under Apartheid* (Knopf, 1986).

ELAINE GOTTLIEB taught creative writing, literature, and film at Indiana University (South Bend) from 1972 until her recent retirement. She has translated many stories and novels of Isaac Bashevis Singer.

SHIRLEY ANN GRAU divides her time between New Orleans and Martha's Vineyard, Massachusetts. She has published eight books of fiction as well as travel articles and book reviews. She has received numerous awards, most notably the Pulitzer Prize for Fiction.

MARTHA LACY HALL has published two collections of short fiction, *Call It Living* (1981) and *Music Lesson* (1984). Her stories have appeared in *New Orleans Review, Sewanee Review,* and other literary journals, and several have been listed among the distinguished stories named in *Best Short Stories* of 1970, 1980, and 1983. Since 1981, Martha Hall has served as fiction editor for Louisiana State University Press.

JEFFERSON HUMPHRIES has published four books of criticism, and his short stories, essays, and poems have appeared in many magazines, including *Michigan Quarterly Review, Massachusetts Review, Oxford Literary Review, boundary 2,* and others.

MAXINE KUMIN, winner of the Pulitzer Prize for Poetry in 1973, is the author of several collections of poems, including the most recent, *The Long Approach,* now in Penguin paperback. *In Deep: Country Essays* was published by Viking in 1987.

MARY LAVIN, of Irish nationality, has published twenty works of fiction, most recently *The Shrine and Other Stories* (1976). She has received numerous awards, including the American-Irish Foundation Literary Award, and has served on several occasions as president of Irish P.E.N.

ALISTAIR MACLEOD, a native of Nova Scotia, is currently professor of English and creative writing at the University of Windsor, where he also serves as fiction editor of the *University of Windsor Review*. Recipient of numerous literary awards, he has recently published *As Birds Bring Forth the Sun* (McClelland and Stewart, 1986).

DAVID MADDEN, writer-in-residence at Louisiana State University since 1968, is the author of *The Suicide's Wife, The Shadow Knows, The New Orleans of Possibilities* and other works of fiction. He is at work on *Sharpshooter,* a Civil War novel set in Tennessee.

PETER MAKUCK teaches at East Carolina University where he is editor of *Tar River Poetry*. He has published a collection of short stories, *Breaking and Entering* (University of Illinois Press), and a volume of poems, *Where We Live* (BOA Editions, Ltd.), with a preface by Louis Simpson.

WILLIAM MILLS is the author of three collections of poetry (*Watch for the Fox,* 1974; *Stained Glass,* 1979; *The Meaning of Coyotes,* 1985), a critical study, *The Stillness in Moving Things: The World of Howard Nemerov* (1975), and a collection of short stories, *I Know a Place* (1976). His latest two books are *Those Who Blink: A Novel* (1986), and a nonfiction book with photographs, *Bears and Men: A Gathering* (1986).

KENT NELSON grew up in Colorado and has lived in Europe, Montana, Texas, and South Carolina, and presently lives in New Hampshire where he is working on a novel. He has published *The Tennis Player* (University of Illinois Press, 1977) and *Cold Wind River* (Dodd, Mead, and Co., 1981).

JOYCE CAROL OATES is the author most recently of *You Must Remember This* (Dutton, 1987). Her last book of short stories was *Raven's Wing* (E. P. Dutton). She is the Roger S. Berlind Distinguished Lecturer at Princeton University and a member, since 1978, of the American Academy and Institute of Arts and Letters.

RICHARD PERRY's most recent novel, *Montgomery's Children*, published in 1984, was the recipient of the QPB New Voices Award in 1985. He is a member of Teachers and Writers Collaborative and teaches at Pratt Institute in Brooklyn, New York.

REYNOLDS PRICE received the 1986 National Book Award for Fiction for his *Kate Vaiden* (Atheneum, 1986). A Rhodes Scholar at Merton College, Oxford, and graduate of Duke University, he presently holds the James B. Duke Professorship of English at Duke. He has published numerous collections of short stories, novels, plays, essays, and poetry.

LOUIS D. RUBIN, JR., has, since 1965, been editor of Louisiana State University Press's Southern Literary Studies series. His own critical work over the last twenty-five years, as well as the work fostered through his series, has been considerable. Among his most recent books are *The History of Southern Literature* (1985), for which he was general editor, and *Surfaces of a Diamond: A Novel* (1981). His short stories have appeared in numerous literary journals.

ELIZABETH SPENCER has lived for a number of years in Italy and Canada but has recently moved to Chapel Hill, North Carolina. She is the author of eight novels, including *The Light in the Piazza*, *The Voice at the Back Door*, and, most recently, *The Salt Line*. In 1983, she received the Award of Merit Medal of the American Academy of Arts and Letters for the Short Story, and has recently been elected a member of the American Academy and Institute of Arts and Letters.

ANNE TYLER was born in Minneapolis, Minnesota. Her books include *A Slipping Down Life* (1970), *The Clock Winder* (1972), *Celestial Navigation* (1974), and *The Accidental Tourist* (1986).

JOHN E. WIDEMAN, professor of English at the University of Massachusetts, is the author of *Brothers and Keepers* and *Sent for You Yesterday*, which was awarded the 1984 P.E.N./Faulkner Award in Fiction.